The Virgin's Prophecy

Colette Murney

AuthorHouse™ UK
1663 Liberty Drive
Bloomington, IN 47403 USA
www.authorhouse.co.uk
Phone: UK TFN: 0800 0148641 (Toll Free inside the UK)
*   UK Local: (02) 0369 56322 (+44 20 3695 6322 from outside the UK)*

Published by AuthorHouse 03/25/2022

ISBN: 978-1-6655-9490-5 (sc)
ISBN: 978-1-6655-9489-9 (e)

Print information available on the last page.

*Any people depicted in stock imagery provided by Getty Images are models,
and such images are being used for illustrative purposes only.
Certain stock imagery © Getty Images.*

*Scripture quotations marked NRSV are taken from the New Revised Standard
Version of the Bible, Copyright © 1989, by the Division of Christian
Education of the National Council of the Churches of Christ in the United
States of America. Used by permission. All rights reserved. Website*

This book is printed on acid-free paper.

*Because of the dynamic nature of the Internet, any web addresses or links contained in
this book may have changed since publication and may no longer be valid. The views
expressed in this work are solely those of the author and do not necessarily reflect the
views of the publisher, and the publisher hereby disclaims any responsibility for them.*

The epoch of evil is about to come to its end. The era of brotherly love is about to commence.
Author unknown

CONTENTS

PROLOGUE

Mount Koressos, Ephesus

(Based on actual events in 'Mary's House')

In the end, she was compelled to come, left with no option. Message after message over recent years, even more frequent in the last few months—sometimes an instruction came in a dream or, when awake, an explicit command, directly into her conscious mind, sudden, electrifying, and always with intense tingling on her skin. 'Go to Ephesus. Go to Ephesus.'

That morning they explored the sprawling ruins without any reaction, spiritually dead like the ancient city itself. Then they climbed the mountain to evaluate the only other possibility and arrived during the afternoon in the neat and simple gardens of Mary's House.

From a professional perspective, Cathrina remained sceptical about the site. A historian specialising in Judaea's Second Temple era, she inclined towards the tradition that Mary died in Jerusalem rather than on Koressos, evidence for the latter sketchy, to say the least. Their visit would need to provide some answers.

'Sit down for a minute,' Josh said as he brought her over to a shaded bench in the courtyard. 'I'll find some water. You should relax a bit if you're going to suss this place out.'

He was right, of course. The hammering sun was killing her. Parking herself on the seat, she searched her bag for sun lotion, and she examined the building as it cooled her burning arms and face.

Broad and solid, the tiny box of weathered sandstone nestled in a grove of bushes and stunted trees. A rocky cliff protected the rear, and the triple-arched entrance opened into the paved expanse before her. Rebuilt as a chapel on the two thousand-year-old foundations, it followed the same dimensions and succeeded in reproducing the simplicity of the original, with a touch of ancient elegance, hints of the Golden Gate in the walls of the Holy City of Jerusalem.

The grounds teemed with visitors, much busier than expected: Muslim women with covered heads; an exhausted little girl with blonde curls and a sunburnt face, her mother gripping her hand, dragging her along; everyone rushing around exploring; different languages echoing across the lawns and pathways. Yet an aura of peace pervaded the place, surrounding her, penetrating.

Tingles stole along her arm, probed her body, increasing and deepening until an explosion of creamy effervescence burst over her, every nerve ending alert and sizzling, as if she'd dived into a deep pool of fizzing soda water. The implications were immediately obvious; the energetic residue of a strong spiritual essence, it indicated the presence of a pre-eminent soul from the higher reaches of the upper realms, the vibration so concentrated it felt pearly white.

Hmmm. Very powerful. Maybe she did come here, after all.

According to the hotel's tourist blurb, Mary arrived with John the apostle some years after the crucifixion, when severe persecution forced them to flee Jerusalem. Settled in Ephesus, they built their home on the slopes of Koressos, and there on the mountain, up above the Aegean Sea, she discovered a lasting serenity. After a quiet and retired life, she died peacefully at age 64.

The archaeology was interesting though not conclusive. Excavations of the first-century ruins found early Christian artefacts, enough to convince the Vatican. Several popes visited, ensuring widespread Catholic support. Cathrina's doubts subsided, even though she hadn't, as yet, confirmed the identity. There couldn't be more than one unconnected soul of this level of power associated with the site. Too much of a coincidence. Although the building might tell them more.

A few minutes later, she caught sight of her grinning husband as he pushed through the crowd with more bottles of water. She collected her things, dumped her empties in the nearest bin, and crossed the courtyard to join him.

They passed through the archway into the cool of the chapel; an altar stood at the top end with Mary's bedroom on the right. In ancient times, the house included more rooms to the left, but they weren't rebuilt. She signalled to Josh she wanted to stay and make some notes. He nodded and headed off to explore. Finding a chair, she sat down, took out her notebook, and drew a plan of the house. Then she sank back to examine the exceptional spiritual atmosphere.

It reminded her of another holy place near Kfar Nahum on the north-west shores of the Sea of Galilee. A tiny oratory, cared for by the Franciscans, it sheltered part of a massive rock on which the Saviour materialised after his resurrection. Every time they went to Israel, she made a beeline for Tabgha, and there, when she touched the blessed stone, her skin tingled with the same piercing sensation. Pure heaven, a sanctuary of total peace.

Mary's little chapel on the mountain produced the identical reaction, power building in the room.

Another scene suddenly appeared with the room rearranged, visually as clear as watching a film. In place of the altar, a fire burned under a steaming pot, and beside her at the back of the room near the opposite wall, a round table and stools filled the corner. A young man sat looking up at an older woman standing behind the table, serving food.

He was very good looking, classically handsome, the image of the actor that played Jesus in one of the old films.[1] Brown hair fell in waves to his shoulders, and he wore a long white tunic with a stripe of gold running from each side of the neckline down to the hem. The woman was dressed in a black gown and veil, her white inner headdress wrapped tightly around her head and neck, like the nuns used to wear in the local convent at home in Ireland. Considerably older, his mother perhaps, her face was strained with illness or suffering, the anguish evident in the dark, wounded eyes.

During their conversation, he smiled up at her with deep love and sympathy; when she responded, Cathrina realised the truth. The woman was Mary, the young man, her nephew John, the son of her sister Salome. Poor Mary. She was drowning in wretchedness.

Surrounded by an almost impenetrable cloud of oppressive sorrow, she lived her life as though carrying an unendurable burden, crawling through a black, never-ending morass that drained her strength with every step. An arduous existence, relieved only when John succeeded in penetrating the darkness to give her comfort and support.

---

[1] Jeffrey Hunter in *King of Kings*, 1961.

Words and impressions became clearer. She grabbed her notebook and scribbled down everything she heard:

'Desolation and hopelessness overwhelmed her. The task given to them by the Holy One had not been accomplished. Her life wasted, she waited now for death. Losing her Yeshu broke her heart, even though she knew the failure to carry out the instructions of the Most High had been the greater disaster. Defeat ground into her soul, gnawed at her mind, binding her with chains of despair.[2]

'How would she face Him, her beloved Creator? She had failed Him. Convinced they would end the rule of evil, she expected humanity to flock back to Him. But it wasn't to be. Their failure entailed terrible consequences: two thousand years before another attempt would be made, two thousand years of Satan, two thousand years of ongoing suffering for mankind. Regrets swamped her, inundating her with self-recrimination and years of heartache.'

The vision changed. She was outside standing under a tree in an orchard, weeping inconsolably.

John wrapped his arms around her and tried to comfort her. 'Don't be despondent, Mary. Be happy that at least the knowledge came to some of us. Our new task is to pass it to the enemy and, therefore, weaken him. We must retrieve what we can from the wreckage. Not all is lost. Please, please listen. Don't cry. You did everything you were able to do. No one could have done more.

'Now you must prepare for the next stage and regain your

---

[2] Yeshua (Yesh-oo-a), meaning salvation, is the original Hebrew word for Jesus. His family and close friends called him Yeshu (Yesh-oo), the Aramaic vocalisation. Prompted by the Mount Koressos visions, I've given him his own name in this book. Others will be called the name by which they are commonly known.

strength. The people we've met here in Ephesus are good people. They will help us. This city is the centre of the world; from here we will send out the love that will conquer all. Nothing will stand in our way. Please listen.'

The power of John's compassion was almost a physical presence. It wasn't just his obvious devotion to his aunt but the innate, loving goodness of the man himself. He radiated kindness. A glow of light surrounded him, and he projected energy, strength, and determination with a nearly ruthless singlemindedness. He would walk, unswerving, the straight and difficult path to his goal. A compelling individual.

The scene disappeared, and she was back in the chapel, the candles burning on the altar, the red lamp above the tabernacle, her mind vacant, her eyes staring. She fumbled with her notebook, found a new page, and tried to recapture the details, forcing herself to retrace her thoughts, adding bits until she remembered no more. Then she collapsed back into the chair and began to analyse the manifestation with a dawning excitement.

By far her most powerful vision, as if she'd been in that room two thousand years ago. Endorsing a religious site came easily to her. A genuine event produced the tingling sensation, and sometimes she received flashes of knowledge or watched a film-like replay of the former incident. This experience, however, was exceptional: sharp, distinct, and very real.

What did it all mean? The rule of evil was a well-known Essene concept from the days of the Second Temple, the time of Jesus, although unusual to hear of it within a Christian context. Yet the ending of the era of wickedness meant the coming of the age of God, which, when she thought about it, could also be called the kingdom of heaven. Was that the connection with Christ?

Getting up to leave, she decided to check the bedroom. Much

smaller than the chapel, the room immediately cradled her with oceanic depths of tranquillity, filling her with much-needed strength. She found a chair in the corner and sat back to rest as the hallowed vibrations sank in.

Again, the scene changed. Mary lay on a narrow bed surrounded by people, one of them John. Propped up with pillows, she wore a white, long-sleeved gown with her white headdress, her arms lying outside the sheet draped over her bed. Even though she was dying, a deep serenity emanated from her, regrets and despair gone at last.

Apart from John, none of her immediate family nor any of Jesus's close companions were present; nevertheless, the men and women who surrounded her deathbed loved her dearly and were deeply distressed by her passing. Her nephew sat on a stool on the far side of the bed with his arms on the coverlet, watching her face. He wore the same white tunic with the gold bands. The vision didn't last long, only momentary and without speech, but this time she appeared happy.

Cathrina finished writing and rose from her chair, dizzy with exhaustion for a moment. She gathered her things, made for the door, and crossed the courtyard, following the path down to the shops. She found Josh with his head in a book, oblivious to everything around him.

His eyes crinkled when he saw her; the smile faltered as he hurried to meet her. 'Are you OK?'

'Knocked out. Worth it, though. They *did* come here. I saw them. I'll be all right when I've had something to eat. Give me a minute and I'll tell you what happened.'

Committed metaphysical explorers, they first met at Tibetan meditation classes in North London. Her husband was a psychologist, and Cathrina's psychic abilities fascinated him personally and professionally. Their marriage opened windows into his own potential, and their commitment to a spiritual path empowered their relationship, each thankful for a partner with similar interests. He was the ideal person to help her process this new experience.

He took her hand and brought her to a little coffee shop away from the noise and bustle of shops and tourists. They chose a table in the furthest corner and ordered cappuccinos and cakes. He listened to her story and read her notes with increasing interest.

'My God, Cathrina. This is phenomenal. Do you understand it? What does it mean?'

'I'm not entirely sure,' she replied between gulps of coffee and bites of pastry. 'I think it must be something to do with the Dead Sea Scrolls.'

'The Scrolls? You're kidding me. How did you get that?'

'The mention of the rule of evil, although I might be wrong. I'm not sure if I took it out of context. You see, running through the writings was the belief they lived under "the dominion of Beliel"—the devil, in other words. The age was coming to a close, and with it, the era of iniquity.'

'You mean they were expecting the end of the world?'

'No, no, no. That's the mistake people always make. We're not talking about the destruction of the earth but the conclusion of an immense expanse of time ruled by evil.'

A blank mask of incomprehension swept across Josh's face.

She grinned. 'Let me explain. You need to understand this. In those days, they didn't see time as going from year to year, from the past into the present and then into the future. To them, time was made up of a series of ages, massive spans of years that continued on from one another. In this case, the epoch of evil was followed by the age of God. Their own time was the cycle controlled by Satan. Something like the Indian concept of the Age of Kali. Does that make better sense?'

'OK. Now I've got it. Go on.'

'According to the Scrolls, a great battle was coming between good and evil, between the Sons of Light and the Sons of Darkness. Light would fight both in this world under the Messiah of Israel and cosmically with Michael the archangel, who would lead the angelic heavenly host. They believed they would win, of course. Satan and the Romans would be destroyed, and that meant the age of righteousness could begin.'

'I knew the Zealots were fiercely anti-Roman, but I thought the Essenes were peaceful.'

'Well, the writers of the Scrolls were certainly prepared to fight physically and spiritually. They were convinced they would destroy the Evil One. It was their total focus. They spent their lives preparing for the Holy War that would cleanse the world of corruption. Their pages are full of battle regulations.

'And then came the Jewish Revolt: the Galilee devastated; the Roman army on its way south, burning everything in a scorched earth campaign; the survivors fleeing before it in terror. Rome's next target was the Holy City of Jerusalem. You can just imagine the scene in Qumran. Apart from preparing for the final confrontation, they desperately needed to hide their precious writings.'[3]

'So they saw the Revolt as the physical component of their Holy War?'

---

[3] There is an ongoing debate about the Qumran buildings. Were they an Essene habitation, a pottery, or something else? And some scholars propose that the Qumran caves sheltered the libraries of many sects and groups from Jerusalem and perhaps elsewhere in Judaea, precious writings secreted before the coming of the legions and never reclaimed.

'Definitely. To them, the Romans were satanic agents. We know they didn't win the war on the ground. The legions wiped them out. And from what I learned today, they lost on the cosmic level as well. Rome and Satan were the victors.'

'I still don't see where Jesus comes in.'

'I'm not sure either. I would never have connected him with this, yet it makes perfect sense, a matter of terminology. Once the epoch of evil ends, the age of God or the kingdom of heaven begins. Any Christian would tell you that preparation for the coming kingdom was the theme underlying all his teachings.'

He relaxed back in his chair, regarding her with an amused smile of anticipation. 'So now you're suggesting the early Christians were Essenes?'

'Not as crazy as you might think. A number of respected scholars, including some prominent Israeli archaeologists, believe there is, at the very least, a strong connection. There are definite differences, of course, especially in their attitudes to violence. The writers of the Scrolls were prepared to take up arms, but all our knowledge of Jesus implies he was a pacifist.

'To be honest, Josh, I don't know enough about links between the Essenes and the early Jesus followers. I'll need to look it up when I get back to London. At the moment, I'm more interested in Mary's belief that two thousand years would pass before another attempt would be made to eliminate evil. That's our own time.'

'I'm finding that part truly fascinating. What's your take on it?'

'Nothing from a historical point of view. Philosophically, is it even possible to destroy evil? And where does nature come in? So beautiful, but you have to admit, incredibly cruel.'

'I know what you mean. It does raise some questions. How do we define evil? And frankly, was there even such a being as Satan?

'Perhaps we're looking at this the wrong way, Cathrina. What Mary said ties up with ancient prophecies: the Age of Aquarius, the coming of the Brotherhood of Man. Many ancient cultures believed we would enter a period of lasting peace in this era. The Mayans certainly thought so. We're back to the 1960s, to John Lennon's "Imagine" and all the new-age beliefs. Wouldn't it be amazing if it was true?

'Anyway, we'll discuss all that later. Let's get to the big question, the one you seem to be avoiding. I'm assuming the messages sent you here to have the visions. Have you any idea why?'

'Oh God, Josh. Don't ask me. I haven't a clue. I'm nearly afraid to dig any deeper.'

'I'm not surprised. The whole thing is mind-blowing. But listen. Don't worry about it. Leave it alone for the moment. Let the information sink in and your subconscious will do the sorting. Then you'll start getting ideas. Just remember this: if you were deliberately sent, you're capable of dealing with it. They wouldn't send you otherwise … whoever *they* might be.'

Rising from the table, he stretched and ran his hands through his hair. 'I'm tired, and you must be exhausted—and starving, from the way you demolished all the cakes, your cappuccino, and most of mine.'

She smiled. 'You've seen what I'm like when I use up a lot of spiritual strength.'

He laughed. 'Don't I know it. We'll go back to the hotel for some real food for you. And for me a desperately needed shower.'

He went up to the counter to pay their bill, and Cathrina wandered out into the sunshine. Thinking over her experience, she tried to make sense of it. So much contradicted the religious teachings drummed into her as a child, particularly the doctrine that Jesus came to die for our sins. For Mary and John, his death was an unmitigated disaster, the destruction of all their hopes to defeat Satan and usher in the kingdom of heaven.

In addition to that, Josh's 'big question' really worried her. She was sent to Mary's House for the visions and the information; that she had to accept. But why? She gazed up the path towards the chapel and chewed her dry lips, as, for a moment, her confidence in her knowledge and capacities deserted her.

I don't understand what's happening. Why was I brought here? What am I supposed to do?

PART 1

The Journey North

1

Escape from an Ancient Harbour

Joppa in Judaea, a Few Years after the Crucifixion

Two ships danced in rhythm beside the quay, prancing shadows in the predawn gloom, long, battered, sea-prowling animals momentarily tethered, brown ropes coiled, hessian sails furled. Out in the night-dark harbour, calm waters reflected the fading moonlight; yet beyond the mole, rolling whitecapped waves crashed over sharp rocks.

On the nearest trader, lamps twitched and plunged among the rigging, casting fluttering light and shadow on the deck below. At the mast, a sailor unravelled lines entangled during the night squalls. Others examined roped anchors stacked at the bow or sorted crates of food and brought them down into the hold. The final mobilisation was nearly complete. To catch the best of the offshore winds, they needed to be on board by sunrise. Her nephew and Simon, the captain, left minutes earlier to collect fresh fruit and should soon return. Then they would embark.

More familiar with the boats on the Lake, the Sea of Galilee, the size of the ship amazed her at first. The tall mast towered above her, standing amidships with a huge square sail. From the mainmast, a long boom with a lashed foresail lay forward over

1

the foredeck. A typical working boat, and a beauty: the long, extended prow curved elegantly upwards, twisting and capering in the hazy half light of early morning.

'Move! You're blocking the plank.' Two men pushed past, each carrying on his shoulders a sheep with nervous, darting eyes.

Staggering back, she almost fell over a pile of boxes. She steadied herself and crept away from the edge of the quay, her red-rimmed eyes searching along the waterfront, wondering where they might be.

A few minutes later she spotted them rushing through the mist, laden with baskets. In front came John, a smile lighting his face, with Simon hurrying behind, bustling and excited. As soon as they arrived, her nephew brought her up on deck.

The captain followed and came over to take her hands, holding them gently. 'Mary, I'm sorry we were so long. You're very welcome aboard.'

Kindness flowed from him, hugging her like a warm, comforting blanket. An old friend from home, he used to fish the Lake before leaving to sail the open seas. Now he owned his own trader, with a successful business among the ports of the eastern Mediterranean and the Aegean. His wife had welcomed them with genuine pleasure the night before, and Mary felt safe with him. She trusted him.

They crossed the deck to the stern and climbed down steps to a tiny cabin, Simon's own captain's quarters. Directly beneath the quarterdeck and away from the main working areas, it would be her home while at sea. He hoped the relative quiet would help her recover after the dangerous journey from Jerusalem.

Then, although it had to be, her throat clutched in fear at the thought of leaving home, separating from everything and everyone she knew and loved. She missed a step, and the rolling ship pitched her forward. John grabbed her, carried her into the cabin, and lifted her up into the bunk.

Her hands held tightly in his, he waited until the rasping gasps subsided and she eased back into the straw mattress. He pushed a soft pillow under her head and pulled the covers up around her. The concern in his eyes forced her to summon a smile: better now; no need to worry. He tidied their belongings as he listened to her breathing. After a minute or two, he went to the door, opened it, and slipped out. She was alone.

The bed was comfortable, and she settled in, the darkness helping to still her thoughts. From above echoed running steps and the shouts of the sailors; below the wooden boat creaked with every gentle movement. A sense of the inevitable crept over her. Impossible now to change her mind. Too late. The ship was leaving Judaea, leaving home. A lump lodged in her throat.

Above, her nephew carefully examined the trader as he stood with Simon at the stern, his sandaled feet balanced and easy on the rocking quarterdeck. The ship's name, the *Galilee*, brought a smile, reminding him of the Lake where his family had lived for all the generations since their return from Babylon. Their home was near Bethsaida, and although boats were second nature to him, this working vessel was something new, a stimulating challenge to explore on the way north.

Used since ancient times, Joppa was a natural stopping point on the southern coast of Judaea, with sufficient depth of water for medium-sized vessels right up to steep, rocky heights. Protected by the jutting rocks of Andromeda and fortified by a mole and quays in the time of Alexander the Great, it was known as the safest refuge along the dangerous Judaean coastline. That is, until Herod built his fabulous Caesarea Maritima.

His thoughts turned to their journey; spring was the perfect time to leave for Ephesus. The winds from the south-east swept across from the desert, and although hot and dusty, they were ideal for the voyage up to the Aegean. Provided they avoided storms, shipwreck, or pirates, it should be a fast sail. Impatient now, he couldn't wait to be underway.

The sun rose behind the village, casting pink and cerise flames of light over the little white stone cottages edging the shore. Men ran to the moorings, untied the ropes, and threw them on deck, leaving the ship held by slip lines.

The plank came in, and the captain called for the foresail to be unfurled, prepared for the rising gusts. 'Man the oars.'

The wind strengthened, the flapping foresail filled, and the boat moved. With the line on the foredeck slipped, the prow pivoted away from the dock towards the harbour mouth, the aft rope was pulled on board and the ship gathered momentum.

'Drop the mainsail'.

Within seconds the brails were released, and the heavy canvas cascaded to the deck. The sailors tightened sheets, while Simon strained on the huge steering oar at the stern. As the crew worked, the wind filled the mainsail, speeding the *Galilee's* escape into the rolling waves of the bright blue sea.

2

Along the Coast of Judaea

At the helm, Simon grinned. 'You enjoyed that. Not too surprising, I suppose. Sailing's in your blood.'

John laughed. He liked the captain, a medium-sized man with straight black hair tied back from his face, a black beard, and dark, mischievous eyes. He was dressed like the crew in a short, Greek-style tunic and was a shrewd and successful trader. His men found him easy, approachable, and worthy of respect. They had complete confidence in his abilities.

A hard existence yet satisfying, and for a wistful moment, John envied his old friend. Such a life might have been ideal for him too, had things been different. Thinking of his aunt below, he rubbed his hands over his face and sighed.

'Try not to worry about her, John. She's still mourning. Don't expect too much too soon.'

'I know. I only wish I could do more to help her. She's not recovering.'

'Are you surprised? The crucifixion of her firstborn son. The shock of that alone would have broken her, and we know how involved she was in his work. The end of all her hopes. Everything gone in a moment.'

'She's suffered so much. Over these last days, it's been a

question of saving ourselves, avoiding the soldiers and Temple guards, then crossing the plain to meet you. Last night was the first time we slept since Jerusalem. We had to get her away from the danger and the fear. It was destroying her, Simon. Now, I'll have to find some way to bring her back to her old self.'

'Poor Mary. All her strength is gone. One look at her face tells you that. Even so, try not to worry. She'll recover; she just needs time. What chance has she had so far? The ship and the sea might be the answer, so when she's rested, bring her up on deck. The men don't know who she is yet. Wait till they hear she's the mother of Yeshua the Healer; they'll be amazed and very keen to help. His fame reached even Joppa.

'Besides that, John, you need to look after yourself and rebuild your own strength. You're exhausted, and you've lost a lot of weight since I last saw you. How can you take care of Mary if you're not in good shape yourself? You're hardly able to stand. Leave her to us now. We'll look after her during the voyage. You're safe. So take the time to rest and relax. And as I said—don't worry so much.'

As he gazed out over the waves, the apostle contemplated his friend's words. He rolled his shoulders and twisted his neck, trying to relieve the aches and stiffness. Maybe Simon was right. Given time, she would return to the woman she once was.

He would need her help in the years to come if he wanted to continue his work with exorcisms and desecrated souls. No one understood Yeshu's task or the plans of the Creator better than she did. She was there from the beginning, and while it was true he'd learned a great deal over the years, he didn't underestimate the depth of her knowledge or experience.

Apart from that, she probably had the best chance of contacting the higher reaches of the blessed realms, and without that direction the followers floundered at times, not sure which turning in the road to follow. At the moment, she didn't believe there could be another path. She fought the possibility of alternative methods to continue Yeshu's work, uninterested in new suggestions. All caused by the agony she endured as she stood below her tortured and dying son, nailed to a Roman cross. It broke her heart. Too much for anyone to bear.

In his own opinion, if they wanted to do anything of value with the rest of their lives, they must put the horrors of the crucifixion behind them and work for the future. There had to be another way, and somehow he would find it. The captain was definitely right about one thing: he needed to rebuild his strength, both mentally and physically. And this sail in the *Galilee* might be the best possible medicine.

Determined to stay focused on the will of the Creator, he jumped up and searched around for something to do, something to help him control his fears for Mary.

'Here, why don't you steer?' Simon said. 'You can be helmsman.'

Pleased with the prospect of handling the vessel, he quickly moved into position.

Immediately after the helm was relinquished, the weight of the sea almost overpowered him. Sail flapping, the ship veered off course. He scrambled to regain his legs and pulled hard on the oar to bring her back under control, the strength needed taking him by surprise. Gradually, as he worked with the wind and waves, he won the battle. The curved prow turned once again to the north.

The captain stood quietly, confident in John's skill yet knowing it would take time and practice to master the ship.

'This one's much heavier than the boats at home, John. There's more to control.' The impish grin on his face, however, gave it away; the apostle knew his old friend deliberately transferred the helm without any real warning of the difficulties. He laughed. They used to play similar tricks on each other as children, and thoughts of those carefree years of fun, on the shores of the Lake, flooded his mind with memories.

Soon, he was exploring the differences between the Lake and the open sea: everything bigger, more powerful, and wonderful. The old excitement of sailing rippled through him, easing the aches in his shoulders, lifting the heaviness. Something new to learn, and by the time they reached Ephesus he would handle this ship as if it was his own boat at home.

He gazed over the blue and turquoise waters, searching the misty horizon. Deep breaths of salty air relaxed him, bringing a touch of exhilaration and delight. Anchored at last, he promised himself he would take his friend's advice and not fret so much about his aunt. She needed time. And so did he.

Relieved that John had a task to occupy his mind, Simon climbed down into the hold. He stopped for a moment outside Mary's door; all was quiet. *Let her rest,* he thought and went forward to check the animals and cargo. Sometimes the crew forgot how easily merchandise moved in strong winds, and storms could still blow up. The safety of the ship was always the priority.

Apart from the two rams destined for a farmer outside Ephesus, the space was packed with bags of Egyptian grain. They should command a decent price now that winter stores in Rhodes and Ephesus were depleted. So would the boxes of spices from Petra, and the precious stones from India would probably give him more profit than all the rest put together. Some of it he would spend on the little sailing boat he promised his son Daniel.

As he took stock, rearranging bags, deciding which merchants to contact and what he should charge, he grinned. *Should be a very profitable expedition.*

His thoughts turned to Mary. Her appearance dismayed them when she arrived at their home the night before: the total desolation, the sunken eyes in the grey face, the bewilderment, the dazed, almost stupefied expression. Severe shock, but not just from the death of a beloved son. Unless he'd misjudged the situation, she had lost the will to live.

His wife reacted quickly, leading her into the house, pulling out a chair, and settling her at the table. She took Mary's cloak and made her comfortable.

They owed an enormous debt to Mary's son, one they could never repay. If Yeshu hadn't come to her so quickly that night, Susannah would have died after Avigail's birth, and probably they would have lost the baby too. Every day, he thanked the Most High she'd been up in Bethsaida with her mother, not down in Joppa on her own. Keenly aware of their obligation, his wife would do everything possible for Yeshu's mama.

Out in the stable, he helped unload the donkeys, brush them down, and give them water and hay in their stall. Quieter and older, his childhood friend seemed stronger than the boisterous youth from Galilee. Experience and responsibility had aged and matured him, although his physical exhaustion was pronounced.

Once they dealt with the animals, they returned to the house where Mary had relaxed during her time with Susannah. Arrangements were in hand to bring their possessions down to the dock. Although the apostle listened, he didn't take anything in. No matter. They had already made the more important decisions.

John had refused the offered free passage, insisting the captain keep the animals as payment, and on the dawn breezes that morning, they left Judaea to make a new life in a strange, faraway land. Simon didn't envy them.

Rocked by the boat, Mary slept. At home in Nazareth, with baby Yeshu in his cradle, she and Joseph sat at the table for their evening meal, talking about old Avner's new villa on the outskirts of Sephoris and the various bits of furniture required for both house and courtyard.

'Benjamin and his sons are coming tomorrow from Tiberius to do the floor mosaics. The younger boy is very talented. I think he'll surprise his father one day.'

Avner, retired now, once sailed the Mediterranean as a successful merchant and was fastidious. Long conversations about the types of wood, the design of the individual items, and how they would meld into the overall structure of the building were conducted over cups of wine in the evening after work.

She smiled in her dream. He pretended he only tolerated these intervals, yet she knew her husband enjoyed them. Always the perfectionist, he liked to see things done properly, and the carved pieces were as important as the design of an elegant house. The deep, artistic streak in Joseph's nature revelled in his craft.

'Mary, you need to eat and have something to drink.'

She woke with a start, surprised, wondering where she was. Then she remembered. 'Come in, John. How late is it?'

The door opened. He carried in a large jug of water and wedged it into a space at the end of her bunk.

'Not far off sunset. You slept all day. You were so exhausted I didn't want to waken you. Why don't you rise now and get some air? We're about to drop anchor. Simon's hoping there won't be too much wind.'

'Is he expecting bad weather?'

'It might get worse during the night. He thought we'd be safer anchored off-shore rather than out at sea. I brought water for you to wash. We'll be able to eat soon. Do you want to come up, or shall I bring your food down to you?'

His mood had lightened, the tiredness gone, and unless she was mistaken, he was enjoying himself. She smiled.

Of course. Playing about in a boat with Simon. They haven't changed much in all these years.

Chasing him from the cabin, she rose from her bunk. Aromas of fresh bread drifted in; her stomach grumbled. Wash first and then food. Reaching for the water, she tried to balance herself on the rolling floor. She felt better. Her time with Joseph had helped.

3

New Friends

She came up a few minutes before sunset, just as the ship turned into a bay. With sails furled, the impetus carried them forward until the released anchors dragged and caught. The *Galilee* slowed, came round into the wind and settled. The crew raced through their duties; thoughts turned to food, and the captain appointed a lookout. The others went below to cook the evening meal.

The ship rocked gently as Mary leaned over the side, the movement slow and restful, and as the flaming orb of the sun began to sink into the western sea, her nephew joined her to whisper their night-time prayers to the Creator.

Mathias and James came with baskets of fish. They uncovered the stove, lit the fire, and fastened a table to the floor of the quarterdeck. Simon joined them and brought her over to a sumptuous seat built against the stern, next to the table. Sheltered by the superstructure, she would enjoy the cooling winds without the overwhelming glare of the sun. Rope hand grips and deep cushions kept her comfortable and safe. His kindness touched her. A dear man.

Next came the food: bread and cheese, a jug of her favourite *tirosh,* and a decanter of *yayin.*[4] James carried over a plate piled with fish, and the men pulled up stools and reached for drinks. The smells tantalised: fresh bread, fried fish, the salty sea, the sharp tang of wine. A feast. With a sigh, she stretched back on her seat and relaxed.

Listening to the conversation, she realised both men lived in Galilee, Mathias in Sephoris, and James near Tiberias. Friendships in common with her nephew were soon discovered, and they laughed and told old tales, the chatter of exiles remembering stories of a faraway and well-loved home.

'What happened to that donkey foal you used to drag everywhere, Simon?' John asked with a grin. 'How it survived I don't know. I remember the day you nearly drowned yourself and the poor little animal. Your mother wasn't too pleased.'

The captain laughed. 'Neither was my father. I sometimes think he was more worried about the foal than me.'

They talked of the storms, how they suddenly lashed the waters, forcing them to abandon work, and old Natan, who sailed with his brother but didn't make it back in time, and the search along the beaches for the boat and the bodies. Their voices were restful, the subjects familiar.

With the sea wind on her face, she remembered her father at the kitchen table, telling stories of his travels and his time in Ephesus, where he lived in the years of his youth.

Joachim spoke fluent Greek and knew the ports and lands around the Mediterranean and Aegean: the slave markets of Apollo's island of Delos; Piraeus, the harbour of once-powerful Athens; the port of maritime Rhodes and the famous lighthouse

---

[4] New wine (*tirosh*) was lightly fermented grape juice used as an everyday drink instead of water, which was usually polluted. Strong wine (*yayin*) was similar to the ordinary wine we have today.

at Alexandria. No doubt, compared to then, travelling to foreign shores was faster and safer, with more efficient boats and greater protection from pirates. The world was getting smaller, with so much of it controlled by Rome.

Her thoughts came back to their own journey and escape. Thanks to her nephew's knowledge of the quick and silent ways to cross the plain, they arrived safely in Joppa and departed. Yet the work didn't succeed. That failure remained, lodged tightly within her like a twisting dagger. John thought there was another way, but how was that even possible? Yeshu was the only person capable of finishing the task, their one opportunity.

Grief gripped her. Black tentacles of despair encircled her, pulling her down into the dark well of remorse. Another two thousand years of Satan. All those poor people suffering. Her throat tightened, and tears flooded her eyes. No one to help them. It was her fault. Guilt burned in her stomach. She should have found a way to prevent the failure. She couldn't breathe.

A cool hand touched hers, and her startled eyes looked up at Simon's face as he reached down into the desolate vacuum and pulled her back to safety.

'Come for a walk with me, Mary. Let me show you my ship.'

With her arm tucked safely into his, they paced the planked deck, the stiff breezes swirling round them. Before long, deep breaths of the salty sea air calmed her. Her throat eased and the pain diminished.

'What do you carry, Simon?'

'Mainly grain from Egypt. Both Rhodes and Ephesus will be low in supplies now. Then we have spices from Petra down in the desert. Fabulous place. Unbelievable. I went down myself a few years ago just to have a look at the temples and palaces.'

His tales painted vivid, magical pictures: camels in caravan with hot, desert winds; harbours with furled sails flapping against masts; exotic faces in crowded, noisy markets; all the haggling, the chaos, the life, and the excitement of the Mediterranean marketplace.

A new world opened before her, so different from Nazareth or even Jerusalem during the festivals. She caught his enthusiasm, and her attitude to the future brightened. Perhaps she would remember her journey as an adventure, something to cherish in the years to come. Grateful for his care, she blessed him in her heart.

They continued around the deck, lingering at the prow as she gazed out into the wind and the softening light over the waves, until the rocking soothed her and she longed for her bed and sleep. The crisis contained, he brought her back to the stern and down to her cabin.

The door closed, and he climbed the steps back to his friends and the decanter of strong wine on the quarterdeck table. It had been a long, hard day.

4

A Proposition

The night passed peacefully; the new day promised moderate east to south-easterly winds. Shortly after dawn the crew came on deck. With anchors raised, sails dropped, and sheets tightened, they sailed smoothly away, heading north-west to Cyprus and the Paphos Port.

Down below, she washed with difficulty in the rolling ship, water spilling from the wooden bowl, slopping over the cabin floor, making it slippery and dangerous. When she crept back into her bunk, it was worse; her head swam with dizziness. She pulled on her clothes and climbed the wavering steps.

Luckily, Simon was still on the quarterdeck, and one glance told him the problem. Taking her arm, he led her to her seat and warned her to keep her eyes fixed on the horizon, the only cure for seasickness.

'The winds are stronger this morning, Mary, and they're coming from the south-east, so we're running before them. That's why we're rolling so much. Soon they'll move to the south, and you'll find it easier. You'll be able to lie back and relax. Try and endure it till then.'

His explanations made little sense. The sickness left her far beyond caring about winds—or anything else, for that matter.

He tucked a bowl into the seat beside her and brought her a cup of tirosh. Even though she didn't want it, he held it to her lips and persuaded her to drink. Holding the stern, she fought as the weakness poured into every part of her. She simply wanted to die. In spite of that, Simon's calm assurance helped compose her, and she concentrated, refusing to let it win.

Over the next few hours, she stared out over the waves, and as the line at the edge of the earth stabilised, the intervals between bouts of nausea lengthened.

The winds changed to the south, as predicted. The ship heeled, but the sickening rolling stopped. Her cushioned nest became a restful haven as the turbulence at the rear relaxed her. The swirling, screeching seabirds amused her, and the frisky dolphins filled her with delight as they leapt and dived in the wake, their smiling faces bringing a sense of joy.

The day advanced, the sun rose overhead, and as noon merged into afternoon, she recovered. Bored with inactivity, she forced herself up and carefully explored, fastening her grip to the sides, gradually gaining her balance. By evening she was carrying tirosh to the crew, smiling and chatting, asking their names and that of the village where they grew up.

The speed of her recovery amazed Simon. As he watched her negotiate the sloping decks, her determination overpowered his deep sympathy with admiration. She had the strength to survive her terrible wounds.

The sailors greeted her with undoubted respect, and the two who had spoken so roughly in Joppa harbour came with apologies. Once they'd learned her identity, they felt honoured to have her on board. Yeshu's fame had spread widely. Both a healer

17

and an exorcist capable of combating Satan, they revered him for his sympathy and compassion for the poor. He even convinced the tax-gatherers (*publicani*) in Galilee to divert Rome's money for distribution among the destitute, and in return, he healed them and their families. The contributions fed widows and orphans, the sick, and those incapable of helping themselves.

It was difficult to imagine the detested *publicani* giving charity, but the Healer wasn't in question. A Jew to be proud of: a Man of God. How wonderful it would be to listen to the stories of his family, something to tell their own children and grandchildren. So they waited with anticipation and watched over Yeshua's mama as she brought them bread and wine, making sure she didn't trip over ropes or become endangered by the heeling ship.

Simon noted the interactions and guessed the thoughts of his men. Mathias had cornered him the night before, after Mary went to bed, and asked him to arrange a get-together with the Galilean couple. He had voiced his misgivings at the time, and now his doubts resurfaced.

The fascination for Yeshu didn't surprise him. So many stories circulated about his birth, his childhood, his life as an exorcist, healer, and teacher—and then, of course, his crucifixion. No one knew the real truth. Still, Simon didn't want to put his passengers under pressure, quite aware of his own profound debt of gratitude.

Some of the men were Galileans, and they, in particular, understood the concept of the Man of God, the human being who brought showers to parched fields, healed the sick, cured leprosy, and even caused someone to rise from the dead, like Elijah did with the widow's son. More recent stories told of Honi the Circle-Drawer, another holy man from Galilee. Imploring rain from the Most High, he would draw a circle on the ground round himself and refuse to move until he was heard. Then, amazingly, a shower would pour down and drench the dry earth.

Reports about Yeshua's activities surpassed all others and spread quickly throughout the land. The people accepted him as someone special. His brother James in Jerusalem was gaining a similar reputation, especially after he successfully petitioned the Holy One for help during a severe drought in the city. As well as that, he spent so much time in the Temple praying for the people, his knees were as calloused as those of camels.

Like Yeshua, he had a strong reputation and following that antagonised the Herodians and high priests, those directly appointed by Rome to rule Judaea. When anyone became too popular, they tried to counteract their influence, fearing the loss of their Roman power and riches, but most of all, they dreaded the coming of the legions.

The family of these revered men were travelling with them, and the crew wanted to find out what really happened. They meant no disrespect to Mary. To them, it was an evening's entertainment, a chance of a lifetime to listen to anecdotes and memories they would talk about for years to come.

The problem went round and round in Simon's mind as they neared the southern coast of Cyprus. He would explain the situation to John and leave the decision to him. Hopefully, an opportunity would arise soon.

Uncertainty resolved, he prepared for their night in port. Without trading, there would be little for anyone to do. It would cost him docking fees, but some time had passed since he'd been in Paphos, a harbour the men liked, as most of them had friends and relatives on the island. He was looking forward to seeing Marcus and his family that night.

※

At the stern, the apostle steered by instinct as he examined the land to the north, the lush, green meadows not yet burnt by the summer sun. The long, low spit to the east elevated to higher mountains in the west, while groves of olive trees on the coastal plain marched into the hills. Above the sandy beach, a village edged the water with tiny houses framing the white sands of a rocky cove. Small blue and white fishing boats sailed the sparkling turquoise water, with men leaning over nets, pulling in the catch.

It reminded him so much of the Lake, even if the dinghies were smaller, more brightly coloured and painted vividly against the blues and greens of the luminous Cypriot seas. Mary would've loved it. No matter. There would be other opportunities. Thankfully, the journey was helping her, the strain diminishing, her demeanour more relaxed. She had gone below to rest and prepare for their excursion ashore. It was their first stop away from home; she wanted to explore.

Paphos was the most important port on the southern coast of Cyprus, popular for travellers going east to Syria and Judaea and for those coming back. The grain convoys from Egypt sailed straight to Italy during spring and summer. In winter, once storms began to rage across the seas and Rome's corn levels fell, traders headed north from Alexandria, hugging the Judaean coast before turning west. Prices might be higher in the cold months, but coastal sailing was safer, ensuring the constant use of Cypriot harbours.

No doubt, the port would be full of travellers: crew from military and trading ships; Roman functionaries visiting other outposts of the Empire; tattooed slaves; freedmen; wealthy aristocrats with leisure, seeing the sights. Around the docks, eating houses and drinking places catered to every kind. Tonight though, Simon wanted them to meet some friends, a family who lived outside the town, and there they would dine.

The captain joined him on the quarterdeck and explained the crew's request. At first the idea surprised the apostle, but he quickly recognised the opportunity to spread the knowledge of loving kindness. He was an experienced teacher, a practised healer and exorcist. He couldn't claim Yeshu's power nor his flair for understanding the human mind, yet for this purpose, he was more than competent.

The longer he reflected, the more the situation pleased him; yes, he would talk about Yeshu, his life and beliefs, and most important of all, he would tell them about the ancient promise from the Creator, explain what it meant for the future.

Then he thought of Mary, wondering how she would feel. Since the crucifixion she stayed apart, seeing only her closest friends and family, never speaking of her son to anyone else. He didn't think she would break her silence; even so, he would have to tell her. You never know. She was getting stronger. Her attitudes might have changed.

When he accepted the proposal, the captain sighed in relief. 'I was worried for a moment, John. I didn't want you to think I'd taken advantage of our friendship. So what now? When will we do this?'

'I'll need to discuss it with my aunt first, Simon. See what she says.'

'Fine. Then let's make it Rhodes. If we leave at dawn, we should be there by noon Friday, at the latest. We'll unload and reload with olive oil. With luck, we'll be finished by Shabbat. Then, dinner on board, and you can talk to us afterwards. Good. That's settled.'

❋

An hour later, the *Galilee* entered the port, the crew ready with their oars to push the ship away from other craft. Simon's control was sure, and he grinned when they docked with a gentle touch. Perfect. Mathias and James jumped to the quay to tie up. Within minutes sails were furled, ropes tidied away, and the deck washed down with seawater, everyone anticipating shore time.

Docked along the quays were traders of various sizes, as well as a *trireme* and several other fighting ships belonging to the permanent Roman navy. The *classis Ravennas* patrolled the coasts of the Empire, keeping brigandage under control and acting as a naval counter to any threat to imperial power.

The waters around the island had been susceptible to piracy in the past. Ships at sea and cities on the coast were attacked, with captives sold in the slave markets of Delos. Initially the Senate took advantage of the increased numbers of slaves and refused to intervene, until predation on their own corn supply forced them into action, initially with uncertain results.

Octavian's decision to reassign the ships abandoned after the Battle of Actium made the greatest difference. Fleets were organised to patrol the seas, giving maritime commerce a more potent protection. Nevertheless, the sea lanes were not immune. Simon appreciated the vigilance of the Roman fleet and hoped to speak to one of their captains, knowing they stayed aware of the trouble spots. Meanwhile, the *Galilee* must be made safe and secure while docked.

5

The Virgin and the Evil Spirit

Finally in port, Mary went below, relishing the opportunity to fill the wooden bowl without spilling water everywhere. As much as she enjoyed the sail, she dreamt of reaching Ephesus and finding proper facilities: to sink into a cool bath, and to have clean skin, clean hair, and fresh clothes, nothing smelly or sticky. When she washed and changed, even with a small amount of water, she felt better, not quite so anxious and afraid.

Afraid? The thought cut short her daydreams and forced her to examine her feelings more carefully. Where were these fears coming from? All through her life she demonstrated courage, one of her most significant characteristics. Anna, her mother, switched from amusement to anxiety at her lack of fear of the animals around their home, but Joachim laughed and encouraged her, proud of his adventurous little daughter. And now she was frightened?

The source of her anxiety had to be identified. Only then could she deal with it. So she lay on her bunk, relaxed as she had been taught by the Wise Ones all those years ago, and began to analyse her spirit, gradually penetrating deep into her being, her very soul.

There in the depths she found the dark, cavernous desolation, opaque and impenetrable, a hard core of hostility and a bottomless well of despair. Dizzy and sick, she felt the sinuous tentacle slide over her neck up into her hair, another rip through her gown, slither round her waist and up her back, sucking and squeezing, dragging her down to the black, sulphurous teeth in the gaping mouth.

Almost paralysed with revulsion, instinctive self-preservation stung her to action, but it took all her newly acquired strength to wrench herself from its grip. As she pulled away and up to safety, she realised the entity in the darkness had come to her when Yeshu died; there on the hill, she'd been forcibly invaded by a powerful, desecrated being.

Afterwards, as she lay exhausted and recovering on her bed, she retraced the sequence of events and their consequences. From the moment the angel told her of the coming Teacher, the infant she would carry, and his role in ending the rule of evil, she had dedicated her whole existence to obeying the commands of the Creator, His wishes the only ones that mattered.

The child, her beloved Yeshu, would teach them how to nullify Satan, and this would allow the age of the Holy One to come into being. The people, the chosen people of God, would be the initiates, the first to understand, and they would open wide the gateways through which the Creator's love would pour down into the world, gradually eliminating fear and unhappiness, bringing humanity back into His care.

They'd given her so much help: Joseph, almost from the beginning, and the Wise Ones from Batanaea and the lands of Damascus, who trained her and helped her gain experience. Yet with all the heavenly direction and earthly preparation, they didn't reach their goal. The Evil One still activated, no doubt stronger than ever since the death of the Messenger of the Most

High. What a tragedy for all mankind. What terrible suffering for all to come. Another two thousand years.

She had every confidence that Satan would eventually be defeated; he couldn't continually thwart the plans of the Father. Earth was intended as a paradise, a school and proving ground, where human beings would absorb knowledge and evolve sufficiently to be with Him forever. And the most important lesson of all would bring them to an understanding of the power of loving kindnesses, the essence of the Great Creator Himself.

Humanity needed to learn how to care for one another and recognise that harmony, not aggression, would eliminate the problems of their world. Even so, this awareness would not be forced on them. They had freedom of choice. They could only come to Him by their own free decision and through the growth of sympathy and compassion.

Why they had failed she didn't, as yet, understand, but the failure must be faced with clarity. At least she was thinking a little more clearly. For the first time, she succeeded in penetrating the labyrinthine mists of sacred knowledge; her intelligence had partially returned, her ability to reach for divine wisdom by following the intricacies of spiritual logic.

'Mary?' her nephew called.

When she opened the door, he stepped back and stared. 'What's wrong? What happened?'

'I'm beginning to see again.'

'What do you mean?'

'My capacity for spiritual understanding is coming back.'

His face cleared, and his tense shoulders relaxed. 'Tell me.'

'I needed to examine myself properly, John, the first time

I was able to try. I'm badly injured. There's a blackness within me, a lower entity and a strong one. I'm sure he came when they killed my Yeshu. He's been with me all this time, impossible for the moment to push away.'

With profound sympathy, he took her hands. 'I know, Mary. He's been with you from the hour of Yeshu's death. We tried but couldn't send him away; he was too powerful. We had to wait until you recovered, at least partially. It's no wonder when you think of all you've been through: the crucifixion, the attacks in Jerusalem, the fear we would be next. It was too much.

'And for us, it was such a shock to watch your strength disappear. Your endurance, always at the core of your being, suddenly vanished, like a stream evaporating overnight in a summer river valley. In an instant, everything gone. It won't be forever, Mary. Your powers will return and I want to help. Yeshu told me to look after you. You're our hope for the future. A lot depends on you.'

Pulling her hands away, she stepped back from him, irritated. 'Don't be foolish, John. What future? My son was the one person capable of dealing with the Evil One, our only chance.'

'I realise that. I'm not talking about ending the age of evil but undermining Satan by weakening his followers. If we teach people how to use love and kindness, we'll prepare humanity for the next time. We need your help.'

'I'm sorry. I can't see what more we can do. It's over.' She choked, pushing down the sobs that threatened.

He reached for her and wrapped his arms around her, holding her tight. Forced to accept the rejection, he knew he'd gone too far, moved too quickly: she wasn't ready. Yet he'd heard that faint whisper of hope; for the first time, something of her old self resurfaced, her ability to synthesise spiritual concepts and find her way through the dark maze of desolation.

Yet when he released her and looked into her face, her spirit had already receded. The black despair returned to deaden her eyes. Poor Mary. He would have to wait, but he wouldn't give up. That momentary glimmer encouraged him, leaving him more determined than ever to help her. One day she would recover, and he would never abandon her.

'I wanted to speak to you anyway. The crew have asked me to talk about Yeshu and his teachings. What do you think?'

'John, you mustn't depend on me for advice. You can't trust my opinion, not while I'm so injured. My judgement isn't what it was; you must decide. You've had exceptional training, and you'll get help from the blessed realms.'

Although she smiled through her tears, it was the final retreat. Mary disappeared behind the mask, the withdrawal total. The tightened mouth and purple shadows under bloodshot eyes convinced him.

He would have to let her go. For a moment, he felt all alone. 'Very well. I'll do as you suggest. You still want to go out this evening?'

'Of course. I'd like to see something of Cyprus. My father always called it the island of love, the home of Aphrodite. Really appropriate for a good Jew,' she said with a smile. 'So yes, let's go. I'm ready when you are.'

'I'll tell Simon.'

He turned for the door, and turmoil churned inside her, as if she was sending her unprotected child out into the world to face all its dangers.

Stop this. He's a grown man. He received the best possible preparation from me and Yeshu. I can do no more. In fact, I must do no more. I might send him in the wrong direction. He'll find his own way.

Now, at least she was aware of the lower soul, a sign she was gaining some strength. So she would concentrate on keeping the entity separate from her own spirit, stop it influencing her thinking or pulling her away from her inner beliefs and duty to the Creator.

It was a hard, dark road, one she must travel alone. No doubt the contamination of Yeshu's mother meant another victory for Satan. Yet the being within, no matter how desecrated, was simply a poor soul who didn't know what he was doing, a soul entrapped in the webs of the Evil One. She would send him love and compassion and never submit to fear again. One day freedom would come, and with it a return to the dear love of the Father.

From that moment she began her lonely journey, determined to tolerate the bodily pain and invading desolation. The dark, heavy presence imprisoned her in a suit of solid metal. With each movement, a mountain of weight encased her body, and the despair, emanating from the soul, battered at the threshold of her own pure spirit, demanding entrance. She wouldn't allow it. That door was barred now. Her long years of coping with evil would guide her, the only contribution left within her power to give. In time, she would succeed.

After what seemed an eternity, John called her. With a smile on her face she drew her mantle around her, prepared for the cooler evening. She went out the door and up the steps to the deck where her companions waited.

'Back in a few hours,' Simon said to Amos as they disembarked.

6

Aphrodite and the Temple Priest

Finally ashore, they ambled around the quays, inspecting vessels and greeting crew, an activity the captain always enjoyed while in port. They passed ships of different sizes and design, each with its own method of crossing the seas. Scrutinising the traders, he searched the rigging for innovations and found, instead, the perfect little sailing boat for Daniel. Imagining his son at the helm, he promised himself he would find something suitable on his return to Joppa.

Further along, John and Mary examined the Roman navy *trireme*, a good example of her class. As she was man-powered and of no appeal to Simon, he hurried on to find one of her officers and an official to pay his harbour fees. A short time later he caught up with his friends as they waited near the road, gazing over the vista before them.

Another pleasantly warm evening, the sun not far from the horizon in the distant west. Quays packed with ships, new arrivals searching for places. Some had empty decks, their sailors already ashore. On others, crews furled and tidied, putting their boats to bed for the night, eager to get away. Laughs and shouts echoed across the water as men came up towards the town in pairs or groups, eyeing Mary with curiosity as they passed. Public eating

29

houses would be crowded that night, no doubt rowdy and violent. He was glad he'd decided to visit Marcus.

His friend's forebears had lived in Cyprus for several generations, since the early years of Herod, and became wealthy by mining the island's copper. Copies of famous bronze statues were prized by the Roman and provincial elite, those who aspired to honour for their education and culture. Sculpture remained an important export throughout the Aegean, and he always maintained friendly relations with the mine owner.

Their villa lay to the east of Paphos, a short distance from the harbour. While they walked up the hill, he told his companions something of his Cypriot patron.

A prestigious family of priests in Jerusalem and prominent in the organisation of the Holy Sanctuary, they supported the Hasmonean dynasty, later ousted by Herod. Considered unreliable, they were pushed from the centre of power to the outer edges of the priestly class and found themselves in danger.

Marcus's adventurous grandfather had no desire to follow his ancestors into the Temple and brought his substantial fortune to Cyprus, where he acquired the mines that ultimately made him very rich. He never regretted his exile, as many of his relatives lost their lives or wealth.

The Empire confiscated the copper mines on the island after the Battle of Actium, but fate favoured Marcus. He had spent part of his youth in Rome and became a close friend of the Emperor's grandson Gaius. The heir's tragic death left Augustus numb with grief, yet he didn't forget the personable young Cypriot who retained ownership of his properties and found his imperial contracts increased.

Over the years, the family grew even wealthier and absorbed the local Hellenic culture. Despite that, the male members of a

Jewish priestly line remained priests, and his friend maintained an interest in the land of Judaea. He would be delighted to welcome them.

The day cooled as Marcus retired to his balcony to enjoy the magnificent sunset, content and satisfied with his life. Alerted by his son to the arrival of the *Galilee* in port, he anticipated a pleasant evening with his seafaring friend.

The room displayed evidence of his prosperity; white marble pillars edged the extensive space and supported a latticed roof, threaded with vines. Gods and goddesses sported on the mosaic floor in fabulous boats, sailing a vivid turquoise sea, dolphins cavorting in their wake. Bunches of grapes sprinkled wall frescoes, mirroring those hanging from the trellis above. Reclining couches, chairs, and small tables gave a welcoming suggestion of comfort and tranquillity.

It was his favourite room in the house, the haven to which he retired during his evenings at home. He watched the setting sun in peace and communed with his God, seeing no contradiction between that and his enjoyment of the fantastic idols under his feet. A Hellenistic Jew, with the prosperity and trappings of the Graeco-Roman world, he used the Greek and Roman names and educated his sons and daughter in the ways of the host country. In private, he lived according to Judaic traditions, faithful to the Most High and to the religion and festivals of his ancestors.

Even though he considered the Gentiles as young in their spiritual understanding and lack of knowledge of the One God, he did not despise them for this. Such matters lay in the hands of the Creator. He discharged his own duties and obligations by ensuring his family understood their priestly inheritance.

Since it was unlikely they would return to Judaea, he took every opportunity to familiarise his children with the people and customs of their ancestral homeland, always pleased to entertain visitors like Simon.

Looking back, he remembered how much he'd taken to the young sailor when he first came to the island, liking him for his intelligence, perspicacity, and considerable charm. As for his boys, they adored the captain, who teased and played with them, treating them like his own, tolerating their almost continual presence on board while the ship docked.

A commotion in the hallway caught his attention. Strange voices warned him of unknown guests, and he rose from his couch to greet the visitors. When the door opened, a smiling Simon came in and introduced his friends.

A tall, handsome man in the long, white, linen tunic of a priest? Or maybe an Essene? The aunt was a tiny woman, no higher than his shoulder. She wore a deep-blue robe with a matching veil over a white headdress, the typical apparel of a reserved and modest Judaean woman.

Rather a contrast to Evia, he thought, amused, glancing over at his wife with pride. As usual, she was unveiled, her hair bound around her head in braids, confidently attired in garments appropriate to a Hellenic noblewoman.

His guests were emigrating from Judaea to Ephesus. The woman wasn't young, and he wondered at her decision to become exiled at such an age. Some reason behind it, no doubt. He smiled as she turned in delight to the sunset, exclaiming at the beauty before them.

They gazed far out to the west, where approaching twilight painted another mesmerising ocean scene, the blazing sun momentarily captured on a flaming horizon, spears of light spitting high into the darkening sky, the blue and green waves swamped by floods of fire. As he listened to their remarks, he stood a little taller. A smug smile curved his plump lips; he was proud of his home.

An unusual couple. This might be interesting.

That first instinct intensified as they sat down to talk. A change from the customary travellers from home. An impression of command and quiet determination emanated from the good-looking young man, a penetrating energy.

Called back from his thoughts, he realised Evia wanted to bring the lady to her own quarters to relax before the evening meal. Dinner would be served within the hour, giving the men a chance to discuss all the latest news from the Roman world.

Smiling her gratitude to her hostess, Mary turned to bow to Marcus. At last he could see her properly.

As he thought, she was old enough to be the mother of either of her companions, not pretty in the accepted sense but striking. Dark, expressive eyes dominated the olive face, a long yet refined nose, with a slightly arched bridge, gave her countenance strength, the full mouth crinkled at the corners with her smile, and the square chin showed resolution.

Probably beautiful when she was young. She intrigued him, surprised at his interest.

The women left, and servants carried in jugs of wine, plates of appetisers, and fresh fruit with delicate portions of honey, figs, and nuts. They relaxed, comfortable in the environment, and Marcus looked forward to stimulating conversation.

The sun set, and the hot day merged into cooler evening. Refreshing breezes blew in from the sea as Simon regaled his host with rumours from Joppa and Alexandria, as well as the talk about Tiberius in his Capri palace. The sudden fall from favour, several years previously, of the hated and feared Praetorian Prefect still held considerable interest. The stories of how the Senate and the mob took their revenge, not only on Sejanus and his followers but also on his unfortunate young children, had spread in whispers throughout the imperial lands.

So many contradictory tales of Tiberius in Capri; some told of cruelty and wild orgies, yet others claimed he was a good man who spent his declining years with philosophers and men of wisdom. Hard to know what to believe. In spite of thinking his servants trustworthy, Marcus dismissed them before the gossip began in earnest, well aware how torture could loosen a tongue, and careful always to appear loyal to the Empire. His continued, lucrative position in Cyprus industry depended on his good relations with Rome and the ageing Emperor.

At last, the conversation turned to John and his journey north. Marcus asked why he was leaving home and awaited his reply with curiosity.

7

The Priest and the Apostle

The apostle, in turn, considered the Temple priest. An agreeable man, bald, overweight, and hedonistic, a congenial companion. Yet behind the self-satisfied mask and social small talk, he sensed a piercing intelligence.

The captain had assured him their host was trustworthy; nevertheless, the crucifixion and its aftermath encouraged a strong sense of self-preservation, especially when questioned by someone he didn't know. Now he wasn't sure how to respond.

The priest watched him expectantly, like a master waiting for his pet monkey to perform a trick. Amused, John decided to trust his friend's judgement.

'Life at home is difficult these days, Marcus. The poverty of the people and the oppressive administration. Judaea is probably worse off under direct Roman rule, but living under Antipas isn't so good either. Sometimes I wonder if we weren't better off with Herod.'

His host regarded him with concern. 'Be aware, John, that Ephesus is equally ruled by Rome. In fact, half the world is. You won't easily escape her. Those countries not controlled at the moment fear they soon will be. There are considerable advantages, of course—the seas are safer with greater availability of grain and other foodstuffs, and there's less chance of being sold off into slavery. However, we live in a world under an iron fist, a situation we must recognise and accept.'

As he settled back on his couch, a frown crossed his face. 'I can only assume the Holy One tolerates it for some reason, and one day He will relieve our sufferings. Until then, we have to endure. Here in Cyprus, we are in a similar position, seen as booty since the time of Alexander, bartered back and forth between empires, the Seleucids, the Ptolemies, and now Rome, trying to stay safe and survive whatever carnage they inflict on us.'

The apostle noticed how Simon agreed with their host, although cynical about the possibility of relief, the Empire's power too strong, too far-reaching.

If only Yeshu had survived to complete his task.

Lost in his thoughts, he looked up to catch his host watching him.

'There's more you could tell us, John. What's on your mind? Perhaps I might even be able to help.' His sincerity dissolved the apostle's doubts.

'If Yeshua the Healer had lived and carried out the task given to him by the Holy One, this conversation would be irrelevant. Satan would be in the blessed realms, and the kingdom of heaven, the era of love and kindness, would have begun to spread over the earth.'

Initially, shock registered on his host's plump face. Then, as hope fought disbelief, he asked, 'What do you mean?'

'For many years, we worked to end the rule of evil by elevating Satan's legions. In the final stages, Yeshua would have captured and held him until his hatred and pride were neutralised, and he recognised the Great Creator as the Lord. But he outwitted us. He used the Romans to kill the Messenger of the Most High.

36

We failed, and it will be a long time before another attempt is possible.'

The priest's black eyes bored into his guest's.

'You speak like an Essene. Do you think as they do?'

'We are Nazoraeans. We don't always agree with other groups within the Essene communities. Some believe in confrontation which, to us, is neither appropriate nor successful. War generates further conflict, and hostility encourages an equally violent reaction. Such activity only increases evil; it isn't our way.

'We know there will be no happiness or real safety on this earth until evil is eliminated. Then anger and aggression will gradually disappear, war and revolution no longer necessary.'

'I don't understand.'

For a moment the apostle wondered if he was wise to say as much. On the other hand, there was something in those black eyes, some inner longing for truth, a deep desire for reassurance that prompted him to explain.

'When evil first came to the earth, it wasn't at the behest of the Father. Humanity chose it. Through the pride of one man, at the beginning of our time, it was brought into being against His wishes. Once created, it spread like a disease, incurable and deadly.

'The Holy One, however, promised it wouldn't last forever. His plans for us were not set aside. Nor did He rescind the gifts of spiritual knowledge and freedom of choice. One day, He told our ancestors, we would choose love not pride, sympathy and kindness, not selfishness, and on that day the epoch of iniquity would end.

'He promised a Teacher, someone who would show us how to defeat Satan and free ourselves from the burden of hatred. Yeshua came, and he chose our people because we already understood the difference between the dominion of Beliel and that of God. He taught us how love can overcome hostility. We expelled desecrated spirits from the possessed, nullified their wickedness, and sent them into the blessed realms. He showed us how these entities caused sickness, both of the body and of the soul, and how to cure physical and spiritual illnesses.

'Although our eyes were opened to phenomenal divine knowledge, we were only partially successful. We hadn't enough time to isolate Satan by penetrating his immediate protection and support. Only Yeshua was capable of completing that last and most important task. Through losing him, we failed.'

Marcus regarded him with fascination, without any sign of disbelief, seeming to understand. His gaze shifted into the far distance as he considered this new knowledge.

Eventually he turned back with a glimmer of unshed tears glistening in his eyes. 'Amazingly, I can accept what you're saying, John. I was aware the Essenes believed the rule of evil was meant to end, a belief and expectation in my own family. I didn't realise such an attempt had been made. What a disaster. But it gives us hope. If it's been tried once, it can be again. What are you going to do? And tell me, who is the lady with you, your aunt? How does she come into this?'

'She is Yeshua's mother, the one who learned from the angel that the era of desolation would end, and the Teacher was about to come. She has been blessed by the Most High.'

The priest stared at the apostle in awe and turned to Simon. 'You have done me and my house the greatest honour, my friend. More than you could possibly imagine. Since childhood, I've been able to sense the presence of the Creator, to recognise whether something is of the Holy One or the Evil One. My father and grandfather had this same gift of discernment; they believed it was priestly, given to us for use in the Temple.

'While you were talking, John, the power of the Most High surrounded you, and I knew you spoke the truth. I've heard a little of Yeshua the Healer from the captain here and from others. If possible, I would like to learn more. When do you go, Simon?'

'I'm sorry to disappoint you, Marcus; we sail at dawn.'

'Don't worry. I'll find a way. And anyway, we still have the rest of the evening.'

Watching him, the apostle was amazed. The veneer of lazy hedonism disappeared, and the black eyes once again fastened on his guest, searching and assessing. He laughed, amused at how cleverly the priest fooled him into believing him a nonentity. Instead, he found a spiritually intelligent man, someone Yeshu would have enjoyed.

At that moment, the noise of doors opening and closing echoed through the house. Their host started, surprised.

'Much later than I thought. Let's go down to the bathhouse and change before dinner.'

They followed him down the corridor to a room on the left where baths were filled with warm water. Clean linen tunics lay on a couch, and he told them to leave their garments to be washed and delivered to the ship before dawn. A generous host.

Later, a servant brought them into a luxurious dining room with pale yellow walls and floors of white marble, an exquisite oasis of golden sunshine. Along each wall, Grecian statues rested on plinths in alcoves, and lovely frescoes decorated the spaces in between. A long, broad table occupied the centre of the room with dark, throne-like chairs, each individually carved, the seats comfortable with generous cushions.

Down some steps, the room opened into a spacious covered

terrace with couches and small tables. Mary reclined as she chatted with Evia. Attired in a silver-grey gown and veil, she had bathed and changed. And, no doubt, she was enjoying the chance to talk to another woman.

He went over to kiss her cheek, relieved to find her relaxed and content.

Their host and his sons Antonius and Tiberius joined them, the boys bombarding Simon with questions: the ship and its cargo, India and precious gems, Arabia and the spice caravans. Used to their antics, the captain enthralled them with stories of huge, dangerous cats and marauding elephants, while their father looked on with a smile.

John wandered out through light, floating curtains into gardens of colour and fragrance. Jasmine and honeysuckle scaled fences, the sharp tang of lemons and oranges wafted over from extensive orchards, and groves of ancient olive trees climbed the lower slopes, reaching for the hills. From there, a stream, still flushed with winter rains, dropped over rocks in a white, splashing waterfall, meandered through flowerbeds and lawns, widening momentarily into a pool to flow down to the waiting sea.

A small stone bridge crossed its course, and he sat for a while on the wall, listening to the music of the falls and watching small fish dart back and forth in the waters below. A peaceful haven, the perfect complement to the beautiful villa.

Marcus is a good man. I wonder why he needs to hide his intelligence.

He heard sounds behind him and turned to see his host coming up the path carrying a box.

'I want you to take this with you, John. A present from Evia and me. Some help, I hope, for you and the Lady Mary in the years to come. I'm organising letters of introduction to prominent Jews who will put you in touch with whomever you need in Ephesus.

Don't open it now, but make sure you bring everything with you back to the ship.'

The weight of the box and the clink of coins astonished John. 'Marcus, we don't need money. We have enough. I really can't take this.'

His host persisted. 'If you won't accept it for yourself, take it for Yeshua's mother, for the Lady Mary. Perhaps it will give her comfort in the times ahead and allow you more freedom to do what you need to do. Please don't refuse me this; I beg you. I would consider it an honour to contribute to your work in some small way.'

His sincerity forced the apostle to acquiesce: no other choice.

'Come back in now. We're about to dine. I hope you don't mind, but when we eat with the children we use our private dining room with chairs, in the ancient way, rather than reclining on couches. The boys prefer it and so do I.' With a smile, he turned for the terrace and took his guest's arm.

'It was such a surprise to listen to your ideas on how the rule of evil would end. Only the Essenes and some priestly families now remember the Creator's pledge, and we've waited for aeons for its fulfilment. In my own family, the knowledge came down through the generations. My father told me, and I will tell my children when they are old enough to understand.

'At times, when I see the suffering in the world and realise there is nothing I can do to prevent it, I think of the commitment from the Most High, and that makes it easier to bear. I do what I can to help, but under Roman rule it isn't always possible.

'Prophecies are made predicting a warrior to lead our people against the invaders, the Romans, the Seleucids, or whatever, yet I always believed them to be a misunderstanding, a garbled version of the real promise, given to us by the Creator so long ago, that one day a Saviour would come and teach us how to banish evil from the earth.

'I'd hoped to learn more of Yeshua and his teachings, but let's just enjoy the evening with the family and we'll meet again. If necessary, I'll go to Ephesus. Simon will be able to find you, I presume.'

'Yes. We're old friends from Galilee. We played together as children, so we'll keep in touch.'

Arm in arm they walked down the scented pathways and into the house. On reaching the dining table, Marcus relieved his companion of the box and left it on a side table. His generosity was unexpected, overwhelming in fact, although John had to admit that the gift might be useful in the future. Gratitude filled him for this strange, intelligent yet simple man, a new friend, he hoped.

While they sat at the table, they enjoyed the jokes, the laughs, the friendship, and the kindness. Mary appeared happier, casting aside her despondency, chatting easily to the Cypriot couple who treated her with undeniable respect and sincere affection.

Servants passed back and forth, bringing in platters of food, confirming their hosts' wealth and his comfort with it. It was interesting to see how such a family lived outside Judaea.

Later, Evia excused herself and her sons as their bedtime approached. The boys said an affectionate goodnight to Simon, climbed on their father's knee to kiss him, and formally bowed to their guests, wishing them farewell. They were lovely children, and Marcus obviously loved and was proud of them. It prompted John to ask him about the problems Jews encountered when living abroad, how difficult was it to thrive within the Empire.

'Ah! That is a complicated question. Are you asking about the freedom to practice your religion, how we are viewed by others, or what?'

'Both, and frankly, any advice you can give us would be valuable.'

'The first thing you must do is contact the synagogue, preferably the president. You'll find a strong and active community in Ephesus. The letters I'm giving you are for prominent members, people in a position to help you. The work you were doing with exorcisms, do you intend continuing with that?'

'Yes. I hope so.'

'Among the Jews or the Gentiles?'

'Only with our own people, Marcus. I know little of other nations.'

'Very well. Let me give you some idea of our presence in the Diaspora.

'At this time, we live in clusters and communities throughout the imperial lands, and the most recent census indicates we make up one tenth of the Empire's population. Although that might give us some influence, it also makes us a target.

'We've been traveling outside Judaea since long before the coming of Alexander. His campaigns stimulated massive movements of people into the new regions he conquered and the Greeks were suddenly everywhere, bringing with them their own civilisation as you know from their presence back in Judaea.

'Where they went, we followed. Many Jews stayed behind in Babylon after the exile, and a substantial number went to Egypt with the Ptolemies. The Seleucids planted Jewish families in what is now Roman Asia, resulting in numerous settlers in Ephesus, Smyrna, and other Anatolian cities.

'Many of our people are in Rome; some are descendants of those captives brought there by Pompey during the conflict with the Hasmoneans, and others followed later, attracted by the enormous economic opportunities. We are everywhere and are protected by law.

'Although the vast majority of us hated Herod, there is no doubt his father gave us one huge advantage: the friendship and gratitude of Julius Caesar. Antipater sent supporting battalions to him from Judaea when he was fighting in Egypt. It saved him from disaster, and we've collected the rewards ever since.

'We can legally practice our religion and meet in our synagogues. We don't have to serve in the army or attend judicial courts on Shabbat. We can gather our Temple tax and send it to Jerusalem.

'These are important privileges and often infuriate those around us. If they cause trouble for us, the authorities tend to come down on our side, because of the Caesarean tradition and because we are an ancient religion. That commands even Rome's respect. So our position legally is good. It doesn't mean we are liked. Mostly we're not.

'The Greeks have their own cities. Except for the few Jews like myself who were specifically granted Roman citizenship, we are seen as foreigners, even when we've lived in a place for generations. You must have seen the same situation in Caesarea, a city in our own land where we have fewer rights.

'That's the position abroad. And indeed the Greeks like to make us feel inferior when they can, something you're forced to put up with, particularly as the Romans identify closely with them. We're the outsiders. In normal life, that shouldn't affect you too much. Does that help?'

'Immensely. You've given me a lot to think about. Thank you.'

'I'll be able to introduce you to the president of the synagogue,' the captain said. 'He's a close friend and he'll make sure you're looked after. But I'm afraid we need to return to the ship soon. I promised James and Amos some shore-time. Do you mind, Marcus?'

'Not at all, Simon. It was a pleasure to see you. And John, I hope everything goes well with you. Until I come to Ephesus, keep me in your prayers, and I will keep you in mine.'

Evia came back into the room in time to join her husband in wishing them farewell, and she gave Mary an affectionate kiss.

They departed and made their way back to the harbour in the darkening shadows. It had been a wonderful evening, and they both thought they'd made some real friends.

8

A Treasure Chest

Back onboard, they descended to the cabin to examine the wooden box and found it packed with Augustan silver denarii—at a guess, at least seven or eight hundred. With them were two sealed parchments addressed to his friends in Ephesus.

Mary's eyes widened. Her hands rushed to her mouth. 'This is far too much, John. Don't you think so? What should we do?'

He considered the gift, a frown creasing his brow. The money alone could sustain them for a considerable period; with their own, there was more than enough to build a house and care for his aunt as her days lengthened.

'We can always give it back. I'll talk to Simon and see what he thinks.' Leaving their treasure chest with her, he climbed on deck to find the captain up the mast at the crossbeam, needle in hand, repairing a rip in the mainsail. As he waited, he relaxed on Mary's seat and gazed over the peaceful harbour.

Warm breezes flowed over the undulating *Galilee*, the decks bright with moonlight. Voices and laughter echoed from ships on the neighbouring quay, their swinging lanterns and dancing lights reflected on the water below. Their new Cypriot friend and his chest of Roman silver filled his thoughts. A magnificent gift, especially from a complete stranger. No doubt, the money would help Mary enormously in the years ahead, yet he wasn't totally comfortable with the situation.

With his work finished, the captain joined him and listened to the story of the coins, his face creasing in amusement.

'How do you think I bought my ship, John? Where would I find that kind of money? I met Marcus in my early years when I captained for another owner. Copper ingots were an important trading product, and he managed the mines, much more involved than he is now. We became friends, and I used to discuss my ambitions with him, dreams I never expected to become reality.

'One Shabbat evening after a meal at the villa, he gave me a box, very similar to the one you carried back tonight. In it were enough Augustan coins to buy the *Galilee*. I stocked her with spices and precious stones from India, went straight to Ostia, Rome's port, and made a small fortune in profit.

'On the way home, I called into Paphos, and Marcus refused a repayment. He was easily able to facilitate the purchase, he said, and therefore it was to him a duty as a priest of the Most High. Although far from home and unable to carry out his Temple obligations, he tries to support his fellow Jews when possible and considers it an offering to the Holy One. He's a good man, John. There aren't many priests in Judaea who would do as much.

'He's very wealthy, and I would advise you to keep the money. He would be genuinely sorry if you didn't. I'm not the only one he's helped. Even though he never spoke to me of others, I've heard the stories. You both impressed him, and he wants to make your life a little easier. Accept his gift. Do something useful with it.

'Anyway, while you're thinking about that, let's talk about tomorrow. We'll leave at dawn. Let's hope the men are back by then. The first job will be getting the ship out and away. That's down to me, but would you helm once everyone has settled into a routine. Take turns with Mathias and James. I'll be on watch from now on. Your help would make all the difference in the morning.'

'You've no need to ask, Simon. Of course I will.'

He was pleased with the request. These days at the helm had been a comfort; they allowed him to regain his strength and learn how to deal with the open seas. The experience might even be of value in the future, which sometimes loomed before him with uncertainty.

Bidding his friend goodnight, he left for his bunk. No point in disturbing Mary. He would tell her everything in the morning.

The ship's heeling woke him at first light, and he rose, washed, dressed, and ran up the steps to join the captain on the quarterdeck. Bleary-eyed but still awake after the long watch, Simon grinned in relief when his helmsman appeared.

The sharp, clear beams of the rising sun pierced the clouds over the eastern horizon. Cyprus receded behind them into the morning mist, and to the north, they glimpsed pale shores on the mainland. With the sails braced to starboard, the strengthening gusts swept over the port beam. The ship surged through the water, the white waves racing beside her, and a cloudless spring morning promised steady-to-strong winds and speed to Rhodes, their next destination.

9

The Maritime Island

Late in the afternoon the next day, the squalls eased, and in the distance land, the maritime island of Rhodes, appeared on the horizon. The *Galilee* approached with slackened sails, heading for the most southerly of the three harbours where vessels from Syria usually docked. Moments after sunset, the ship edged past the Kayston Rocks into the port, the heavy-eyed crew waiting with oars poised. An official called greetings and directed them to their docking space.

Mary came on deck to watch, relieved to arrive after the long, blustery days, eager to disembark for a meal. Simon had told them of a hostelry that catered for travellers from Judaea, providing not only food but baths and a laundry service. Only minutes away, it gave them the last opportunity to bathe and have clean linen.

The captain wouldn't join them, too busy organising transportation of cargo and contacting merchants for olive oil. They had until the morrow, lots of time to explore. She hid Marcus's chest in the cabin and pulled her mantle around her, ready to depart. John lifted the basket of clothes, following her up the steps and down the plank to the quay.

They searched the harbour inns until they found the one

Simon recommended. A pleasant-faced woman hurried over. 'Well, my dears. I'm Sarah, the wife of the owner.'

She took Mary's arm and herded them to a table in the corner, chattering amiably without waiting for answers, drying her hands on her apron.

'Now what can I do for you? Something to eat and drink, yes? Just landed? Where are you from? Yes. Yes. You just sit here. Perfect for you. Now, what would you like?'

She pulled out stools and wiped down the table. 'I have some nice roast lamb. What about that? Or fresh fish? What do you think?'

They explained their requirements: baths, food, their garments washed and ready for the next day. Almost in an instant a servant girl arrived to take their basket, and Sarah's husband came to collect John. On her way to the women's quarters upstairs, Mary glanced back to see her nephew scarcely controlling his laughter as he hurried after the innkeeper in the opposite direction. She grinned.

At least we know she'll get things done.

Later, she crept down the steps, tightly clutching the walls, reinvigorated but still unbalanced on dry land. She looked forward to their arrival in Ephesus, hoping to settle into a more normal life. For the moment, she was managing to keep herself stable, thanks to the Most High, finding it a little easier to tolerate the physical pain in her body and the heartbreaking despair and desolation emanating from the desecrated soul within.

Even so, when she slept, she descended to deep, murky caves with the sweet, sickly odour of decomposing bodies, to be chased by salivating wild animals or men with blood-stained knives, fleeing in fear to awake exhausted and lie in the darkness until dawn.

On other nights she stood shaking before the cross on the hill: a jagged knife twisting in her gut, the scorching midday sun, the metallic smell of blood, the stink of faeces and urine, the streaming sweat; his face ripped and torn, battered black, encrusted; the thorns digging deep into his scalp and brow; his eyes swollen, barely seeing; his head and shoulders hanging, the nails tearing, ravaging his wrists; the feeble gasp as he laboured to breathe.

And the lizard eyes beneath the red-plumed helmet of the Roman soldier who flung her back, John's arms as he caught her. On those mornings she awoke to a pillow drenched in tears and lay there, unable to move, insensible, until her nephew found her and held her while she wept.

The heartache and dejection that followed often lasted for days. Eventually, the spiritual discipline trained into her soul by the Wise Ones during Yeshu's childhood came to her aid, and with her nephew's constant support, she dragged herself up to some sense of normality and the ongoing fight for her freedom.

In time, she would strengthen and consciously direct her night-time actions, learn to neutralise the attacks in her dreams. And there would come a day when she would send the entity back to the realms of the damned, back from whence it came. Those tasks were still in the future. She wasn't capable as yet, although stronger than she had been when she embarked in Joppa, much more in control.

The apostle, of course, understood what was happening, but she didn't think anyone else would guess. She didn't want to be a burden or cause others distress. Attacks from Satan littered her past; over the years, she learned how to deal with them. Experience and determination would help her cope with this one.

Down on the terrace next to the gardens, still spring-green and full of scented flowers, their table cooled under an overhanging tree. He ordered a bean stew with onions, just what they needed. They didn't stay long. A quiet, peaceful night to be followed by a day of discovery on the island.

The next morning they explored, but after hours of walking around markets, harbours, and the ancient city of Rhodes, she was glad to return in the afternoon. The others spent the day unloading and reloading. Then they went ashore and would return later for the promised dinner.

Apparently, they were anticipating an enjoyable evening, especially with the prospect of tales about Yeshu. As well as that, it was unusual to have a woman on board for Shabbat, someone to oversee the evening as would a mother or wife. It created an atmosphere of comfort and home, better than the crowded, impersonal eating houses along the harbour.

She went down to leave the clothes collected from the inn and the little items from the marketplace, things to remind her of the journey north. They had bathed and changed, but she was tired and rested for a moment on her bunk, falling asleep almost immediately. Awakened in the early evening by voices and laughter, she rose, tidied her appearance, and climbed the steps to be with her friends.

On the quarterdeck, they'd organised a second table with extra seating: bowls piled with bread, grapes, and figs; jugs and decanters filled with wine. Tempting aromas wafted up from the hold, and her mouth watered. She poured some tirosh and sank back into the soft cushions on her couch, listening to the others as they told the adventures of their day. The twilight breezes swept over the waters, swirling around the ships, sweeping away the dust and debris that accumulated since morning.

Amos and Samuel sauntered along the dock with even more drinks, followed closely by Honi and Jude. They gathered at the tables. The sun was about to touch the earth when James emerged with the long-awaited tray of roasted lamb, a platter of fish, and dishes of vegetables. They were ready to begin.

10

The First Teaching

She lit the lamps, and, prompted by the captain, her nephew said a prayer, asking the Father to bless the feast before them, protect them from the dangers of the sea, guide their ship into the harbour of Ephesus, and home safe to their own port of Joppa. A simple and heartfelt blessing, spoken with such trust and authority that the connection between him and the Creator was palpable.

It shivered through those who sat at the tables on the quarterdeck. Wide-eyed, Simon stared at his friend, and Mary smiled, aware how fully John had come into his abilities. Even with her injury she felt the power. She searched the faces of the others; the surprise on Simon's, the glimmer of tears in Mathias's eyes, and the wonder and question with James, Samuel, and Jude. Only Honi and Amos stayed oblivious to the change, interested only in the food and wine, pouring drinks and reaching for bread.

The apostle, she noted with amusement, remained totally unaware of the effects of his prayer. Conscious of many holy souls around him, she thought through the implications and wavered. Had she been wrong? Was there still a chance? Questioning hope battled with the physical pain within. Did the Father sanction the search for another way? If so, what it meant for the future she didn't understand, as yet. She needed to listen to the apostle's

54

thoughts and examine them carefully, to remain to the end of this special evening and perhaps discover something of what lay before them. Conversation stayed quiet and thoughtful, everyone waiting for him to speak.

Finally, his meal finished, John gazed at his friends and knew what he wanted to say. 'You asked me to talk about Yeshua the Healer, but first let me say this: we have lost the Teacher and Messenger of the Most High, yet the mandated task from the Holy One still must be completed. No one can prevent it. It will take longer than originally hoped, but its accomplishment is destined.

'When the human race first walked the earth, the Creator gave them two important gifts: the capacity for spiritual knowledge, and freedom of choice—the right to accept or reject His wisdom. Greater understanding would teach man to love his brothers and sisters, as well as all the other creatures that shared his world; thus a paradise would emerge on the earth. Throughout the aeons, humankind would progress and absorb the lessons necessary to be with the Father forever.

'At that time, a man was born with unique abilities, gifted above all others, and sent to accelerate our evolvement. Instead, he began to believe he created his own potential, that his capacities were innate, not from the Holy One. In his overwhelming pride, he sought to place himself in opposition to the Creator, to attract all worship to himself, and he turned humanity away from the One who made them. By doing so, he brought disaster to mankind.

'He grew to hate the Father and led us to suffering and destruction. As he gained strength, he attracted many loyal adherents by healing their illnesses and giving gullible people what they thought they most wanted; he restored to a partial form of life those who had passed over and for whom the loved ones left behind mourned in sorrow. Satan thrived on the adulation of those who believed him omnipotent, until nearly all humanity turned its face from the One who gave them life.

'This is how the rule of evil came into being. Despite this, the Holy One didn't withdraw His gifts, neither freedom of choice, nor the potential for spiritual knowledge. These will always be freely available to mankind.

'Some of our ancestors remained faithful, a remnant who kept their belief in the Father. The era of desecration wouldn't last, He promised them. One day it will end, and from that day onwards, the season of love and kindness would reign upon the earth.

'A Teacher would come to show us how to defeat the Evil One. For this reason Yeshua walked among us, the Messenger of the Most High. Had he lived, the age of wickedness would have ended; the kingdom of heaven would have begun to spread. But it wasn't to be, so the task has fallen to us.

'Two things we can do now: remind our own people to care for each other, as taught by the prophets, and continue Yeshua's work with the possessed. We can exorcise desecrated souls, nullify Satan's influence within them, and send them back, elevated and cleansed, to the Father in heaven. In this way we will do all we can to prepare for the next attempt.

'Although we no longer have Yeshua to hold and control Satan, there will be another way to deal with him. In time, we will learn what to do. Meanwhile, we can weaken the throngs of his followers, the cohorts and battalions who support him and keep him strong. In the future, when we are ready to begin again, he won't have the same sources of sustenance and will be easier to elevate.

'This will be my work in Ephesus, the measures I will take for the rest of my life. The love we will create in so doing will send out a power that will change the earth. Nothing will stand in our way. The Creator has given His word. The dominion of Beliel will end, and we will build a different future and a new world.

'May the Holy One guide us and help us to do His will.'

A stunned silence fell on the group as they stared at the apostle.

He waited for a reaction. A small, uncertain voice came from his left.

'Is there anything I can do?' Mathias asked. A smile curved Simon's mouth.

'Yes, you can,' the apostle replied. 'Treat people with loving kindness as we've been taught by the prophets.'

'No, no. I mean, can I join you in whatever work you will do in the city?' Aware of the sailor's senior position on the *Galilee*, John glanced over to the captain in surprise. A smiling nod answered.

'Mathias, I don't know, as yet, what will happen. I need to meet the members of the synagogue and assess the situation. Certainly, when we are settled and begin to work, we'll need all the help we can get. We can talk about this later, if you like.'

James watched and listened.

'I'd like to know how this started. How did Yeshua know what to do? Who told him he was the Teacher?' John studied his aunt, amazed she hadn't excused herself and left. Yet there she sat, encouraging him to continue.

'Mary, his mother, received the first knowledge. She was still a young girl when the angel came and told her of the babe she would carry, the promised Teacher who would show the people how to defeat Satan and bring an end to his rule.'

Gently, she interrupted. 'Would you like me to tell this part? If that would help.'

Delighted, he concurred.

'Soon after Yeshu's birth, the Wise Ones came from Batanea, from over the hills to the east of the Lake, members of our own Nazoraean clan who were extremely well versed in spiritual matters, far beyond normal knowledge. Their communications from on high warned them of the coming Messenger.

'The child would need help, they told us. He must be educated, his talents nurtured and prepared for the task he would undertake. Initially they came to Joseph and me, and then later to others in the family and community. They gave us spiritual knowledge and taught us how to raise the babe in the ways of the Father.

'Those of us with appropriate abilities were shown how to recognise and cultivate his gifts, supervising him until puberty when the Wise Ones came again to evaluate his progress. They found in him a strong healer with a formidable ability to send hence evil spirits. On returning north and east to their own lands, they brought my son with them, and there he grew in power and strength.

'Often he came home to spend time with us and impart the learning to relatives and friends who would help him in the future. When he finished his training, he already had a nucleus of supporters who understood his work, and he was able to begin the elimination of iniquity.'

Nodding to John, she asked him to continue.

'When Yeshu returned, his spiritual gifts had already matured, especially physical healing and the capacity to combat evil, immense, inherent aptitudes honed over many years to the greatest possible degree. A highly evolved soul.

'In my opinion, his most impressive talent was the way he radiated the pure essence of the Creator. Everyone in his company sensed it: his kindness and understanding for those who had done wrong; his heartfelt compassion for the suffering, the blind man, the leper, those who mourned a loved one; for the woman who gave away her last coin to the poor. We were surrounded by love.

'Even the depraved souls felt it, and this gave him incredible command over them. They couldn't resist him, would do anything he asked. In his presence, evil weakened and didn't influence them to the same extent.

'Through love and understanding, he drew them away from Satan and helped them ascend to the Father. He aided them by removing the sickness from their souls, just as he removed physical illnesses from the bodies of those who lived.

'This was the most important lesson he taught us, the core of all his work. These poor beings are sick. In the depths of their pain they don't know what they are doing. If we reject them with anger, we condemn them to more suffering. On the other hand, if we treat them with love, sympathy, and patience, we bring them to a greater awareness of the Father in heaven. This is how the rule of evil will end.

'You must understand this: these entities are the souls of those no longer living, people who ended their lives with the guilt of wrongs committed during their time on earth. They wander among men and women who live, searching for the spiritually weak or those with a tendency towards wickedness. Much of their power is gathered by encouraging their living victim into greater and greater corruption.

'Hatred and hostility is to them the breath of life, the desire for material riches a fine wine which leads to drunkenness and the empires of our world, whether Seleucid, Roman, or Parthian, are an unending feast leading to spiritual destruction.

'The road before us is difficult, and in time we will receive, from the blessed realms, clear instructions for the times ahead. In the meantime, in the city of Ephesus we will find many who are possessed and lower souls who need our aid to return to the Father. Much can still be done, and people of compassion will support us in our work.

'May the Holy One guide us and help us to do His will.'

Silence fell once more. This time, a calm serenity settled over the group. The lamps flickered, throwing light and shadow on their faces, and beyond them, as the sky darkened, the port grew peaceful.

The apostle sat back and relaxed. Only a little knowledge could be absorbed at a time. The more dangerous teachings must be kept for those capable of sustaining them and even then could only be given when they strengthened their defences against Satan. Over the next days, some would come to discuss everything further. He would wait.

11

North through the Blue Aegean

The *Galilee* left Rhodes on the second dawn and sailed north to Ephesus. The passengers and crew settled into a routine, pulling into quiet coves at night-time, eating their evening meal together at the stern, as they did on Shabbat. During the day John helmed, and the senior crew took turns, often in conversation with the Galilean couple.

The captain gave them time and opportunity, transferring many of their responsibilities to the younger men. He expected Mathias would leave on this trip, James at some stage later, and considered the capabilities of the others, wondering who might be advanced enough to take their places.

At no time did he consider making it difficult or persuade them to stay. It would be hard to lose them, not only for their experience but because they reminded him of home and his youth. He would miss them and wished he could do more, envying them their freedom. At any rate, he was determined to do everything possible to support John and Mary and be satisfied with that.

Mary was stronger, more relaxed and optimistic, although on a few occasions the evil within overcame her, bringing back the old despair and hopelessness. The loss of her son punished her with guilt, leaving her stricken. Going below, away from her nephew's solicitous eyes, she would curl up in her bunk and sustain the physical pain, the sense of desolation, the dragging numbness and grief.

In spite of that, a change had come. A small part of her separated and calmly watched the suffering woman as she fought the presence. Aware of the cause, she no longer became lost in her mind and endured the long hours of agony from which there was no relief. She persevered and waited, praying to the Father for her freedom.

Surrounding her with love, the apostle resigned himself to the fact he could do no more. Feeling the fluctuations of the entity, he sensed the battle being waged for Mary's soul and poured his strength into her, convinced she had the will to succeed. Many times it crossed his mind that Yeshu knew how his mother would suffer, and he hoped one day she would regain control of her soul.

As they sailed north, Mathias and James questioned him about the Teacher and his beliefs, drinking in the knowledge like parched men in the desert. A joy to teach. Both exhibited definite capacities for kindness that reinforced his faith in their abilities, their potential for the future.

With regard to his own life, the road ahead remained blind, with no indications as to what he should do.

Then he remembered his cousin saying, 'Don't anticipate. Don't worry. Deal with what is to come, one step at a time. All will be well.'

On the fourth day they turned to the east and continued down the straits separating the island of Samos from Mount Mycale on the mainland and entered the Bay of Ephesus. Hugging the coast to the right, Simon related the histories of the white marbled cities that sprawled along the coastal plain. Finally, they approached the narrow estuary of the Cayster River, which led to the city on the southern bank. They had arrived.

PART 2

The City of Ephesus

12

Present Day: North London

Out on the patio, Cathrina lay back in her cushioned deckchair at the terrace table and surveyed the garden below: roses spreading in swathes of pinks and reds, scurrying up and over fences, smothering the shapely arch which covered the steps leading down to the lawn. The scents wafted around her. She knew she ought to do some deadheading, but she had neither the energy nor the motivation.

Books and pages covered the table. Perched on a pile of files, Susie, the black-eyed tortoiseshell, purred like a tiger cub and batted her paw at the encroaching white butterfly, while her mistress gazed blankly over the empty playing fields that stretched into the distance. Cathrina's brain had simply shut down.

On returning from Ephesus the previous weekend, she immediately began her research. There would be no time after she went back to work on Monday. Josh was lucky; a psychology lecturer at a North London college, he still had the rest of July and most of August. At times she envied him his summer holidays.

She had finished her reading and arrived at final conclusions. At first, she concentrated on discovering connections between Jesus and the rule of evil, but the more she delved, the more she focused on the undoubted links between his early followers and the Essenes.

Now, she wanted her husband to read through her notes and give his opinion. In the meantime she would relax and try to bring her brain back online.

Jesus and the Essenes

Some early church writers assumed the connection. Eusebius (260–339 CE), bishop of Caesarea and advisor to Emperor Constantine, appeared to view the Christian gospels and epistles as Essene writings. Epiphanius (367–404 CE), bishop of Salamis, believed two branches existed: the Osseans (from the Hebrew, *Osei ha Torah*, meaning 'doers of Torah'), the celibate branch, and the Nazoraeans, who married and lived in cities and towns.

The Jewish historian Josephus (37–96 CE) gave the greatest detail and positioned them within the four main philosophies in Second Temple Judaea: the Sadducees, an aristocratic group to which the high priestly families belonged; the legalistic Pharisees, who followed both the written law and the oral tradition; the peaceful Essenes; and the Zealots, passionate, even vehement, in their allegiance to the One God, yet willing to kill or die in their attempts to eject foreigners and idolaters from the land.

Hippolytus (160–235 CE) identified several Essene groups, all committed to righteousness but with different attitudes to the use of physical force.

He included the Zealots among them. In contrast, he regarded the Nazoraeans as pacifists.

Although he found it difficult to trace their origins, the eminent scholar Jerome Murphy-O'Connor believed the Essenes evolved as a rigorously pious sect in Babylon in response to the divine punishment of the exile. Their beliefs show Mesopotamian influence; facing eastwards before dawn they beseeched the Creator for sunrise, they studied the healing effects of plants and stones and became star gazers, experts in astrology, divination, and foretelling the future.

From Zoroastrianism they learned of the two spirits that control man, one of goodness and the other of evil, and proposed two spiritual kingdoms: the realm of the good angels, the servants of God led by Michael the archangel, the Prince of Light, and that of the demons under the leadership of the Angel of Darkness, Satan the king of wickedness.

They didn't return to Judaea when Cyrus initially released the Jews from exile but remained within the Persian Empire, until the Maccabees invited them home during their war of independence in the mid-second century BCE.

They expected to find the land free of Gentile influence, but Greek culture had spread widely in the east after the conquests of Alexander the Great. The community rebelled against any possibility of assimilation, and although they dispersed, they kept to themselves, separate, exclusive, and insular. They grew in numbers. According to Josephus, four thousand lived in villages, towns, and cities, marrying and having children.

In the early days after their return, they questioned the validity of the Temple sacrifices, the legitimacy of the non-Zadokite high priests, and their use of the Babylonian lunar calendar instead of their own pre-exilic solar version. The changes meant that unauthorised priests celebrated the most important feasts, including the Day of Atonement, on the wrong days, and this caused the Holy One's covenant with Israel to be revoked. The people were left ritually impure and without protection from Beliel, the devil.

A new covenant with the Most High was inaugurated, one which assumed responsibility for obtaining atonement for the people. But there were differences among the Essene groups in their attitudes to the Temple. The celibates spurned the Sanctuary and replaced the sacrificial activity with a daily communal meal, preceded by ritual immersion. Practising voluntary poverty, they followed the Law, with particular care in regard to the Sabbath.

Those living in the cities and towns reacted differently and continued with Temple worship, sending votive offerings and paying the required tax. However, in principle, they rejected animal sacrifice and considered the practice a temporary measure. Josephus tells us they replaced it with a third method of purification, perhaps similar to the rites performed by the desert community.

According to the Scrolls, the sectaries ate their meal together at least once a day, but we don't know how often the Nazoraeans gathered for theirs, a ritual which anticipated the Christian eucharist.

Early church writers report that, after the crucifixion and possibly for some time beforehand, Mary and her family James, Simeon, and Jude, with her nephews James and John, the sons of Zebedee, lived in the Essene quarter, now Mount Sion in south west Jerusalem. (Before 70 CE the walled city enclosed this area.) The question therefore arises: Were the ancestors of Mary and Jesus both Nazoraeans and Essenes?

Hippolytus and Epiphanius describe the Nazoraeans as a pre-Christian Jewish clan which returned, with the other Essenes, when the Maccabees persuaded the exiles to colonise the latest conquest, Galilee of the Gentiles.[5]

Although the situation isn't clear, there is some evidence that a number of Nazoraean families came to live in the area later named Nazareth or Nazara. The majority settled in Batanea, Old Testament Bashan and Gilead, the lands east of the Sea of Galilee and the Jordan, extending as far north as Damascus and south through Perea to 'Bethany beyond the Jordan' where Jesus was baptised.

---

[5] The title 'Nazoraean' is based on the Hebrew 'to keep or observe' and possibly means 'keepers of the covenant'. The early clan expanded into the Nazoraean Assembly led by James the Just, the brother of Jesus. Within Judaea, the Jewish Christians were known as Nazoraeans.

Descendants of David, they were the royal family from which the Anointed One would come.

Their understanding of the end times connected directly with the Koressos visions. The Messiah was about to come, the anticipation widespread in the intensely messianic atmosphere of Second Temple Judaea. The era produced various and contradictory descriptions, although the accepted version assumed he would vanquish the invading Romans and allow the righteous to repossess the land. Many claimants to the title appeared during this period and they all, including Jesus, met the inevitable end of those seen to rebel against Rome.

The Essenes had a specific scenario for the last days, supplemented biblical prophecy with their writings and planned for their own community, the final faithful remnant, to fulfil the prophetic expectations. Whether in the desert or in towns, they treated their dwellings as messianic war-camps and lived their lives in preparation for the confrontation between the Sons of Light and the Sons of Darkness.

They waited for the Anointed One of Israel and Aaron: either two Messiahs, one from the Davidic line and the other a priest or someone both royal and priestly. The predictions included the possibility of a prophet, the returned Elijah, the precursor and divine guide who would counsel them in the final days.

As Michael's angels moved among them, they conducted themselves at the highest level of ethics and morality, abhorring criminal and immoral activities, practicing charity to the needy and loving kindness towards their fellow man. Wearing only white linen, they carefully followed the Law, obeyed the purity instructions and kept the Sabbath holy. Voluntary poverty prevailed, and they earned a living by pastoral activities, agriculture, and the handicrafts of the artisan.

The celibate group held goods and property in common, while those in towns donated two or three days wages per month towards the public purse. This was used for those in need and to provide accommodation, food and clothing for traveling members.

For the Essenes in Judaea and their fellows, the Therapeutae in Egypt, the most important day in the year was Pentecost, the feast of renewal, and it was always celebrated on Sunday, the first day of Creation. At that time, they gathered in general assembly to celebrate the new covenant, which replaced the ancient one of Moses.

Old members reaffirmed their pledges, and those entering made their vows of initiation. Although Jewish by circumcision, a separate ritual was required. After a long noviciate and final acceptance by the gathering, a baptising immersion brought total remission of former wrongdoing. Afterwards, they joined their co-members in the community meal.

The similarities to Christianity became more than tantalising; combined with the experiences on Koressos, they compelled. Was it a coincidence that the Jesus followers, on that first 'Christian' Pentecost in the Essene Guest House on Mount Sion, received baptism by the Holy Spirit with tongues of fire, as gatherings of the sect in other locations initiated their new members through the Holy Spirit and a baptism of water?

Other features in common followed: the concepts of the new covenant, the initiating baptism, the Holy Spirit, the forgiveness of sins, and the sacrificial meal, all central to the practice of both.

The Christian eucharist and the sacred communal meal of the Essenes commemorated the establishment of the covenant that replaced the Temple sacrifices. In each rite, the bread and wine were blessed by the priest, and unlike normative Judaism, the former was sanctified first.

Another variant was the prominent position given by both sects to the Holy Spirit, mentioned not only in the Community Rule and Damascus Document but called upon frequently in Essene hymns and blessings. At times, the title referred to God, on other occasions to the spirit within the human being.

'And He made known His Holy Spirit to them, by the hand of His anointed ones...' Damascus Document, 4Q266, column II, (page 130).[6]

---

[6] These two references come from *The Complete Dead Sea Scrolls in English* by Gaza Vermes. The page numbers given are from the fiftieth anniversary edition, published by Penguin Classics in 2011.

'No man shall defile his holy spirit since God has set them apart.' Damascus Document, 4Q266, column VII, (page 134)

Like the twelve apostles, and Peter, James, and John, the three pillars of the followers, twelve men and three priests led the desert celibates. They owned property in common with strict rules against lying about the extent of an applicant's possessions, as reflected in the story of Ananias and Sapphira when they tried to hold back moneys promised to the early Christian community (see Acts 5:1–5).

An elected individual held the Essene public purse and paid all community expenses, just as Jude was responsible for the twelve. And when Jesus sent out those who would preach throughout Judaea, giving them the unexplained instruction to take nothing with them as all would be provided, was he referring to the custom of the communities to welcome other Essene travellers as brothers, providing accommodations, food, and clothes?

Furthermore, the emphasis he placed on healing, exorcising, and teaching was replicated in the sect's drive to holistically cure ills in body, mind, and soul, especially by the Therapeutae, who were considered experts in the cure of the whole personality.

The more esoteric concepts of exorcism are not mentioned in the Scrolls, although, according to some scholars, the writings we have inherited were used to instruct newcomers. The sect transmitted their secret advanced knowledge orally.

There were differences, of course, yet these can be explained by the diversity of thought and attitude among Essene groups, particularly to the use of physical force.

For instance, we know the Nazoraeans believed Jesus was the Messiah, the long-awaited descendent of David, but they saw him as a pacifist who would save them from spiritual evil, not the military general expected by the Essenes of the Scrolls or indeed by most Jews of the time.

The Saviour didn't support a physical war; he envisaged a battle for souls, one he began by exorcising desecrated spirits as he walked the shores of the Sea of Galilee. He was the Teacher who came to free humanity from the predations of Satan, and as he emphasised in the Sermon on the Mount and elsewhere, he was a man of peace, not the expected military man of violence: 'Blessed are the peacemakers, for they shall be called children of God' (Mathew 5:9). 'Love your enemies and pray for those who persecute you' (Mathew 5:44).

The rule of God, the kingdom of heaven always remained his goal and focus, a task which would only be achieved by eliminating evil through love and compassion, concepts that reach back in time to Leviticus: 'You shall not take vengeance or bear a grudge against any of your people, but you shall love your neighbour as yourself: I am The Lord' (19:18).

This instruction throughout the centuries had stimulated care for the destitute, the widow, and the orphan. Within Essene philosophy it expanded. Treating their companions with immense loving kindness, they forbade even the expression of anger: 'And he shall love each man, his brother as himself; they shall succour the poor, the needy and the stranger' (The Damascus Document, 4Q266, column VI).[7]

Yet for the writers of the Scrolls in the last days of the age, that precept applied only to their own group. They had no tolerance for their enemies, whether foreign or of their own people. All who opposed them would be destroyed. Curses against the enemy, both physical and cosmic, fill their writings.

'They may love all the sons of light, each according to his lot in God's design and hate all the sons of darkness, each according to his guilt in God's vengeance.' (The Community Rule, IQS column I).[8] They still envisaged the Most High as, potentially, a God of revenge, not the God of Love that Jesus reflected, and the kindness he showed to all, friend or foe, did not characterise their philosophy.

Furthermore they excluded certain people. 'No madmen, or lunatic shall enter, no simpleton, or fool, no blind man or maimed, or lame, or deaf man, and no minor, none of these shall enter into

---

[7] *The Complete Dead Sea Scrolls in English* by Gaza Vermes, Page 134.
[8] Ibid. Page 99.

the community, for the Angels of Holiness are in their midst.' (The Damascus Document, 4Q266, column XV).[9]

Although the Nazoraeans accepted women, there is no mention in the Qumran library of their association with the celibate group, and in the Damascus Document they were banned from Jerusalem, except for short visits.

In contrast to the rigidity we find in the Scrolls, Jesus welcomed everyone as an equal, and his prominent followers included women. He cured the blind and infirm, associated with the ritually impure, tax collectors, prostitutes, lepers, the woman with the discharge, those in mourning, and even, on occasions, Gentiles. Yet there is no evidence he immersed or purified himself after each contact.

Deeply moved, on occasions to tears, by the sufferings of the *am ha-arez*, the unlettered multitudes of the people, those despised by rapacious landowners, chief priests, and Roman overlords, Jesus deliberately identified with them. He treated them with respect, with love and kindness.

And this helped release them from the oppressive burden of their own perceived unworthiness. No longer did they fear their predestined destruction as portrayed by the writers of the Scrolls, but by accepting the Saviour's help and healing, the cripple took up his bed and walked.

---

[9] Ibid. Page 138.

With a revolutionary way of thinking, yet deeply rooted in his Jewish heritage, he was powerfully influenced by the social needs of the people and the religious and philosophical thought of the age.

Josh came in an hour later to find her down in the garden, with Susie at her feet, in among the bushes, deadheading roses, her blonde hair gleaming in the sunlight. He laughed. She'd been promising herself that 'treat' for ages.

He put on the kettle and arranged her favourite white-china mugs and plates on a tray. A jug of milk with spoons and forks followed, and he unpacked the fresh cream and chocolate eclairs he'd bought down in the bakery in Hendon. With the silver teapot filled, he brought everything out to the patio. Calling his wife, he poured and sat down to enjoy the rest of the afternoon.

She dragged herself away and joined him, laughing with delight when she saw the cakes. When he finished, she searched for her final notes and passed them to him. Sometime later he turned to her, almost in exasperation.

'Cathrina, there's something I don't understand. How did Christian celibacy come from Judaism? It's almost incongruous. Our religion reveres family life. The rabbis are married, and the exhortation to go forth and multiply is still foundational. It might be a bit off the point here, but can you explain it?'

'Ah, but you're talking about present-day Rabbinic religion, which evolved from the lay Pharisees after the destruction of Jerusalem in 70 CE. Very different from religion in the Second Temple era, when the Sanctuary was still functioning under the priestly class. Yet, funnily enough, it isn't as irrelevant as you might think.

'A priest couldn't approach the sacrificial altar while "impure". This didn't have the sexual overtones of today's Catholic confessional. It was ritual, not immoral. I think it originally indicated the absorption of an "unclean" vibration from a place, an activity or another person, something that rendered the priest spiritually contaminated.

'For instance, he could become affected through crossing a graveyard, touching a corpse, a Gentile, a leper, and lots of other ways, including having sexual relations. This applied even when the couple were married. After sex, both the man and woman became "impure" but could cleanse themselves by immersing in a *miqvah*, as described in Leviticus 15:16–18.

'That's why the priests conducting the morning and evening sacrifices in the Temple remained celibate. In practice this wasn't too difficult. They came from all parts of Judaea for a period of duty in the Sanctuary and afterwards returned to their normal lives and relationships with their wives. Continual abstinence wasn't required.

'Even the high priest had to live apart from his wife for seven days before entering the Holy of Holies in the Temple on the Day of Atonement. A nocturnal emission during that time meant he was "impure", and his deputy would take over his duties.

'The Essenes were even stricter; it required three days to "purify" the couple. Among the celibates in the desert, the priests were in permanent residence. As the communal meal replaced the Temple sacrifices, constant celibacy was necessary. The laymen of the community presumably accepted the condition in order to minimise spiritual contamination.

'The Egyptian Essenes, the Therapeutae, took vows of poverty and chastity. They lived solitary lives dedicated to prayer, fasting, learning and the practice of their healing arts. Eusebius even thought they were the first Christian monks. They certainly were the forerunners of Egyptian monasticism that influenced the early non-Roman monasteries found in places like Ireland.

'So yes, Josh. I agree that celibacy didn't derive from Rabbinic Judaism. But one could argue that both the celibacy requirements for priests in the Holy Sanctuary and the asceticism of the Essenes, as detailed in the Scrolls, produced the pattern for Christian celibate life. The two religions either directly evolved from or were strongly influenced by two very different Judaic sects in the Second Temple era. It explains a lot of the differences.'

'That's really interesting and makes perfect sense. Now, what's the story with the Nazoraeans? I thought the early Christians were called Nazarenes.'

'This isn't clear-cut either. They were called Nazoraeans, Nazareans, Nazrenes, Nassenes, names derived from Nazareth or based on Essene, although it's more likely that the name Nazareth came from the Nazoraean clan name. They have the same Hebrew root.

'When I read about the Jesus followers escaping north to Pella of Perea, on the east bank of the Jordan, before the outbreak of the Revolt, I always wondered why. What made them think they'd be safe there? But if it was part of the Nazoraean homelands, then it makes sense. They would be safer there than anywhere else.

'John's Gospel tells us that many people east of the Jordan believed in Jesus, and Epiphanius says the sect still existed there in his own time, the fourth century, living in the lands from Pella up through Batanea, as far north as Aleppo, in present-day Syria. It was the fabled land of Damascus mentioned so often in the Scrolls. And remember, this was where the Essene John the Baptist worked and where Jesus was baptised.

'The whole story is fascinating, much more complicated than I originally understood. I think Mary's ancestors must have been Nazoraean Essenes. There are too many similarities with early Christianity to ignore the connection. Over the years, they moved away philosophically from those Essenes prepared to use violence and evolved into a peace-orientated sect, dedicated to ending the rule of evil by non-violent means.

'But, Josh, what I would really like to know is this: How were Jesus and the Nazoraeans going to end the rule of evil? What were they planning before he was captured and crucified?'

13

A Roman City with a Greek Goddess

One of the major harbours of Roman Asia, the city was easily accessible from the Aegean, sandwiched between two ports, Smyrna to the north at the mouth of the Hermus valley and Miletus where the sinuous Meander finally reached the sea. Although smaller than its neighbours, the Cayster River commanded a wealthy hinterland which extended into the Anatolian plateau to the east, with connections both to the Black Sea and the Fertile Crescent.

The old Persian Road followed the River Hermes to Sardis and then cut through the Tmolus mountain range to Ephesus. Another route, to the south, crossed the hills into the Meander floodplain and joined the Great Southern Highway, with direct access to Syria, Judaea, the Euphrates and beyond. Pivotal geographically and the most important metropolis in the eastern Roman Empire, the city reigned both as a commercial hub and the seat of government for the provincial administration.

As they approached, the magnificent harbour buildings lay before them, the quays packed with traders and several ships of the imperial navy. With the mainsail furled, sailing gently on the foresail, Simon eased his way in, following the instructions of the official on the dock, the crew over the sides manoeuvring. A laughing face with a prodigious, black beard called him, waving him over. Within minutes the *Galilee* was tied up beside his friend, with long lines secured to bollards on the quay. A grinning captain climbed over the gunnels to a boisterous reception.

Mary surveyed the scene from her usual perch, absorbed in the colours and noise, listening to the foreign voices and their languages, scanning the towering, columned buildings, the broad streets and wide, paved spaces: everything afloat in a marble sea of cream.

The place seethed with activity, filled with people rushing to mysterious destinations: stately figures with purple-edged togas; tattooed slaves carrying boxes; turbaned, black-eyed, swarthy merchants pushing and hustling. A feverish port and a noisy city.

They had arrived at last, ready to begin their new life. Suddenly, without warning, fear and dread flooded her. *What am I doing here so late in my life when I should be at home preparing for a quiet old age, rather than this stupid journey away from everything I know?*

Her body trembled. With her arms wrapped tightly around her, she slipped from her seat, made for the steps in the hope that no one would notice, and found her way down to the cabin. There, she fought for control and gradually separated herself from the entity, calming the rage building within her.

Later in the evening, they went with the captain and Mathias for a meal in a restaurant a short distance away, and afterwards they discussed what they should do over the following days.

'The synagogue first,' Simon said. 'That's where you need to start. Joseph will be around the market tomorrow. His son owns a shop there. I'll talk to him about finding you somewhere to live. On the fourth morning, we leave at dawn, so that gives you some time. You can stay at an inn or find a small house. He'll have the contacts.

'Don't go too far from the synagogue, Mary. It's the centre of Jewish life here. It has a meeting hall, a library, baths, and somewhere you can wash clothes: everything you'll need. More importantly, you'll make friends and become part of the community.'

'What about work?' John asked. 'I'd like to buy a boat and learn about the local waters.'

'You shouldn't have a problem with that. There are families from home who fish the bay, even the Aegean. I'll make sure you're introduced to the right people.

'Tell me this. What are your plans for Yeshu's work?'

'I need to assess the situation first, Simon. Helping the possessed is the priority, so I'm hoping the president will have some ideas. Exorcisms I can do myself, but I'll have to train people to help with the elevations.'

Mathias interrupted. 'One more trip to Joppa and then I'll join you. I can repair boats. I'll find work around the harbour.'

'That would be a beginning, Mathias, and I'm grateful. Our task won't be easy, so let me give you an idea of what we're going to do.

'When he came to us after his death, Yeshu told us to weaken the heart of the enemy. Some of the followers thought he meant the Romans, but they are only instruments. If vanquished, they'd be replaced. After much discussion, we decided to remove the strength of the Evil One by neutralising his legions.

'It's important you understand this. Satan is surrounded by adherents, both the spirits of wicked men who died and went to the realms of the damned and those who still live but are under the influence of hatred, the desire to control others, and hunger for material riches. Taking away his support will cripple him. His power derives from the adulation of his armies. Without them, his capacity to harm would disintegrate.

'The followers are continuing with this work in Jerusalem, and I want to do the same in Ephesus. It means I'll have to find the lowest evil spirit here, probably Artemis.'

The captain's eyes widened. 'The goddess, you mean. You're going to attack the goddess?'

'No, no, not attack, Simon. If she is the most powerful, we can nullify her by kindness, not anger. That wouldn't succeed. Hostility would only make her stronger. We aim to do the opposite.'

Simon's brow creased in puzzlement. 'I must admit I don't understand.'

With a smile, John reached for his arm and apologised. 'I'm going too quickly. Let me explain. Yeshu gave us knowledge our people didn't have. The Pharisees teach the spirit is immortal, but they also believe the dead, both good and evil, go to an underworld until the end of the age. That's when the physical body resurrects and re-joins the spiritual being. The whole person, body and soul, is summoned to a last judgement, when the righteous are sent to the realms of the blessed and the desecrated are destroyed.

'We learned a different way from Yeshu. All souls are immortal, both good and bad. After death, a human being doesn't go to Hades or wait for final arbitration by the Holy One. Judgement is immediate and carried out by the person's own high spirit. If he judges his life as good, he will go into the gardens of the

Holy One. On the other hand, a harmful life will send him to the realms of the damned.

'Sometimes, lower entities are drawn back to the earth-plane and they attach themselves to living people, encouraging them to do wrong. In this way, they experience anger, power, and lust, continuing spiritually the existence they enjoyed while alive. The idols of our world are often such fallen souls, and they are capable of giving desecrated energy to those who identify with them. They can even give physical healing.

'Not all gods or goddesses, however, were wicked during their lifetime. Some performed brave deeds for their people and were declared divine when they died. Others are intrinsically corrupt, and this I must discover about Artemis. If she is a lower soul, she must be weakened and elevated. Afterwards, the city will be a more contented place. Of course, it will depend on how low she is. That problem is for tomorrow, not tonight. At least, this has helped me clarify what I need to do over these next weeks. By the time you return, we'll have an answer.'

His friends nodded, seeing the future a little more clearly. Their meal finished, they left for the ship.

Outside in the darkening street, the harbour lights twinkled in the distance, and when they turned the final corner, the dancing lamps hanging from the rigging of the ships painted a welcoming sight. Long before they reached the *Galilee,* they heard the laughter of James and the crew, all crowded together on the quarterdeck with decanters of strong Rhodian wine, celebrating their arrival and a night in port.

Mary went below. Later, in her bunk, she listened to the buzz of conversation above, their familiar voices a comfort, and strangely enough, they brought a sense of home. She would miss them.

14

A New Home and New Friends

Over the next few days, John and Mary walked the roads and pathways of Ephesus, up the main route to the theatre that snuggled into the foot of Mount Pion, round past the *agora* to the Praetorium and the colossal Temple of Augustus.

A splendid marble city, a jewel in the diadem of the eastern empire, streets lined with magnificent public buildings, theatres, and temples, like rows of white luscious pearls on swathes of cream linen, the perfection a betrayal when they gazed into the dead eyes of the tattooed slave and caught sight of the bloodstained whip in the hand of the soldier.

They stayed away from the Artemision, around which lay a cloying heaviness, a whiff of decomposing death. The apostle was certain now; the goddess was a dangerous evil spirit. She would be difficult to subdue, but one day he would have to face her. He would need help, which meant training new people until they could confront her with the necessary sympathy and understanding.

He kept Mary away. It would be difficult to sustain both the entity within and the perversion seeping from the temple.

Instead, they looked at inns and houses and met Joseph, the synagogue president, a plump, smiling man with a bushy beard and a twinkle in his eye. Assuming the stories of Yeshua the Healer had filtered into the community, Simon informed his old friend of the identities of the new arrivals and emphasised John's abilities as a healer and an exorcist.

'Keep it quiet for the moment, Joseph. Let them settle into the city first and see what happens.' His wish to whet the president's appetite for such useful and interesting newcomers met with considerable success.

He worked tirelessly to discover suitable houses nearby. Two days later he found a small, comfortable dwelling with two bedrooms and a kitchen-living room only a few streets away.

The thought of her own home delighted Mary, and the pleasant atmosphere reassured John, although he was glad to be a considerable distance from the temple. At a reasonable rent, they took the house for the next three months. By then, the future would be clearer.

He employed two young girls to clean their new home, and in the market he bought a table and stools, beds and bedding, pots and bowls for the kitchen and had them delivered. Mary arranged the rooms and befriended her helpers, learning about their families and the community. By Friday afternoon, everything was in place, except for their belongings on the ship.

She lit a fire to roast the fish and cook the lentil stew for Shabbat that night. During the morning, a visit to the market with Joseph's wife, Hannah, amazed her with the choice of food available. Her new friend directed her to shops owned by Jews, where produce would be fresh and meat properly prepared, not previously offered in sacrifice to idols. She returned home with baskets packed with fish, loaves of bread, vegetables, and lots of other items. Working contentedly in her kitchen, she prepared enough food to last several days and looked forward to their first Shabbat meal.

A noise in the courtyard alerted her, and she found her nephew and the captain unloading a young donkey. She gathered up a box full of her clothes and possessions from Nazareth, knowing the sight of familiar items would make the house a home. The men followed with the rest and left to go back for more.

That evening at sunset, she lit the lamps and sat down to their first meal with Simon, Mathias, and James. Their friendship was now enduring; in some ways, they felt bound together for life. When the three men departed that night, they did so with reluctance, realising how much they would miss their friends.

Mary and John relaxed at the table afterwards, strangely at peace. Noises from outside disturbed the quiet.

He jumped to his feet and made for the door. 'I forgot about the donkey.'

'What? A donkey? Did you buy one?'

'No. The captain did. As we paid for our passage with the animals in Joppa, he wanted to repay me for my work on the ship. I enjoyed the helming, but he insisted. She's a lovely little animal. She'll be useful and company for you when I'm away.'

With that he left, looking back with a grin.

She laughed. *Three of us now. I wonder what he'll bring home next.*

She quickly settled into her new house, and her own little treasures gave her comfort. The sculpture of their home in Nazareth, a present from Joseph so long ago, stayed in her bedroom, the first thing she saw in the morning. The sparrows Yeshu carved with such sensitivity looked as though they would burst into song. They brought a sharp stab of grief.

On the bed lay the coverlet made by her mother and given to her on her wedding day. Again a long time ago, a lifetime really.

Everything so different now. Only the most precious things came with her, the things impossible to leave behind, everything small and irreplaceable, memories and mementos. They gave her solace. At night, when she stroked the material, her mother kissed her, and her father smiled from her bedroom door.

She kept busy. Since the *Galilee* sailed, John left early in the morning and often didn't return until sunset, walking the streets of the city, exploring and assessing. On Shabbat they went to the synagogue with Joseph and Hannah and met some of the locals. The building was well endowed as Simon promised: a central hall, baths, *miqvahot*, washrooms, and toilets, all under the same roof, and as they were connected to the city's water supply, the facilities were splendid.

Hannah showed her around, bursting to tell how much her husband contributed over so many years. She was a likeable, homely woman, kind and gossipy, dressed like Evia and most of the other women in the Greek style, her hair uncovered and braided.

There was little she didn't know about the community, and Mary soon became lost in marriages, babies, deaths, who had gone back to Judaea, and who made a fortune at one thing or another. She nodded now and again, smiling appropriately. No point in trying to sort through the stories or remember the characters. She would get to know them all in time.

In the meantime, John met the Jewish men of the city. Addressed to two wealthy merchants, both major supporters of the synagogue, the letters from Cyprus surprised Joseph; he was intrigued to find the newcomers with such important contacts. He delicately inquired about Marcus, who he was and what he did. John only revealed a little. But it was enough to ease their acceptance, and the respect with which the president and his wife treated them helped to absorb them into local society. It wasn't long before people discovered their connection with Yeshua the Healer.

'Oh yes,' Hannah said to her best friend, Miriam, whose husband was a dealer in precious stones. 'They came with Simon from Joppa. He introduced them to Joseph and told him that Mary is Yeshua's mother and John is the son of Mary's sister. Don't say anything though. It's just between us.'

The whispers danced from family to family, magnified as they went, until everyone knew that the relatives of the Teacher from Galilee had arrived in their city. Some had family members back home who had been cured by Yeshua.

One old man had an ageing aunt who suffered from a skin ailment. Thinking it leprosy, they forced her out of her village, as if she was worthless, and compelled her to live in a cave in Arbel, near Tiberias on the Sea of Galilee. She and two other women, similarly afflicted, heard the stories about the Healer and waylaid him on the road to Kfar Nahum. He cured them; he took away their pain and distress.

'My aunt wept in shame and fell on her knees to the ground. But he knelt beside her, and with his own hands, he wiped away her tears and talked to her until she was calm. He told them to bathe, change their clothes, and as soon as possible, get examined by the priest and declared clean. One of the women who followed him took the three to her house, fed them, bathed them, and gave them new garments in place of their old rags. They went home to their own families with honour, without the shame of their affliction, and that I won't forget.

'When I was a boy, my aunt Ruth told us stories of the kings of

Israel and the history of our land. She was a scribe and read from the scrolls. Yet they banished her, forced her to become a beggar, she who taught the children of the village and gave them pride in their heritage. Some years afterwards she died, but it was natural, in the company of her family, a woman to be respected and loved. When I learned of her cure, I offered my prayers in gratitude to the Holy One. I never thought I would have the chance to thank Yeshua's mama.

'And then I heard what happened to this good man. How could the high priests allow the Romans to do such a thing? The killing of a Man of God.' Simeon broke down in real distress.

Others grumbled about the Roman occupation of their homeland, and anger arose against the Rome-appointed high priest Caiphas and his father-in-law, Ananus. Joseph heard of it and quietly intervened, calming the indignation. He talked to those who murmured and convinced them it would be another tragedy if Mary discovered what was happening and decided to leave.

'Let her live here in peace. Don't force her away'.

In fact, he wanted no trouble with the authorities. Although their people were protected by law, any rebellious words or activity would be squashed violently, and the Jews would pay for it in blood. Experience taught them to be inconspicuous. He gave a sigh of relief when the agitation ceased.

Thus Mary found a home in her new community. They took her to their hearts and gave her a place of honour and respect, as well as an acceptance of her desire to live retired. Yet the women still invited her to their homes or called for her on their way to the market, where she exclaimed over the spices, the foreign vegetables and the plentiful supplies of grain. She ran her hands over carved tables and chairs, made by the local carpenters, or examined the intricate tapestries and carpets, woven in the mountains from the fine-haired sheep that grazed the highlands.

The most amazing marvels, for her, were the faces she met, the people from so many lands: the familiar, elegant togas of the Romans; the strange trousers of the yellow-haired, pale-faced men from the north; the swarthy merchants of the east; the black glistening skin of the tall, proud Nubians; all mingling in the streets or in the *agora*.

It helped her keep busy, contained the entity within, and only at night in her bed did the evil emanations spew over her, burning her flesh, leaving her in great physical pain, exhausted, unable to sleep, lying awake until dawn.

It was easier on the ship. The sea calmed and strengthened her. She missed the *Galilee*.

John arranged with Joseph for the delivery of Marcus's letters to Samuel the spice merchant, and Jacob the physician. He was surprised when several nights later a servant came with an invitation to dinner the following evening. Mary declined, pleading tiredness. John accepted; he was curious about Marcus's Ephesian friends.

He enjoyed a sumptuous meal in a beautiful villa on the outskirts of the city. Samuel welcomed him warmly, and they dined with his wife, Ruth, and their son, David. They talked about Marcus, Judaea, Ephesus, and the community. Although genial and enjoyable, he sensed no compelling affinity, as with their Cypriot friends. A nice family, but continued communication would be a strain. Disappointing.

Jacob the physician was traveling when the new arrivals reached Ephesus. When he read the letter from Marcus, he immediately called on Joseph at the synagogue, wondering what he would discover. He went home that night with much to ponder, amused yet pleased that his friend had alerted him to the presence of the Galilean couple.

He first met the Cypriot on the Maritime Island when they were boys studying in the famous philosophical schools of Rhodes and Camiros, where, to his surprise, the philosophers also revered the Supreme Being. His family had lived in the Diaspora for several generations, and like Marcus, he was a Hellenised Jew, enjoying both the intellectual interrogation of his Greek studies and the undoubted spiritual connection he experienced with the One God.

He pursued knowledge and tried to fathom the depths of the Holy One's interaction with His creation, with human beings, with all His other creatures and with the earth itself. An avid reader of philosophy, he probed the writings of the Greek masters and stayed aware of the current Jewish thinking: the prophecies, the thoughts of the Sadducees, Pharisees, Essenes, and all the other sects that flourished in Second Temple Judaea.

Stories of Yeshua the Healer had penetrated Ephesian circles, and from what he understood the Nazoraean seemed more genuine than most. A Man of God following in the steps of Elijah, Elias, and more recently, Honi the Circle-Drawer, the holy men from Galilee who produced healing and other 'miracles' so embedded in reality they could neither be ignored or explained.

All these men enjoyed unusual, personal relationships with the Creator. He wanted to hear more about this latest Galilean and maybe something of his beliefs.

In his letter, his old friend asked him to help the newcomers, and he would certainly try. An informal meeting on Shabbat would be best. At his desk, he wrote a short note, rolled the scroll and sealed it. He called Avrom, his personal servant, gave him the letter, and told him to deliver it to Joseph the next morning. He smiled.

If I know Marcus, this will be instructive.

On the following Saturday, Mary and John walked over to the synagogue and met their new friends. The ladies questioned her about her activities, the furniture she'd bought, and whether she liked the house. It was relaxing and good natured and gave her a sense of acceptance.

The men stood round in casual groups discussing business and all the latest news. Leaving his aunt with her friends, John joined those with Joseph, and soon afterwards a man with dark hair, streaked with grey, came over. A hand on his arm caught the president's attention.

When he turned, his face broke into a delighted smile. 'Jacob, how good to see you. I wondered when you'd be here. You know Simon and Reuben, of course.'

He greeted the two men with evident pleasure, giving the apostle the opportunity to examine Marcus's friend.

He studied the handsome face with the laughing eyes and sensed the dynamic energy of a powerful personality, a strong yet benign spirit. He waited until he was introduced. They looked at one another, evaluating, until simultaneously they laughed and reached forward to clasp arms, like two old friends long since parted.

Jacob wanted to know all about Marcus and how they'd met. They were soon involved in conversation, and Joseph slipped away, taking his companions with him. Rarely had John felt such a connection. Mary and Yeshu were exceptional and very close, but this man was like a brother, maybe even the one who could provide the help he needed.

The physician worked for the city, although in his youth he had travelled extensively in Arabia and the east, studying the properties of herbs and drugs, learning the latest medical techniques and treatments. His ships traded in the eastern Mediterranean and brought back a continuous supply of medications from Syria, Judaea, and Alexandria to be marketed in Ephesus and other centres in the Aegean. He was wealthy yet unassuming, more interested in John and his meeting with Marcus.

The apostle said little about himself but told Jacob all he knew about the Cypriot family, their beautiful villa overlooking the harbour at Paphos, and how the mine owner and Simon became friends.

'Now, that could be interesting. Perhaps you would introduce me to the captain. We might be of use to each other, especially if he comes regularly to Ephesus. Tell me though, is there anything I can do for you here in the city? Anything you need?'

'Not at the moment, Jacob. We've just arrived. Still getting used to the place and settling in. We have no idea how things will turn out, so we're taking it slowly.'

'Fine, but let me know if the situation changes. At least, come to dinner someday next week. I'd like you to meet my wife, Martha, and the family.'

'We'd love to. Come over and I'll introduce you to my aunt.'

Hannah and her cronies greeted them with delight, preening in the presence of the two handsome young men. It was some time before Jacob could turn to Mary, immediately recognising her amusement at the ease with which he charmed all her female friends. He grinned at her, like a young boy caught in mischief, but the warmth of her greeting reassured him.

Later, on their way home, her nephew told her how delighted he was with the introduction. She agreed. She liked Jacob.

15

A Many-Breasted Monstrosity

The apostle continued exploring the city to assess the spiritual condition and judge the overall level of desecration. The worst emanations came from the Temple of Artemis. He climbed the hill behind the theatre to examine the vast edifice and identify the spirit who ruled there. His thoughts returned to the festival procession on the previous day, his heart clutching with sympathy for all those caught, so inescapably, in her web.

The golden chariot of the goddess led the parade and carried her enormous cult statue, the breastplate laden with the testicles of her sacrificed bulls, the cloying smell equalled only by the sickening spiritual stench. Her castrated chief priest and the virgin priestesses followed with the Ephesians in their tribes. Young men and maidens of marriageable age led the procession with their hunting spears and bows, all richly dressed and accompanied by their finest horses and fastest dogs.

Through the marble streets, they circled around Mount Pion to the Magnesium Gate and back to the Artemision. And there, in the wide spaces of her unholy precincts, they frolicked and feasted all through the night.

He had no doubts in his mind; she was a strong lower entity. How many thousands did she affect, filling them with a lust for power and riches, her devotees totally unaware she was evil, unconscious of their own spiritual seduction? His compassion strengthened into determination. She would be elevated, and he would work to neutralise others like her.

The moment to face her arrived. Over several days he prepared, increasing his strength to the maximum. He found a place to sit and focused his concentration on the interior of the building, on the colossal statue in the centre of the colonnaded edifice, the essential core of the cult.

Standing before her, he gazed up at her, the many-breasted Artemis, magnificent but obscene in her pungent lushness and promise of fertility. When asked to give she gave, but she wrapped her gifts in silken threads that bound the receiver with powerful chains to languish in her service throughout the ages, until released by more profound understanding, or a power greater than hers.

The world belonged to her, worshippers bowing and basking in the heat of her seductive but destructive beauty, the giver of lecherous passions and uncontrollable cravings.

Her eyes moved. She saw him and began to work her magic. He felt the attraction, the stirrings of lust. Remaining calm, he allowed her to come towards him, to entwine herself around him. Just another petitioner, a supplicant wanting something she could give.

But she laughed—he would receive, possibly not all he wanted, but yes, she would let him have a little, enough to bring him back for more. And he would pay, oh, indeed, he would pay, her servant forever. Sliding over and around him, confident of her victory, she entered and filled up his vastness, his cavernous being.

And he acquiesced, remaining still and calm, knowing all her thoughts, allowing the invasion until he absorbed the fullness of her soul, the totality of her desecration. Thinking him weak and of no consequence, she concentrated all her energy on him.

Then he bound her, restraining her with his mind and his disciplined spirit. Holding her firmly, he turned on her the force of his compassion, the pity of his benevolent soul. And finally, he demanded her name. She screamed in agony and fought his hold and his mastery, his kindness like daggers in her breast, her barren essence squirming in the light of his loving heart.

It is so easy to take the first wrong step towards evil. That simple movement is almost casual, not so important. The second is much easier. The third and fourth create the habit until the web of guilt enfolds the spirit, making it more and more difficult to return to the paths of righteousness that lead to the pastures of the Holy One. Greatly to be pitied is the one who takes that first, fatal step.

Such was the being worshipped as a goddess by enslaved human beings, those who surrendered to her their freedom of choice. They filled her with strength and left themselves chained and fettered, their life blood leached from their souls.

He held her tight, and she struggled against the love and understanding, full of fear and dread.

Yet as the enveloping layers of corrupt miasma began to disintegrate, the screams lessened and softened to a whimper. When she revealed her true identity, his compassion penetrated to the spark of purity at the centre of her being, that remnant of innocent beginnings betrayed to iniquity so many aeons before. After what seemed an eternity her essence changed, became lighter and stronger, until the tingling effervescence enfolded him.

Many beings of light surrounded him, and the goddess was no longer the many-breasted monstrosity but a young and beautiful girl lying on a marble floor, white of face and stricken with exhaustion. They approached her from all sides and lifted her gently.

Others came to him, carried him from that desolate place, and returned him to his body on the hill where he awoke, exhausted and suffering. Every muscle and bone was sore. His back and shoulders ached with pain. Unable to rise, he fell back to the ground with a groan, drained of power, refusing to even think of the elevation in case he pulled her back to her hell, her magnificent mausoleum.

Holy souls relaxed him into sleep and strengthened him during those long hours of repose while he lay stupefied on the ground. Well after sunset his eyes opened, and for a moment he knew not where he was. Every part of him was in agony. Later, he managed to stand and stumbled down the paths, past the theatre and the synagogue, slowly making his way along the streets to his home.

16

A Severe Reaction

Worried, Mary rushed to the door when she heard him in the courtyard.

Hair matted, his face streaked with dirt and sweat, he looked as if he'd endured countless days in the desert without food or drink. He staggered as she led him to a stool at the table. With a soaked cloth, she washed his face and hands, quietly talking to him until some colour stained his skin. No wounds visible, so he hadn't been attacked physically. Something spiritual? If he was badly weakened, he needed rest.

First of all, food and drink. She poured tirosh and held the cup until he took it and drank thirstily. She found bread and cooked fish and fed him like a child. He chewed slowly, and swallowing was difficult. His eyes were red, his handsome face old and drawn.

When she helped him to his room and pulled down the bedcovers, she tried to pull off his tunic, but he fell on the bed, entrapping it. She kissed him on the forehead and left him, her much-loved nephew. At the door she looked back; he was already asleep.

During the night, the moaning wakened her. She jumped from her bed and grabbed a wrap. When she opened his door, the room stank and flies buzzed around him. His upper body

103

ran with perspiration and his forehead burned with fever. He flung his arms around, thrashing and shouting in some strange language as he fought the demons of his delirium. She attempted to wash his face, but his arm crashed into her, throwing her against the wall, the situation beyond her physical ability.

She ran to her room, pulled on a gown, wrapped herself in a warm cloak, and hurried to Joseph's. A bleary-eyed servant answered her knocking and went for her master. He came quickly, and hearing what happened, asked her to wait. Within minutes he returned, dressed and in control, issuing instructions for Jacob the physician to be called.

At her home he took charge—lit the lamps and built up the fire to heat water. It gave her the chance to dress properly. When she returned to help, he had washed down the fevered patient and found clean sheets, the flies and odour banished.

In the kitchen she collapsed on her stool at the table. Her hands shook, and a sharp pain stabbed behind her eyes. The sudden onset of the illness and the speed of his deterioration bewildered her. Thinking through everything he said in previous days, she found nothing to account for it.

She knew he protected her and avoided anything that might exacerbate her condition. Even so, she wished he'd warned her if he was going to attempt something really dangerous. It had to be a spiritual battle. He focused on neutralising the corruption in Ephesus, but surely he wouldn't deal with anything strong without help.

Jacob's arrival interrupted her thoughts. She told him what she knew and brought him to the bedroom, where Joseph watched over a calmer patient.

Over the next days he improved under the care of the physician and the synagogue president; eventually, he told them about the confrontation in the Temple, the battle with the entity. Their initial scepticism graduated to respect, especially when they considered Yeshua's reputation as an exorcist.

But the apostle fretted; had he gone too far, too soon? Would Satan pull down the newly elevated holy soul? If she fell, she would be a lot stronger than before. He should have raised her over several weeks and watched for deterioration. Yet that course required trained helpers. Even Mary couldn't help with anything hazardous.

What was done was done. If he'd made a mistake he would have to bear the consequences. With that, his thoughts stilled, and he began to regain his strength.

During the following weeks, he recovered and spent time down at the harbour, finding a fisherman with whom he sailed the Bay of Ephesus. He met others and absorbed the local lore: the best fishing areas and where to sell his catch. They liked him and told him when a good boat came up for sale. Now he had work, a source of income, no longer dependent on their savings or the silver coins in the carved box under his aunt's bed.

They finally went for the postponed dinner and met the cool, intelligent Martha with their three children: Simeon, a young man of 20 who was studying to be a physician, and two younger girls, Elianna and Alona, both of marrying age and searching for husbands.

To John's delight, a friendship blossomed between the two women, although it didn't surprise Jacob; he already sensed the potential. It stilled an ache in Mary's heart, fostered by the separation from her family in Judaea, the loss of all she loved except for her nephew.

It was to her new friend, she told the stories of Yeshu: the message from the angel, the end of the dominion of Beliel, the coming of the Teacher, and so on. She described the joys and the sorrows, how they were taught by the Wise Ones, how her son had striven to fulfil his mission, and finally, how her beloved child died, crucified on a Roman cross, the dream interrupted, the task incomplete.

Martha listened, aware of Mary's continuing agony, and she grew to care deeply for the indomitable little lady from Galilee. She admired her courage and determination, inspired by her commitment to the Most High, and her profound, almost familial love for the Great Creator. Those who worship the One God often exhibit some measure of fear and trepidation, but with Mary it was pure, loving affection, like that of a daughter towards a beloved father. She had an unwavering desire to carry out His wishes.

Martha felt humbled, with new insights into her own relationship with the Holy One. On a more mundane level, the social circle of the new arrivals enlarged, giving them an extended family, and their friendship with the two couples strengthened.

John recovered his spiritual condition but stayed away from the Temple, although he didn't sense any increase in desecration within the city. In fact, everything seemed lighter. Despite that, he wasn't ready to test the results of his work and sent all thoughts of Artemis from his mind.

He concentrated on familiarising their new friends with Yeshu's teachings and the promise from the Most High regarding the rule of evil. They met in Mary's house and she enjoyed the conversations, the inevitable discussions and arguments of a typical, Jewish intellectual gathering, contributing her own opinion when asked and proud of John's mastery of the mechanics of elevation.

Their people fiercely debated the problem of death and its aftermath: the Sadducees and high priests assumed the spirit perished with the body; the Pharisees believed in Hades, the physical resurrection and the last judgement. Even some of the Essenes thought the rule of evil would end with the annihilation of the Romans and all the enemies of Israel in a great conflagration of fire.

Nothing was further from the Teacher's beliefs. He, and the Wise Ones who trained him, taught that evil could only be neutralised by kindness and compassion. Love was the only true antidote. In this way, he calmed the angry man and pacified the depraved entity, although more time was needed to deal with the cold, implacable aggression and power of Rome.

Even so, he never advocated a physical battle. Anger and violence produced more of the same. Hatred and hostility directed towards another, whether Roman or Jew, strengthened the overall desecration and delayed the coming of the kingdom of heaven, the rule of the Most High.

To eliminate evil, a human being must learn how to love others, to treat them with care and kindness. 'An eye for an eye and a tooth for a tooth' was an ancient saying, but when taken literally it led to war and destruction.

The greater mandate from the Torah instructs thus: 'You shall not take vengeance or bear a grudge against any of your people but you shall love your neighbour as yourself. I am the Lord' (Leviticus 19:18).

This instruction led to a culture of charity among the Jews—care for the widow, the orphan, and the less fortunate, for all those unable to help themselves. Within their belief system, they understood the Creator's command as an imperative to be honoured.

On this foundation Yeshua based his ideas. Love towards others, including the Romans, helped to end the era of iniquity. The apostle told them the story of the learned teacher who asked which commandment was the greatest.

Yeshua replied: "You shall love the Lord your God with all your heart and with all your soul and with all your mind. This is the greatest and first commandment. And the second is like it: You shall love your neighbour as yourself"[10]

They were the bedrock of his teaching, the gateway through which everyone entered the kingdom, the rest an elaboration on this basic theme. For the simplest person to understand, he often explained his lessons through little stories. The Teacher lived again for those who listened and brought a cool balm to Mary's grieving heart.

On other occasions, the memories threatened her self-control, and she would slip away to her bedroom or out to the stable to brush down the donkey, distracted and calmed until able to return. Her nephew noticed but said nothing, although he did wonder if she was deteriorating.

A nucleus of helpers gathered. The physician was fascinated by the Teacher's ability to heal the sick and exorcise strong evil spirits. He bombarded John with questions, especially as he was similarly experienced but, as the apostle insisted, nowhere near the level of Yeshu.

'Most of the time, it's not too difficult to push a desecrated

---

[10] (Mathew 22:37-39 New Revised Standard Version. NRSV)

spirit from a victim, easier still if you have several people working with you. Making sure the person doesn't get into trouble again, takes a lot more time and effort.'

'How does it work?'

'You must identify the soul, discover his name. Not everyone can do it. Yeshu obviously could, and thankfully so can I. Once you have the name you have more control.

'Then you send the invading spirit back to the realms of the damned. To prevent it infecting someone else, we call it back at a later stage and elevate it. That's a lot more complicated. We use love and compassion to neutralise the surrounding evil until it dissipates completely. Then the cleansed soul is able to ascend to the blessed realms.

'The person's spiritual healing is vital and takes time. If he doesn't learn how to purify his thoughts and actions, he will either nullify the elevation, or another lower soul will take advantage of his spiritual weakness and enter. So the whole process has three parts of equal importance, but interdependent.'

The possibilities for the possessed of Ephesus were obvious: poor, stricken people banished to dismal places well away from the city, somewhere they could do no harm except to themselves.

The apostle promised to help them once the group had more experience, and as they listened to his plans, his new friends felt privileged to have the Galilean couple in their community.

Exactly a lunar month after his encounter with the goddess, John climbed the hill overlooking the Artemision. It was twilight, and a new moon hung in the deep-blue sky. A warm breeze blew in from the Aegean, the salty tang of the sea mingling with the scents of wild flowers scattered across the scrubland. Peaceful and quiet: no activity around the temple below.

His spiritual condition had returned in full, and he was ready to test his work. He settled on the ground and called the young girl. Immediately, an effervescence surrounded him, the creamy tingling of her holy soul. Not only had she elevated successfully, but she remained in the blessed realms.

There had been the possibility of her desecration, either by a more powerful lower spirit or through an inadequate elevation. Neither had occurred and she was safe. He sent her away gently, and with a sigh of relief, said a prayer of thanksgiving to the Most High.

He knew he'd been lucky. At first, he only wanted to examine the entity, but the assessment became a full confrontation that severely taxed his abilities and power. He owed its success to the many holy souls who came to aid him.

I won't try that again. And hopefully I won't have to. If all went well, he would have his new trainees, and Mathias would be back soon. A reasonably sized group, enough for both exorcisms and elevations.

He was looking forward to the arrival of the *Galilee*. Although glad to have his new friends, he missed the Lake and home. At times, something would remind him: the way the water lapped on the beach, the scents on the wind, even the smell of the fish. That's when he had to find a distraction and refocus his mind on his mission.

Still, it would be good to see the Galileans again.

17

A Deterioration

However, his aunt wasn't doing so well. At first, she loved her little house near the synagogue, but the negative effects of living in a noisy, crowded city crept in, leaving her stifled and besieged. The overt battles with the entity increased in frequency, and the defence of her soul grew more difficult. The strength she had gained during the voyage dissipated; nothing compensated, neither her nephew's care or the kindness of their friends.

One morning, as they sat at the kitchen table, Martha commented on the change and Mary's eyes glistened.

'In the beginning, I was just glad to be on dry land. The ship I enjoyed, even though it was cramped and impossible to keep clean. Here I can wash, cook, and be on my own to do what I want.'

Martha laughed. 'That I understand. I need time by myself as well. But what happened recently? You're not as content and you look tired. Are you ill? Is there anything we can do?'

'No, no! Physically I have nothing to worry about—except, of course, I'm not so young anymore. The real problem is living among so many people. I'm not used to it. I spent my life in a small village where we all knew each other. I would walk down and sit by the stream, pick wildflowers in the spring, or simply relax and think without any interruptions.

'In Ephesus, you have thousands of people rushing around, and no matter how hard I try, I can't find peace. I think John realises there's something wrong, although he hasn't said anything. I don't want to be a burden. It was different in Jerusalem. There, I had the family and lots of friends. I felt safe. Here, in this marble city, I can hardly breathe.'

Tears streamed down her face, and Martha pulled over her stool and wrapped the little Galilean lady in her arms. How much more could she take: the crucifixion, the years afterwards often in hiding and fear, the mad escape to Joppa and the flight from Judaea? John's illness didn't help either. Yet she had the feeling there was more behind the deterioration.

For the moment, they would have to find some way to make her life easier, to give her greater peace. In the kitchen, she found a jug of tirosh and cups, brought them to the table, poured the new wine, and tried to reassure her.

'You don't have to live in the middle of Ephesus, you know. Yes, John is working, but why do you have to be here all the time? Let's think about it. I'm sure we'll come across a nice, quiet place away from all the activity and noise. I'll help you. We'll go and visit lots of places. Don't despair.'

Mary smiled though her tears. 'Thank you. You do make me feel better. Still, I must do more for myself. I'll talk to him.'

As it happened, the physician's wife saw him first. When she left Mary and walked over to the synagogue, she met him on the way. Within minutes they were sitting in Hannah's kitchen, immersed in the tempting aromas of baking bread. Martha told them of the conversation and the need for a more peaceful home.

'I thought she was deteriorating. Fortunately, we have enough coin to build a house, if we can find a suitable place.' He considered them for a moment. 'There's more to the situation than you realise. Maybe it's the right time to tell you.'

They stared at him, wondering what was coming.

'When they killed Yeshu, the shock for his mother was severe. The crucifixion itself was brutal beyond words. But her suffering was intensified by her belief that she failed in the task given to her by the Great Creator. It was to Mary the angel brought the message about the end of the rule of evil and the coming of the Teacher. And from that moment, she dedicated her whole existence to fulfilling the wishes of the Holy One. Then her son was dead, the work unfinished.

'As she stood before the cross, her despair nearly destroyed her. In her grief, her normal discipline deserted her, and she lost control. Her spiritual being was suddenly open, unprotected and vulnerable; evil always watches and takes advantage of such an opportunity. A strong, desecrated spirit forced an entry and attached himself to her. He is one of Satan's closest affinities, one of tremendous power, and he's still with her.

'Initially she was very ill. In fact, we wondered if she would survive. Then some measure of awareness returned. Most of the time, she appeared rational. At other times, her grip on reality weakened and she didn't recognise us. We tried again and again to cleanse her, without success. The soul had too strong a hold. Yeshu would have managed it but we couldn't. We were forced to wait until she was stronger.

'That's why I brought her to Ephesus. I had to get her away from the memories and the attacks from the Herodians and high priests. Even though the people of Jerusalem did everything they could to protect us, her fear worsened her condition.

'The sea journey helped enormously, and she recovered enough to know the truth. She realises a lower entity is with her, and she believes, in time, she will push it out. Her old courage has returned. Although the soul is attached, thankfully it isn't a full possession. Only her knowledge and determination to carry on gives her demeanour a semblance of normality.

'When she's with people who care for her, the attachment is temporarily weakened by the love we give her, and the physical effects are not so strong. When she's alone she experiences the full torture. It burns like acid on her skin, she told me, a black, viscous scorching, and from it, there's no escape.

'Because she is now aware of her injury, and to some extent separate from it, she suffers the pain more intensely. Living in the city is only part of the problem; being on her own isn't an option. She would only survive for a short time. Wherever she wants to go, I will go with her. I promised her family I would look after her.'

They stared at him, lips parted, eyes wide in horror, amazed that Mary endured so much yet appeared so calm. Hannah's heart ached, her mouth trembling.

'Does she talk about it?' she asked.

'Only that once on the boat. When I ask how she is, she tells me not to worry. But I can judge her condition from her eyes and the colour of her face. And over these last days, she doesn't look too good.'

Martha gazed down at her tightly clasped hands. During the previous weeks as she learned about Yeshua, the elimination of evil, and the coming of the kingdom, she experienced a profound joy, the pure exaltation of divine revelation. And at times, she recognised that same spark of sheer delight in Jacob's eyes. The Galileans had changed their lives.

The work of the Messenger of the Most High must continue, and Martha was determined to play her part. How could they help Mary? 'John, what would happen if she died in this condition?'

He turned to her in surprise, pleased with her unexpected understanding.

'If that happened she would probably fall into the realms of the damned. It depends on her inner strength, although I have to admit the entity has created a strong link with her. He is capable of pulling her down and holding her, at least for a time.

'Then she would become an evil spirit and a dangerous one. All memories of goodness and compassion would leave her. The desecration surrounding her would impel her to do enormous harm in this world. If Satan succeeds in this, our work would have a formidable adversary.

'So you understand why I must do everything I can to save her, apart from the fact that I love her very dearly. She's my mother's sister and Yeshu's mama.'

Martha reached over and gripped his arm. 'We'll help. Try not to worry. We're with you now. The priority is finding her a peaceful place to live, somewhere on the outskirts of the city, yet near enough to allow you to continue your work. I want to think about it, and Jacob might have some ideas.'

'Joseph always knows about houses for rent or sale,' Hannah added, tears in her eyes.

He smiled. Martha sensed the relief as he slumped on the stool, his brow clearing. He'd decided to trust them, and for that she was grateful. They would share the burden now and find an answer. Poor John.

✳

That evening, Jacob's response amazed and amused her.

'What about up where my aunt lives? We've been there. To the south in the foothills of Mount Koressos.'

A picture flashed into her mind of her father-in-law's wealthy and eccentric sister with her rambling house and gardens overlooking the Aegean.

'Yes, of course. What a lovely place. Are there other houses? Where would Mary live?'

'Rachel owns property up there, and I'm sure we could persuade her to part with a little, enough for a house, a stable and some land.

'That isn't the problem. It's a long walk from the city up a steep hill. No question of John traveling up and down on a daily basis. If she likes it, we'd have to find a girl to live with her, to cook and clean. A kind person to keep her company.'

'I think that might be the difficult part,' Martha said. 'Although a house on the mountain, yet near the sea, would be ideal. Let's see what he says.'

At the synagogue, the president listened to his wife's tale with interest and pondered the explanation of Mary's condition.

So that's how it works. Fascinating. His depth of knowledge is amazing.

'Joseph, are you listening? Do you know of anywhere quieter for her?'

'I'll need to think about it.' Such a pity she didn't want to stay. Hannah liked her and he didn't want to lose John. He could do so much good in the community and had already opened windows into Joseph's own potential, stimulating both his intellect and his soul. His wife was right, though. They had to do something. Nothing came to mind. He would ask around on the morrow.

Mary prepared the evening meal: fried fish with leeks and onions, bread to dip in olive oil. More optimistic since Martha's visit, she was determined to find ways to help herself. In the morning, she would go down to the beach to the west of the harbour. She had an affinity with the sea, and the voyage from Joppa proved how much it strengthened her. A walk along the sands towards the bay would help her find somewhere quiet to sit and concentrate on the incoming waves, pull from them the power and strength of the Holy One.

Her nephew came in at sunset, and they enjoyed a quiet evening, his presence giving her some relief from pain. She told him of her desire to leave the city.

'Yes, I met Martha on my way home. We'll find somewhere quieter. We can build a house if you like. Let's see what's available. You're fond of both her and Hannah, aren't you?'

'Yes of course.'

'Good, because I explained your spiritual condition to them. I hope you don't mind, but I thought it would help if they understood the situation, particularly as they are learning more about our work.'

She stared at him. How could he do such a thing? Her private business discussed by others. A surge of anger flooded through her. Rising abruptly from the table, she grabbed the dishes and brought them over to the bowl near the fire. She poured hot water from the pot over the cups, scalding herself as she tried to control her annoyance.

Why can't they leave me alone? I don't want everyone finding out

I allowed such an invasion. Oh dear Father, please help me. The tears began to flow.

John ran to take the pot from her shaking hands. He put it down beside the fire, took her arm, and brought her back to the table.

'Mary, please don't be angry with me. I thought it would be better if they knew what actually happened rather than thinking you didn't like the house or Ephesus. We can trust them. They want to help and would do anything to spare you further pain. As I would. You know that, don't you?' He held her hands, and control slowly returned.

He'd made a bad mistake. He remembered her independence, how she and Joseph were true partners, equal in every way, with no desire of one to dominate the other. She also guarded her privacy, and he should have talked to her before speaking to the others. On the other hand, they needed them. He poured a cup of tirosh and closed her hands around it, coaxing her to drink.

'Mary, we need all the help we can get. If we're going to succeed, we must trust them. I'm truly sorry. I should have talked to you first. But Martha was so worried. She assumed it was the crucifixion and everything that followed in Judaea. I wanted to be honest. I thought they deserved that.

'They were so upset for you. It helped them understand how desecrated souls can cause us harm. It isn't only those who do wrong. It can be someone like you, someone who has such a powerful connection with the Holy One Himself. If they see that you can be invaded, through no fault of your own, does that not give encouragement to those who are weaker?

'Those who are attacked by evil deserve our love and

compassion. Your friends will do all they can to help you, Mary, and through their efforts become stronger themselves. We can't do it all by ourselves. We must work with others, give what we can and accept aid in all humility.'

He stopped, thinking she was the last person to whom he should preach. Then he saw the glimmer of amusement in her eyes, the trace of an ironic smile curl her mouth, and he sighed with relief. Somehow he'd managed to pierce the barriers. He chanced a grin and took her hands, and through her tears she smiled.

'You're right. At times I feel so besmirched. Still, you *are* right. It can be hard sometimes to pretend all is well. It would be easier to relax a bit more.'

She rose from her stool and went back to the dishes, heating the water and stacking the cups and bowls. Cleaning and tidying would give her time to recover and decide how to deal with the subtle changes in her relationships with her friends, because, as no doubt she realised, the women would discuss everything with their husbands.

Out in the stable, he brushed down the donkey, the rhythmic sweeps relaxing him, pushing aside his concerns. He cleaned out the stall and laid down a fresh bed of straw. When finished, he was pleasantly tired and ready for sleep.

In the house, Mary had gone to bed. He called good night as he went to his room. Her immediate response and the tone of her voice reassured him. She had forgiven him.

18

Exploring the Possibilities

During the following morning, her two friends arrived. Mary's worries fled from her mind when Martha swept her into her arms and held her tight, as if she would never let go. Their concern was palpable, and she knew they wouldn't treat her any differently.

They sat at her kitchen table, talking about the house on the mountain and whatever Joseph might find. No one spoke of the evil attachment. She relaxed and felt safe.

Over the next days, they viewed houses and places where they might build. Jacob's mule cart climbed Mount Koressos, and John was impressed with the intelligent, provocative Rachel, a nice-looking woman with wonderful bone structure, her hair braided around her head, her gown elegant in aquamarine and teal, the tones of the Aegean Sea. She teased them outrageously and told her nephew's friend she would be more than happy to sell him land if it gave her such a handsome neighbour.

They stayed the night and explored the next day. The area was populated with little groups of houses, surrounded by fertile gardens. Considerably cooler than the city, John thought it ideal. Several Jewish families lived nearby, neighbours and perhaps future friends. That evening they discussed the potential, and Rachel suggested they bring Mary up to stay to see if she liked the place. Jacob thought they should all come; pleased with the prospect of company, she immediately agreed.

On the way home, the apostle probed for more information. Jacob's aunt was the widow of Drusus, a wealthy merchant and shipbuilder who sailed the seas as a young man before graduating to the captaincy of a trireme in the Roman fleet that patrolled the eastern Empire. He eventually succumbed to his father's persuasions to return home, and he met Rachel.

The marriage was arranged between the families, both prominent in Ephesian Jewish circles. What surprised everyone, however, was how much the enterprising sailor and the beautiful young girl adored each other. She discovered an unsuspected desire for adventure that delighted her new husband. And although he worked hard in the business, his love for the exotic did not desert him.

The family expanded into shipbuilding, assembled a fleet of small traders, not unlike the *Galilee*, and extended their range into the far corners of the Aegean and Mediterranean. When he captained a ship, he took his lovely wife with him, and after their son was born, hammocks were strung in the captain's cabin and on the quarterdeck. Rachel and little David loved the sea; she always claimed he stayed quieter and more content in his swinging nest during rough weather than he ever did in his proper bed on dry land.

They were an original couple, well known in the trading ports and among the notables of Ephesus. Hellenised Jews and comfortable with Gentiles, they did not refuse to socialise with the Roman and provincial elite. As well as the beautiful old home on the mountain, they owned a house in the city which, when her beloved Drusus died at forty two, she closed up to live permanently on the hill overlooking the Aegean.

Later, when David managed his father's business, he reopened the house near the harbour, and although his mother sometimes visited she gladly returned to her retreat on the slopes of Koressos. There she found a lasting peace. Listening to Jacob, John wondered would Rachel and Mary become friends. There was no point in worrying. His aunt never failed to surprise him. He would leave the matter in the hands of the Father.

One morning two weeks later, not long after dawn, the physician and his family arrived with the mule cart packed with baggage. More bags and baskets were added, and they attached the donkey's bridle to the rear. They took it easy climbing the hill. The men and girls walked part of the way. The little animal was unhitched and gambolled beside them, trotting back and forward, braying loudly and keeping them amused with her antics.

It was approaching noon when they arrived at a broad, cultivated plateau. Further off to the right, a long, rambling house perched on a hill, the expansive central section built in stone on two levels with wooden extensions on each side, protective wings curving around a spacious terrace. Well-tended lawns and gardens swept down the hill to a low wall bordering steep cliffs. Rachel's farm.

To the left a little green valley nestled among the hills, and behind them, the Aegean sparkled blue in the distance beyond the island of Samos. Directly below, the city sprawled along the river. It was paradise: the air fresh and clean, the peace broken only by the laughter of the girls, the sharp clip-clop of the boisterous little donkey and the jangling harness of the mules.

They drove through wooden gates, up a drive bordered by sweet-smelling orange trees and arrived at the side of the house. There Reuben waited to help with the baggage, and Rachel came over to wrap her arms around Martha and her daughters. When she turned to greet her Galilean guest, her eyes twinkled in welcome, and Mary was jolted by the certainty she was meeting an old and much-loved friend.

They walked down through terraced lawns to a covered garden pavilion; from there, they examined the plain of Ephesus below.

Dotted with marble buildings, colonnaded temples, large squares, and formal gardens, the city stretched before them. To the east, the imposing Artemision caught the sunlight, the marble pillars sparkling in the retreating, morning mist. A ship sailed down the Cayster to the bay, and in the west lay the Aegean, islands speckling the sea as far out as the Cyclades. Straight ahead on the northern coast, the white temples of the coastal cities led Mary's gaze into the distant haze and another island—Chios, Rachel told her.

She breathed the scented air and felt the tingling blessing of the ocean. Heaven. Absolute heaven.

She walked down to the bottom of the garden and stood alone, her arms leaning on the low wall. It was blissful. The power of the Creator, coming in from the sea, was almost beyond belief. She was totally cut off from that help in the city and would need it if she wanted to push away the entity.

They watched her leave, and Martha was about to follow when Rachel stopped her.

'Let her go. She needs to decide if this is what she wants. We'll talk to her later. I like her, you know. She's unusual. You must tell me what you've discovered, especially if she's to become a neighbour. Come on. We'll go up to the house. I'll send Susannah down to watch and bring her in when she's ready.'

Panelled with pale oak, the spacious entrance hall cherished the memory of Rachel's husband with a treasured collection of model ships, relics of their sea-faring days and Drusus's passion for boats: warships, triremes, traders, all sorts of sailing craft, every surface a harbour and everything still positioned exactly the way he liked it.

She brought her family through and up the stairs to their rooms on the upper floor, leaving them to settle in. At the end of the corridor, she checked the one she'd chosen for Mary, hoping she would like it. She laughed to herself. She didn't often take to women, but this little lady stirred her interest. You could tell she had suffered. Hid it though. Didn't want to bother anyone. Wise really. People so often get bored with the problems of others.

Back downstairs, she turned left through the main, reception room into the extension wing where she liked to relax. Doors opened to the terrace; she could see Mary down at the wall and Susannah waiting on the steps.

At least that situation is under control. I'll sit down, and they can join me when they're ready. She curled up in comfort on her favourite chair, knowing the well-trained servants would take care of her guests.

When Martha came in, she was dozing but instantly awoke, alert and eager for gossip.

'Tell me. What do you know about them?'

'Didn't Jacob tell you anything?'

So Rachel learned Mary's story: the angel, Yeshua the Messenger of the Most High, his task and teachings, how the Romans crucified him and prevented the elimination of evil. She heard of the attempts by the chief priests to destroy the

Nazoraeans, seeing them as a threat to peace and their Roman riches. And then the escape of Mary and her nephew to Ephesus. Martha told her everything she knew, with the exception of her friend's spiritual condition. That secret she kept.

Rachel sat in her chair, her hands clutching her face, her eyes half closed, trying to make sense of it, overwhelmed by the horror. Jacob slipped in beside his wife and held her hand when the pain of the telling became too much, encouraging her to reveal all so his aunt would understand.

'The city, with its crowds and noise, is depleting her strength,' he added. 'She needs somewhere quiet and peaceful, somewhere to rest and feel safe.'

Rachel wiped her eyes and nodded. 'I've heard about Yeshua the Healer. The last time I was down with David, one of his captains came to dinner and told us how the Galilean had cured his father from some disease. He was horrified and angry about his crucifixion. I must admit I didn't really listen. There are so many reports of killings in Judaea that you end up closing yourself off. We're lucky here. We Jews are relatively well treated.

'Anyway, what would you like me to do? I'll help all I can. Where is Mary now, by the way? Is she still in the garden?'

'She's in her room lying down. I think she likes the place, Aunt Rachel. You might have a neighbour.'

'Good. I could make sure she's well looked after. What about John? It's too far to go up and down to the city every day.'

'Frankly, I'm not sure of his plans. They have the house although they only intended that as a temporary measure until they made up their minds about the future.'

'Well, let's not worry about that for the moment. Let's talk about now. How long can you stay?'

'At least half a moon. I don't often take a proper holiday, and

Avron knows where I am if I'm needed. So your house will be full. I hope you won't become bored with us.'

She smiled. 'On the contrary. It will be a great pleasure. It's a bit lonely at times even though I do socialise with the neighbours. Having my own family to stay is always a joy.

'Now, I suggest we make some arrangements. You've met some of the servants. Susannah looks after the house and Devorah is the cook. You'll find her in the kitchen if you're hungry. Ruben works in the gardens and manages the farm. You probably came across him in the stables. Tell him to put the mules and the donkey out in the fields, although I'm sure he'll think of that himself.

'As for meals, we have bread, cheese, and fruit late in the morning. Come down when you're ready. There's no set time. Our main meal is in the evening around sunset. Usually in the dining room. In the afternoons, I like to have something out on the terrace. But if you are hungry at any time, speak to Devorah and make sure the girls know the kitchen is over in the opposite wing. Young people are always looking for food. Tell John and Mary as well. I want them to relax.'

Jacob smiled at his aunt. So organised in her arrangements. Always the good hostess. He remembered the stories of her banquets in the city when he was young. The servants would do all the work, of course.

I must remember to give them some drachmas when we leave. He was glad she didn't have slaves. They always made him uncomfortable. He refused to have any in his own home, and thankfully, Martha agreed.

Footsteps in the hall broke into his thoughts, and a plump,

smiling woman carried in a tray piled with small loaves, cheese, and different kinds of fruit.

Rachel grinned. 'Thank you, Devorah. Well timed. Take everything out to the terrace. Jacob, find the girls. We'll eat out there.'

He went off to obey and discovered his daughters in the stable giving the donkey and mules buckets of water. This was a treat for the girls. Why hadn't he thought of it before? They must come up more often. He prised them away and brought them inside.

Mary was lying on her bed when the door opened and Martha peeped in. She began to rise.

'No. Don't get up. I'm sorry to disturb you. You're tired. We're about to have some food, and I wasn't sure if you wanted to come down. Why don't you rest for a while longer?'

'No, no. I'm much better. I've hardly spoken to Rachel. Give me a minute and I'll be with you. Where is John? Have you seen him?'

'No. I was about to see if he's in his room. It's next to yours if you need him.'

'I know. Susannah told me. Such a sweet girl.'

'You get ready and I'll see where he is.'

Mary tidied her appearance and joined them to go down to the terrace, where the family gathered round a table covered with food and drinks.

Rachel came over immediately to lead her to her chair. She poured tirosh and made sure her guest had everything she needed. The little acts, so simple yet so kind, reassured Mary, and she knew she was genuinely welcomed. The two women exchanged a silent glance, and the slight nod from each recognised the budding friendship and whatever the future might bring.

Peaceful days followed for Mary. Much of the time she

spent quietly in the garden pavilion, gazing out to sea, her eyes following the ships as they sailed the estuary.

She reflected on her life: the coming of Yeshu, the love she felt for him as she gazed at him sleeping in his cradle, his long, dark lashes and dimpled cheeks, his little hands waving in the air as he reached for something in his dreams. And then, over the years, watching him grow into everything the angel foretold.

The joys and responsibilities: Joseph and the children, studying with the Wise Ones, learning not only the lessons to teach the child but also how to expand her own spiritual potential, increase her self-discipline and power. And after all the work, the planning, and the dedication, her beloved child was crucified, just as success lay moments before them. All gone in an instant, the regrets leaving her breathless with grief and despair.

Since his death, she now realised, only part of her remained fully conscious, the rest locked away, confined behind strong, barred doors, protected from the possibility of feeling, from the sword that pierced her heart that day on the hill. She had sleepwalked through those early years, barely aware of the world around her, expelled from life, surface walking, existing but not living.

The threats of death in Jerusalem forced a partial acknowledgement of reality, and the voyage on the blessed sea with Simon and his crew gave her lengthening moments of normality, a long-forgotten memory of family.

The months in the city nullified even that tentative recuperation, leaving her plagued once more by anxiety and fear. Most of the problem sprang from the growing control exerted by the entity. And she knew, if she wanted to be free and regain her own soul, she must find a peaceful place like this idyllic haven on the mountain. On these heights overlooking the Aegean she could continue the recovery she began on the *Galilee*.

19

A Secluded Valley

One afternoon while they were alone on the terrace, Mary admitted her feelings, and Rachel, remembering her cold, lonely existence after the death of her Drusus, reached for her hand and held it tightly.

That evening, she took John aside and described a small valley cut into the hills further along the heights, not far from the farm gates. To the north and the sea, it was protected from the worst of the prevailing winds by a wall of rock, parts of it twice the height of a man. A mountain stream fed the flat, fertile ground.

They walked over to see it the next morning, and Jacob went with them. They thought it ideal. She wanted to give him the land, but John refused, knowing Mary's fierce independence. If she liked it, they would buy it.

Later in the afternoon, the whole family returned with the mule cart packed with blankets, cushions, and baskets of food and drink. The men unhitched the animals and let them forage, while the family explored. Rachel and Mary examined the seawall and discovered an access to the top where they found a flat stone. They sat and gazed over the vista below.

'I noticed this little valley when we first arrived, and it's paradise, true paradise. Thank you. It's exactly what I want.' Mary stayed still, eyes closed, lips moving in prayers of thanksgiving. Finally she rose, her decision made. 'Let's go find John.'

In an instant, a new chapter opened in Rachel's life. She'd been given a purpose; she would watch over and care for this little Galilean lady who had come so late into her life, glad to be alone no longer. Sometimes it amazed her how fate wove such intricate patterns, and she wondered if the Creator had designed a special one with all their lives. If so, she hoped she would play her part, whatever it might be.

The picnic became a celebration. The girls and Susannah went off to gather wildflowers while the others demolished Devorah's cakes, drank tirosh, and tried to decide the best site for the house; what size should it be, and how much ground would they need for vegetables and fruit trees?

Mary smiled as she listened, happy to leave the details to her nephew. She was simply delighted to have found such a wonderful place.

The men examined the land more carefully and marked off a rough perimeter. Reuben would advise on the exact placement of the house and surroundings, but John hoped they would find some way to take advantage of the phenomenal clifftop views.

The sun was setting when they left for home, and that night, Mary dreamt of the house in the valley and showed Joseph around. They climbed the cliff to her rock and from there scrutinised the panorama below. She was happy.

They stayed for a month, and although she was aware of the entity, she enjoyed an ease of mind unimagined since the crucifixion. They planned the house and gardens and found a local artisan who quarried stone. The invaluable mule cart transported materials, and the men came home at night, tired and dirty, but excited at the prospect of finishing before winter set in.

Meanwhile, the women talked about their lives and became firm friends. Rachel loved Mary's gentle composure, the validity she emanated even through her pain, while Mary delighted in Rachel's adventurous spirit, amused at the stories of their voyages. It reminded her of Joachim in his younger days; she smiled as she listened.

Much of the fear and anxiety she experienced in the city had gone; she strengthened every day. The physical pain, more severe after sunset when the lower soul was stronger, became bearable and she slept easily. Nevertheless, waves of despair swept over her at times, grief at her son's death and the sharp stab of defeat at the curtailment of the work.

Her hostess noticed the change during these episodes and was so concerned that Mary finally confided the cause. This led to a barrage of questions, and Rachel's fascination persuaded her to reveal the spiritual teachings given by the Wise Ones during Yeshu's childhood.

She explained initially how evil came into the world and spread to such an extent that awareness of the Great Creator disappeared from human knowledge.

Rachel's eyebrows shot up. 'I thought a group of angels led by Lucifer rebelled against the Most High and were the bringers of iniquity.'

'No. No. Angels are His messengers, much closer to Him than we are. They do His will. They would never separate themselves or betray Him in any way. No. The fallen angel stories are fables, Rachel. Evil was brought into our world by a human being, one designated by the Most High to bring knowledge and understanding, to help humanity break through ignorance. He should have been the Light Bringer.

'I often think of his own father with the greatest sympathy. He was a pure soul with very special abilities, born among the first humans—a healer, and more importantly, he could hear the Father's voice, receive His instructions. He became the Leader of his tribe and taught his people how to be kind and to care for one another even when old and decrepit. They built a community based on love and kindness, the first one on the earth.

'The knowledge spread through other villages and tribes, slowly at first, then more speedily when the people recognised their increased success through cooperation rather than conflict. For the first time, humans separated themselves spiritually from the animals. They cared for the old, and in return, they found minders for their children and learned the wisdom of the elders' experience. They tended the sick, and the Leader healed their wounds and cured their diseases.

'It was the beginning of civilisation, and this good man led his people out of darkness into the light. His son, the future Evil One, was born with phenomenal capacities but he used them to turn his followers into spiritual slaves with no minds of their own, unable to escape his lust for domination and control. And no matter what his father said or did, he couldn't save him. Just as humanity began to grow into the light, evil come into being.'

'What exactly did Satan do, Mary? Were you told?'

'Yes. The sages revealed the full circumstances of his fall and that of his followers. But Rachel, it's much too dangerous for you, as yet. Joseph and I waited many years before the Wise Ones believed us strong enough to learn the whole story. We had to practice nullifying evil directly, through concentrated loving thoughts..

'And you must do the same. Understand and master the knowledge of good and evil. Then corruption won't harm you, and you'll be able to protect yourself from Satan. Sometimes, those who think themselves immune underestimate the level of their strength. Study the lessons of love and practice spiritual discipline, and that will reinforce your defences.'

Her friend looked away, her lips pursed.

'Rachel, I'm sorry. I don't want you to think I don't trust you. I do. But you need to realise that evil can latch on and control you before you're even aware of its presence.'

'No. Forgive me. I shouldn't demand so much. I'll wait. Can you tell me what happened to you?'

'Normally a lower soul is drawn to a living person with similar desires, and when given the opportunity, will attach himself. In my case, the shock of Yeshu's crucifixion gave the entity an opening. My recovery depends on my determination and my ability to send love to the poor soul within. As my son said, as he hung on that Roman cross, "Father, forgive them, for they know not what they do".

'When we understand that these entities are themselves victims, we learn to sympathise. In this, Yeshu was a master. He loved and cared for the fallen, and his compassion empowered them, allowed them to escape the webs of Satan and return to the Father.

'Taking the first step into wickedness can be surprisingly simple. The second and third steps are even easier. For those who aspire to be with the Great Creator, self-discipline is the path, and we need the strength to turn back when mistakes are made. The desire to be with the Holy One, the longing for eternal happiness must always remain before you. It is the only way to protect yourself.

'Although this is a world of temptation, Rachel, it is also a place where your soul can strengthen by resisting the pull to degradation, and through loving others, find the straight and narrow pathway that leads into the lands of the Most High.'

The time came for them to return to Ephesus. John gave final instructions to the stonecutter, and Ruben finished the initial planting. Another month would finish the house.

With the cart packed and everyone ready to leave, Rachel stood at the gate, her hands clenched. She would wait impatiently to see them again. Mary hugged her and climbed aboard. She waved until a bend in the road hid the farm from sight. Then she turned towards the city in the distance.

During the following weeks, she packed boxes and baskets, amazed at how much they'd accumulated since their arrival. She wouldn't bring much furniture. Her nephew needed it. Reuben's brother was a carpenter and lived not far from the valley. He had offered to make all the essentials, and they would add extra pieces later, as required. So she concentrated on her own personal items and whatever John might need during his visits.

They resumed their normal city life. John went to the harbour, met up with his fisherman friends, and spent time in the estuary or on the Aegean Sea. Joseph asked him to read a lesson at the synagogue and talk about Yeshu's beliefs, especially those concerning the possessed.

The two couples were an adequate foundation for an elevation group, and they understood the underlying theory. Now they needed experience. But nothing could be done until Mary left for the mountain. Dealing with such souls entailed absorbing at least some lower vibrations; he didn't want to compromise her vulnerable condition. If the president wanted him to talk to everyone on Shabbat, however, he would be happy to do so.

20

The Galileans Return

After nearly four months, the long-awaited *Galilee* returned to Ephesus. Out fishing in the bay, John noticed the ship coming up from Samos under full sail, and he wondered. As she approached, he was certain. Abandoning plans for the rest of the day, he turned for the harbour. He tied up, collected his catch, and reached the trader as Simon was launching the boarding plank.

He climbed aboard and threw his arms around his grinning friend. The noise alerted the others. Soon cups and a jug of strong wine landed on the quarterdeck table, all work at a standstill. They exchanged the news, and the apostle invited the captain and whoever was available to the house that evening. Luckily, he had a reasonable catch but went to the market for extra food and hurried home to tell Mary to expect guests for dinner.

James and Mathias came with Simon. They opened the door to aromas of fried fish and onions, a table laden with figs and dates, bread and olive oil, jugs of tirosh, and a decanter of Rhodian wine. They sat down to a meal with their friends, eager to hear all the news of the previous months.

There were no messages from Jerusalem, to Mary's disappointment, although perhaps a good thing, a sign that all was well with the family. Their friends listened to the stories: the people they'd met through the synagogue; John fishing the Bay in his new boat; and, of course, finding the idyllic spot on the slopes of Mount Koressos, where they were building their new home.

During a lull in the conversation, Mathias asked about progress in the spiritual work. Had anything happened?

Hearing the controlled eagerness, John smiled. 'Yes, there've been some changes. Jacob, Joseph, and their wives are now with us, and we hope to start dealing with the possessed soon. At the moment, I'm teaching them the theory behind elevations.'

He glanced from face to face, trying to guess their decisions.

James grinned. 'We both want to work with you, but we can't leave the *Galilee* until we find capable replacements. Simon's nephew is one, and we found another good man. They'll come on board in Joppa. So Mathias is staying as from now, and I will join you after the next voyage. So what do you think?' His eyes twinkled.

John laughed, his face creased in delight. Friends from home. 'Wonderful. Seven of us now. Potentially an effective group. It will take time to train you, but we'll soon be able to deal with possessions as well as begin work on Satan's strongest supporters. One day he will elevate.'

'When will that happen?' Matthias asked. 'Will it be in our lifetime?'

Mary reached over and touched his hand. 'You must understand that Satan's elevation requires not only the elimination of his legions but a method of capturing and holding him until he's weakened. Only then will he ascend to the Father. Although Yeshu was born with extraordinary abilities, they had to grow slowly. The Wise Ones trained him from early childhood: years of study and practice, learning how to tolerate stronger and stronger evil spirits.

'Now that he's gone, we have to find another way. We hope to receive instructions from the blessed realms, but the process will take longer.'

Mathias persisted. 'When you say longer, will it be in our lifetime?'

She took his hand in hers and gazed into his eyes, wondering how to answer. She didn't want to burden him with the knowledge which caused her such despair: two thousand years of suffering before the next attempt.

John quickly intervened. 'Matthias, here's something that might interest you. When I first came to Ephesus, a strong corruption pervaded the city. Over the first weeks, I searched for the origin. It came from the Temple of Artemis, from the goddess or rather from a strong lower soul masquerading as her, using the adulation of her supporters as a source of power. When I examined her to discover her original identity, it became a full elevation. Thankfully, the Artemision is now clear.

'She's gone, although it took all my strength, and I was ill for weeks afterwards. The care from Mary, Jacob, and Joseph saved me. I should have waited and acted with support, but at least now the temple will no longer corrupt the people of Ephesus. I'm sure in time they will benefit, even though they won't know the reason.'

Simon stared at his friend, almost expecting to hear that the Great Temple had collapsed. 'What does this mean?'

'Superficially, nothing has changed. The cult still operates; her officials still function, the processions progress through the city as usual. Her priests don't seem to realise she isn't there anymore.

'It's difficult to predict what will happen in the future. Among the Gentiles, their priests are chosen from the local elite. Their spiritual knowledge is nonexistent. They are more concerned with profit and power, how they can use their position to their material advantage, desires nurtured by the goddess. Whether this is true of those who served Artemis, I don't know. They might be more aware and sense the change. But we shouldn't worry about that, for the moment.

'The important thing is this: one month after the elevation, her spirit was still in the blessed realms. Recently, I went to the building to confirm my examination. The goddess no longer occupies the Artemision.'

His listeners regarded him with awe; he waved it aside.

'No, it wasn't all me. I had tremendous help. In fact, I made a bad mistake taking on so much. I was lucky not to be injured and the work delayed, if not terminated. I'm telling you this for another reason.

'You can do this. I have considerable abilities, but they aren't extraordinary like Yeshu's. You both have talents we can work with, and as I helped neutralise the evil here, you can do the same for other places. I will teach you, and you can pass on the knowledge to others. You will learn how to elevate desecrated souls, and we can begin as soon as you are able.'

A gleam of excitement and determination sparkled in Mathias's dark eyes. He had waited patiently, and now this new task lay before him. He turned to share his exhilaration with his friend but stopped when he looked into James's blank face.

Simon interrupted. 'James, you must stay. You want to do this and I won't put difficulties in your way. There are enough of us to get the *Galilee* home to Joppa, and we'll pick up the new crew there. We'll be here for three or four days. That should give you time to find a place to live.'

'Are you sure?'

'Of course he's sure,' Mathias said, to Simon's amusement.

'We'll find somewhere down near the harbour. It'll be a different life. You'll enjoy it.' John went to find another decanter of wine; it was a night for celebration and hope for the future.

The next few weeks were busy. The Galileans found an inn near the harbour, owned by a Jewish couple, and before he left, the captain spoke to the *agoranomi*, the officials who managed the market and port. Soon Matthias was repairing damaged vessels. Small jobs at first, but when positive reports filtered back to the harbour office, they added him to the list of repair specialists they recommended. Then Jacob met him and sent him to David's shipbuilding yard with letters of introduction, resulting in more work which he juggled with existing contracts. A promising start.

At first, James helped Mathias but soon realised it wasn't for him; he preferred sailing his own craft. His father had been a fisherman on the Lake, and the freedom of life on the water attracted him. John suggested they spend a few days fishing in the bay together, for a share of the catch. Their success persuaded them to continue the arrangement, and when James bought his own boat they would work as a team.

Meanwhile, Mary prepared to move, and one afternoon the men took the mule cart up the mountain to pay the workers and check on progress. They stayed at the farm and completed the financial arrangements for the land. Early the next morning, they went over to examine the house.

It was perfectly positioned. The back nestled against the sheltering seawall while the front entrance opened into the green expanse of the valley. Built of well-dressed stone with a roof of wood and layers of woven reeds, the body of the building was divided into a living room and kitchen, with bedrooms on both sides. To the right, Mary's room was spacious and airy: the music of the trickling stream was just outside the open window. The two rooms on the left were smaller but adequate: one for her nephew when he came to visit and the other for the servant they still had to find.

He talked with Avram the carpenter and organised the furniture. A price was agreed, and all would be in place within a month. Rachel offered to get blankets of wool, the winters were colder than in Judaea, sheets of linen, embroidered bedcovers, and perhaps some wallhangings. John took the farm manager up to the rock where his aunt loved to sit. What about a pavilion, similar to but smaller than the one in Rachel's garden? Reuben grinned. He knew exactly what was needed.

They took a final survey of the house and gardens, imagining what it would be like in a year's time when everything matured. It had all the promise of a delightful home, not unlike the one in Nazareth, John told them. It wasn't far from Rachel and other neighbours, yet withdrawn enough to be quiet and peaceful, a retreat from the world. They would move in during the following month when the temperature dropped for the autumn, giving them time to prepare for winter.

As they were leaving, he remembered the servant and hoped they would find a local girl.

'What about Susannah?' Rachel asked with a smile.

John gazed at her in surprise. 'Are you serious? Don't you need her? And would she want to come?'

Jacob was amazed, knowing his aunt treated the girl like an adopted daughter. 'Why are you suggesting her?'

'It was her own idea. She would be near her family. Even though her younger sister would like to work, she's too inexperienced for

Mary. She's to marry Reuben's son and live on the farm, so she'll come to me.'

'Susannah likes Mary and wants to help. She would be ideal, hardworking and an excellent cook; Devorah trained her. She's a kind girl, quiet and peaceful. You couldn't find better.'

'I totally agree,' John said, giving Rachel a kiss on the cheek. 'Do you want me to talk to her?'

She laughed. 'I'll deal with it. You would leave her tongue-tied.'

The two men climbed into the cart. Jacob shook the reins, and they left their hostess standing at the gate with an amused smile on her face.

That should keep everybody happy.

PART 3

The Mountain

21

Present Day: North West London

Cathrina stood back to survey the attractive mock-Tudor house in the quiet tree-lined street.

'Are you sure this is it?'

'As far as I know.' Her husband closed the black gate and walked up the path. He reached for the knocker on the bright-red door. 'Let's see what happens.'

Roses and petunias bordered a minute square of perfectly trimmed grass. Clematis and honeysuckle climbed the railings and covered the fence, which divided the house from its neighbour. Everything well cared for—pristine, in fact.

She must have a gardener or family nearby.

The porchlight came on and the door opened. A tiny, smiling lady with short white curls stood on the threshold, peering out. Smartly dressed in a navy jersey suit and a cream-coloured silk blouse, she certainly didn't look older than 80, her face soft with hardly a line.

'Hello. You must be Josh and Cathrina. I'm Jean. Come in. You've timed it nicely. There's a fresh pot of tea waiting for us.'

She linked Josh's arm and turned back into the house, leaving his amused wife to turn off the lights and close the door. She followed them down the hall, through the sitting room, into an extensive dining alcove with a table set with delicate bone china, silver cutlery, napkins, and plates of tiny sandwiches and cream cakes.

Gosh. Afternoon tea.

"I hope you don't mind coming in here; it's so much easier for me. Do sit down.' She directed them to their seats, found her own, and began to pour.

A traditional and elegant room: the walls painted in cream, plump sofas and armchairs strategically placed, with a lovely Turkish carpet on the light oak floors. Bookshelves lined one wall, and several original paintings were positioned on the others. French doors opened to an immaculate patio and garden. Gloves and pruning shears lay on a table outside the window.

So she does the gardening herself.

Even more intrigued, Cathrina settled into her chair, ready to enjoy the afternoon with this interesting old lady. A glance at Josh found him regarding their hostess with an equal air of expectation.

They'd heard a little about her when they went over to Golders Green for dinner after their return from Ephesus. During the meal they entertained his parents with the tales of their holiday, including that of Cathrina's visions. It fascinated Manny, and he questioned her on the Essene connection, but Ruth said surprisingly little. Afterwards, Josh noticed how she watched his wife. Not sure what to make of it, he regretted saying anything, thinking he'd exposed Cathrina to criticism.

Later, his father disappeared into the lounge to watch TV. And while they stayed to drink an extra cup of creamy coffee, his mother related the story of the rescue circle she joined all those years ago in North London and left when she fell pregnant with her youngest son, Jonathan.

Josh stared at her in disbelief. 'You never told me any of this, Mum.'

'I'm sorry, love. I wanted to be careful. I learned not to push anyone in a specific direction, especially not someone from my own family. You can so easily send them away from their designated future. Your obvious interest in spiritual matters warned me not to put a foot wrong. You're still too young to be involved with us.

'Look, Jean's the one you need to talk to. About the rule of evil, I mean. That was the basis of our work. And from what I remember, she wrote a book.'

'What? About your work?'

'No. About Satan's era of iniquity, what it meant, how it came into being, how it would end.' A mischievous smile played around her eyes as she regarded her son's exasperation.

'Why didn't you tell me this before?'

'God knows, Josh. So many times I began, but something always stopped me. The situation didn't feel right. I just followed my instincts and years of experience taught me to trust them. You're both so young with all your lives before you. Rescue work is based on a highly advanced form of spiritualism. University level. A more accurate description would be "metaphysical exploration". Nothing frivolous like fortune telling.

'For me, it was a wonderful time, as well as a profound spiritual education. Our membership was mainly Jewish, so I felt safe somehow, although we dealt with some very dangerous stuff, really desecrated souls. We had a few Christian members including Jean, the secretary. She took the notes and instructions, kept the records, and acted as one of the elders, the more experienced members, a general overseeing committee.'

Cathrina interrupted. 'Yes, but what did you do?'

'We elevated souls that fell into the lower realms after they died,' Ruth said with a smile.

She stared at her mother-in-law in astonishment. How could this middle-aged, sensible, Jewish housewife from middle-class Golders Green become involved in anything so outlandish? Yet she appeared to be sincere.

'How did you do these elevations?' Josh asked, intrigued.

'We called the lower soul into the circle and sent him to a trained medium who allowed him to speak. We talked to him and sent kind thoughts until he ascended into the upper realms—heaven, in other words.

'If a lower soul came in, I sensed it as a black, heavy cloud, full of anger and depression. As we surrounded him with love and kind thoughts, the darkness slowly dissipated until it completely disappeared. At that stage, some of the others would get the tingles on their skin, similar to you, Cathrina. They confirmed the rescue.

'Members reacted differently; a few felt the tingling, others a warmth or they saw increasing light in the centre of the circle. Some of us had nothing. I couldn't feel upper vibrations at all, for instance, but my abilities with desecrated vibes were useful. I could always tell when the soul left the lower realms.'

This new knowledge fascinated Cathrina. It ran parallel to her own experiences. 'How long did you stay with them?'

'Nearly four years. In the beginning I went with a friend to see what it was all about. A bit of fun to be honest, pure curiosity.

Yet the more I learned the more interested I became, until I joined them and stayed right up to my pregnancy. Then the Guide told me to leave. The lower vibes could harm the growing foetus.'

'Did you go back, afterwards?'

'I tried, but they said another path would open up for me in the future. In the meantime, I should concentrate on bringing up my family.' Her eyes filled with tears. She quickly wiped them away.

Josh took her hand, amazed to see his down-to-earth mother so upset. 'Did they tell you what you would do?'

'No. The knowledge would come to me. They didn't forbid me to return. It was up to me, but to stay at home was the better choice, at least for the time being. The desecration might affect you children, they said. And we did deal with some awful souls. If I remember rightly, we were rescuing Nazis at that time.'

Her son's mouth fell open. 'Nazis? You're not serious, Mum?'

She laughed at him. 'I thought that would get your attention. We neutralised evil with loving thoughts, my dear, and what is more desecrated to a group of Jews than the SS?

'The Guides suggested it. We had important but very difficult work coming up, and they believed elevating Nazis would strengthen us, in particular those who suffered so much in the war. Some of our members lost their whole families in the gas chambers. Imagine the pain of such rescues. We needed to learn self-control, however, and how to use objective kind thoughts.

'Of course they were right. It took deep commitment to be compassionate to those souls, to send them loving vibrations. Eventually we were expert, until sending them kind thoughts became as natural as breathing.

'The Nazis made it difficult once they realised we were Jews. They taunted us, boasting of the torturous things they did to our people in the camps, anything to provoke an aggressive reaction. If they'd succeeded, we would have fallen to their level, and they would have gone down even further.

'Sometimes I look back, and that particular work fills me with genuine satisfaction and pride. I learned how to be sympathetic to Nazis, to view them as poor souls who didn't know what they were doing. We raised quite a few of them, and some truly vicious entities left the lower realms, which meant we weakened the overall level of evil. So you can understand why they warned me about the possible effects on my unborn child.'

Josh watched the expressions on his mother's face and smiled. 'You had a lot of respect for these high souls?'

'Oh God, yes! You couldn't help it. I felt so safe with them. When a high soul took him over, our medium went into full trance, completely unconscious. Members, sensitive to upper vibrations, described sitting with a Guide like being in a cloud of effervescence. Again, similar to you, Cathrina.'

'I'll never forget those years. It satisfied a yearning in my soul, Josh. I loved it, and I learned so much. It made me a better person. But to get back to your situation, you need to talk to Jean. She'll help you.'

He tried to dig deeper, but she stopped him. 'No. No more. I'm afraid to say too much in case I harm you.' With that she clammed up, and even her darling son couldn't persuade her otherwise. Their only option: meet with this white-haired, 82-year-old lady with whom they were having afternoon tea.

Jean chatted with Josh, catching up with all the news from his mum and dad. Cathrina was only involved superficially, but when their hostess at last turned to her, she became aware of a laser-like inspection and knew this lovable old lady shouldn't be underestimated.

'Well, my dear, tell me what happened. Ruth said you had some kind of manifestation.'

'It wasn't quite like that, Jean. I think I tuned into a series of past events involving Mary and John, the apostle. I'll read you the notes I made at the time.'

Jean listened, nodding every so often as the story unfolded. 'I hadn't realised she'd gone to Ephesus. No doubt the persecutions after the crucifixion forced them to leave Judaea. Poor Mary. She must have gone through hell.' She stared out into the garden, thinking.

The silence lengthened, and Cathrina finished her tea, glancing over on occasion to Josh, wondering what they should do. He continued watching their hostess with interest and gestured not to worry, to give her more time.

Eventually, she turned back and considered them. 'I'm not sure what you want from me.'

'We hoped you would answer some of our questions. We've been through these notes so often, and there are bits I don't understand. I was brought up as a Catholic, and these visions contradict a lot of the teachings I received as a child, in particular the doctrine that Christ died for our sins. In fact, it's almost as if the basic premise underlying Christianity is up for question.'

She faltered as Jean's face broke into a smile. 'Sorry. Don't mind me. Many years ago, I began to write a book on what would have happened if Jesus hadn't been crucified. What if he'd succeeded in his task? Then we became involved in important work, and I never finished it. And now the subject is coming up again. Interesting.'

'Do you know what he came to do?' Cathrina asked with a touch of impatience.

Jean smiled. 'Oh yes. He came to end the rule of evil, just as Mary said. But the lowers stopped him. Satan, the devil or whatever you want to call him, rallied his forces, both the dead and the living, men and women he influenced and controlled, the Romans, and their supporters, the Herodians and high priests. They arrested Jesus and killed him.

'They didn't understand what they were doing, of course, no idea of the consequences, concerned only with their desire for material riches. So they did exactly what Satan wanted them to do. They eliminated the one person who could have saved humanity.'

'How though?' Josh asked. 'That's what I want to know. How would he have ended the rule of evil? And more to the point, what exactly is the rule of evil?'

Jean looked at them and smiled. 'Tell me this. Do you believe in objective wickedness? Do you think desecrated spirits can influence us to do harm?'

They glanced at each other, not sure how to answer.

Cathrina laughed. 'I grew up with the devil and all his works. A typical Catholic upbringing with Mass on Sunday and a convent education. All hellfire and brimstone. He was intensely real to me, in my childhood. In fact, he terrified me.

'Nowadays, I have some understanding of the workings of the human mind and that changed my attitude. So I suppose I now tend to dismiss him. A great deal is explained by psychology. Where does he fit in anymore?'

'What about you, Josh?'

'Although I'm a psychologist, I don't think anyone could be Jewish and not be aware of evil. The stories I've listened to all my life convinces me something consciously malevolent is active out there. If it came from the subconscious, I would hope mankind would evolve and change. The problem is, it doesn't explain everything.'

'OK. Do you believe in life after death?'

With the nods, she continued. 'Right. Let me briefly tell you how it works, lessons our Guides taught us. Seven sunsets after a person dies, he judges himself. Note: he does his own judging. No one else has the authority. Only one's own inner spirit is capable, and that spirit is totally just. It sends itself either up or down to be with others on the same vibrational level, like birds of a feather. They gravitate towards the vibrations they are used to, like a spiritual gravity or attraction.

'One point might interest you: there are no everlasting fires in hell. That belief comes from the memories of the unending furnace in the Valley of Gehenna, outside the walls of Jerusalem, where the ancient Canaanites burned children as a sacrifice to their god Moloch. In the lower realms, it's freezing cold. No warmth down there, no love. And the further down you go, the colder it gets.

'The important thing to remember is this: both "uppers" and "lowers" interact with the living. High souls try to influence us to acts of kindness, and many people are aware of these beings of light, assuming they are angels: probably the source of the guardian angel concept. The task of the highest realms, the home of the Seers, is to guide humanity towards physical and spiritual evolvement and a greater connection with the Great Creator, the Supreme Being.

'The lowers have a similar structure, but their goal is destruction. A desecrated spirit absorbs power from those under his control and will cause depression, illness, and on occasions, death to the one to whom he succeeds in attaching himself.

153

'In rescue work like ours, we call the entity into the circle, and by sending kind thoughts, we neutralise the evil surrounding him. We have trained mediums capable of holding the soul and allowing it to speak. Over time we reach the pure essence at the centre of the being, the spark of the Creator that resides in every one of us, and the spirit is then able to ascend into the upper realms. There, it will strengthen and graduate further upwards.

'There is no doubt, Cathrina, that psychotherapy plays an important part. Much of one's negative behaviour has roots in childhood trauma, lack of love, abuse, and other factors, and often the damage is beyond the person's conscious control.

'When we are damaged spiritually, we attract lower souls who are comfortable in the heavy, dark atmosphere surrounding us. Effective psychological help can increase our confidence and self-acceptance. We begin to think more positively and emanate purer vibrations which are unpleasant, even painful, to the lowers around us. They leave. We recover emotionally and spiritually. A difficult procedure but especially effective if the patient has a strong affinity with the psychotherapist.

'Ask your mum about elevations, Josh. She's had a lot of experience, a competent lower medium.'

'She wouldn't tell us anything. She insisted we talk to you.'

Jean smiled. 'I suppose she was trying to protect you.'

Cathrina's patience evaporated. 'Jean, what has this got to do with the rule of evil?'

'Ah! Now we get to the crux of the matter. You must understand that the Creator never meant evil to come into this world. Earth should have been a paradise where we would evolve in body, mind, and spirit.

'In the days when humans first learned to rise above their animal instincts, a man was born with the ability to help mankind

154

in this initial transformation. He inherited phenomenal gifts and would have been of inestimable value. Instead, his arrogance and pride in his abilities grew to such an extent, he placed himself in direct opposition to the Supreme Being. He created evil and became known as Satan.

'His story is a long and complicated one which I'll explain in detail at another time. What I want to emphasise now is this: man brought moral evil into our world, not God or fallen angels, and what man originated, he can eliminate. Such human wickedness isn't here permanently. In ancient times, the Creator promised it would end, and in time, we will realise it is within our own power to neutralise the Evil One.

However, the real question you need to ask is this: what is evil? The answer lies in the understanding of suffering. There are two types: one comes from lack of knowledge, the other from man's malice.

'The former is experienced through the normal process of learning how to interact with nature and our material world: a child lifts a burning coal from the fire; a lion mauls a hunter in the African savannah. In neither case is malice involved. The little one explores but lacks information. The animal is hungry, follows its instinct and hunts for food. Its victim is careless, reckless, or unlucky. If they survive, both child and man will, hopefully, learn from their mistakes. In these cases, pain helps prevent the repetition of a dangerous experience and contributes to evolution.

'The second type, moral evil, is caused by the deliberate desire to harm another sentient being: an angry young man kicks his dog to death; a woman is knifed in a dark alley and her few coins stolen; a father sneaks into his daughter's bedroom and sexually abuses her; Jews are thrown into a gas chamber. These are cold-blooded acts, committed in full knowledge. You will find greater or lesser expressions, but the suffering experienced will always lead from hostility, the wish to inflict damage on another, different spiritually to that resulting from ignorance.

'To be brief, the spiritual effects of moral evil are neutralised totally and permanently by love and compassion. It doesn't come in the blink of an eye, of course. Time and sufficient kind thoughts are required. Jesus understood this. He came to teach us the Golden Rule of loving one another.

'Unfortunately, he only completed part of his task. The full flowering of the kingdom of heaven didn't happen. Today, Satan still influences humanity. Sometime in the future, however, he will elevate, and at that stage, suffering caused by human malice will very gradually diminish. It will take time, through further human evolution, but there will come a day when deliberate evil will fade from mankind.'

A scraping noise interrupted, as Josh abruptly pushed back his chair and burst into the sitting room. He paced up and down muttering to himself, agitation in every movement. 'I don't believe it. I just can't see it.'

Cathrina stared at him with wide eyes, her mouth open. She glanced at Jean, but she was regarding him quite serenely as he tramped her wooden floor.

After a few minutes, he made an effort and pulled himself together. The pacing stopped, and he returned, sheepishly, to his place at the table.

'Forgive me, Jean. I didn't mean to be rude. But the whole idea is so crazy and against everything I've learned about human beings.'

'Josh, I completely understand. Look at the last century with the world wars, especially Hitler and the Holocaust, and then today, these new explosions of aggression from the old authoritarian regimes. I'm not surprised you find it difficult to accept.

'Even though human moral evil didn't end two thousand years ago, it will at some point in the future. We've been working on this since the 1950s. Our Guides told us about the imminent coming of the Brotherhood of Man. Cathrina's visions and Mary's prophecy confirms this knowledge, and it isn't some fairy story for babies.'

Although still agitated, her firm conviction forced him to break through his irritation and consider the proposition. 'Are we back to the new-age concepts of the 1960s?'

'Some of them, yes. The ideas came into western public consciousness at that time, but the prophecies go back millennia to major civilisations.

'We're not alone, Josh. The great souls in the upper realms, our ancestors and those who have gone before us, are trying to help humanity. To put it somewhat crudely, they don't sit around on their fluffy clouds all day, twiddling their thumbs. They actively enable our progress.

'Our own Directing Guide, an ancient and very wise soul, came to facilitate this advance, to bring us knowledge. During my own time with our group, almost fifty years now, we've dealt with continuous threats to our civilisation with amazing success. But our work is far from finished. Incredible efforts are still being made.'

'Then why isn't it stopped? If there is a good and just God, why doesn't He prevent the suffering, stop the wickedness?'

It was the eternal question, and she looked at him with heartfelt sympathy. 'How can that be, Josh? Humans have the freedom to choose. A man created moral evil, and others deserted the Most High to follow him. The Creator won't go back on His plan for us or wave a wand to take away humanity's freedom because He doesn't like our decisions. He won't deprive us of our ability to think and decide, abilities we've gained and further expanded through human evolution.

'God is a being of pure love. We've become very aware of this, over the years. We've spoken to many high souls, and the further up you go into the upper realms, the more powerful the love.

'The universe or universes are evolving, and we humans are growing with them. We've reached the "point of reflection", the stage where we can intellectually consider our options and refuse to respond to instinct. If we are surrounded by hatred, we can stand back, and instead of reacting automatically with anger or fear, we can choose to act differently: we can love, and we can have compassion.[11]

'This is an important stage in our evolution. On a world or even an individual level, we haven't yet learned how to control our emotions. Until we do, we're stuck. To evolve further, we need to pass through this point. To a certain extent, we're still like our animal ancestors. We're partially carnivore; we see our existence and survival as depending on the destruction of others, other humans or other sentient beings. In the future, we hope that will change.

'We don't know what the Creator has planned for us, or why the whole process began in the first place, but we are moving in a specific direction. How long it takes is up to us. He can only work through people who want to do His will: people here on earth and those on the other side in the upper realms; people like your

---

[11] In his book, *The Phenomenon of Man*, the evolutionary theorist, respected paleontologist and visionary theologian Pierre Teilhard de Chardin explores the physical, psychological and spiritual changes that occurred during our evolution into *homo sapiens*.

mum, Josh, or high souls like our Guides. Human beings have to change. We have to reject evil; we have to learn to leave hostility, malice, aggression, and most of all, fear behind. We have to take the next step.'

He looked at her for a long moment, this white-haired old lady who compelled him to confront some difficult truths.

He smiled at her, not sure what to think of it all. 'I'll make us a fresh pot of tea.'

Jean watched him as he disappeared into the kitchen, aware of the inner battle being waged, and turned briskly to her other guest.

'Are you beginning to understand why I'm so interested in your experiences, Cathrina? Mary confirms what we've been told. It looks as though another attempt will be made to end the rule of evil in our own time; if successful, the brotherhood of man or, as Jesus put it, the kingdom of heaven will finally come into being. It's exciting and wonderful. I can only thank you sincerely for coming and telling me.

'But why you? I'm wondering why you, in particular, had these visions. There must be a reason. Have you any ideas?'

'Not a clue, to be honest. Although, I think they sent me—as Josh says, whoever "they" might be. For years, every so often, I would hear a voice in my mind saying: "Go to Ephesus. Go to Ephesus". Eventually I went, and this happened.'

'So it wasn't a coincidence. No doubt intended and part of the pattern.'

'Do you think so? I've always considered myself a spiritual explorer because I can feel both upper and lower vibrations, an ability that runs in my family. And I know I'm supposed to do something with it. Any further than that, I just can't see.'

'Ah! You believe you have a task. Even more interesting. Well, look. I'm going to help you. That's what you want, isn't it?'

'God, yes. We're a bit out of our depth here, Jean. Your support would make such a difference. I need to understand what I'm dealing with. I want to find out if I'm expected to do something in particular.'

'Okay. Don't worry too much about it. The answer will come. Although I'm wondering if you should write.'

Cathrina laughed. 'You must be psychic. I've been thinking about a book.' She glanced over at her husband, who was leaning against the kitchen door, listening.

He said, 'It's a good idea, especially when you consider your work on the Essenes and the Nazoraeans.'

'Marvellous,' Jean said. 'It's time this information was out in the world. And if you really mean to write about this, I'll give you my book, *The Coming of Evil*, the full story of Satan's original fall and the early surge of his power, in considerable detail. A wonderful sequel, or in this case, prequel for you.'

They both grinned, finally delighted with each other.

'Let me write mine first. Then we'll deal with yours,' Cathrina said with a laugh, amazed at how her experiences in Ephesus had become a spiritual and historical project.

'Before we go any further, let's have this cup of tea Josh promised us.'

He brought clean cups and a fresh pot into the dining room and settled back in his chair, thinking about their discussion and the decision to cooperate. He was the first to break the comfortable silence.

'What I still don't understand is why none of this came down to us. Surely there must be a record.'

'Our Directing Guide asked the very same question, Josh.

Why didn't we have at least an oral tradition of soul elevation? We told him that some of the Christian churches, like the Catholics and Anglicans, retained specially trained exorcists who used a formula for possessions.

'He was disappointed and presumed this was all that remained of a considerable body of instructions intended for people in general, not for the chosen few. We learned that during the first years of Christianity, when the leaders died and discovered they'd stopped this knowledge from being freely available, many recriminated themselves and fell into the lower realms to years of suffering.'

Josh gazed at her in astonishment. 'Wow. You mean they believed they were to blame and ended up in hell because of it.'

Focusing his eyes on her serene face, he couldn't decide whether it was all this new knowledge or the old lady herself that fascinated him more. She opened doors into a world he realised existed but had never heard explained so clearly, with such intelligence and command.

'Why did it all die out, Jean?' Cathrina asked.

'It's phenomenally dangerous work. Not something you play around with. You need to know exactly what you're doing, otherwise you end up in trouble, with an attachment or a possession.

'In our rescue circle today, we are given a powerful protection from the upper realms, and a Guide always examines us before and after we elevate a lower soul. Being a rescue worker requires constant self-discipline. And frankly, it's really hard work. It takes a long period of training, under the guidance of the upper realms, to learn how to deal with lower souls and years of experience to elevate the really deep ones.

'After the crucifixion, I assume it was an oral, esoteric

tradition, kept among the capable few. Those who stopped its continuation were probably trying to protect their people from spiritual damage.

'According to the Guide, however, that decision didn't pass scrutiny by their own inner spirit. When they died and learned the truth, they blamed themselves. Perhaps for not having greater courage.'

'That sounds a bit tough,' Josh said, frowning.

'Yes, but you must remember we judge ourselves after death, and we do so with clear-sighted justice. No rose-coloured spectacles, no desire to minimise our faults. A spiritual lapse to me might be of no importance to you.

'No doubt, they were good people with high standards. Their failure to measure up to those standards caused them to fall. They prevented the future elevation of lower souls, and as well as that, they stopped the use of knowledge brought to us by Jesus. If they lacked personal bravery that's even worse. Our work requires courage. Cowardice makes the lowers stronger. They feed on fear. The guides continually drummed it into us: "There is nothing to fear but fear itself".'

Cathrina sat thinking, trying to integrate these ideas into the history of early Christianity. 'The "fear" idea is interesting, Jean. It fits with the historical situation. The Roman elite were suspicious of the charismatic, oriental cults coming in from the east. Their own religion was ritual. They used animal sacrifice to appease the gods who gave them victory in war and protection for the Empire.

'The eastern acts of worship were different. They demanded an emotionally charged belief and identification with the god or goddess. They were considered outlandish with too much influence on the people, particularly women, including senatorial women. Potentially a threat to Roman authority.

'The emperors came down hard on them. Augustus banned Egyptian Isis and destroyed her temple in Rome. The Jews were expelled from the city by both Tiberius and Claudius, although they soon returned. Like Christianity, eastern religions sought converts, and the Empire viewed them as an attack on stability and political control.

'The Romans disliked Christians because they wouldn't respect their idols, the irreverence seen as an attack on the Empire's divine protection. They suspected the new religion's members of killing babies (the Eucharistic blood) and cannibalism (eating the body of the Lord).

'When the Great Fire broke out in Nero's reign, many thought the Emperor started it. He needed a scapegoat and blamed the Christians. As it happened, the sight of burning bodies, used as torches to light the palace gardens, helped turn the dislike of the ordinary people of Rome into sympathy.

'The persecution ended, but episodes like this might have forced them to be careful. Perhaps accusations of necromancy, or rites connected with the dead were a threat. Although we don't know if knowledge of soul elevation reached Gentile Christianity. This might be an area of research. I'll see if there is anything in the ancient writings. What do you think, Jean?'

'You're the historian. I'll leave it to you. Keep me informed though. I can always give a spiritual perspective. I must admit, I'm delighted you're doing this, Cathrina. If there's going to be another attempt to end the rule of evil, this knowledge needs to come into the public domain.'

Josh interrupted. 'I would like to ask you something, Jean. Who were your Guides? Anyone we would have heard of?'

'If you mean historically, then no. They are simply some of the many unrecorded souls and saints in the highest reaches of the upper realms, those who have dedicated themselves to the evolution of humanity.

'Over time, as I said, we've spoken to quite a few. However, it was a very special privilege, and we don't identify them or do anything to cause them harm.'

'I understand. At least, I think I do.'

22

Paradise Discovered

On her terrace one morning in late summer, the jangle of harness and the echoes of girlish laughter warned Rachel that her family had arrived. She alerted Devorah in the kitchen and went down to meet them. John drove over to the valley with the last of Mary's boxes and explained to Susannah where everything should go. On his return, he left the animals and cart in the stable with Reuben and joined the others for a late breakfast. They didn't linger.

When Mary first saw her new home, she felt almost dizzy with surprise and excitement: the cream sandstone walls surrounding the entrance, the rose bushes in tubs on either side, the curved path leading to Susannah, who stood waiting at the open door, smiling in welcome.

Gardens stretched down to the middle of the valley, where a stream, born from mountain springs, brought fresh, cold water throughout the year, even on the hottest day. Reuben had planted fruit trees and prepared others for the cooler weather. With these and her garden she would be well supplied with food by spring, and the extras, such as fish, grain, and lentils would easily be found in the local market.

The changes inside thrilled her. Susannah had cleaned and scrubbed, all the building dirt gone, the rooms immaculate. Mary hugged her tightly and thanked her. It was perfect. She smiled at Rachel, aware of the little touches her friend had added: the bright bedspreads, the wall hangings, the woven covers on the couch, the movable partitions. She ran her fingers over the table, amazed at the quality of the furniture, the beds built specifically for each room, the closets carved with flowing shapes. Joseph would have loved it all.

Susannah brought drinks to the table and took the girls away to explore, leaving the others to rest and talk. But as soon as she sat down, exhaustion overwhelmed Mary, and nothing seemed to calm the evil spirit. A burning irritation stewed within her, the entity rising in anger, impossible to control. She had to get away from everyone, to be on her own to deal with the pain.

Seeing the strain and guessing the cause, John quickly intervened. 'Why don't you lie down for a few hours, Mary? You've had a long day.'

He took her arm, shaking his head at Rachel and Martha when they tried to help. In her room he moved the partition across the window and left her sitting on the bed, removing her veil. He brought her a cup of tirosh. She smiled in gratitude and lay back into the pillows.

He closed the door and returned to the others.

'Don't worry. She just needs time, and Susannah's here. Let's go back to your place, Rachel. I want to talk to Reuben.'

The house was still and Mary rested. Later she heard bees

buzzing outside her window and pondered the possibility of honey. Joseph kept a hive. With enough flowers and plants in the garden, she might try.

Eventually sleep came. Hours passed as she dreamt of Nazareth and her home on the edge of the village. Even there she was tired, her clothes stained, her sandals scuffed and dirty. Thirst forced her to the well, and as she drank the refreshing water, Joseph brought white cloths to wash her face, hands, and feet. Cleaner now, he held her in comforting arms and sent her back to waken in her bedroom on the mountain, a little stronger, a little calmer, more ready to face the years ahead.

The cooler breezes of early evening whispered through the rooms; she awoke feeling well recovered, smiling when she remembered the dream. She washed, changed her clothes, and hurried out to climb the cliff face.

There on the platform she discovered the most delightful surprise of all. It had been enlarged by cutting extra space into the rock, and a small pavilion built of latticed woods, covered with woven reeds. The path held ceramic pots of roses and other flowering plants. Inside were stools, a small table, a high-backed chair, and a small, cushioned couch where she could lie back and relax yet still see the Aegean. John's idea, of course. He was so thoughtful.

She sat down and surveyed the vista below, soon lost in fantasies of ships and voyages, in memories of Joachim, Anna, and the beloved family she had left behind. She was in Ephesus now for the rest of her life, and with the realisation came acceptance. So much had gone, but she still had her nephew and these wonderful new friends. And now they'd found this haven, this beautiful mountaintop sanctuary. The peace would aid her recovery, and perhaps, in time, she would help John with the tasks that still remained.

Instantly, as on that first day, the effervescence of a divine blessing tingled on her skin. She thanked the holy one who came and, once again, committed her devotion and duty to the Most High, asking only for the strength to endure whatever was to come. Time passed, and she fell asleep in the cool shade of her pavilion.

John found her there, later in the evening. He organised food and drinks; she awoke, hungry, to delicious aromas. He unpacked the basket and settled in the high-backed chair beside her couch, ready for their first meal in the new home.

They spent an enjoyable few hours searching down the coast and out to sea, trying to identify the various islands. They talked about the future, his work in Ephesus and what still had to be done in the house. Avram the carpenter lived nearby, and Rachel would bring her to the market to see what was available locally. She shouldn't want for anything.

'We are safe, Mary, certainly as far as coin is concerned. So make yourself comfortable. I will keep on the house in the city for the moment, although I'd like to build on the hill behind the theatre, up where I did the elevation on the goddess. That area is now a great source of spiritual power. It would mean you could come down and stay.'

He smiled, thinking it would be a long time before anyone could drag her away from this heavenly place.

'We've been well cared for,' she said. 'It's amazing when you think back: all the killings in Jerusalem; that terrible night when they broke into the house and poor old Simon died. James pulled me out of bed, and we escaped. I thought I'd never see peace again. You were right though. This has been a new beginning, and I do believe I'll recover here, find my real self again.'

He reached over and took her hand, playing with her fingers as he did when he was a child.

'I know you will, Mary. If anywhere, it's here. You have the house, the gardens, the orchard, and this little pavilion. Susannah will look after you, and Rachel is only a short walk away. Peace yet company when you want it. You're independent. The workers are paid, and I've settled the final payments for the land. I'll be up regularly, and I'm sure Matthias and James will want to come too.'

They watched the sun descend in the west and said their prayers of thanksgiving. Later when the shadows deepened and twilight moved into cooler night, they gathered everything into the basket and returned to the house. Mary lit the lamps, bringing the darkening rooms to life, and when Susannah came back, they spent the first night in their new home.

She awoke soon after dawn to the smell of baking bread and the sound of the trickling stream outside her open window. She rose, washed, dressed, and turned her mind to her Creator, saying the Shema, the ancient hymn of worship and thanksgiving, grateful for all her blessings. Then she spoke the Prayer to the Father,[12] given to them by the Wise Ones and taught by Yeshu to all the followers, the song of hope that called for the end of the rule of evil and the inauguration of the era of the Most High, the kingdom of heaven.

With anticipation she went into the kitchen, greeted Susannah, poured herself a cup of tirosh, and brought it out to her own little domain. She examined everything in detail. The orchard was big

---

[12] The Lord's Prayer.

enough for at least twenty trees, ten already planted. The olives, fig, plum, and cherry were familiar, but she didn't know the others. Holes were prepared for further planting, and she must ask Reuben what he intended, eager to be involved. In the garden, onions and leeks grew in tidy beds. The rest of the area had been dug and turned over, ready for spring. She laughed with delight.

Later they walked over to join their friends, finding them as usual on the terrace. They told the stories of the pavilion on the clifftop and how, the night before, they had a meal there among the scents of roses, high above the world, looking down on the sea and the valley below. Her happiness was infectious, and Rachel smiled as she listened, glad she'd sold the land to John. A new life for all of them.

Work required Jacob to leave the following morning, but Martha and the girls would remain. They enjoyed the cooler air and the freedom from noise and dirt, even though, as the physician insisted, Ephesus was well organised and clean compared to most cities.

John also stayed to make sure Mary and Susannah settled in. Reuben went regularly to the market, and a few days later, they both left with the donkey at dawn. They returned in the afternoon with baskets packed with basics, such as lentils, peas, beans, nuts, and cheese, as well as fresh fruit and vegetables.

A jenny goat peeped from behind the donkey's rump, and around her neat black hooves gambolled two tiny female kids. The nanny would supply them with milk and cheese, invaluable in the winter months ahead, and would be mated again the following spring. Still, they needed to control her. With a long rope, he tied her to a tree beside the house. Goats would eat anything in sight, and on the way home they'd stopped with Avram to arrange for fences to enclose the land.

The next morning he milked the nanny and moved her further down towards the valley entrance where the shelter was greater and the grass greener. The kids jumped and played around him, knocking his legs with their hard little heads, sucking his fingers when he bent to stroke them. They were continually under his feet, but they amused him. He smiled when he glimpsed the little white bodies running to and fro among the bushes.

The fencing would enclose the animals with sufficient grazing yet protect the gardens and orchards. While he diverted water from the stream into the vegetable garden and soaked the plants, he pondered on their own washing facilities.

The fishermen at the market talked of pools in the mountains, and he wondered if any were near. He walked up the valley and eventually came to a waterfall that splashed into a broad expanse of cool, fresh water. Contained on either side by steep cliffs of rock, it was deep and private. He stripped off and immersed himself, enjoying it more than any marble bath in Ephesus or Jerusalem. He must take Mary and Susannah soon. Bathing facilities, a private miqvah, not far from the house. What a blessing. Rachel would know who owned the land.

At home, he changed his tunic and told his aunt of his discovery. She wanted to go straight away, and when she told Susannah, they grabbed clean clothes and abandoned the cooking.

At the pool, he laughed at their joy and left them. Somewhere to bathe gave that last, finishing touch. They were well supplied with everything they needed now, and he wouldn't worry when he was down in the city.

As their friends were expected for Shabbat dinner that evening, he walked over to join them on the terrace, amusing them with the antics of the goats and the thought of Mary with her own special bathing place in the mountains.

When he described the area, Rachel recognised it immediately. 'That's part of the farm. They'll be safe there. No one goes up that way.'

She laughed, amazed how nicely that helped her new neighbours. She hoped Mary would be happy on the mountain, glad she'd come there to live. Later, as the sun dropped towards the horizon, they left John to find the girls and get ready.

Mary and Susannah returned clean and refreshed to finish the preparations. Baked fish, lentil stew, fruit, and fresh bread would be a suitable thank you to Rachel and Martha for all their help, as well as a celebration for their arrival on the mountain. With the table prepared and the lamps in place, she sat down to wait for her first guests. She poured a cup of tirosh, and hearing voices, went to the door to welcome her friends.

23

A White Pavilion

That first winter on the mountain brought increasing peace to Mary. Although still aware of the evil presence, the physical pain diminished. Even so, at times the despair took hold, and she tortured herself with the broken faces and bodies of those who would suffer in the centuries to come, wondering what they could have done—no, what *she* should have done to ensure the success of the work.

At night when she slept, it was *she* who dragged the cross through the streets of Jerusalem, *she* who suffered the sting of the whip on her back, on her bare breasts, *she* who writhed in pain as the thorn pierced her brow. She gazed into alien faces who did not love her—deserted, abandoned, alone, and inconsolable.

The first time it happened on the mountain, Susannah thought her mistress was losing her mind and ran to the farm for help. Rachel came immediately, and seeing Mary's ravaged face, took her by the arm and walked her up to the pool. She took off her veil and headdress and pulled her into the water where she floundered, slipping on the stones, trying to break free.

Rachel held her tight, bathing her face and head until she came back to herself and stood sobbing in her friend's arms. They remained there until the cold penetrated and Mary shivered in shock.

Rachel wrapped her in her own cloak, gathered the discarded clothes, and brought her down the valley to her home. She found a clean dress and head coverings, helped her change and be herself again. All that day she stayed, reluctant to leave her alone. Later they went up to the pavilion, and Susannah carried up food and drinks, thanking the Most High for Rachel's help, begging Him to save her poor, suffering mistress.

In her friend's calm, sensible care Mary regained her self-control and remembered. Overcome with shame, she tried to apologise, but Rachel stopped her, saying it wasn't necessary, admitting she hadn't completely understood evil until that day. She'd felt the entity at the pool, experienced the desecration and power as he fought to dominate Mary, battled for continued possession of her soul.

He was dark and vicious, and there were moments when she feared for her own safety. Mary's eyes were slits of rage and fury, her mouth spitting white, an animal's growl in her throat, her nails ripping at the face before her. She had the strength of a powerful man, and only with difficulty had Rachel held her off, prevented any real damage to her own body.

She pushed her down, forcing her poor, naked, greying head under the water, shocking her with the piercing cold. Her respect and love for Mary reinforced her total refusal to let this power have her, and it gave her the courage to resist.

Somehow she remembered the words Yeshua had spoken on the cross: 'Father, forgive them, for they know not what they do.'

She repeated them to the evil spirit, with deep and genuine

compassion; Mary screamed in terrible agony. A short time later she opened her eyes, recognised Rachel, and collapsed in tears. The power, however, was gone.

When she heard what happened at the pool, Mary finally recognised it was the desecrated soul that was pulling her down into despair.

Rachel took her hands. 'Listen to me, Mary. I don't know if I'm right, but I want you to hear what I have to say. You are only one person. No matter what task the Most High has given you, you cannot do it alone. You can only succeed with the help of others. And if they don't cooperate and you fail, even though you strive with all your strength and all your soul, you mustn't blame yourself. Humanity wasn't ready. They are not sufficiently purified. They need to go through further suffering. Your task, your only responsibility, is to prepare for the future, for the work still to come.

'There is always more than one way to accomplish a goal. And if the first one fails, the next one must be found. To despair at this stage is self-indulgent and not worthy of who you are.'

Rachel stopped, her eyes wide open, her hands to her mouth, as if to pretend the words had never been uttered. 'I'm so sorry. I don't know where that came from. I didn't mean to hurt you.'

Mary gazed at her with a calm and thankful smile. 'I know exactly where it came from, my dear friend. It was something I needed to hear, and I'm so grateful you said it. You helped me today more than you can possibly imagine. I've been lost for a long time. I am only beginning to realise it. Thank you for your kindness. I'm sorry I put you through so much.'

She leaned over and gently kissed Rachel's cheek. 'You're tired. Let's go back to the house, and we'll take you home.'

In the weeks and months that followed, all through the rest of the winter and early spring, Mary grappled with her thoughts. When despair attacked, she fought not to succumb. On the days when mourning for Yeshu threatened her bruised soul, she climbed to the pavilion, gazed out to sea, and pictured the *Galilee* with Simon and his crew, wondering where they sailed, wishing she was with them. Or she took Susannah and searched the hedges and pastures for wild herbs, for rocket, mallow, chicory, and endive, and as the rains fell, they ran to the pool for mushrooms.

Although it taxed the depths of her strength, her self-discipline slowly re-emerged, and she governed her mind. She didn't try to restrain the entity or weaken him. That would have been too much. She simply wanted to be herself again, to be Mary, committed to the Great Creator, watchful for His wishes, ready to obey His commands.

Her despair departed, her mourning ended. A full acceptance entered her soul; she had accomplished all of which she was capable in the sight of the Most High, and that knowledge left her whole once more.

John came up regularly, and alerted by the rapid changes, wormed the details from a reluctant Rachel. He spent time with her, explaining that Mary was, at last, pushing out the lower soul, aware how influential her intervention had been at the turning point. She told him of her terror at the pool, ashamed of her weakness.

He disagreed. Everyone experienced fear when they first faced the viciousness of a powerful desecrated soul. Her subsequent actions defined her true character. When one is attacked, the usual response is to return anger for anger, hostility for hostility. The person receiving the hatred senses it and returns it with equal, if not greater, force. It's a common human reaction, but it's the way of Satan.

Rachel didn't act like this. Even when the evil spirit intimidated her with his fullest malevolence, she realised how much he needed her pity, the victim of all the hatred he endured during his time on earth, and afterwards, in the realms of the damned. She returned compassion and understanding, a reaction the entity answered by fleeing, unable to withstand the power.

'Rachel, this is the basis of all our work, why Yeshu always said, "Love your enemies. Do good to those who hate you". Evil cannot sustain itself for long in the presence of concentrated loving kindness. I commend you for your strength and courage. You are a true daughter of the Father.'

She gasped in delight, tears shining in her eyes. Her shame and self-reproach evaporated.

After a moment or two, her thoughts turned to Mary. 'Is he gone?'

'No. I can still sense him. When he recovers, he'll come back. Through her shock and grief at Yeshu's death, she became open spiritually, and the soul forced an entry. Part of him is still with her, and she must now push out that presence, clear out the nest so he can't return. She's reached the turning point, thanks to you, Rachel. She finally understands what happened and what to do.'

He laughed. 'You haven't seen my aunt when she's determined

about something, have you? She's the most resolute, obstinate individual I know, and I promise you, when we were children, that wasn't always easy. When she makes up her mind, nothing stops her.'

His face relaxed in memories, his love and admiration obvious. Rachel smiled. 'Will it be long?'

'I'm not sure, but it doesn't matter. It will happen. She has both power and knowledge, and her confidence will return as she works. She won't allow herself to be so vulnerable in the future.'

'But John, what mother wouldn't grieve the killing of her own child?'

'That's not what I mean. It is normal and right to mourn. However, you must understand a difficult truth, Rachel; Satan and his followers don't respect such conventions. They feel no pity, no love of family. They simply used Mary's shock as an opportunity to invade her spirit. Now, she has to clean out the invasion and break the link with the soul.

'As Yeshu was a target, so is his mother. They want to destroy her. This entity is very powerful. That's why we couldn't expel him long ago. It's an indication of how much they fear her.'

'Poor Mary.'

'Yes. I know. But now she's recovering.'

'Tell me. How will she push out the evil spirit?'

'Through the strength and discipline of her mind. She can't force him out directly, that would weaken her. It wouldn't be successful. Instead, she will make herself so strong he won't be able to sustain her pure emanations. She needs to concentrate on who she is, a servant of the Great Creator, and push aside all despair and sorrow, bring her conscious mind into a peaceful place.'

'So she can no longer mourn her son?'

'Her pain after Yeshu's death was undeniable, but it's gone on too long. The greater suffering was caused by the failure of the work, and those attitudes were misplaced. This she now accepts, and the grief will end.

'In bringing peace to her mind, in refusing to accept the desolate thoughts of the desecrated being and making herself available to the Father, in all her power and determination, she will recover her soul. You can't do the will of the Most High if you are under the influence of evil, and she knows that. When you are with her, Rachel, be happy. That will help her more than anything else you could do.'

With her doubts dispatched, Rachel's friendship with the little Galilean lady deepened, and Mary was relieved, knowing her friend had experienced her own catharsis. They spent time together, talking on the terrace, searching the market stalls for fish and fresh vegetables, but not too much time, each busy with her own obligations.

Life settled into a rhythm. During the morning, Susannah pounded the grain into flour, baked the bread, prepared the bean or lentil stew for the evening, and tidied the rooms. Mary cared for her animals; she milked the goat, brushed down the donkey, and if the new trench didn't bring enough water to their troughs, she carried more in from the stream. The kids gambolled and jumped around her, on occasions catching her with their sharp little horns. But like her nephew, she enjoyed them and felt peace in their company.

After breakfast in late morning, they walked up the valley to bathe or wash clothes. The animals went with them, grazing the tender grass and herbs. The baby goats scrambled up steep cliffs, jumping from rock to rock, disappearing from view. On a few occasions they didn't return and their pitiful cries echoed around the pool as they called their mother for rescue. Usually she ignored them, to Mary's amusement, but once or twice, perhaps sensing some danger, she bleated continuously until the two little white bodies emerged from behind a rock.

When they returned home, they would rest. Susannah sometimes visited her sister, and Mary would go up to the pavilion to gaze out to sea and watch the ships glide up the estuary.

On other days visitors called; the fisherman from the mountains with a fresh catch, or Reuben to see if they needed anything. They would come in for a cup of tirosh, with figs and dates, and gradually Mary learned about her neighbours. They too found out about her, and when she visited the market, someone greeted her with a nod or a shy smile.

A number of Jewish families lived in the mountain valleys. Inevitably, they discovered that the mother of the crucified Galilean had come to live among them. Furthermore, they learned that the angel foretold the end of the rule of evil.

Mary noticed a subtle difference in the gentle nods and smiles, an increase in deference, even a touch of awe behind the greetings. She was used to this from the followers in Judaea, but now, considering her condition, she decided it was better to avoid direct contact with strangers. She went less frequently to the market, spent more time with Rachel on the terrace or took the donkey and goats for walks along the lanes or to the pool.

Only John's visits every Shabbat interrupted their peaceful life, and he was there the night she had the dream.

The angel came and took her by the hand to a place high in the mountains where a brightly glowing pavilion with square pillars of white marble was perched on the edge of a sheer cliff.

Yeshu stood there, his face wreathed in smiles. With him were Joseph, Anna, Joachim, and many others she couldn't later recall. In a white dress, embroidered with sparkling threads, they took her to a throne-like golden chair and placed a crown on her head. Her son served her delicious food and told her she was free, her soul her own again.

When she woke and remembered, she realised it was true, not just a dream. The sanctity of the blessed place remained, tingling on her skin, fizzing on her scalp; a golden light suffused the room. She called her nephew and he came in, a broad smile on his face. He knew, summoned by his cousin to be with her and afterwards bring her home.

She rose, dressed, and poured a cup of milk, and they climbed to their retreat on the clifftop where they talked and talked, each trying to recall the details. Then they prayed their heartfelt thanks to the Father for His help in bringing her home.

Later, they walked over to tell Rachel. She hugged Mary in delight, relieved it was over. She listened to all the memories, the essential and the trifling: Yeshu, Anna, Joachim; the white, square pillars; the throne and the crown; her sumptuous dress. John told them his mother and father were there, as well as many of the Nazoraeans and old friends from Galilee and Jerusalem.

She tried to control her elation, knowing it too might be dangerous, and her nephew decided to stay a few extra days to make sure all was well. Gradually, a lasting tranquillity, an enduring peace, entered her heart, leaving her safe at last.

A period of joy ensued. Free from contamination, she grew strong, and an effervescent aura surrounded her, as if she walked in a calm blessedness that nothing penetrated.

No longer concerned about her condition, she resumed her visits to the market and the women greeted her, smiling and nodding. A group came to Rachel's to enquire about Yeshua's mother, and one of them, the daughter of an Essene elder in the Holy City, asked if it was true that the Healer had talked about the end of the rule of evil.

Rachel related what little she knew and could repeat without breaking confidences; she promised to find out more. When Mary heard of the visits and the questions, she began to impart further knowledge to her friend. Initially, they met informally when available. Then Devorah asked to join them, and later, Rivka, Susannah, and her mother, Adora. The news of the teachings spread, and more local women, including the Essene daughter, wanted to learn. They decided to meet more formally every seven days, on Shabbat.

She explained the rule of evil, the promised kingdom of heaven, the angel, the teacher Yeshua and how Satan instigated the killing of the Messenger of the Most High. It was now inevitable, she assured them, that the epoch of iniquity would leave the earth. Yeshu taught his followers how such desecration could be neutralised by concentrated loving thoughts, a knowledge built upon their own ancient law: 'We must love our neighbour as we love ourselves' (Leviticus 19:18).

She now agreed with John that another way would be found; although she still believed a long time would pass before the accomplishment of the task, a beginning would be made. It was wrong not to hope. When John came, he went to see those who were sick, and many were healed. The men talked to him and throughout that year, a small gathering in the mountain valleys followed the way of Yeshua. They remembered the ancient commands of the Torah to care for their neighbour and do good to others.

✳

Down in the city, the apostle began the exorcisms. Already familiar with the method of expulsion and the theory behind soul elevation, the group experienced the realities of raising a desecrated soul. They worked slowly, ensuring they weren't overstretched and had time to regain their strength between meetings. Those who recovered from possessions were cared for, sometimes by the physician or John's healing, but mainly through learning how to live in such a way that the evil spirit would not return.

They had successes and failures, as not all stayed free of new contamination. Nevertheless, it was a beginning. Jacob was jubilant as he learned the techniques of physical healing and merged them with his own medical knowledge. Martha watched as his fulfilment grew and felt joy in her own sensitivity as her skin tingled each time a soul ascended into the blessed realms.

Hannah and Joseph looked after the possessed and learned how to choose those they might help. They reintegrated many into the community, re-establishing links with their families. John supervised calmly and quietly, healing when asked. He found a tranquil peace within himself and was particularly close to fellow Galileans Mathias and James, strengthening their understanding until their confidence in facing evil grew stable and sure.

Gradually, Yeshua's teachings became more widely known, and John gained a reputation as a Holy Man of God, in the tradition of his Galilean predecessors. Often, members with problems were introduced, and his kindness and loving acceptance of those who strayed became known and honoured. No one feared to speak to him, and through his actions the community accepted that the instructions of his Master, Yeshua, must have come from the Holy One.

Some of the older women tried to arrange a marriage for him, thinking to give him companionship and love. But John had a secret, one he never discussed, even with Mary although she knew the circumstances. He once loved a beautiful young girl from Galilee, and they married in his youth. They experienced a happiness they believed would last forever. She died suddenly, stricken by disease, and no one was able to help. He was desolated and for a time did not want to live. Then Yeshu returned and assigned him responsibilities which filled his soul and gave him a reason to go on.

He never wished for another love, knowing it would be the moon to his blazing sun. On occasional blessed nights he met her in his dreams, and they walked hand-in-hand on the shores of the Lake, talking of his days as if they'd never been apart. Afterwards, her presence remained with him; at last, it was enough. It gave him peace. One day they would be together in the lands of the Father.

The women sensed his lack of interest, realising he didn't want to marry, and wondered what happened to him when he was young. So he found a place of honour in his adopted community and a role as teacher and healer with the group on the mountains.

He spent most days with James on the estuary, and later they met Mathias to enjoy the delicious meals in the inn at the harbour. On Shabbat they went to the synagogue where the matrons found new sources of speculation, two young men, friends of the respected John, with well-paying jobs in the city and as yet unmarried.

He was left to follow his own inclinations, an honoured member of the community but curiously apart, his real companions the healing group which he led and inspired. With them, he opened his heart to acceptance and understanding.

24

Unwrapping a Gift

In the later part of one summer, Jacob came to the apostle with a question. A physician friend from Sardis in the Hermus Valley to the north heard of their success with the possessed and asked for help.

A member of their Jewish community had fallen from a clifftop, and afterwards didn't recover in his mind. The poor man raged through the streets, yelling and fighting with anyone he met, injuring several people before escaping into the hills. Antagonism erupted between the Greeks and Jews; the city council held their community responsible. They were desperate.

'What do you think, John?'

'Do we know anything more? What was he like before the accident?'

'I don't know. Antonius sent the message, and his man is waiting for an answer before he goes back over the mountains.'

John thought through the implications. There could be brain damage. If so, he might not recover. But what if a lower soul was using him? 'How long would it take to get there?'

Jacob grinned, already planning the journey. 'Two days

probably. So we're going. It will give you a chance to see more of Anatolia.'

A week later, Martha packed the mule cart with everything she and her daughters required for an extended stay with Rachel, now a much-loved friend. It would give her a chance to see Mary, whose departure from the city had left an empty space which nothing filled. She missed her every day.

Life had changed so much since the letter arrived from Marcus of Cyprus, and she looked back in amazement at how she blossomed, become more confident in her role in life. She discovered, within herself, a deep desire to help others, almost an extension of her love of family. To her delight, she also found a consistent and reliable spiritual sensitivity.

The sizzling cloud of effervescence always indicated holiness, and desecrated souls brought the gritty heaviness around her shoulders. Other identifications were not so easy: the unexplained headaches, the tiredness when well rested, the waves of depression. Were they external or part of her own being? As she dealt with a wider range of desecration and carefully noted the effects on her body and mind, her discrimination matured.

When she discovered the logical structure underlying the organisation of the upper and lower realms, it gave her immense intellectual satisfaction. Rational steps solved spiritual problems; when applied with sufficient determination, they succeeded, unless prevented by outside interference. One and one always equalled two, two and two made four. She soaked up the knowledge, slaked her thirst, and found her oasis in a desert of ignorance. The mathematical precision reassured her enquiring mind, gave greater depth to her spiritual role, and the times of pure happiness expanded in her life.

She remembered when John first asked her to evaluate a desecrated spirit and how it unnerved her so much, she almost panicked. Only his calm, confident presence gave her the courage to go on. It wasn't too low, he told her, no different from an irritable man she might meet in the marketplace. Even so, when the heavy miasma came towards her, her body and spirit closed against it instinctively.

Understanding her fear, he encouraged her to relax and allow a full experience of the presence. If it was too much, they would push it away. Trusting him, she let the soul penetrate. It was heavy and bad-tempered, and to her amazement, she clearly heard in her mind the angry words of a separate personality. Yet within a few minutes, she realised they were similar to her own thoughts when annoyed or depressed. It was easier than expected. She registered the level of strength for later comparison with other lower souls, and then her colleagues sent the being away, clearing her until she was herself again.

Slowly, she conquered her nerves and learned her craft. She examined stronger and stronger souls and developed enough confidence to remain calm and resolute with even the most depraved evil spirits. She accompanied the apostle when he exorcised the possessed in their dismal hideaways outside the city, and her sympathy grew for both the living person and the invader.

Her greatest satisfaction came when he asked her to hold a soul and let it speak, so they might discover how it first fell to evil. Through her eyes, the entity stared at her friends with hatred and contempt, furious they had pulled him from his den, searching desperately for a way to break out of the snare.

He swore at them. 'Just wait till I get out of here. You'll pay for this. You won't get away with it. I'll make sure of that. No, I don't want anything. No, no. I'm not thirsty. Give me some strong wine. Yeh, I'd like that. No, I don't want your filthy drink. No. Leave me alone.'

He fought the kindness, pushed away the love, but she sensed the cold, dark emptiness of his existence, the grinding fear beneath the bravado. Trapped within her and held there, he was unable to escape their pity. Hesitantly at first, she spoke his words and her companions listened to the whole sad story of how evil entered his life. Wickedness came slowly at first, and then with more and more insistence until he lost his soul to desecration.

As he talked, their compassion penetrated; he accepted some food and a warm cloak, and the layers of chill lessened. Eventually, when he considered his life, he regretted the harm, asked for forgiveness, and learned how to forgive himself. The coldness dissipated, and he absorbed the loving warmth of that first step into recovery.

The holy ones came, those who knew and loved him in happier days on earth. His mother stood smiling with open arms, waiting to hold him and bring him home to the blessed realms. There he would strengthen until capable of rising a little further, gaining knowledge and stability in a new and better place.

Sometimes she found the emanations hard to sustain and took a long time to recover. However, as the weeks and months passed, her resistance built and John monitored her progress, never allowing her to try too much. Still, she was glad of the opportunity to go to the mountain and rest. She had so much to tell her friends and looked forward impatiently to her chair on Rachel's terrace.

25

Over the Tmolus Mountains

In the blazing sun, approaching noon, two days after Martha's departure for Koressos, the exhausted men reached the high pass in the Tmolus Mountains. They found a cool forest, and at a clear pool fed with springs, they unpacked the mules and let them roam to search for grass and wild plants. For the remainder of the day they rested, eating the greater part of the food and draining the wineskins. By evening they recovered, and the apostle asked his companion to tell him something of the land they would reach the following day.

The most fertile and prosperous valley in Roman Asia, the Hermus plain was dominated by Sardis, the ancient capital of the kings of Lydia and Persia's seat of power in the west. It straddled the Royal Road which led from the Persian capital to the Aegean Coast. Since olden times, mighty armies marched its wide expanses. Down this highway, Croesus began his ill-fated attempt to demolish Cyrus and returned defeated and destroyed. Later, invincible Alexander followed to avenge Xerxes's attacks on Greece and, in a drunken rage, burned beautiful Persepolis to the ground.

After his death, the region suffered the murderous competition of his successors, until the Seleucids emerged triumphant and established Sardis as their regional base. Prosperity followed, although not for long. Rome forced its surrender as the Empire expanded eastwards. But the fall of the Republic, the civil wars, the murder of Caesar and the flight of the assailants led to devastation for Anatolia.

Cassius and Brutus stripped the city of its gold, and only after the battle of Actium, when Octavian eliminated Mark Antony, did the devastating internecine turmoil end.

'It's not surprising, John, that they build temples to the emperors. Except for our teachers in Rhodes, the philosophers who acknowledge the Supreme Being, the Greeks have no belief in the One God. Their idols resemble powerful human beings with all their vices and virtues. To them, Octavian was "the saviour", the one who brought lasting peace. No more wars or destruction. They declared him a god, which is a tradition here in the east.

'As for Sardis, its wealth originally came from goldmines here in the Tmolus. The kings like Croesus were famous for their riches. The mines are long gone, and the wealth of the region now depends on the phenomenal fertility of the Hermus basin, its grain and fruit, the wines exported all over the Empire, as are its carpets and tapestries. On top of that, its position on the main trade routes, between east and west, is a major advantage.

'The temple of Artemis, below the Acropolis, was the original focal point until the city expanded towards the river. As Hellenism spread, the city acquired the usual trappings of a substantial Greek *polis*: the *agora*, stadium, theatre, and baths. Like most Anatolian cities, the people are content and view the Romans as benefactors.'

'What really puzzles me, Jacob, is the difference between government here and the system back home in Judaea.'

'The two states are completely different. Here we are near

the imperial centre and the two cultures, Greek and Roman, are similar, their gods more or less interchangeable. And as I said, they see the emperors as peacemakers. The old city states lost some measure of freedom but gained stability and prosperity.

'Judaea is sandwiched between two empires, Rome and Parthia. Cyrus set our people free to come home after the exile, and a tradition of support for the old Persian empire has been transferred to the Parthians. Many would welcome them as overlords. The Roman Emperor is well aware of that.

'Furthermore, look at our concepts of God. We have no patience with their idols, and they can't understand our beliefs either, although they have to respect our traditions, partly because of the Caesarean law but also because we are an ancient religion. Even Rome respects that.

'Here we live side by side with a reasonable level of tolerance, but in Judaea we are a threat. That's why the high priests fear any anti-Roman activity. They know it won't lead to freedom as it did when the Maccabees rose against the weakening Seleucids. This time rebellion would result in the destruction of our people. Rome is ruthless. We wouldn't win.'

'I know that and so did Yeshu. He saw their desire for wealth and domination as a manifestation of Satan and hoped, if we were successful, the craving for power would diminish. But it wasn't to be.'

The physician looked at him with sympathy. 'It's all in the hands of the Most High now, my friend.'

'I know. We can do no more for the moment. Anyway, let's concentrate on Sardis. Are there many Jews?'

'More than in Ephesus, and they maintain reasonable relations with their Greek neighbours. Back in the time of Augustus they tried to prevent us sending our donations to the Temple in

191

Jerusalem. Herod intervened, and the old laws of Julius Caesar were upheld. They released the gold. Since then we've had no trouble. We keep to ourselves, though. It's safer. So I understand why they are worried about this damaged man. I hope we can help him.'

Early next morning they left the camp and rode the refreshed mules through the forested pass and down the meandering road that fell steeply between sheer cliffs of rock, from the heights above to the Hermus Valley far below. By late afternoon they reached the city, once more exhausted.

26

Sardis

Small, plump, and full of energy, Lucius, the synagogue president, soon attended to the needs of his guests: the animals stabled and fed, the baggage in cool, well-furnished rooms, baths, clothes changed, and a meal prepared by the tall, slim Esther, with the calm, still expression on her pretty face. Unlike her husband, it was hard to read her thoughts; she kept those and her opinions to herself.

The family came from the Holy City, of priestly descent like Marcus. Lucius returned occasionally for the autumn festivals, standing proudly in the court of the priests. Next time he would bring his son and introduce him to his heritage. He kept in touch with relatives and talked with some knowledge of his native land but was more interested in Jacob's telling of the rumours circulating the Jewish communities of the Empire.

With the social preliminaries satisfied, they discussed the possessed man, Benjamin, one of several similarly afflicted, who lived as outcasts in the hills to the north of the city.

'One man came and charged us a large amount of coin to deal with him. He went up to the caves, and I think he used the ancient rites of Solomon, but he got nowhere. In fact, he was nearly killed, and we had to rescue him ourselves. At least he returned our drachmas, but we are back in the original situation. We'll pay whatever it takes if you can assist us.'

John reassured him. 'Lucius, don't worry about money. We don't take coin, although we will need food and somewhere to stay.'

'That won't be a problem. You'll live here and eat with us.'

'We'll also need some support.'

'Tell me what you want me to do.'

'Can you find at least four or five people, either men or women, who are kind and sympathetic, strong in character, calm in demeanour, with no impulse to anger or frustration?'

Lucius's eyebrows rose. 'What will they have to do?'

'Let me explain. When a desecrated spirit is sent from a living person, it tries to find a new home, someone with whom it has a similar desire to do wrong. If he discovers a suitable victim, he attaches himself and enters. Often he returns to the original host, becoming even more bonded. So an exorcism can put others in danger. Do you understand?'

'I have to say I don't. I thought the evil spirit returned to his master, Satan.'

'It is possible to send such a soul directly back to the realms of the damned, and once I saw Yeshua the Healer do this, by sending entities into the bodies of swine. They fled over a cliff and died. In that case, apparently, the lower souls did return to their designated place in Satan's domain. However, there is a better way. We neutralise the desecration around the soul and send it into the lands of the blessed. That will reduce the power of evil on the earth.'

Lucius and Esther looked at each other in consternation. What was he talking about? Pigs and cliffs. They began to think they'd made a huge mistake. This was all a waste of time.

Seeing their disbelief and disappointment, John laughed. 'I'm sorry. I've confused you. Let me explain properly, and then you can decide. Let's have some more tirosh. It's going to take some time.'

And so, they heard the story of Yeshua the Healer, the promised Teacher who brought to the world the knowledge of how to combat evil. They talked for most of the evening until the apostle was sure they both understood.

'Jacob and I will identify the name of the invading spirit and expel him. Later, we will call him back and elevate him. At that point, we'll need others to sit quietly with us. They will send love and compassion to the poor soul. We might need to do this several times. It depends on how strong he is. Sending him from Benjamin might be the easy part.'

The president leaned back in his chair and thought through everything he'd heard. He didn't know whether to be terrified or excited. It was fascinating, so wonderful if successful. Something within him responded to the challenge, his priestly heritage perhaps. He had to see it done and wondered who would help. Antonius definitely. People who wouldn't take fright: that might be the difficulty.

'Can we practice this, John?'

'That's a good idea. The entity with Benjamin is strong. When you talk about him I can feel the desecration. We won't know for definite until I examine him.

'I suggest you gather your people and see if they're prepared to help. We'll find a soul that isn't too far down and raise it. That will give them experience. And if you like, we can heal the sick. Can't we, Jacob?'

'Why not? Make sure Antonius knows; they're his patients.'

※

COLETTE MURNEY

So it began. News of the healer and exorcist from Ephesus spread through the community, and two days later they packed the synagogue with the sick and diseased. John explained Benjamin's situation and asked for help. Quite a few came forward, including the man's mother and sisters. They told the story of his accident.

The family owned herds of sheep and grazed them in the foothills of the Tmolus. Benjamin worked hard and hoped to marry a lovely young girl, a neighbour's daughter. One night he didn't come home. They searched for him, knowing something was wrong. They found him at the bottom of a cliff, unconscious, with a wound to his head and a dead sheep beside him. He regained consciousness and seemed to recover but never returned to them in any other way. He talked as though he didn't know them, and the young girl's father forbade the connection, fearing for her life. Eventually, he left in a rage to live in the hills.

His mother was in tears. 'I lost my son that day, and now we have this trouble with the council. Please help him. We'll do anything, pay you whatever you ask.'

John tried to calm her. 'You don't need to give me money. This is my holy work. We'll do what we can to save him.'

She looked into his eyes, desperate to believe him. Her daughters came over. He asked them to take care of her.

'Do all you can to rest tomorrow, so you are strong in the evening. I need your help, but if you are distressed it would be too dangerous. The evil spirit would attack you, exploit your weakened state. If you are calm and determined, he won't penetrate your guard and you'll be able to help Benjamin. Do you understand?'

Almost bereft of hope, they agreed to do everything he asked and led their mother away.

Esther overheard the conversation and brought them into

a quiet corner to sit down and rest. She told them what she knew of the men from Ephesus, their well-known success with possessions, and persuaded them to have faith.

John asked those who wished to help to return the next evening and then turned to the sick, going from patient to patient, laying hands on each. One man had a large swelling on the side of his head. Yet when the cool fingers touched his brow, a liquid burst into his mouth, almost choking him, and yellow pus poured from his ear. The physician cleaned the eruptions and gave him herbs, to be soaked in boiling water and consumed morning and night.

Another had difficulty walking. The healer took his hands and helped him rise; his limbs lost their stiffness and the pain almost disappeared. During the afternoon, they eased the suffering of many, resting between patients, taking food and water often.

Antonius, initially sceptical, worked beside Jacob, amazed at the obvious physical changes in those under his care. When they could do no more, they told those remaining to come back the following day. No one would be left unaided.

John's undoubted abilities impressed all those present, and a considerable number arrived to offer assistance and hear what he had to say. Some were frightened at the prospect of confronting a dangerous evil spirit and departed, but others found it fascinating, eager to hear more. He spoke to each in turn.

One woman was with child and came with her spouse.

'Care for your unborn babe,' he told her. 'Keep it well away from evil. Surround it only with love and joy. Make your home a centre of happiness, a worthy home for a newborn soul. I can't accept your aid, in case the contamination damages your little one. However, your desire to help another in distress does you great honour. There are others, enough to do what is needed.

Thank you both for your kindness, and may the blessings of the Most High be upon you and your child.'

Two brothers, neighbours of Benjamin, offered to join them, but John felt strong hostility around them. He asked their names.

'Tiberius and David, listen to me. What happened between you to cause such hatred? Why do you detest one another so much? Before you do anything, make peace and mend the fences that are broken. If you joined us, all would be lost in chaos. Only love and compassion can elevate an evil spirit, and if you have no sympathy for one another, how can you give kindness to a desecrated soul? He would feed on your hatred and fall even further. Go and forgive one another for whatever harm was done. Do you want to be stricken like your friend? Save yourselves or you too will be lost.'

They stared at him in surprise, taken aback by his awareness and the stern note in his voice. Looking embarrassed, they left but spoke to each other on the way, and the apostle hoped they would see sense.

Once he had spoken to all and chosen ten strong participants, he reiterated the procedure. 'I will go to the cave with my friend here, identify the invader, and expel him. Then we must take Benjamin back to the synagogue to deal with his physical injuries.

'That evening we will meet. I'll call the soul to myself, and Jacob will speak to him. You will sit quietly and feel pity and kindness. He will probably scream and shout but ignore it. Concentrate only on thoughts of goodwill towards him. I'm sure you had sympathy for your neighbour when he was injured, and this poor soul too is damaged. He needs our help. Feel for him as you do for your friend, and both will be released from evil.

'To give you familiarity with the process, we'll find other souls you can elevate. They won't be as difficult, and raising them will give you valuable experience. If anyone doesn't want to go on, don't worry. I will understand. Our work isn't for everyone. Those who want to join us with the lighter elevations, come back in two days, after dusk.'

The next day they explored the temple of Artemis in Sardis, with their host as guide. It wasn't as contaminated as Ephesus. John found one area where several souls gathered and identified a mother and her son. Lucius watched with increasing interest, amazed at the abilities of the two men.

In the evening, those who were unaided returned with at least the same number of new people. The apostle concentrated on the original group and also managed to help some of the later patients, but his diminishing strength prevented him continuing. Lucius went to explain the situation and asked the rest to return on Shabbat.

One old man, stricken with pain, became obstreperous, and the president had to use all his diplomacy to calm him. 'The healer has only so much power, Jotham. There's a limit to the number he can help.'

'I'll pay him well. Plenty of drachmas.'

'He won't take your money. You will have to wait your turn with all the others.'

'Tell him I'll make him rich if he comes to my house and heals me. Tell him.'

'I'll tell him, but I know he won't come.'

Later in the evening, Lucius told his guests the story.

'His rage is contributing to his physical condition. I won't be able to heal him.'

'Why is that, John?'

'The healing wouldn't penetrate the hostility. He would need to push the anger aside and show consideration for others.'

199

'I don't think he is likely to do that.'

'No, I thought not. Poor man.'

'He's not so poor. He's rich and, to be honest, obnoxious. He's a member of the community but expects everyone to give him special treatment. Not too well liked, I'm afraid.'

'Don't worry about him, Lucius. I'll speak to him when we meet and try to make him understand what he's doing to himself. I can do no more.'

For John, the time spent with the Sardis family became a wonderful source of relaxation and strength. The president owned orchards of vines and a wine fermentation complex to the west of the city. Slightly dry with a fruity aftertaste, the product was light and refreshing. As he explained the process, especially his grandfather's addition of a small amount of Aegean seawater, his face lit up with excitement, his hands flying around in the air.

His wife would glance at him, a twitch of amusement at the corner of her mouth, yet there was love in her eyes, a pride in her feisty little spouse. Their happiness vitalised those around them, the effects apparent in the intelligent, inquisitive son, on the cusp of manhood, and the beautiful younger daughter with black curling hair and those startling bright-blue eyes. She would smile enchantingly and besiege him with questions, while her mother looked on with a grin, ready to intervene if she tortured him too much.

He was glad they'd come, and that reminded him. 'Lucius, what about Antonius? Will he help with Benjamin's injuries?'

'We'll see him tomorrow. He was so impressed with the healing.'

Jacob laughed. 'He pestered me afterwards. Wanted to know how it all worked. So I'd be surprised if he didn't join in.'

'He has considerable spiritual abilities,' John said. 'Capable of holding an evil spirit, maybe even a strong one. Very useful if you decide to continue this work after we've gone.'

They turned to him, intrigued by the unexpected comment.

'You have the same ability, Lucius. However, both you and Esther have another quality that's equally important: kindness and understanding for those who have taken the wrong path. Probably why you are so well liked and respected. You must have someone to hold a soul but you also need others to talk to it, to guide it towards an evaluation of its life. You two are ideal for this.'

Excitement and wanting filled Esther's eyes. The children almost grown, her intelligence demanded something more than caring for her family and mothering the community.

Lucius observed and understood. She wasn't fulfilled. A loving wife and a wonderful mother, she deserved the best, and if possible, he would give her whatever she needed.

Watching the exchange, John recognised the bond and waited.

'I wish I'd met your Yeshua. What an honour and privilege to sit at his feet. I spent my life worshipping the Most High, and we've taught our children to do likewise. Yet, in my soul, I miss my native land and regret I didn't follow the traditions of my ancestors. It's difficult to be a priest without an outlet for that heritage. That's why I care for our people here. I hope I fulfil my duty to the Holy One, in some small way.

'Everything you've told me strikes a tone in my heart, like the ram's horn, summoning me to prayer, wakening me from a deep sleep. I hear the call, but I can't ignore the anxiety, the fear of what we will do and whether we are capable.'

John smiled. 'Lucius, it took me many years, under Yeshua's guidance, to learn the secrets we will teach you. It will take dedication, but in time you will absorb the knowledge, both of you.'

With tears in her eyes, Esther reached across the table and touched her husband's hand. 'You are the kindest man I've ever met, Lucius. You have sympathy for others, especially those most people despise. If anyone can do this, it's you, and I want to help.'

John reassured them. 'You don't need to decide immediately. We will be here for a while. Let's see what happens with the elevation tomorrow, and then Benjamin.'

On Shabbat, the community gathered at the synagogue, and the apostle read from the Torah. Afterwards, he talked about the Great Creator, the loving Father who gave them everything, including life itself. He spoke of the coming of evil, how humankind turned from the Most High to immerse themselves in material riches and the exercise of power over others, activities that led to pride and anger and, in turn, resentment in the less fortunate.

'They forgot the lessons of compassion and sympathy, the instruction to care for their neighbour, taught to their ancestors in the misty days of the distant past. Hence, over time, humanity degenerated further and further into fear. Even so, the Father's love remained unchanged, and He sent the Teacher to show us how to combat the evil encompassing our world.'

The members listened quietly, believing him a good man, although the more cynical thought he asked too much. Only the old man showed open hostility, the one who grumbled when not given preference. And later, when the healing began, he became so vociferous they were forced to stop.

'Jotham, it's impossible to heal in an atmosphere of hatred; furthermore, there's no point in doing anything about your physical condition until we send from you the depraved spirit that consumes you. If I tried to help you, it wouldn't work. You're so full of anger all attempts would fail.'

In a rage, the old man attempted to rise, and John could clearly see the lower soul that controlled him. Gathering his strength, he focused on the invader and demanded his name. The host struggled out of the chair. Jacob and Lucius quickly moved to restrain him as his fury mounted. The healer persisted, his kind face growing stern, his sympathy supported by power. For some minutes, the soul fought the opposing determination until the defiance weakened and the name was uttered amid foul curses and filth.

'Depart from here,' the apostle commanded with concentration and strength. 'Go back from whence you came,'

The old man writhed as the entity resisted, but his surrender was inevitable. Finally it went, leaving Jotham collapsed in his seat, sweat streaming down his face, blood dripping from his bitten tongue. The two physicians lifted him and carried him from the room, with orders to do everything possible for his physical body and not to leave him alone, even for a moment.

The apostle turned to scrutinise the Sardis community. He would use the situation to clarify his ideas. Some were shocked, some excited, a few looked at him in awe, and others regarded Jotham with disgust as he was taken away.

'Be careful. Don't despise him. We don't know how he absorbed such a malevolent entity, but whatever happened, he's to be pitied. If you condemn him now, it will make it easier for a desecrated soul to reinvade. If you show sympathy and understanding, his own spirit will build fences against further attack.

'Remember, it's very easy to deride those who have fallen but difficult to recognise our own faults. How many of us can say we have not carried out harmful deeds in our time?

'Only by love and kindness can we neutralise evil. Now that the desecration is gone, two things must be done. We will elevate the lower soul and return him to the realms of the Father. Secondly, we must teach Jotham how to prevent a similar invasion, show him how to be kind and do good to others. And you in the community can help. Much of the harm he did may not be his fault. He acted under the influence of a malicious entity, and as I said, we still don't know how it came to him. Please don't attack him for past differences. Give him the chance to grow strong, and you might be surprised at the man you will find.'

A man from the back shouted, 'That's easy for you to say, but you're a stranger. He was vicious to people here. You can't expect us to forgive and forget. He certainly wouldn't.'

'Let me say this to you. If you act in this way, he won't recover. He'll quickly revert to the man you abhor, and you'll bring down further harm on yourselves. If you accept that a lot of what he did was not his own doing, you could, in time, have a good man in your midst.

'Don't make a mistake here or undo what we've done today. We all know the tradition of an eye for an eye, but the rule of the Most High says something else: "You shall not take vengeance or bear a grudge against any of your people, but you shall love your neighbour as yourself. I am the Lord." You'll find it in Leviticus.' (19:18)

A woman in the front interrupted. 'You were angry with the evil spirit.'

'No, you misunderstood. I bore the soul no animosity, but I was determined he would not remain with Jotham. It's not his place. Being kind and understanding doesn't mean you allow the desecrated spirit to have its way. It mustn't be allowed to dominate. For the moment it's weakened and will take time to regain its strength. We'll use that interval to neutralise the desecration and elevate the entity. All will be well.'

They stopped for food and tirosh, bringing a level of normality to the gathering. Lucius answered questions about the men from Ephesus, and some enquired if their possessed relatives might be helped.

'They'll be here for a while, and John believes we can do this ourselves. He's teaching us. We already have a group to clear Benjamin, and we hope to gain experience from that and go on to aid others in the same situation.

'Let me tell you this. Since he's been with our family, we've recognised he has wisdom and abilities far beyond the usual. He promised to teach us the secrets given to him by Yeshua the Healer, knowledge on how to release people from possessions and even physical illness. We need to learn from him. He's a good man and he's trying to help us.'

The calm demeanour of the president and the trust with which he and Esther treated their visitors convinced those present, and after the meal they left to go home, stimulated by the unusual events in the synagogue.

The shock of the exorcism and physical collapse created a spiritual vacuum in Jotham's soul, a hollow, barren place vulnerable to repossession. In the days that followed, the apostle filled the emptiness with sympathy and taught him how to use loving kindness, gradually strengthening his defences against evil.

At first, the old man thought he would drown in a quagmire

of guilt as he blamed himself for his cruelties to all he knew. It took all John's strength to prevent him falling, once again, under the weight of his own self-reproach. Eventually, he grasped the advantage of a more appropriate alternative, a life dedicated to helping others. He grew strong, and his companions learned how to revive those who were, in essence, born into a new life.

A sharp businessman, familiar to those in the community and in the Gentile world beyond, Jotham had grown, over the years, in both wealth and enemies. Yet long after the visitors return to Ephesus, those who knew him noticed his changed behaviour in amazement. Tenants in his properties received an element of consideration. His nephew told of an affectionate gesture, a kind thought.

Although he still managed his business interests with efficiency, the outbursts of anger ceased, and those who spoke to him no longer sensed unease or fear in his presence. In time, the first tentative approaches of friendship came, the beginning of a more contented life.

The new group sat to elevate the mother identified at the temple. John called her to himself, and Jacob directed the activity, prompting his companions when kind thoughts were needed, persuading the soul to tell them how she fell into darkness. Gradually they raised her, until the tingles crept along Jacob's skin, and holy light replaced the shadows.

Their satisfaction increased when the son was called and found already with his mother, the power of her elevation sufficient to carry him too, into the blessed lands.

The men stayed in Sardis for three months, and the evil spirit with Jotham ascended. They met many times, and each sitting left everyone drained of strength. Jacob's experience and determination calmed the abusive entity, his tranquil demeanour ensuring the group didn't disintegrate in fear. They persevered, and the soul weakened. The night he elevated was a time of profound relief, compounded seven days later when an examination found him still safe and stabilised in the realms of the Father.

Benjamin was a different story. They went to the cave with some neighbours, captured him, and gave him an effective herbal concoction which rendered him malleable. The apostle obtained the name of the entity and sent it hence. Afterwards, they brought the poor man down the hills into the care of the physicians.

The skull was badly damaged, forcing Jacob to create a small hole to relieve the pressure in the brain and reduce the headaches. Over several weeks with medical treatments and healing, he slowly recovered on a physical level. Some damage remained; scars crisscrossed his head, and he walked with a limp for the rest of his life. However, his thoughts and decisions were clear; he was whole in his mind.

The elevation of the invading entity was an easier process. Less desecrated than Jotham's attachment, it was raised within two settings.

The young man went home to be cosseted shamelessly by his overjoyed mother. He returned to the foothills, his sheep around him, and in the spring, new lambs gambolled and played, racing from hill to hill, until exhausted they ran to the teats of the ewe. And although he lost his first love, he met another with whom he was happy. In time, he presented his mother with grandchildren.

On a cool autumn morning, mules bridled and saddled, baskets securely fastened, they were ready to depart. Esther and the children came to see them leave, tears streaming from her eyes as she kissed John goodbye. He had given her a new joy, a purpose in her life, and she loved him dearly.

May the Holy One bless him and keep him in His care.

Lucius walked with them to the outskirts of the city and stood by the gates watching until they disappeared into the distance. He turned for home and his Esther, contented with their achievements but happy to have a little, less excitement and manic activity, both in the synagogue and among the family.

I definitely need a rest and make sure all is well with the vines. I haven't seen them in weeks. I only hope Joseph is looking after them.

27

Home Again

On Koressos, life continued at a peaceful rate. Martha and her daughters remained at the farm and sometimes Elianna's betrothed came to stay. In general, the days passed quietly. As autumn and harvest-time approached, they cleaned containers to hold their winter stores.

The valley's well-matured orchard and gardens supplied the household with fruit and vegetables throughout the year, and on occasion, they sold the surplus in the local market. Reuben came to help with the grapes, piling baskets of dark purple on the living room table. It was enough work for the moment, he told them, and promised to come back later to pick the figs and dates.

They crushed most of the grapes and stored the new wine in skins. The rest, dried as raisins, they pressed into blocks or boiled to make the thick, delicious honey they used as a sweetener. Their fruit was similarly processed, the greater part squashed for eating with chunks of bread.

Although exhausting, they often relieved their work with visits to the equally busy farm. Mary's arrival allowed Rachel and Martha to escape down the garden to the pavilion or, if they called over to the valley, they climbed to the clifftop with a jug of tirosh and a basket of Devorah's sweet cakes. And as time passed, they wondered when their men would come home.

On other days, with Susanna, the girls, and the animals, they ambled up to the pool to enjoy the cool waters before the winter months closed in.

One afternoon, Rivka came running. The mule cart had arrived; Jacob and John were on the terrace with food and a decanter of wine.

That evening, he slept in his high-backed chair in the pavilion, and she stayed with him, thankful to see him home and safe. Later, Susannah brought up their evening meal and left to visit her sister.

Well into the starlit night, they told all the news of their time apart, and he relaxed, glad to be home; he'd missed her. The changes amazed him, especially her strength, although he noticed a touch of the ethereal, her spirit almost too compelling for her physical body. Being with her was an experience of tranquillity, a cool, serene lake under a moonlit sky.

Her negativity gone, she radiated a pure, deep love that encompassed everything and confirmed her acceptance that one day all would be well. She had stabilised in her own being, at peace with her past and unconcerned for her future, focused only on the present moment.

Over the following weeks, he brought in the rest of the cherries and olives, prepared the ground for new plants, pruned the trees, trained the vines over new structures, and tied them into position. In the evenings, every limb ached, but he was content. Peace, with no time to think and no demands on his mind or his spiritual strength.

Wrapped in the cocoon of Mary's gentle and undemanding love, he slowly revived, and one night, up on the clifftop, he suggested they resume the meetings, postponed since his return.

She looked at him and thought for a moment. 'No. I don't think that's a good idea. You've been through a lot in the last few months, John. You don't want to force your recovery. Sometimes these experiences need to settle in your mind and sprout like seeds in the garden. If you crowd them with other plants, they grow out of shape.

'You're only home a short time. You're stronger but you're not right yet, not at a level to get the guidance you'll need from the blessed realms. Why don't we invite the Galileans up for a few days? Reuben goes down to Ephesus regularly; he can bring them. What do you think? We'll have to buy a tent though.'

He was delighted and amused at how well she knew him. Having his two friends to stay, men from home, would be wonderful.

It was exactly what he needed, and several nights later, his aunt smiled as they recalled memories of childhood and the crazy things they did when their mothers weren't looking. She grinned when Rachel came for the evening meal and related her exploits at sea with Drusus on the Mediterranean and the Aegean, matching tales with the Galileans of ports they'd explored and people they met.

It was late when the men walked Rachel home. When they returned, the apostle settled his friends into the new, spacious tent in the orchard. As he couldn't find Mary in the house, he climbed to the pavilion and sat beside her, knowing she wanted to talk.

'John, did something upset you in Sardis, something you didn't mention?'

211

He laughed to himself. She missed nothing. 'Why do you ask?'

'It's just that, for a fleeting moment when the others talked of their adventures, you seemed envious, really envious. I thought about how much you'd been caught up in our lives. You were swept along with us: we had the task, and then Yeshu's death left me injured and you took care of me. You had no life of your own.'

'It's not too late, you know. I'm safe here with Rachel and Susannah. You don't have to worry.'

He burst into a laugh of pure delight. 'Of course I would love to go sailing around the ports of the Mediterranean with all the carelessness of a vagabond. Who wouldn't? Do you think I would exchange one minute of my time with Yeshu or with you for something so unimportant? You two have been the joy of my life. I wouldn't change a thing, neither the good times nor the desolation, for anything the world would offer. You won't get rid of me so easily.'

He rose, tossed back his cup of tirosh, put the jugs and cups into the basket, and reached down for her hand, pulling her out of her couch.

'You must be tired to think such thoughts. I assumed you wanted to know what *did* happen during our time away. You'll have to wait for that now.'

She laughed, glad her mischievous boy was home again. She kissed him and went to bed, content.

PART 4

Return to Jerusalem

28

Present Day: North West London

It was a hot June afternoon, summertime in London. Cathrina relaxed under the canopy at Jean's garden table, the patio bathed in the scents of roses and honeysuckle, the only sounds the distant hum of buzzing bees and the intermittent clipping of gardening shears. Everything was quiet and peaceful.

Josh was dealing with the last frantic days of college exams while she'd taken some time off, partly to watch Wimbledon, but mainly to concentrate on her final research and discuss her findings with Jean. Their collaboration over the previous year amplified her understanding of events two thousand years ago. Combined with her own expertise, Jean's encyclopaedic knowledge clarified her grasp of both the historical and spiritual realities. Her Ephesus visions now made sense.

Let's see what she comes up with, she thought, as the sprightly old lady crossed the lawn, pulled off her gloves, and threw them into the box on the patio.

'Good girl, Cathrina. I'm ready for a cup of tea. Let me wash my hands and I'll be with you.'

Within minutes she was back, demolishing sandwiches and cakes, asking about Josh and Ruth, talking about her roses and Whiskas, her much-loved but straying black-and-white tomcat, delighted with summer, and so pleased to spend time in her garden.

Cathrina listened with affection, responding where appropriate, smiling to herself, waiting, until her companion spoke.

'Enough of all that. Where did we get to?'

'Although the research is quite detailed, Jean, I'll only give you a synopsis. I tried to integrate the Koressos information with my historical understanding of the Second Temple era. Apart from your knowledge of the rule of evil, your explanation of the purity regulations made a definite difference. You're the first person I've met who actually understood what they meant.'

'Good. Glad I was of some use.'

'The research divides into three: James and the relatives of Jesus; Paul and the beginnings of Gentile Christianity; and finally, the Jewish Revolt of 66 CE and the effects on both the Jews and the first Christians.

'James and the family are key. Luckily the sources for him are relatively plentiful, an important Jerusalem personality in his own right, the records not so overwritten as those of Christ.'

'Overwritten? What do you mean?'

'A lot of the history is gone, Jean, lost or destroyed. Much of what survived, such as the works of the Jewish historian Josephus did so because the early Christian monks copied works that mentioned Jesus, James, or some other apostle. The problem is, they inserted bits of text or rewrote parts to align the contents with contemporary religious teachings. So now, historians have to try and separate the insertions from the original.

'The church banned other writings as heretical and often destroyed them. That happened at Nag Hammadi in Egypt. We still have the Gospel of Thomas and other texts because a monk refused to burn his books and buried them instead. Now, we're left with only scraps of once-valuable historical knowledge. Even the gospels and the Acts of the Apostles suffered revision, with stories of Paul's activities directly contradicted by his own letters.

'So we must be careful. History is written by the victors: in this case, the Roman Empire and the new Gentile Christian church living in an imperial world. They reimagined the original story so their religion would survive.'

'Sorry, Cathrina. You'd better explain that as well.'

'Early Christianity speedily discarded its roots, or at least changed the background to make it more acceptable to a Gentile audience.

'Thirty years or so after the death of Jesus, the Jewish people, like the Dacians who lived in present-day Romania, had the unbelievable audacity to rebel against Rome. No way would this be tolerated. To do so would destabilise the Empire itself. The answer was ruthless.

'The Roman legions wiped out the Dacian rebels, and the same thing nearly happened to the Jews. More than one million slaughtered in the Holy Land, 97,000 sold as slaves to be scattered throughout the imperial lands. Those in the Diaspora lost their previous protected status, and henceforth the authorities suspected them as sources of rebellion.

'The new Gentile Christians found themselves in a dicey situation. After the Revolt, anything coming out of Judaea was anathema, especially a new eastern religion, and how could they present this "Saviour"' to potential converts in an atmosphere of virulent anti-Jewish aggression?

'So they played the party line; to encourage the Gentile expansion of Christianity, particularly into the equestrian and senatorial levels of society, they diverted blame for Jesus's death from Rome. The scapegoat was obvious; they blamed the Jews.

'Scholars still argue about who wrote the gospels but most accept they weren't written by close associates of Jesus or the apostles. We don't know for sure, but it's more likely they were composed by Gentiles, not Jews, and when examined from Mark through to John, they display increasing anti-Semitic belligerence. They forget that Jesus, Mary, Joseph, and their family, as well as all the apostles, practised Judaism, always faithful to the Law and the traditions of their ancestors. These gospel writers did their best to minimise this unfortunate truth.

'For instance, we are led to believe that the "good and just" Pilate tried to save Jesus during his trial, but the "Jewish crowd bayed for his blood, calling it down on themselves and their children, insisting on his crucifixion."[13] We know from historical sources that Pilate was the most bloodthirsty of all the Roman governors in Judaea, later recalled and exiled because of his disastrous and murderous administration. To him, the Nazoraean was just another so-called Messiah rebelling against Rome. His death would have meant nothing.

'Furthermore, the "Jewish crowd" that witnessed the trial weren't the ordinary Jewish people. If there even was a Jewish crowd, they would have been associates of those in power—in other words, collaborators. The people of Jerusalem wouldn't have been allowed near the place.

'From modern historians we learn that Pilate and the high priests had responsibility for the crucifixion, a Roman method of execution. The Emperor himself appointed and dismissed both the Herodian kings and the high priests. They carried out his orders and held Judaea as a buffer state between the Parthian and

---

[13] Mathew 27:22-25. NRSV.

Roman empires, with legions in Syria to enforce imperial will. They simply saw Jesus as a threat to governance and their own riches. So they got rid of him.

'They remind me of the Vichy government in France under the Nazi occupation, but, after Germany's defeat, no one blamed the French people for Vichy activities. In fact, we admire the work of the resistance, their courage and dedication. Yet for two millennia, we've reviled and persecuted the innocent Jews for the activities of Pilate, Herod Antipas, and the high priests, all of them puppets of Rome.

'In part a successful operation in misinformation, the gospels appeared after the Revolt, while Rome flushed out remnants of messianic activity in Judaea. James was already dead. Emperor Vespasian and his successors continued to fear the rise of another revolutionary descendent of David; Jesus's other brothers Simeon and Jude were discovered and executed. In Trajan's reign, Jude's grandsons met the same fate.

'Yet after two millennia of Christianity, from our altars and pulpits, we still hear this same fiction about "innocent Rome" and the "guilty Jewish people", even though our scholars have long since exposed the truth.

'No doubt Jesus was a challenge to the status quo, his popularity among the people rendering him dangerous, his removal a necessity. Afterwards, James became the leader of the Nazoraean Assembly, directly appointed by his brother according to the Gospel of Thomas. Not many of the early writings about him are overwritten, although few Christians know much about him.

'Most assume Peter was the principal apostle, surprised when they learn James succeeded as leader of the Jesus-followers, or Nazoraeans, after the crucifixion. As Peter went to Rome and preached the new religion there until his martyrdom under the Neronian persecution, his Gentile converts believed he was the leader of the Church, the Roman 'bishop' had to be more important than anyone else. During the centuries that followed, this view became embedded as fact.'

'I was brought up in the Church of England and didn't realise James was Jesus's full brother. I thought he was a son of Joseph by a former wife.'

'The same thing happened with the Catholics, Jean. It all goes back to the developing doctrine of Mary's perpetual virginity. It's as if they believed the baby miraculously appeared outside Mary's body without being born in the normal way.'

'Interesting. I might have something to add here. A bit of information our Directing Guide gave us. I remember his words exactly: "In Judaea at the time, it was common knowledge that Mary was purported to be in virginal state at the birth of Jesus". Specific terminology, isn't it? He tended to be very precise in his wording of such important information. So I take it someone, a midwife perhaps, attended her, subsequently told the story, and it spread like wildfire.'

'What happened afterwards? Did he tell you anything more?'

'No. I always assumed she led the normal life of an ordinary married woman. You have to remember that the Guide was speaking to a predominantly Jewish group, and there was general scepticism about Mary's virginity. So he gave us this very firm confirmation: the conception of Jesus was supernatural, but the birth was normal.

'He also told us that this occurred on other occasions, although rarely. When a great soul needed to come to earth to aid the evolution of mankind, there was a virgin birth. This also happened when a lower entity came to desecrate humanity. Rare, but true.'

Cathrina stared at Jean. 'Wow. Fascinating but scary. A bit like the film, *Rosemary's Baby.*'

'I know. It makes you think. Anyway, I interrupted you. Go on.'

'I can say with some historical confidence that Jesus had full brothers and at least one sister. The early drive to designate Mary a "perpetual virgin" didn't start until the third century. The letters of Paul, the earliest Christian writings, talk openly of the "brothers of the Lord" and the gospels of Matthew and Mark list them as James, Joses, Simeon, and Jude. Mark also tells us that Salome was present at the crucifixion and mentions the "brothers and sisters of Jesus" when he went to Nazareth to preach, so there might have been more than one girl in the family.[14]

'What is surprising is that we can find them among the apostles, although disguised or viewed as unimportant: James the Less, Simon the Canaanite or Zealot, and Jude Thaddeus.

'Another question is this: it's claimed that James only began to accept Jesus after his resurrection. If you think about it logically, he had to be more closely involved beforehand. How did he suddenly pop up out of nowhere without any experience and expect seasoned healers and exorcists like Peter and John to obey him without question? His non-involvement doesn't add up, and strangely enough, Acts supports this theory. When electing an apostle to replace Judas, it specifies the candidate must have been with the Movement from the beginning. Don't you think this would apply much more stringently to the new leader?

'A Nazoraean and a Nazrite, James had definite similarities to his cousin John the Baptist. Nazoraeans and Nazrites are not connected, by the way. The two words have different Hebrew roots. Nazrite was based on the phrase "to set aside or consecrate"

---

[14] Mathewr 13:55-57. Mark 6:3-5 and 15:40. NRSV.

and their vows could be taken by anyone. For James, they became extensive: he didn't cut his hair or beard; never drank strong fermented wine or ate meat, although I presume new wine, tirosh, would have been acceptable; a daily bather in the Jewish miqvahot, not the Roman baths; and he wore only linen.

'A truly fascinating man, revered in Jerusalem as James the Just, or the Righteous, and so loved by the ordinary people they would try to touch the fringes of his garments as he passed in the street. He had an immense reputation for holiness, spending hours on his knees in the Holy Sanctuary praying for the people, and in early Christianity he was called the *Oblias*, the protector of the city from Satan. Even Josephus the historian believed the death of James led to the destruction of Jerusalem and the Temple. Had he lived he would have saved them. And another thing: he made rain.'

Jean laughed in delight. 'How wonderful. And very useful in a hot country like Israel. Anything to support the claim?'

'The early Church fathers report it. It's every similar to the abilities of the Holy Men of Galilee like Honi the Circle-Drawer, of course. Apparently during a severe drought, James went out into the open and implored God to send rain. It came immediately. What do you think of that?'

Jean gazed into the distance. 'It does make you wonder what capacities and capabilities lie undeveloped within us. Like Jesus himself said, we could move mountains if we truly wanted to. I'm sure these abilities will come as we evolve. But back to the Lord's brother: did you find a connection with the rule of evil?'

'Yes. That wasn't a problem. It was a commonly understood concept at that time, and as he was a Nazoraean with Essene connections, James would've known about the epoch of iniquity. But something else caught my attention. I tried to pinpoint the methods they used to end evil and two areas stood out: their own personal righteousness and their overwhelming desire to keep the Temple clear of spiritual contamination. I wondered how these contributed to their objectives.'

'How do you mean?'

'I'll explain in a minute, Jean. Before that, I'd like to give you a rundown on the political situation in Judaea at the time, including how James and the Nazoraeans fit into the picture. Then we'll talk about my ideas and you can tell me what you think.'

'Perfect. My background knowledge is scanty, to say the least.' 'OK.'

'Rome firmly controlled Judaea. Pilate was recalled in disgrace in 36 CE. Historical sources reveal the Roman Prefect to be a vicious, ruthless man, not the weak compromiser portrayed in the gospels. Other prefects followed until 41 CE when Agrippa I became king of Judaea, a direct descendant of Herod the Great and Mariamne, a princess of the Hasmonean royal house that her husband replaced.

'Over the years Herod killed off the surviving royals, including his wife, but not before she bore him sons, giving him a royal bloodline to be used by him and Rome. A descendent of the native dynasty would more easily command the affection and loyalty of the people. From Rome's perspective, Agrippa had two functions: farm the taxes and keep the people under control. The Empire didn't tolerate unrest and stamped it out ruthlessly. But they expected the new king to be more popular than a Roman governor. He received the right to appoint the high priests; together they acted as Rome's ruling arm in Judaea.

'On the other side, we find a people divided. The opportunities for wealth attracted some, and they formed the Herodian party in support of the king and high priests. But the ordinary people detested their overlords. Genuinely religious and dedicated to the One God, they believed in the messianic prophecies. The land belonged to the Great Creator, and they fiercely opposed control by the Gentile Romans, who were seen as idol worshippers and servants of Satan.

'The Nazoraean Assembly, led by James the Just, the brother of Jesus, philosophically confronted the Herodians and their adherents. Claims of five thousand members are considered optimistic by modern scholars, yet there is evidence that the people of Jerusalem and increasing numbers of the minor priesthood supported them. This gave James an influential position within the religious opposition to the establishment.

'Under him, the movement remained firmly within traditional Judaism, although with an ascetic and righteous flavour, influenced, no doubt, by the strict philosophy of the many Essene priests who backed him. They followed the law to the letter: the commandments plus the purity and dietary laws.

'The Assembly interpreted the ancient Levitical instruction to "love God and love your neighbour as yourself" as piety towards the Father in heaven and a commitment to the welfare of their fellow man, with a social and financial component. Traditionally responsible for the development of charitable activity, the law focused on the care of the widow, the orphan and the destitute. James and his community expanded this with a drive towards a personal and monetary equality, similar to today's socialism or even communism (see Acts 4:32).

'Like his brother, everything he believed in brought him into direct conflict with the Roman establishment that defiled, in his opinion, the people, the Sanctuary and the Holy City. He fought against three pollutions: evil riches gained through oppressive taxation and other methods that terrorised the people;

pollution of the Temple by the acceptance of contaminated wealth brought into the Treasury from Gentile foreigners, including the Herodians; and lastly, "fornication" by which he meant taking a second wife while the first one lived, divorce, polygamy, incest, or any other forbidden sexual relationship.

'The Herodians were particularly guilty: as tax farmers they exploited the people, causing suffering and death; some indulged in illicit relationships with close family members such as marriages between uncles and nieces; and they believed Agrippa to be sexually involved with his sister Berenice, who had previously married two uncles, brothers of her father.

'Some ancient writings suggest that Simon Peter attempted to forbid them entry into the Temple, considering them Gentiles, although technically they claimed to be Jews. He also tried to bar Agrippa and Berenice from entering the Holy City itself. No doubt the apostle incurred the enmity of the king, possibly the underlying cause of his imprisonment and later departure for Rome.

'The high priests proved to be equally difficult. Doubts existed with regard to their genealogy and entitlement to high priestly status. But more importantly, they acted unrighteously, mainly interested in the accumulation of wealth through their share of the taxes imposed on Judaea. The people also hated them for their treatment of the minor priesthood. Josephus tells us they sent out violent thugs to the threshing floors to steal grain from the ordinary priests, causing starvation and the death of many.

'Their disrespect for the norms of their office was even more of a concern as they directed Temple affairs and Nazoraeans, like Jesus and James, endangered their lives in their attempts to prevent contamination to the Sanctuary. And this is where I think the connection with our subject lies.

'Ending the rule of evil was the primary goal of the Nazoraeans. This required the maintenance of their own, spiritual condition but also the continued sanctity of the Temple. Many scholars believe that when Jesus expelled the moneychangers from the courtyards, thus interfering with the cult's financial organisation, the enmity of Caiphas led to the plan for his crucifixion. Later, an attempt by James to protect the sacrifices from another contamination fostered the idea of his death by stoning. This was known as the Temple Wall Affair.

'In 62 CE, Rome ruled Judaea directly, but Agrippa II, king of Galilee, obtained the right to appoint the high priests and acquired the Hasmonean Palace, situated next to the Holy Sanctuary in Jerusalem.

'On the side overlooking the priestly courts, he built a balcony from which he observed the sacrificial activity while he dined with his non-Jewish guests. To treat a holy ritual as entertainment for idol worshippers was, to many, a diabolical contamination; a well-publicised decree, upheld by the Roman administration, specified that no Gentile could enter the inner courts of the Sanctuary, under pain of death. To bypass this edict in such a manner angered many of the people, especially the minor priests conducting the rituals.

'An extension was built to the wall between the courts and the palace, the view blocked. An enraged Agrippa demanded its destruction and brought the matter to Rome. Surprisingly, Nero's verdict went against him. But James, considered the leader of this righteous indignation, made a fatal enemy.

'Soon afterwards, the king appointed Ananus as high priest. When the procurator Festus died, Ananus took advantage of the interregnum, called a Sanhedrin, accused James of blasphemy, and had him stoned to death.

'James lost his life when the establishment no longer tolerated his popular opposition. His attempt to protect the Temple failed. We don't know what activities or rituals they intended using to end the epoch of iniquity, but whatever they planned, it didn't happen.

'What we do know is this: a few short years later, Rome destroyed Jerusalem; the invaders burned the Holy Sanctuary of the Creator to the ground and stole all its treasures; more than a million Jews died or were sold as slaves, to be scattered throughout the imperial lands; but most importantly, the rule of evil didn't end, and the kingdom of heaven didn't come. Satan was triumphant.'

She stopped reading, surprised she felt so upset.

But Jean understood and reached over to grip her hand. 'It can get to you after a while, Cathrina. Such a phenomenal opportunity that didn't succeed, even with all their efforts. To me it indicates how much of a threat they were to Satan. He engineered the deaths of Jesus, then James, and did everything possible to wipe out the Jewish people.'

'What do you mean?'

'They must have been on the right track. Otherwise, the lower realms wouldn't have gone to so much trouble. They used a massive amount of lower power to kill Jesus, then his bother, and followed that up with the destruction of Jerusalem and the Temple. The Nazoraeans were on the point of success two thousand years ago.

'I think Satan feared the Chosen People then and still fears them today. He's trying his best to eradicate them. Look at the persecutions over two millennia and the Holocaust in the last century. I realise it might be hard to grasp, in this day and age, that he operates in this way, but I promise you he does. I've come across too much evidence of his activities during nearly fifty years of rescue work.'

'You think they still have a part to play?'

'Yes, I do. They're connected with the drive to neutralise evil and made the first attempt during the Second Temple era. And in the 1955, when our own rescue circle was first formed by a group of Jews, they were instrumental in bringing back the techniques of soul elevation that Jesus brought to humanity two thousand years ago. We don't know what further tasks have been assigned to them.

'Let's leave that for the moment. You wanted to talk to me about what Jesus was going to do.'

'Yes. I think both the asceticism of the Nazoraeans and the Temple itself were important for some reason. I'm trying to find out why and hope you'll be able to help.'

'I'll do my best.'

'OK. You said the rule of evil would end when Satan, and every other soul in the lower realms, elevated into the upper realms. Yes?'

'I don't see how else it can be done. All souls are immortal. Desecrated souls can't be destroyed. You can't destroy energy, in this case consciousness. Nor can they be separated from humanity and contained indefinitely, as that would strengthen the evil. The only option is to purify and change the energy, neutralise the negative vibrations surrounding lower souls so they can elevate. The answer is still yes.'

'And those attempting to raise the lowest souls, especially those immediately around Satan, would need to be in strong upper condition.'

Jean smiled, impressed by Cathrina's growing spiritual

understanding. 'Yes. Otherwise they wouldn't have the power to neutralise the lower vibrations.'

'Well, everything about James indicates that this was what he tried to do. He lived a strict, ascetic life and kept lower contamination to a minimum. In fact, this is where your explanation of the purity laws comes in. They describe ways a person might protect themselves from pollution. You agree with that, don't you?'

'Yes. From everything you told me, they are quite pertinent. We all absorb contaminated energy every day from stress, tiredness, illness but also from negative emotions like anger and hostility. That's why we sometimes feel that heavy exhaustion we instinctively know is more than physical depletion. Normally, we push out these vibes in a spiritual parallel to the physical excretion of faecal matter, and in time, we "clear". But if we do something against our conscience, through rage or hatred, you have a different situation. We might become spiritually injured. From that, it's more difficult to recover.

'To avoid contamination, the Nazoraeans needed to live a conscientious life, not just keeping the commandments and the law but staying away from people and places contaminated with lower vibrations. Otherwise their ability to deal with evil would be compromised. The purity laws give specific directions on how to protect oneself. They hold deep, ancient, spiritual knowledge.'

'So they knew how to keep themselves clear and free from spiritual pollution, and they stayed strong to elevate the most powerful lower souls.

'Then answer me this, Jean. Why oh why, in God's name, did they risk everything for the Temple? Why not stay quiet and do their work to end the rule of evil in secret? Why did both Jesus and James come out into the open and physically confront the high priests and the Herodians over the Holy Sanctuary?'

Jean's eyes widened as she stared at Cathrina, caught unawares by the question. Then, she sat and thought, gazing off into the distance, fiddling with her silver bracelet, lines on her forehead deepening, her eyes screwed up as she focused.

After some time, she turned to her friend with a look of delight, of dawning understanding. 'You clever girl. You have something here. There's information from our Directing Guide that might be relevant, something we were told many years ago, and frankly, I'd forgotten all about it.

'The Nazoraeans tried to elevate a key lower entity, one of four who acted as the primary security barrier around Satan. Those involved had so much difficulty raising him, that Jesus, who was holding the soul, had to use a lot of his own power to successfully complete the elevation.

'The rescue weakened the devil's circle of protection to a dangerous degree. With Satan at the centre, the four souls stood at the points of the compass, north, south, east, and west of him, each a forceful, compelling affinity with the other three, like identical quadruplets, their spirits so tightly intertwined and interwoven that penetration through them was next to impossible.

'Their strength, however, was also their weakness. The rescue impaired the protective fabric of the remaining three souls and allowed a partial passage of upper vibrations to Satan—in other words, holy emanations from Jesus, from faithful Jews all over the world, as well as spiritual power from the upper realms.

'Furthermore, many souls, possibly thousands, above the rescued entity and directly connected to him went up into the upper realms with him. It was a potential disaster for the lower realms. Their leader suddenly became vulnerable.'

'Yes, but where does the Temple come in?'

'They probably needed the extra power to deal with the soul.'

Cathrina looked totally confused.

Jean laughed. 'Look, let me explain the Holy Sanctuary of Jerusalem from a spiritual point of view. To the Jews of that era, it was the abode of the One God, the Great Creator, and a source of immense upper power, mainly because it was the centre of focus for the Jewish people, not only those in Jerusalem and Judaea but also for the Diaspora, the exiles scattered throughout Europe and beyond. Their spiritual aspirations converged on the Temple itself, the earthly seat of the Most High.

'During the festivals, the thoughts and prayers of thousands and thousands of fervently religious Jews joined those physically in Jerusalem. Their focused minds would cause an upsurge in spiritual power that Jesus could use to help him elevate the four guards and eventually Satan himself. Like concentrating the rays of the sun through a mirror to create fire. A holy laser beam, if you like. Surgical precision.'

'I still don't understand how it works.'

'It's all to do with the effects created by a given number of concentrating minds. They conducted experiments with transcendental meditation during the war in Lebanon some time ago. As long as they maintained a certain level of meditators, fatalities and injuries decreased, intensity of the conflict lessened, and communication between the opposing sides followed.

'When the levels of concentration dropped, deaths went back up and cooperation stopped. It's a similar idea. With sufficient numbers of people centred on one objective, you can create potent results. Huge numbers of minds concentrated on the Holy Sanctuary would produce tremendous upper power.'

'That's strange. I remember Josh telling me they conducted

a similar experiment in Washington DC. A ring of meditators encircled the city, the concentration continuous. And in that time, murders, robberies, and all unlawful acts took a dip. It was definitely confirmed that the meditation made the difference. It's fascinating to think they were doing that two thousand years ago. But would it have worked?'

'Yes. It probably would have. In fact, I've seen it done.

'During the 1980s we prevented a major spiritual attack on humanity, something we'd prepared for over many years, the most difficult work we ever attempted. It was 1985, the summer of Live Aid in Wembley—the summer of compassion, I always thought afterwards.

'Bob Geldof stirred up sympathy for the starving in Ethiopia, and countries all over the world joined together to help, including Russia, and that was unexpected as it was during the Cold War. Nearly two billion people from 150 nations watched the concert live, the first time compassion for our fellow man activated on a world scale.

'And in Ireland, statues of the Blessed Virgin Mary moved.'

'I know about this, Jean. The excitement affected everybody. People went out in droves to see them, praying and saying rosaries. It was happening all over the country.'

'According to a university study, there were more than thirty recorded incidents, a religious response, they believed, to social angst caused by fear during the Cold War. They were certainly right about how frightened people were at that time. The atmosphere in London darkened. We were sure a nuclear attack was coming.

'Instead came Live Aid, the spectacular upsurge of compassion from all over the earth, the moving statues of Mary and the people of Ireland praying beside them. And in the middle of this, we finished our spiritual work. It almost goes without saying: we were successful.

'We neutralised the attack from Satan, and the world found itself on a different course. But it wasn't only us. The universal sympathy made the difference. So many people contributed money to feed the starving in Ethiopia. For the first time in history we recognised ourselves as one human family and we loved our brothers and sisters. We wanted to help.

'How could Satan fight that? We stepped back from the brink of disaster in those days and created a new future for humanity. A few years later, the Berlin Wall came down, and soon after, the Cold War ended.

'I'm sure the upper realms were involved in the statue phenomenon and in stimulating Bob Geldof. He, in particular, did more good in this world than he could possibly imagine. So, Cathrina, I think you are right about the Temple. I can imagine how massive levels of spiritual energy could be generated by the festivals. They probably carried out their most important elevations then.'

Jean paused, thinking, questioning the possibilities. Were they about to work on the second Satanic guard during the Passover Feast, when Jesus was captured?

No wonder the Holy City and the Sanctuary were destroyed. Nowhere else on earth was the Great Creator worshipped with such faith and in such numbers. Jews from all parts of the known world, concentrating on the Sanctuary at specific times, producing spiritual energy for the upper realms to use.

Satan and his cohorts were on a knife edge, in danger, and they fought back with everything they had. A series of well-orchestrated tragedies followed: they used the Romans to kill Jesus; Agrippa and Ananus had James stoned to death; Titus and Agrippa devastated Galilee, killed the people, and butchered the fishermen, the tranquil Lake streaked red with their blood; the legions surrounded the Holy City, besieging and destroying men, women, and children; the noble white and gold Sanctuary of the Most High, the one and only centre of worship for the Great Creator, burned to the ground.

Such inimitable nuclei of knowledge and sources of spiritual strength couldn't continue. Satan found them too dangerous. To allow them to survive and spread the knowledge was too much of a threat. Everyone and everything was annihilated, wiped out, especially those in Galilee and Jerusalem, who had listened to the Lord and received the wisdom. Not many of the Jesus followers cheated destruction; they were slaughtered in the lands bordering the blessed Lake, starved behind besieged walls or pierced by a Roman sword.

Judaism persevered under the rabbis, with the people scattered throughout the Empire, gathering in synagogues without the centralising core of their Temple. And for two thousand years their descendants were intimidated, persecuted, and killed, never allowed to become too strong again.

29

The Dusty Roads of Home

There came a time when memories of Judaea and Jerusalem saturated Mary's thoughts, even her dreams, and with them grew a longing to go home. At first, she dismissed it, thinking it impossible if not unimportant. Still the niggling desire persisted.

She told John the next time he visited.

'Perhaps it's time, Mary. I have the same feeling. I want to go back. Should we go when Simon's next in port? Normally, he only stays a few days, so we would have to move quickly.'

Surprised by his prompt response, she laughed. Yet as she considered the possibility, her heart filled with longing. Although she delighted in her home and life on the mountain, she wanted once more before her death to walk the dry, dusty roads of the land of her birth, to stand in the Women's Gallery of the Temple, to watch the spiralling smoke rise to heaven as the priests sacrificed to the Holy One, and to wait at the Nicanor Gate and arrange an offering of thanksgiving for her escape from the clutches of Satan.

Most of all, she needed to see Hannah and her sons James, Simeon, and Jude and hold her grandchildren in her arms. All these years she buried them deep in the recesses of her memory, hoping to keep them safe not only from Rome but from the probing of the Evil One. And now they filled her mind, full and fresh in their beloved presence, and her yearning for them intensified.

She had felt the sharp, stinging pains in her side and knew she wouldn't live forever. Yet death was not something to fear; it would reunite her with those she loved and missed, at times bitterly. When it came, she would welcome it, glad to return to her first and most precious home. So in a way, the sudden desire to see her family didn't surprise her. It was a parting, an opportunity to give her love and blessings to those she would leave behind. As long as she didn't draw to them unwelcome attention, it would be a crowning joy.

She smiled at her nephew and reached over to touch his hand. 'Let's go home, and as soon as possible.'

Fate forced them to wait nearly a month before the *Galilee* arrived in port. Two mornings later, the ship sailed away from Ephesus harbour. Their friends came to bid them farewell, and as Mary watched the sobbing Martha on the quay, her throat tightened. Was this a final separation? She waved until they disappeared from sight and then scanned Koressos, trying to find the heights behind which her retreat lay hidden. Eventually, she identified Rachel's farm and the slight ridge to the left where the pavilion perched. She regained her soul on the mountain, but whether she returned to it would be in the hands of the Father.

Her journey to Joppa filled her with well-being. Sitting on her bench, she chatted to Simon and John or spent time with the crew, bringing them jugs of tirosh.

Sometimes, she went below to help Amos, now responsible for meals. She taught him simple stews, easy to prepare while sailing, and when anchored, the more complicated recipes that required a stable fire. Her pupil became quite the expert, delighting in the rough appreciation of his shipmates. But mainly he enjoyed

Mary's affectionate company, the sense of family she brought to the voyage.

The captain looked on in amazement and near disbelief, comparing the gaunt, grieving, grey-faced creature who stumbled aboard his ship all these years ago with this contented woman, with the twinkle in her eyes and colour in her cheeks. She emanated a gentleness that drew others to her like a magnet. His graceless sailors became obedient sons in her company, and her presence on his ship bestowed on it a blessing.

When John explained the circumstances, he was glad for her, pleased she'd found peace at last. But he was aware of an insubstantiality, a touch of the ethereal around her and questioned his friend about her health. Was that why she was prepared to chance the undoubted dangers of returning home?

As usual, imperial affairs directly affected their homeland. After the death of the Emperor Tiberius, his successor, Caligula, rewarded the loyal Agrippa, grandson of Herod the Great, with territory north of the Lake and later with Galilee and the province of Perea, east of the Jordan.

The new imperial reign was a disaster for the Jews. Only the prevarication of the governor of Syria prevented the installation of the Emperor's huge statue in the Holy Sanctuary and the revolt which inevitably would have followed. Caligula's mental health deteriorated, however, and to general relief he was assassinated by his own praetorian guards.

The fortunate Agrippa, in Rome at the time, acted as intermediary between the praetorians, the Senate and the potential heir, Claudius, a man of unfortunate physical appearance, but intelligent and a direct descendent of the divine Augustus. This latest ascendant to the throne repaid his Jewish friend by including Judaea and Samaria in his kingdom, now of similar size to that of his grandfather.

'The news spread like wildfire throughout the country,' Simon said, 'and they expect Agrippa to arrive in Caesarea at any moment to take control. There's jubilation everywhere. He's Mariamne's grandson and therefore a native Hasmonean. The people think he'll protect them from the Empire. But I wouldn't trust him. He's been educated in Rome, a Herod through and through. Neither he nor the high priests will turn on their Roman masters or risk their power and riches. They'll do as the Emperor orders.

'And we don't know how they'll treat the Nazoraeans. The Assembly has increased in numbers and the minor priests in the Temple support James. But they'll be seen as followers of a rebel, already judged and crucified. Their popularity won't save them. You need to travel quietly. Tell no one who you are. Wait until you meet the family and judge the situation yourself.'

The *etesian* winds blew strong, and they soon reached Joppa. They stayed with Susannah that first night and left early the following morning, John with his robust staff and Mary perched on her donkey, baskets packed with their belongings, reins in her hands.

It was late summer. The dusty roads and the yellow-brown grass told of a sweltering season coming to a close. She didn't see or care. She remembered the last journey to the port, those cruel days of grief and failure, the fear and dread. Would the soldiers overtake them? Were they already ahead, waiting to ambush and kill them? At the end of her strength, a terrible desolation filled her, everything wasted and destroyed. The Father's love was gone; the warming Presence no longer surrounded her. Utterly forsaken, she experienced a tiny measure of the piercing isolation and loneliness of her Yeshu's final hours.

Her nephew saved her; he brought her back from the edge of the abyss. Without him she would have fallen. And now they were home once more, on the way back to the Holy City. The barren, burnt paths and bare, rocky hillsides were green and fresh, a paradise of streams and fountains, a land of beauty and promise. Joy erupted in her heart, bringing tears to her eyes.

She had survived, regained her connection to the Father and her belief in herself. Everything she was capable of doing for the task she had done. And she also believed what Rachel said at the mountain pool: now was not the time. Success would come in the future, and for that they must prepare. For this she was returning, this sense of renewal and confidence in what the years ahead would bring.

In the meantime she remained at peace, listening to the clip-clop of her little donkey, to John humming to himself as he strolled along, sandals covered in the dust of Judaea, staff in hand. She drew her mantle around her and settled comfortably into the saddle, rolling with the movement, knowing she was exactly where the Father wanted her to be.

They travelled the road on the northern edge of the densely cultivated Plain of Ajalon and stayed overnight at an inn on the outskirts of the town of Lydda. Late the next morning they journeyed on, stopping often at wells to water the donkey and give Mary a welcome break from the saddle.

Eventually they reached a rugged road that rose with a line of trees and narrowed into a ravine. It brought them to the lower Beth Horon village, the beginning of the pass that led to Jerusalem. They stayed for several days at a small inn, having a complete rest in preparation for the difficult climb.

The pass was the main conduit through the Judaean hills, and due to its strategic importance, many ancient battles were fought over its terrain. When Joshua claimed the land and defeated the kings of the Canaanite cities, they fled before him down the gorge. Centuries later, Judas Maccabeus confronted the Seleucids in a final attempt to prevent the eradication of the worship of the God of Israel, a rebellion that became a war of independence.

In the days before the well-maintained Roman road, it was a death trap; soldiers, wounded and terrified, struggled through jagged rocks, and crazed horses catapulted into the deep ravines on either side.

To Mary, the ascent was a marathon through hell itself. They almost made it to the top when she collapsed. Holding her upright in the saddle, John pushed on into the upper village and the courtyard of an inn. In a panic, he pulled her from her seat, her eyelids fluttering in the bloodless face, her lips blue. He yelled for help.

A woman of middle-aged years came running, and reading the situation, beckoned him to follow as she hurried into the building to a large bedroom on the ground floor. She pulled down the covers, and he lay his aunt carefully on the bed, searching her frozen face as the woman took her hands and rubbed them briskly.

'You came up the pass?'

'We did. It was too much for her.'

'She'll recover. Her colour is already coming back. You go take care of your animal and your belongings. You'll be in the next room, right beside your mother. I'll look after her.'

He stood immobile, hardly able to breathe. He felt sick. His stomach churned; he thought his legs would melt beneath him.

All he saw was her white face, no breath, no life. She was going, leaving him.

The woman tried to bring him from the room, but he pulled away and returned to the bed. In the end, she forced him back, her hand firmly on his chest, and compelled him to look at her.

'Listen to me. You're in no state to help her. You'll only do harm. You managed to bring her here, and now she needs rest. I'll look after her. I promise you.' At last, the sympathetic determination penetrated; he realised he could do no more.

'Mary, her name is Mary. She's my aunt.'

Sensing the deep fear, she took his arm and brought him into the room next door.

'I know it's frightening, but you must try not to worry. I've dealt with this situation many times in the past. She's overstrained herself. It will take time, but she'll recover. It's not too serious. You go settle your donkey. Ask the boy in the stable to feed her and rub her down. Make sure you rest before you come back to see your aunt.'

Her serene demeanour reassured him, and he nodded. 'Thank you. I'm sorry, I don't even know your name.'

She smiled in relief. 'I'm Hannah. My husband, Jacob, and I own the inn. You're in good hands.'

She gave him a gentle push towards the courtyard, turned back into the room and closed the door. She undressed Mary and wrapped her in linen sheets, crooning to her as if to a small babe. Gradually her patient relaxed until the regular breathing confirmed she was asleep. Yet she sensed when Hannah tried to rise and grew restless, muttering in her dreams. The nurse remained and soothed her until her repose deepened.

Mary walked the rooms in Nazareth, searching the deserted house, looking for Joseph, for Yeshu and James. Where were they? The furniture was all gone; even Joseph's workshop was bare. Where was everyone? The panic and distress gathered momentum, and the throbbing in her chest intensified. Sinking to her knees, she sobbed. Why had they gone and left her all alone?

A warm glow came with the familiar smell. Strong arms surrounded her and carried her, she knew not where. She didn't mind. She was safe. The pain diminished as she snuggled into his robe and fell asleep in Joseph's care.

Sometime later she awoke to see his face smiling down at her. 'Rest now, Mary. It's not yet time. You still have work to do. Then you can come home. We'll be waiting.'

Disappointment pierced her for a moment, but then she relaxed. She knew it wouldn't be too long.

In the room at Beth Horon, the woman on the bed gave a deep sigh and her breathing stabilised. Convinced the crisis had passed, Hannah rose to leave. She tiptoed to the door, watching for any reaction, but all was well. Mary slept peacefully.

The innkeeper's wife was a herbalist, born in the Judaean hills and familiar with the properties of the plants to be found among the rocks and crannies all around the inn. After some hours her patient awoke, and she questioned her about her health. Noting the pains in her side, she treated her with herbs appropriate for a weakened heart. Under her care, Mary steadily improved, regaining her physical power and strength over the next few weeks.

Meanwhile, John explored and contemplated, no longer concerned about his aunt's condition. He recognised the powerful healer in Hannah, and when Mary revealed the dream, it confirmed his relief.

While having a meal with Jacob and his wife, he learned that Gibeon was a short distance down the road, the ancient High Place where the Tabernacle of the Lord stood in the time of Saul, before David brought it down to Jerusalem. There, in the distant past, his ancestors sacrificed to the Creator, and he knew he had to go.

He left early one morning, taking with him a skin of tirosh, some fruit, and small loaves of bread. Well before noon he arrived and climbed the rock-strewn hillside to the platform above. He gazed with amazement on Judaea stretching in all directions, the lookout point of the ancient tribes.

The wide Plain of Ajalon spread below him, the paths of their recent travels, and beyond, in the far west, the thin blue line of the sea traced the horizon. To the north, the hills reached into distant mountains; there lay Galilee and the much-loved Lake. More uplands faded into eastern desert, and when he searched further south, he picked out on a ridge the gleaming white towers of the Holy City.

Settling on a clump of burnt grass with a rock at his back, he took out the food and tirosh. A fig peeled, he broke a loaf and examined the vast plain below, thinking of their journey and wondering if it was Mary's last. He considered going down to the city to find James and bring him to Beth Horon; he wasn't sure what to do for the best.

No doubt, the answer would come. Here, in this blessed place, where the Tabernacle once stood and the Holy One spoke to Solomon in a dream, he would find the solution. As he relaxed, the emanations from the highest spheres overcame him, and he fell asleep to awake far up on a mountaintop with Yeshu's arm around his shoulders.

'When Mary is stronger, take her to the High Place and we'll help her. She'll live a little longer, certainly until she finishes her tasks. She must speak to the followers and we'll tell her what to say. Then take her back to Ephesus. She'll be with you for a while. When she leaves, try not to grieve too much. You saved her. The love between you protected her so strongly, the evil spirit became ineffective. That loving attachment kept her safe; it stopped her succumbing.'

He woke with Yeshu all around him and returned to the inn with a deep sense of peace. During all the years in the north, he'd waited for this clear direction from on high. And thankfully it came before they entered the Holy City. For this they were called home. She had the ability to penetrate high into the blessed realms, much higher than anyone else, except Yeshu, of course. If she brought back information and instructions they would be genuine, worthy of decision and effort, a gift for all the Nazoraeans, jewels beyond price.

Hannah met him at the door and reported the improvement in his aunt's condition. The herbal infusion made a considerable difference, and she promised to scribe the details to be replicated in Jerusalem. He went immediately to her room where he found her sitting up in bed, supported by pillows. She grinned when she saw him, listened carefully to Yeshu's message, pulled her mother's coverlet up around her, and lay back with a contented sigh. Over the next days, she improved steadily until she could walk without help.

Two weeks later, they left. With tears in her eyes she kissed Hannah goodbye. They would return at some stage and hoped to see her in the future. Afterwards, she turned with determination to face the final stretch of road to the Holy City. A shiver went through her as she remembered the last time they'd been there, but she pushed away her fears. What needed to be done, must be done. She would place her soul in the hands of the Father. Nothing else mattered.

A short time before noon they arrived at the High Place, and she gazed, amazed at the panorama before her.

At the western edge, John removed the baskets and saddle and left them in the shade of a rock. He took the donkey down to a pool fed by springs and turned her loose to graze. While Mary explored, he arranged covers on the ground and unpacked Hannah's breakfast of figs and small loaves of bread. When she returned, full of questions about the places she saw, he persuaded her to sit down, worried she might be overdoing it.

Mary was responding to the energy on the blessed hill, to the warm, loving Presence that gave her physical and spiritual healing. When she turned her head, sparkles flashed in the noon sky and feathers brushed her cheek. A special, wonderful place, inundated with the love of the Father. She laughed, easy in her limbs, all memories of pain and dread gone.

For the duties still to come, they prepared her.

The glow around her head had grown in the years since her release from evil, but that morning, a golden aura completely encased her, white light shimmering in the air.

'Have something to eat, Mary,' he said gently, passing her

food, knowing it would stabilise her, give her body sustenance without disturbing her elevation.

Within moments of finishing, she was unconscious, still sitting on the coverlet with her back against the rock, her eyes closed, her breathing almost negligible, her spirit no longer present. He remained immobile in case he disturbed her, and from the depths of his heart he surrounded her with love and support, wishing her courage and endurance wherever she travelled.

Sometime later, she stirred. He shifted to her side and held her steady with his arm around her back. When she opened her eyes, he reached for her cup and persuaded her to drink. Mary slowly realised she had left the blessed kingdom and sobs of disappointment and loss erupted.

Later, when she recovered, she spoke. 'Thank you, John, for staying with me. I wouldn't have returned if you hadn't been there to bring me back.

'The angel said this to me:

> You must now look to the years ahead. What has passed, is past. The future holds all our hopes. There was always the chance that Yeshua would not complete the task. And there is no doubt; the Evil One still rules.
>
> However, we have accomplished an irreversible victory. For the first time since the commencement of the epoch of iniquity, the power of love has activated in your world and created a chink in the armour of the Evil One. He has learned how love overpowers evil, and that chink, that fatal flaw, will grow and grow. He will fight love with all his fury, but he cannot overcome it. It is the essence of the Holy One, and it will prevail.

You can weaken evil through your love for one another. But anger and hostility consumes your realm. The people of the earth are selfish and greedy. And they desire power. In this way, the Evil One maintains control over you, resulting in suffering, destruction, and death for those without, disease and degradation of the spirit for those who have. You must persuade humankind to do good to one another, to care for their neighbour, to feel pity and compassion for those who tried to harm them. All the lessons Yeshua taught while he was with you.

In your world there are influential centres of power, and like massive, gluttonous spiders pulling all into their webs, they promise the delights of your material world. There must you send your healers and leaders to neutralise desecration as Yeshua taught them. This is your great task, to safeguard the future of your race.

There will come a time when he will return as promised, and then Satan will ascend to the Father. However, it cannot be done without your help. You have freedom of choice. You must choose liberty from evil. It cannot and will not be imposed on you.

Send out your soldiers of loving kindness, not your legions of destruction. Not all is lost. Much can still be achieved. It is within your grasp, yet it is your right and freedom to choose. Remember, it was the Father who created you. His essence is the core of you. Use the healing love and compassion of which you are innately capable to reverse your soul's race to destruction. Return to the paths of the Holy One, as must the Evil One himself, one day.

Go out and strive to save your world.

'John, this is the message I must bring to the followers. And although he didn't say it directly, the knowledge came to me again: it will be two thousand years before the next attempt.

'My son once warned me: if we failed, a time of suffering would come for our people. Satan will do his utmost to wipe out all those who received the wisdom. He won't let them live. The high priests thought they saved us by allowing Yeshu to be captured, but I fear they may have brought to us our destruction.'

When she thought of her children and grandchildren, all her friends and neighbours in Jerusalem and Galilee, all those who had followed and supported them in the task, her heart constricted in agony, and she was unable to breathe. How they would suffer, and there was nothing she could do to help them.

He wrapped a blanket around her and held her. They would stay there that night. The power pervading the ancient site would protect them and keep them from harm. And it would give her a chance to recover her composure and strength. He made a bed for her where they sat. Pacified by the holy emanations, she slept.

Sitting with his back against the rock, he guarded her as she relaxed into healing and restoration. He thanked the Father for her recovery, for His words of advice and direction. Some ideas were familiar, others surprising, with new momentum away from Judaea, out into the unknown world.

What would it mean for them, the family, their closest companions? Where would it lead them? Thoughts and questions tumbled through his mind until he too fell into a dreamless sleep, deep and sound.

30

The Holy City

They awakened with the sun rising over the mountains of Moab in the east, and after their prayers, they packed everything for departure. The donkey came running when called, soon saddled, bridled, and laden with baskets. John helped Mary to mount. As they descended the hill, she looked back to the blessed place and thanked the Father for sending the angel. Once more, she turned to face Jerusalem, now only a few hours away.

They travelled down through the steep-sided valleys until the city walls appeared in the distance, and beyond them the white and golden towers of the Holy Sanctuary shimmered on the Temple Mount.

Bypassing the crowded streets, they took the western road to the south and east, entered the city through the Gate of the Essenes, and reached the steep, narrow passageway on their left. The little animal attacked the difficult climb with John leading, Mary clinging to the mane, twisting and turning until they finally scrambled up the last few steps through a wooden door on the right into a small courtyard. They were home.

Aware of the signs of strain and exhaustion, he lifted her from the saddle and carried her over to a table beside the wall, leaving her there on a stool while he checked the house.

'I won't be long. Don't move.'

She nodded, too tired to speak. He found the key in its usual place in the stable and grinned when an inquisitive black donkey came over to push at his hands for titbits, a tiny foal trembling at her rump. He crossed the courtyard and opened the door calling for James. No one answered.

The spacious living room remained exactly as it was when they abandoned it all those years ago: the large table to the left, the fireplace flanked by tall cupboards on the wall to the right, even the old couch still there in the far corner. Memories of Yeshu and Mary with all their friends gathered around the table, deciding what to do next, arguing and organising, full of fervour and hope. His stomach clenched in a moment of grief. He pushed it away. No point now. Look to the future.

He searched everywhere—the bedrooms, the workshop at the back, everything empty but clean and well cared for, as though someone had left moments before. Her old bedroom next to the living room was still unused and only required blankets and pillows. With her clothes in the closet and her keepsakes on the bedside table, she would soon feel the inviting warmth of home.

He carried her in and settled her on the couch, pushing cushions behind her head. Rummaging through the baskets, he found the herbal infusion, poured a measure, and held the cup to her lips until she drained it.

Back outside, he stripped the donkey of her gear and led her into the stable with the others, checking there was enough water and hay. Later he would brush her down and examine her hooves. Getting to know her new companions would keep her busy in the meantime.

Food next. A few of Hannah's loaves remained, and when he searched the cupboards he discovered fig cakes, olive oil for dipping, and fresh apricots, a little feast to celebrate the end of a long and difficult journey. They needed time to recover, especially Mary. The physical deterioration had pinched her aquiline nose, the face more lined, and dark circles under her eyes; the tightened mouth spoke of ongoing pain.

Her heart was failing and the crisis in Beth Horon wouldn't be the last. He doubted her ability to return to Ephesus, and this house, ideal for his cousins, no longer suited her condition. She couldn't deal with the steep streets, confined in reality to the house itself. He would speak to James.

Looking up, he found her scrutinising him.

'Don't worry about me, John. I'm not finished yet. You heard what Joseph said. It isn't my time. I'll be here for a while longer.' She laughed at his frowning face. 'Seriously. Don't be so concerned. I'll be strong enough to do what I have to do. You'll see.'

He rose, leaned over to kiss her cheek, and went to prepare her room.

A while later she walked in, and a smile curved her mouth. 'It's wonderful. Thank you.'

She touched her mother's coverlet on the bed and lifted from the table the little sparrows Yeshu carved all those years ago. Tears filled her eyes but no longer those of despair. That was in the past. All would be well. They were in the hands of the Blessed One.

She kissed him on the cheek, wished him good night, and turned to undress for bed, happy to be back in Jerusalem, whatever it might bring.

Keen to establish a routine as soon as possible, she arose before dawn and began her day as usual with the Shema and the Prayer to the Father that called for the end of evil and the coming of the kingdom. Too hungry to wait for a later breakfast, she found food in the cupboard and brought it to the table. She collapsed heavily on a stool, weakened after this small effort. Laughing to herself, she remembered how she'd boasted to her nephew the night before. And now she couldn't even organise her own breakfast. She would need to rest a lot more and get someone in to help. Ruth might be available. Her sons would know.

With that she dismissed the problem from her mind and considered how she would spend her time. The family first, of course: James, Simeon, Jude, and the children. Perhaps a message could be sent to Hannah. Then the Temple; a purification offering was necessary after the expulsion of the entity and a thanksgiving to the Father for all He had done for her and given to her. Although they didn't finished the task, they took one important step forward; as it would be her last visit to His Holy Sanctuary, she would pray for a successful conclusion.

Too tired to clear everything away, she shuffled over to the couch and lay back on the cushions. Within minutes she was asleep.

He found her a few hours later when he came down from his room, still exhausted from the journey and amazed she had risen so early. He was fetching bread and figs for breakfast when the door opened and Ruth walked in.

The unexpected sight of her old friends stunned her, eyes flickering back and forward between John and the sleeping Mary. She ran to him and hugged him tightly, kissing him on both cheeks. A plump, pleasant woman, about ten years younger than his aunt, she emanated kindness and had looked after the family since they moved to Jerusalem. During the agonising years after the crucifixion, she stayed with them almost continuously, right up to the night the house was invaded and they had to flee.

While his aunt slept, he related the stories of their time in Ephesus and how she had recovered almost completely, only to collapse a short distance from home. She could do very little now and needed support.

'Do you think you could help, Ruth?'

'Of course I will. My own mother had the same problem and I looked after her for years. So don't worry. I'll take care of her.'

It was an enormous relief.

When Mary awoke, she smiled with delight to find her old friend preparing breakfast.

Positioned beside the table was the high-backed chair from her bedroom. Comfortable and easier to manoeuvre than the heavy couch, it was more useful in the living room. He carried her over, settled her among the cushions, and she caught up with all the news, learning that James and Jude would return later in the day. They were down in Pella with Hannah. She relaxed, content; her loved ones were safe and well.

'They'll get a shock when they walk in and find you home again.'

During breakfast, they arranged Ruth's extra hours.

Mary interrupted. 'Ruth, I need a physician. My herbal drink is almost finished.'

'Jacob the herbalist here in the community is the best. I'll ask him to call. You have a list of the ingredients? Yes? Give it to him and see what he says. I'll go directly after breakfast, and I'm sure he'll come later on today.'

In mid-afternoon she returned, accompanied by a heavyset

man with dark, bushy hair and beard, a ruddy face, and kind eyes. He wore the white rough-linen tunic of the Essene.

Mary had gone to bed, so her nephew took him in to see her. Afterwards, he came back to the living room to read Hannah's list.

'John, you know her heart is affected. The damage can't be repaired. I think we can slow the heartbeat down a little; hopefully that will give her an easier life. The draught is effective. I'm not surprised it helped her. With a few additions, maybe we can improve it. She'll have to be careful though and take things slowly.'

The apostle examined Jacob as he spoke, sensing the healer within. A kind man, dedicated to his patients, not unlike his namesake in Ephesus. Satisfied, he made arrangements, and Ruth promised to collect the concoction to give Mary that night.

By evening they were settling into being home in Jerusalem. Ruth cooked a lentil stew before she left, promising to return in a few hours. John put bread, olive oil, figs, and dates on the table and was about to ladle food into Mary's bowl when they heard a clatter in the courtyard.

James opened the door. He was of medium height, slim and wiry with a long nose, a thin face, and large, black, expressive eyes. A Nazrite from a young age, his black hair was long and shining with health; he wore the Nazoraean linen tunic, belted with a pleated rope.

His usual serious expression dissolved into a delighted grin when he saw his mama and cousin, his pleasure mirrored on their faces. He crossed the room to her chair and wrapped his arms around her, the questions tumbling out. When did they arrive? What decided them to come home?

Looking into her face, he noted the deterioration and pulled up a stool to sit beside her, taking her hand. 'How are you, Mama? Tell me what's happened.'

Her eyes glistened, but she didn't allow the tears to fall. He shot a worried glance at John.

'She was fine until we reached Beth Horon. The pass was too much. We stayed at an inn until she recovered. Jacob was in today. He's good, isn't he?'

'The best we have. What did he say?'

'Her heart is damaged, but he can help. The innkeeper's wife was a herbalist and prepared a drink that made a considerable difference. Now that he has the list, he'll be able to add a few ingredients to slow down the palpitations.'

Although overjoyed to see his mama, the thin face and body dismayed him, her delicate hands like fragile birds, trembling and weak. He tried to keep his tone cheerful, to spare her the extent of his concern.

'Jude will be so upset. Originally, he was coming back with me, but he was tired and went home. He'll be here in the morning. You'll see him then, Mama.'

'What about Simeon?'

'Down in Perea, helping with the olives. He loves to work on the land. He should be home in a few days. But listen, let's have some food. I'm starving.'

With another bowl and cup, he joined them, spooning lentil stew for Mary, breaking bread and pouring tirosh.

'Does Ruth know you're home?'

'She does,' John said. 'I've arranged extra hours for her.'

'Good. I'll see if she'll move in for a while. All her children are grown now and her husband is away meeting the spice caravans on the road between Petra and Palmyra. So he'll be gone for a week or so. I'll ask her. She'll be a definite help.'

John watched the mother and son, the latter obviously shocked and trying his best to hide it. Even so, she sensed his distress, her head bent over the table.

She looked up into his black eyes. 'I am not well, James. I haven't much time left. But please don't worry about me. I'll be happy when it comes. I'll be with those I love dearly. I was so damaged after Yeshu's death, but now I'm in a place of unimagined blessedness. No regrets. A wonderful life and an extraordinary family. You brought me real joy. So don't be upset, my beloved son. I'm very happy.'

Hurrying over, he dropped on his knees beside her chair and pulled her into his arms. Tears came, hot and strong. She hugged and kissed him, mumbling words of comfort.

John quietly stood up, took his bowl with a chunk of bread, and slipped out the door into the courtyard.

Over the next days, the household settled into a routine. Ruth came to stay, on hand when Mary needed her. The new drink lessened the pain, allowing her to undress without discomfort and carry out the simple, caring duties so important for her self-respect. Her friend helped when asked but didn't intrude unnecessarily, her presence appreciated more and more.

The house in the city soon became home again. Inherited by James on the death of her mother's youngest brother, it always brought fond memories of visits for the festivals. It didn't bring her the happiness and contentment she experienced in Nazareth or on the mountain, yet it had always been a welcoming centre for their family and friends.

Initially, she worried that news of their presence would reach the ears of the high priests or Herodians, but James assured her that the original agitation had subsided, more recent years quieter. For the moment at least, they were safe.

Her first visitor was Jude, of course. Warned by his brother, he didn't allow his shock at her condition to show, but when he left later, visibly shaken, he questioned John about her collapse.

Very different in appearance to James, he was shorter and more solidly built, with curly, almost frizzy hair to his shoulders. His eyes told of his relationship to his eldest brother; they twinkled, and like Yeshu's, nearly disappeared when he laughed. He wore the traditional white tunic of the Nazoraean, was married with a daughter and two sons. His wife and children came with him the next day, and Mary spent an hour of happiness with her grandchildren, although she tired quickly and went to bed to rest, drained but content.

James contacted Peter, Andrew, and Thomas, and the closest of Yeshu's companions gathered with the family around the big table. Her heart tightened to see them all together, so much loved yet so different.

Short and stocky with heavy, broad shoulders and arms, Peter's slightly stooped posture produced a purposeful, almost intimidating appearance, strengthened by the determined gleam in his eyes. Combed back from high temples, his straight brown hair reached to below his ears.

Unlike the traditional white-linen tunic of his companions, he wore a knee-length, greenish-brown version, his fishing clothes, displaying strong, hairy legs. A working countryman, reared to a life on the Lake, a man who dealt honestly with everyone he met. Although a successful businessman, his boats now in the hands of his youngest brother, he rarely donned the more formal, long garment, claiming the short one gave him freedom.

His brother Andrew, tall, almost stately with a well-developed physique, walked slowly and deliberately in an upright stance. His long face, strong nose, brown wavy hair, parted in the middle and falling below his shoulders, always reminded her of Yeshu. They were very alike and, on occasion, were mistaken for each other, especially at a distance. Her eyes misted when he arrived, unable to look at him for too long.

Thomas, another big man with a powerful energy and presence. He had short, dark curls, a trimmed beard, a prominent nose and large, black, darting eyes that absorbed everything at once. Highly intelligent and eternally curious, he interrogated John, fascinated by every little detail, amazed at how much they'd accomplished both in the city and on the mountain.

However, John's telling of the angel's message provoked the greatest reaction. As he only remembered some of it, Mary asked him to find, on her bedside table, the scroll she'd scribed that afternoon.

When he returned, she gave it to James and suggested copies should be made. He read it to the others, and she observed their faces: the wonder, the hope. Was there still a chance?

'This means Yeshu is coming back. Yes?' Peter asked, joy and amazement in his voice. No one answered.

'Do we know when he'll be here?' Andrew asked eventually.

She dropped her head, hating to disappoint them.

James regarded her steadily. 'Mama, if you learned anything else you must tell us. It will affect our decisions.'

'I'm sorry about this, but I was told it would be two thousand years. The original information came to me when I still had the evil spirit, so it might have come from Satan. Yet while the angel spoke at Gibeon, the span of two thousand years seemed to be part of the message.'

Peter gripped his hands together, his knuckles white, his head bowed, a hope unrealised.

Continuing his perusal of the writings, James read and reread in silence, deep in thought. He raised his head and gazed off into the far distance, oblivious to all around him.

Well used to his cousin's methods of deliberation, John grinned and awaited the outcome with interest.

'Mama, are these the exact words of the angel?

'Yes. Why do you ask?

'The exact words. You're sure.'

'Yes. They impressed them strongly into my mind so I wouldn't forget. I'm sure I've remembered them correctly.'

He relaxed, read the message one more time, and then rolled it up, his understanding satisfied, his decision made.

'Well, we have a task ahead of us. The holy spheres used a lot of power to bring Yeshu into the world to neutralise evil. It will take a similar amount for him to return. In some ways, I am not surprised it might take another two thousand years. That's another spiritual year and timing is everything in our work. Our limited hour of opportunity may have passed, but it doesn't mean we can't continue with what he began. He's no longer with us, so we must find another way.

'In fact, the message concentrates on what we have to do, not Yeshu. He brought us the knowledge and showed us how to use it. Therefore, we'll concentrate our efforts on this; Satan is injured. I presume the elevation of the guard at the northern gate weakened his immediate protection so badly that blessed emanations penetrated directly to him, especially Yeshu's concentrated love. That means we still have a slight chance in our own time.'

'You're right,' John said, almost to himself. 'I missed that. Do you think the northern guard is still in the blessed realms?'

'I don't know. I thought he would fall after Yeshu's death. But why would they give us these instructions if he had? We didn't dare examine him and jeopardise you, Mama. You were in no state, and frankly, at that time, neither were we.

'We knew he was on the same level as the evil spirit with you; the two of them were strong affinities, powerfully connected with each other. It was too dangerous for you and for us. We were much weaker without Yeshu.'

'I can hardly remember those days. I was in another world. I didn't even realise the soul with me was as low as Satan's guards. Did you, John?'

'Yes, but I didn't want to remind you. You had enough to deal with.'

'Anyway I am strong now, at least spiritually.'

Her son laughed in pure delight. 'Strong? Mama, you pushed away a desecrated entity that we, as a full group, couldn't begin to handle. I'm in awe of your strength.'

The others smiled at her as they nodded their agreement.

'I was surrounded by love and care. John here and all our friends in Ephesus. And then, Rachel at the pool.' She told them how her friend intervened and forced her to recognise how the lower soul was controlling her.

'Tell me what happened with the other guards. There were four at the gates surrounding Satan, weren't there? North, south, east, and west. An impenetrable barrier. Nothing could get through to him until Yeshu managed to get their names. Did you do anything more with them?'

'No, Mama. We decided to wait for instructions. I'm not Yeshu. I can hold a very strong soul, but not to his extent. And remember, he had to participate in the elevation while containing the entity. I couldn't do that. We'll have to weaken the others before I can deal with them. And unfortunately, we have no one who approaches Yeshu's ability. Unless I'm mistaken, however, the angel's message gives specific instructions on how we can tackle this.'

'What?' Peter asked.

'It tells us to go out into the main cities of the world and elevate the strong souls there. Don't you see? If we neutralise all those on the level above the four guards, who are in turn above their master, we will deplete his three, remaining protectors and also the Evil One himself.

'Remember, his power comes from the adulation of those around him. As we eradicate his support, his own strength will dissipate. Eventually, the pure essence of the Creator at the centre of his being will be released from its prison of evil. He will start to absorb loving kindness and return to the Father.'

'Evil he created himself.'

'You know that doesn't matter, Peter. It was at the beginning of human development when our souls were changing and in many ways, circumstances conspired against him.'

James thought back and remembered how Yeshu always had great compassion for Satan and his own reluctance, at first, to see his brother's point of view.

At that time, humans depended on hunting. They killed to live. They saw no other way. The concepts of kindness and cooperation were only beginning to be understood. Satan inherited phenomenal psychic and spiritual powers from his father and possibly from his mother as well, but the innate drive of the hunter overwhelmed him.

There's a huge difference between inheriting abilities and having the maturity to use them wisely. He was only a child, no more than 9 or 10 when he first became aware of his gifts, far too young to exercise them without destroying himself. What chance had he?

His father tried to teach him, but by the time he grew into manhood he had already succumbed to his desire for things. If he wanted something he took it, no matter who was hurt or how he did it. Would his mother have made a difference? As far as they knew, she died when he was young. She might have been able to persuade him away from the disastrous path that lay ahead of him.

Unfortunately, he knew, at least to some extent, what he was doing. He knew he was acting against the Holy One. He wasn't completely innocent, and that, combined with his unparalleled spiritual potential, allowed him to create evil.

'We mustn't blame him. Our task is to save him and bring him home to the Father. And by doing so, we'll make sure humanity returns to the path the Creator intended for us.'

'We need to consider something else,' Mary said. 'It's just come to me. His confidence in his invulnerability is gone. We've shattered it. There is doubt now, and that's another weakness. He's no longer impervious but diminished in his own eyes, permanently vulnerable.'

The old friends sat long into the night, deciding the future, their morale raised by the angel's message. She relaxed and listened, joining in when asked, remembering the years with Yeshu there beside them, planning the elevations and what to do next.

James asked his cousin if he would expand his area of responsibility to all of Anatolia.

'Yes. That shouldn't be a problem. We already have a developing group in Sardis. Seven of us work in Ephesus, with another gathering with Mary on the mountain. Although the strongest effects, so far, resulted from the raising of Artemis.'

Thomas laughed in delight. 'Artemis? The goddess? How did that happen?'

'Not in a very disciplined way, I'm afraid,' John said, screwing up his face. 'I only wanted to assess her but was forced into a full elevation. I was seriously weakened and lucky not to be severely injured.

'She stayed up, thankfully, and no longer contaminates the city. The temple is clear, but her priests don't realise she's gone. They continue sacrificing and processing through the streets, even though there isn't a goddess.'

The story intrigued James. 'Are all Roman priests insensitive?'

'Mostly yes. They are selected because of their wealth and standing within their community and are expected to pay for the sacrificial animals and the festivals. They rarely have any real spiritual abilities.'

'That might be to our advantage. We could work in secret without disturbance.'

Peter would go to Rome where he had relatives in the Jewish quarter. Initially, his brother would accompany him; afterwards, he wanted to concentrate on Greece.

'Bring with you at least one companion already experienced in both exorcism and elevation,' James said. 'You're an exorcist, Peter, while Andrew is a healer and can send strong loving thoughts to a desecrated soul. That's an excellent combination, a stable centre for an inexperienced group.

'Thomas, you're like Andrew, compassionate and a healer, but not as strong as Peter in sending hence lower souls. Have you thought of someone to go with you?'

'My nephew, Joseph. What do you think?'

'Good choice. Young but with a lot of potential.'

Although interested in the developing campaign, Mary grew tired. She rose to leave and James helped her to her room.

He returned moments later. 'Andrew, would you give Mama healing?'

'Of course.' James sat down, his mouth tight, his brow creased in a frown.

Jude was sitting beside him and gripped his arm. 'Things are changing, my brother. We've taken a new turning, and it will challenge all of us. The holy ones see much further than us. They assessed the possibilities and believe this path will produce better results.

'Yeshu says Mama has work to do in Ephesus, so allow her to do it with joy. The failure of the task broke her heart. To be given something new will feed her soul like manna from heaven. He knows this. There's no point in trying to keep her safe. That's not her way. Let her do what she can. We have no alternative.'

James nodded. 'I know you're right. I just hoped she would stay with us a little while longer. It was selfish.'

Andrew came back and James searched his face. 'Tell me.'

'Her heart is swollen and beating irregularly.' Even so, he smiled. 'If only you could see what's happening. She is completely surrounded by healers from the blessed realms and getting all the help it's possible to give her. They are looking after her. There wasn't much I could do, although I think Jacob's herbs are making a difference.'

'Thank you, Andrew.' He turned to the others. 'That's all we can achieve at this time. Simeon will be back in a few days. He,

Jude, and I will remain in Jerusalem as I'm sure the Evil One is concentrating his forces, and the most dangerous battles will be here. We'll begin work on weakening the entities standing at the other three gates.'

He was sure the souls immediately around Satan knew they were using the power from the Temple during the festivals. The living upper affinities of the satanic guards made all the difference with the last elevation. They provided the extra boost they used to raise the first guard. Unfortunately, it made the Sanctuary vulnerable; they had to protect it.

'At least here we have many friends to support us, whereas all of you will build from new foundations. John has made a promising start in Ephesus, but I fear for you and Andrew in Rome, Peter.' A shadow crossed his face. 'We thought the Greeks were unholy in their passion for combat and violence, yet they are civilised compared to the Romans. Thirsty for blood with a carnivore's desire to rip and rend, they take real pleasure and delight in another's suffering, their games a cold, ruthless altar for human sacrifice.

'I don't understand them. At times I find it hard to feel compassion for them. It's my most difficult task, even though I know it's the only way. I have to remind myself they've been desecrated by Satan and can't help themselves.' His head in his hands, his composure nearly deserted him.

John pulled his stool over beside him. 'They'll change over time, James. Not all of them are corrupt. Here in Judaea you only meet those befuddled by power and crazed by the desire for riches and of course the army, trained over many years to be harsh and pitiless, dry-eyed as they destroy.

'Your task here in the city will be difficult, because Satan now sees you as the greatest threat. You have Simeon, Jude, and some very experienced supporters. As well as that, your talks on the Temple steps are bringing the people to a greater understanding. So try not to worry. You will protect Jerusalem.'

James looked up and nodded, hoping he was right. Then another thought struck him. 'John, my brothers and I never thanked you adequately for everything you've done for Mama. We knew how ill she was, and I was so torn, my responsibility to the people and Jerusalem, as well as to my mother.'

His cousin interrupted. 'Don't say another word. Thank the Father for the dream that warned you to send her away. They would have killed her, James. She was a unifying force, both for the family and the Nazoraeans. If they'd succeeded in eliminating her, we wouldn't be such a threat. We did the right thing. We got her away in time.'

'And now you must take her away again.' He turned to his brother. 'Send for Hannah, Jude.'

'I'll arrange it tomorrow. She might return with Simeon.'

It was the beginning. Over the next days, old friends came to meet Mary and John and discuss the plans to disperse into the Empire. Gradually, groups formed with destinations assigned. And as the angel's message spread more widely, others came forward, asking to be trained and sent into the cities of the world to prepare the way for the coming of the kingdom.

It was an exciting time, but James made sure they proceeded slowly. Outside the leaders, only a small number could claim sufficient experience to exorcise or hold an evil spirit, and these became core members of potential groups who might go abroad. The newest exorcists were chosen carefully from those with appropriate ability and a calm, stable temperament. They needed time to expand their skills, as they would be far away in a strange land, and if they made mistakes, they had little help.

The leaders finally decided to make the following year a period of training and consolidation. Nevertheless, only those who displayed consistent competence would be allowed to venture away from home.

The return of Simeon gave his mother immense joy. A big, solid man not unlike Yeshu in stature, although a little heavier and shorter, he had a square, clean-shaven face with short, dark, curly hair, kindly brown eyes, and a loving smile. He hadn't taken Nazrite vows or married but followed the ancient Nazoraean traditions faithfully and supported his eldest brother with a steadfast, unobtrusive conviction. In many ways, he became the solid centre of the family after his father's and Yeshu's deaths and never wavered in his belief that their path led to the Father.

Where James was an incisive, spiritual thinker and charismatic leader, Simeon stayed in the background, quiet and thoughtful, deeply concerned with humanity and its relationship with the Holy One. Mary teased him and called him her philosopher, but she recognised in him a character so much like Joseph's, intelligent, solid, and dependable, a safe anchor in a sea of storms.

He arrived after sunset, just as they were sitting down for their evening meal. Dropping his bag and staff by the door, he strode quickly to Mary's chair, pulled up a stool beside her, looked into her delighted eyes, and took her hands. He searched her face but showed no signs of shock at her obvious condition. The messenger from James met him on the road and told him of his mother's arrival and illness. Having come too far to return to Perea, he sent Ephraim on to Hannah and asked him to bring her back with him to Jerusalem.

Ruth prepared a place for him. He was glad to join them,

as he'd walked since dawn and eaten only lightly at noon. He questioned them about Ephesus and they spent a pleasant, few hours discussing their adventures, especially how they built the lovely, little house on the mountain where his mama regained her soul.

When they mentioned the angel's message, he simply smiled, more interested in their experiences at sea and how did his cousin find sailing such a heavy ship. He introduced a lightness to the table, missing in recent days, and when the others noted Mary's laughter they followed his example.

Eventually she tired, and he brought her to her room, staying until Ruth came to help her undress. He kissed her goodnight and promised to look in later. She smiled, happy to see him so well and strong. Their connection had always been deep, their love embellished by solid, mutual admiration.

My beloved boy.

In the living room, the conversation sobered. Simon asked about her physical condition and the arrangements for her care. He admitted his shock at her deterioration and listened to the messages from Joseph and Yeshu, especially his brother's wish for her to return to the north.

'I hoped she was back for good, but no doubt he's right. He usually is,' he said with a rueful grin. 'She might be safer there, and her work on the mountain will give her focus and satisfaction.'

He read the angel's message and pondered their decision to form groups for the cities of the Empire.

'The future drive is definitely away from the centre, even though we know the attacks will concentrate here, especially on the Temple. I wonder why they're doing this?'

James listened with interest and a deep respect for Simeon's intellect. 'What's worrying you?'

'I can't pinpoint it. I'll have to think it through. It's connected with Mama's belief it would be two thousand years before they try again, yet they're sending us out into other lands. I don't understand it.'

'Do you think Mary's original information came from the entity?'

'No, John. I don't. Why then did she sense it so strongly in Gibeon? Evil wouldn't penetrate to the platform. Either the Holy Presence or the angel would eliminate it. No, the two thousand years came with the message and confirmed what she already knew.

'And as we've learned from experience, her ability to receive instructions from the blessed realms is formidable. Her words must be evaluated carefully.'

He put down his cup and rubbed his eyes. 'I'm tired and probably not thinking too clearly. But this is what I don't understand; there are two distinct streams of information. First, we've weakened Satan and we must neutralise his close protectors so we can possibly elevate him. Secondly, evil will last for another two thousand years when Yeshu will come back and finish it. Can both be true? Where are we?'

James regarded his brother and grinned. 'Just when we thought we knew what we were doing. But you're right. The two ideas contradict one another.'

'And here's something else to think about. We Nazoraeans inherited the Creator's promise to end evil. The benefits would then go to everyone, the Gentiles as well as us.'

'Yes, but we didn't end the epoch of iniquity. When we do, the advantages will go to them automatically.'

'I know that. But why can't we give them the knowledge of love and kindness? Look at the message. It doesn't say: "Go out and save your people". It says: "Go out and save your world".

'Our new task might be more difficult than we think. The Father is a father to all. We are simply the carriers of the wisdom. Do we let them continue in their ignorance for another two thousand years? I have the feeling it was their future suffering that left Mama so distraught after Yeshu's death. It was all too much for her.'

James stared at his brother. 'What do you think, John? You have more experience of other nations than any of us.'

'I don't know what to say. I agree with Simeon that the potential pain and torment for the peoples of the world did overwhelm Mary with grief. Working with them directly would be a very, different proposition. I've met some God-fearers in the synagogues of Ephesus and Sardis, but I wouldn't want to deal with them on a regular basis. I don't know enough about them, how they think or what they believe.'

Simeon broke in. 'Let's forget it for the moment. We have time to consider our options. I definitely need to rest, and I want to see Mama before she falls asleep.'

He rose, picked up his bag at the door, and went out the back.

James laughed. 'Trust him to upset everything.'

John grinned. He was sure they would find an answer. The continual input of new ideas exhilarated him, reminding him of the years with Yeshu. He began to clear the table while his cousin went out to check on the animals and bar the courtyard door for the night.

A few days later Ephraim arrived back without Hannah. Little Joses was ill, although not seriously. Once he recovered and Isaac's mother came to look after the household, she promised to be on the road. The news disappointed Mary, but she put it behind her and concentrated on her physical recovery.

Over the following weeks she improved steadily, and by the Feast of Hanukkah she was strong enough to go to the Temple. At the Nicanor Gate, James helped her give her offerings to the Levite, and with Ruth, she entered the Women's Gallery to watch the sacrifices.

The white and gold towers glowed and sparkled in the late-afternoon sunlight. Smoke rose from below where the priests toiled silently, preparing the meats, depositing the fats, pouring the blood on the sacrificial altar that stood before the magnificent, golden door of the Holy Sanctuary.

She remembered when she first came with her mother and father and how, over the years, they dutifully followed the traditions of her people, coming to Jerusalem for the festivals, the centre of their devotion to the Most High, a time of holiday and celebration. Here, as a young girl, she first sensed the power of the Creator, His loving Presence all around her.

And she was here in the Gallery when she so sincerely consecrated her life to His service, a dedication that led to the angel and Yeshu, to a life of joy as well as the inevitable pain and despair. Yet her troubles and sorrows were no worse than those of so many others in the land, and she put them firmly from her mind, thanking the Most High for all the times of happiness.

Joseph and she brought the children to the Sanctuary and watched with pride their growth into maturity. Yeshu inherited the love of the holy place and it became the vibrant living core and power source of the work to eliminate evil. This visit would be her last. She would never return, no longer capable physically. Even so, she was content. To the best of her ability she had fulfilled the promise she made to the Holy One all those years ago, and in the depths of her soul she was satisfied.

However, the journey to and from the Temple drained Mary's reserves of strength, and she collapsed on the way home. Simeon pulled her from the saddle and carried her up the steep streets into the courtyard while Jude ran for Jacob.

She lay on her bed, her face white and strained, her breath rasping. Simeon supported her head and shoulders as Ruth spooned a few drops of the herbal liquid into her mouth. Gradually, a slight wash of pink began to tinge her blue lips. Ruth prepared her for bed, and she lay there unable to move. Only her eyes acknowledged her friend's care and tried to smile her appreciation.

When Jacob arrived, he confirmed the further deterioration and prescribed a sleeping draught to give her complete rest. He could do nothing more, except advise them to let her sleep as much as possible over the next two to three days. It was now in the hands of the Father. Jude went for Andrew, the healer, and Simeon decided to go for Hannah.

For several days she hovered between life and death. The herbalist attended regularly, admitted the situation was beyond him, and healing from Andrew made little difference. Jude inspected the family tomb and prepared it.

On the third evening, Hannah arrived to find the streets and courtyard filled with friends, neighbours, and many of Yeshu's followers. She pushed through, with Simeon behind her leading the donkey. Peter, Andrew, and Thomas sat at the living room table with the other leaders of the Nazoraeans. Ruth saw her and helped her through to where the family kept vigil beside her mother's bed.

When his sister entered, James rose and gave her his stool. She nodded to the others and settled on her seat as she gazed at the thin face in the white headdress, propped up against the pillows: the narrow, blue lips; the fluttering eyelids; the cold, delicate fingers and hands. She held them carefully in her own and tried to infuse them with warmth and life. Her mother was almost unrecognisable.

If only she'd managed to leave earlier, but Joses relapsed, and with Simeon's arrival she had to relinquish the sick child into the care of Isaac's mother. But she couldn't worry about that now. Her little boy would recover.

Jude stood at the foot of the bed where Simeon joined him, his eyes filling. John remained at the other side, opposite Hannah, finally beginning to accept that this was the end. She wouldn't return to Anatolia. He would miss her and wondered what his life would be like without her.

And then, in the depths of his misery, he sensed a familiar presence and heard a well-loved voice. 'Fear not.'

Mary shuddered and sudden colour flooded her face. She breathed deeply several times and opened her eyes to see her family all around her and her daughter gripping her hand. She smiled at them, held tightly to Hannah, and fell into a peaceful sleep. Shocked, they looked at each other, questioning, wondering.

'I'm sure I felt Yeshu,' John said, 'and he told me not to be afraid. They're helping her. She'll recover.'

James nodded. 'I definitely sensed his presence, but I didn't hear anything. Although I agree. The physical difference already is remarkable.'

'They want her to come back to Ephesus.'

'I know. She will leave us soon but at least not in death.'

Some hours later, she awoke, found Hannah's calm face before her and her delight overflowed in tears. She hadn't the strength to talk, but she listened to all the news of Isaac, the children, and her husband's very competent mother who would, no doubt, spoil them outrageously while their own mother was away in Jerusalem. Mary laughed and although Hannah amused and cajoled her, the extent of the deterioration gave her a jolt. She decided to stay as long as possible, certainly for a few weeks.

There followed a period of immense peace for Mary. Hannah's arrival made the difference. They spent time together, and her recovery progressed at a steady pace, as if her desire for life had returned; that reason to go on revitalised her body and health.

They talked long during the day and often into the night; the latest stories of the grandchildren, the cuts and bruises of the younger ones, the studies of the oldest, the very intelligent Natan, the lovable, funny Joses, and their hopes for their daughter Salome, growing up to be a beauty, although a handful, with a decided mind of her own.

Mary smiled with sympathy for the girl, remembering her own youthful determination, her iron will. Hannah was lucky; she had married a man who loved her dearly and was immensely proud of her and their children.

May the Holy One take care of them always.

The winter weeks passed quickly, and eventually Hannah had to return to Perea. Mary held her tightly in her arms, believing it unlikely they would see each other again. On the steps at the wooden door, her hands clenched at her breast, she watched as Simeon led the donkey down the street with her daughter on its back, until they disappeared around the corner into the valley that led south to the Gate of the Essenes.

31

A Mission to the Gentiles?

Spring came, and the Nazoraeans met regularly in the Essene synagogue or in James's house to prepare for the coming exodus. The brothers continued debating the angel's message without reaching a decision on the Gentiles, until one day Peter arrived at sunset, in time for the evening meal.

The family were discussing the proposed marriage between Jude's only daughter and a handsome young man whose parents had supported Yeshu throughout the troubled years. Pleased for her son and granddaughter, Mary listened although soon grew tired and rose to go to her room. Ruth followed; she no longer needed to help, but the women enjoyed their time together in the evenings, talking over the day's events and deciding the needs of the morrow.

In the living room, the conversation continued until Peter interrupted. 'I had a visitor, and I don't know what you'll think about it.'

James glanced at him, realising he had been unusually quiet throughout the evening. 'What's wrong?'

'I'm not sure. You remember some years ago when the high priests attacked us, a particularly obsessive man called Saul accused us of destroying the beliefs of our ancestors. He tried to stop us preaching in the Sanctuary.'

'How could I forget. He lashed out at me on the Temple steps and threw me headlong into the courtyard below. Luckily, it knocked me out and he thought I was dead. Otherwise, I think he would've come down and finished me.'

'I don't remember any of this,' John said, searching their faces. 'When did it happen?'

'It was sometime after you left with Mama,' Simeon said. 'James had a broken leg, and we managed to get him across the Jordan and north to Hannah. Quite a number of our friends came with us and travelled on to Batanea and the lands of Damascus.

'Jerusalem was a dangerous place for us at that time. We were still under attack and this man was prominent among the agitators. He was connected to the Herodians in some way, always with them. And then he disappeared. In fact, I thought he had died because the violence suddenly stopped.'

'Well, he is very much alive, and what's more, he wants to meet with you, James.'

Silence fell as they stared at Peter.

'Meet with me? Why? What does he want?'

'He says Yeshu is with him and he's been given a mission to teach the truth to the Gentiles. It sounds crazy, but I think you should see him. There is something about him. He's changed.'

Completely disconcerted, they looked at each other.

Eventually James asked, 'Do you believe him?'

'As I say, there's something about him. One minute I can sense Yeshu, and then he's gone. I don't like the man, but I can't dismiss him. If it is your brother, he wouldn't want us to ignore this.'

Simeon interrupted with decisiveness. 'Peter, start at the beginning. Tell us how you met this man, everything he said to you, why he believes Yeshu is with him, and what exactly is the task with the Gentiles.'

A strange tale followed about the troublemaker who once attempted to eliminate the followers and prevent the spread of their beliefs. That morning, one of the Nazoraeans came to Peter's home. A tired, travel-stained man from Arabia had approached him in the Temple court, saying he needed to see Peter and James, asking him to arrange a meeting. Thinking nothing of it, Peter went back with him to the Sanctuary, assuming the stranger was one of the many looking for information about Yeshu or someone in need of healing.

In the outer court, he approached the man sitting on the bench along the wall and immediately recognised the slight, thin, brown-clad figure with black, penetrating eyes and receding hairline. He spun around, seeking a way to escape, thinking he'd walked into a trap set by the high priests or Herodians.

Then his name rang out across the court, and something in the voice forced him to stop and turn, something familiar and well loved. For a moment he thought it was Yeshu and he stood transfixed, unable to move while the man walked towards him.

'I'm sorry, Peter. I didn't mean to frighten you. I can tell you recognise me, but I promise you, I am not the man you once knew. I am changed, and Yeshua ordered me to come to you and listen to your words.

'I was well versed in the details of his life and death in those days when I opposed you, although now I realise he came to save us, not destroy us. At the time I didn't understand, and it is my shame and regret that I tried to do you harm. I beg your forgiveness.

'He gave me a task to which I've promised my life. I will go to the Gentiles all over the world and teach them what he taught you: to love one another, to forgive one another, to treat each and every one they meet as brothers and sisters, children of the same Father in heaven. We don't have much time. I must work speedily, but before I begin I needed to come to you and to his brother, the one I attacked, and tell you of my task and mission.'

'To be honest, I didn't know how to react. He had a wild look about him, an overwhelming, almost obsessive determination that was frightening, but I recognised that look from the one I sometimes see in your own eyes, James,' Peter said with a grin that broadened with the answering glimmer of amusement on his friend's face. 'So I brought him home, fed him, and gave him a bed where he's sleeping at present. He knows I'm coming here, so now we must decide what to do.'

'What do you mean when you say you sensed Yeshu?'

'Not all the time, Simeon. It comes and goes. At times, I get the tingling effervescence of Yeshu's spirit and then the man is kindness itself. I would do anything he asks of me. Then, minutes later, Saul is back, and him I don't even like. It's hard to forget the lives he took, the people he destroyed. Even so, there is no doubt something happened to him.

'Apparently, after the attack in the Temple, when they thought you were dead, James, the high priests decided to round up the Nazoraeans, now without a leader. They didn't discover you were alive until later. But they were determined to take advantage of the situation and asked Saul to gather a group of his friends and follow you across the Jordan and north to the lands of Damascus.

'On the way, Yeshu came to him in a flash of light and asked him why he was trying to kill us. The encounter shocked him. It changed him. He says when the Lord is with him he understands everything clearly. Otherwise, he's as lost as a motherless child, bereft of knowledge and guidance. He realises he's done great harm and must strive for forgiveness. He hopes his spirit will come into balance if he applies himself to this task.'

Simeon was concerned for his brother's safety. 'Why does he want to see James?'

'James needs to know what Yeshu requires of Saul.'

'Perhaps you should go, brother. Do you want me to go with you?'

'I'm sorry, Simeon, but he only wants to meet James.'

Concern became real suspicion. 'Will he be in danger?'

'No. Don't worry about his physical safety. Something else is going on here.'

James arranged with Peter to meet at his home the following evening. They decided to say nothing to Mary until the situation was clearer. A strange story, intriguing; Simeon wondered if Saul could be the solution to his problem with the Gentiles.

Several hours after sunset, when his brother still hadn't returned, he and John left to wait at the end of the street and met James on the way. He said little as they walked home, asking them to leave the full discussion for the morrow as he wanted to involve his mother.

'Yes, Yeshu's spirit was with Saul intermittently, and I wonder if even he will be able to change the man. He is arrogant and argumentative in his inner essence and this side is blatantly obvious when Yeshu isn't with him. When he's present, the man is kindly and understanding. I found it difficult to cope with the competing personalities. I don't know how it's going to work. Let's not talk now. I'm tired and I'm going to bed.'

On the next afternoon after Ruth went home, Mary joined her family at the table and heard the story. She vividly remembered the violent firebrand who opposed them all those years ago and listened, amazed.

'Why speak to you, James?'

'Because Yeshu thought we should know what was happening, and Mama, there's no doubt he is with the man at times.'

'Yes, but he might be keeping him from doing you further harm. Does it necessarily mean he has a mission to the peoples?'

'That's what I'm trying to decide.'

'James, does it really matter?' Simeon asked. 'If he's prepared to go out and teach the Gentiles about loving one another, isn't that what we need?

'Let's think about it. The message tells us to weaken the evil in the world but it also says, "Send out your soldiers of loving kindness". Perhaps this is an extra method to be combined with what we've already planned. If we'd neutralised the realms of the damned, all would be different, but we've only taken the first step. As Mama's friend Rachel said, the world wasn't ready. The kingdom can't and won't be imposed on us. Humanity must agree to it, and that means not only us but all mankind, or at least enough to let the change happen.

'Now it's up to us to choose how to proceed. Our own efforts in weakening the other three Satanic protectors and neutralising the power of the temples might succeed. Satan might elevate. What if he doesn't? Preparing for the next attempt in two thousand years means instigating a change in humanity itself.

'The Romans desire for blood, death, and conquest must be dealt with, preferably from within. If Yeshu is using this man, then his choice is a clever one. He's familiar with the Gentiles in a way we Nazoraeans would never be. He understands them, and there is every possibility he will be effective, especially if he is as obsessive as Peter says.

'Think about it. His judgement was proven wrong. He called Yeshu a destroyer and now discovers he was sent by the Father. That's a difficult lesson for an arrogant man to accept. Yet he has done so and now follows Yeshu's guidance. I would help him if I were you, James. He won't be easy but definitely worth the effort.'

Mary listened to her philosopher and smiled. Although she disliked what she remembered of Saul, her son's arguments were convincing. 'What do you think, John?' she asked.

'I agree with Simeon. And if we do our work to neutralise the Empire's temples, it will give the concepts of loving kindness a better chance to spread among the peoples.

'James, tell me this. Do you intend teaching him the deeper knowledge of soul elevation?'

'No. Of that there is no question. He has blood on his hands. He must elevate himself before he can directly confront evil. And moderate the anger I sense within him. Part of me still wonders, with Mama, if Yeshu is trying to remove him so we can proceed with our own tasks.

'On the other hand, Simeon's point is compelling. Let's be honest; without Yeshu, we only have a very, slim chance of elevating the other guards. If we don't succeed, the decision to teach the benefits of loving kindness to the Gentiles might make all the difference in the future. It makes me think it could be the underlying reason why the blessed realms are sending some of us away from Jerusalem to deal with the temples. As you say John, neutralising them will help the spiritual evolvement of the nations.'

'Another question,' his cousin said. 'Will these Gentiles become God-fearers or Jews even?'

'Certainly not Jews. Why should they? Surely they only need to follow the laws of Noah. Our own laws don't apply to them. They were intended to set us apart, to show us how to protect ourselves from evil, to strengthen our focus on the task to neutralise corruption. The Noahide Laws apply to all mankind. Nothing more is needed.'[15]

The discussion continued, but Mary began to tire. John helped her to her room and promised to tell her all later. She lay down, pulled her mother's coverlet up around her, and within minutes was asleep.

In the living room they talked long into the night. They would support Saul's venture and finalised what knowledge and advice should be given to help him.

During his time in the city, James went to see him on several occasions, answering his questions, teaching him what he could, and finding Yeshu's influence quite strong at times. They finally parted on good terms, and John turned to organise the departure for Ephesus. They would leave after the feast of Pentecost.

---

[15] AccordIng to the Jewish Talmud, the Seven Noahide Laws are a binding set of laws given to Noah by God for all humanity. They are: 1. Not to worship idols. 2. Not to curse God. 3. Not to commit murder. 4. Not to commit adultery, bestiality or sexual immorality. 5. Not to steal. 6. Not to eat flesh torn from a living animal. 7. To establish courts of justice. Non-Jews who follow the laws are known as Righteous Gentiles.

PART 5

Back to the Mountain

32

Present Day: North West London

The promised Indian meal, with lots of poppadums, arrived with Josh at 6pm. Exhausted after days of marking papers and overseeing exams, he sat heavily at the table with Jean, glad to relax for the weekend. Another two weeks before college broke up for the summer. No, they hadn't decided, as yet, where to go, but he would love to spend some time at the Kinneret.

In the kitchen, Cathrina's ears pricked up. Fantastic. She would love to see the finds from the Mount Carmel caves: some very early discoveries; archaic *Homo sapiens* and Neanderthal burials with evidence of rituals; continuous habitation from Palaeolithic through to the Neolithic and animal domestication. Phenomenal excavations.

She'd have a chat with her former archaeology professor and find out who they knew at Haifa University, see if she could organise contacts in Israel before the end of term. Grinning, she carried in the plates and cutlery.

Half an hour later, Josh appeared more relaxed and rested. They cleared the table, made a fresh pot of tea, found some mugs, and settled back to hear the final part of the research.

'Where did you get to? Did I miss anything?'

'Nothing you haven't heard already. I promised not to start

on Paul until you arrived. That's the next bit. Before we deal with him, I want to brief you on the Revolt and how it affected the Nazoraeans, or the Jewish Christians, as they were called in later years.

'James was stoned to death in 62 CE. The Jewish Revolt against Rome that had simmered under oppression for so many years finally exploded in 66 CE. By the year 70, the Holy City was destroyed, with hardly a stone left standing, the Sanctuary of the One God burned to the ground, the treasures stolen, the gold and precious objects melted down and used to build that malevolent altar of torture and martyrdom, the Colosseum in Rome.

'Before the conflagration, an "oracle" warned the followers and some escaped to Pella of Perea on the other side of the Jordan, but so many of those who had listened to Jesus and James died of starvation during the siege of Jerusalem or were slaughtered in the fighting. In the scorched-earth campaign of the north, the Sea of Galilee ran red with the blood of the fisherman butchered by Titus, Vespasian's son, and by Agrippa II, the Herodian king of Galilee.

'Altogether around one million Jews died and a further ninety-seven thousand were scattered as slaves to the four corners of the Empire, their descendants only recently able to return home.

'This changed everything. If the Jesus movement in its original format and ascetic ideology ever had a chance of surviving outside Judaea, the Revolt and the destruction of Jerusalem nullified that hope. The Gentile Christian Church side-lined Nazoraean beliefs. James is almost unknown, and much of their knowledge is buried and forgotten.

'Yet I have to wonder: had there really been any possibility of success in the imperial world of the day? Remaining emphatically within Judaism and a rigorously, righteous sect, they were respected and popular among the people. They believed in the One God, the Great Creator, not the multiple superhuman beings that thronged Rome's pantheon.

'More importantly, their declared philosophy of "loving one's neighbour" totally opposed the underlying imperial drive, the ruthless desire to control and exploit other peoples. To the Nazoraeans, Rome belonged to the Evil One, his active agent in this world, and it was their declared intention to neutralise him.

'What they believed was this: if they succeeded in establishing the kingdom of heaven, the Empire would in time become irrelevant. The hunger for military control of immense swathes of the earth would slowly diminish, the lust for riches eventually replaced by cooperation among peoples and a willingness to eliminate the sufferings of mankind. Although spiritual ignorance and lack of understanding would remain, harmful acts would gradually lose the sharp, vicious edge of malice. Concern for one another would begin to grow.

'Such an idealistic future and one that didn't materialise, their leaders destroyed: Jesus crucified as "King of the Jews", James the Just stoned by a high priest and a Herodian king.

'In the spiritual battle between the opposing sides, Rome won the day. They annihilated the first base of Christianity, their numbers decimated by the Roman terror. Few survived to impact the future growth of the new religion. Their descendants emigrated into present day Syria and Iraq to influence Islam. The Ebionites and other groups revered Jesus as a prophet and James as a righteous man, all of them inevitably declared heretical by the successful Gentile Christian Church.

'Fortunately, the sayings of Jesus were remembered and recorded. The authentic teachings of care and compassion, as in the parables and the Sermon on the Mount, came down through the centuries. The Lord's Prayer speaks of the hope for the coming of the kingdom, that the will of the Most High would supplant the will of Satan and the rule of evil would end, although few today would understand the original message. As John said to Mary: not all was lost. Enough survived to teach us the essential lessons of loving kindness.'

'So you're saying a lot of their ideas died out,' Jean said.

'Partially yes. Yet this is where it gets interesting, although it took me a while to understand. I thought through the Koressos visions again and connected them with the parable of the weeds. They all point in the same direction.

'The initial plan to neutralise Satan could work through Judaism. Here you have a people who fervently worshipped the Creator, a monotheistic religion that already separated good from evil and had, through their prophets, a deep understanding of how to avoid spiritual contamination as indicated by their purity laws. The ideal, if not the only nation at the time that was capable of helping Jesus to carry out his task, especially if we are right about the connection between his work and the Temple.

'However, once the plan for Judaism failed another one replaced it, this time a long-term one with two parts: the direction taken by the surviving Jewish Christians and the path that led Paul to initiate Gentile Christianity.

'Let's consider the Nazoraeans first. In my vision John said, "Be happy that at least the knowledge came to some of us. Our new task is to pass it to the enemy and therefore weaken him. We must retrieve what we can from the wreckage. Not all is lost". The "enemy" had to be Satan and the "knowledge" refers to the concept that love and compassion neutralises evil.

'They needed to degrade the support around Satan and that meant elevating the idols in the temples of the Empire. The early

Church writers tell us that missionaries went out from Mount Sion to Rome, Alexandria, Athens, Carthage, and the cities of Roman Asia.'

'If I could interrupt here, Cathrina. It's interesting you should mention temples. In the 1980s we worked on a project in Greece and during some free-time the Guide suggested we examine local temple ruins and evaluate their spiritual condition. In some cases the altars held severe desecration with souls at a lower animal level, very far down. We also found traces of human sacrifice. We cleared several sites but with enormous difficulty.

'Work like that would produce valuable results for the Nazoraeans. It would raise the spiritual condition of that particular city and the effects would extend outwards to cover a vast surrounding area.'

'This reminds me of something strange that happened in Ephesus, Jean. When we visited the site of the Temple of Artemis, it was spiritually clear, no heavy vibes. I even felt tingles there.

'A few days later we left the main ruins to explore the site of the original city. Ephesus was moved in ancient times when the river brought down silt from the highlands and blocked the harbour. We climbed the Acropolis of the first city where they sacrificed during the foundation ceremonies, and something truly horrendous remains there. I was physically very ill, and if Josh hadn't been with me, I might have been in serious trouble. It took days to recover.'

'God only knows what happened there, Cathrina. It's heartbreaking to realise that if humans were sacrificed, perhaps war prisoners, their souls are still trapped there and will remain so until the hill is cleansed.'

'Why wasn't the Artemision as bad?'

'Evidence, perhaps, that John and Mary cleared the temples.

But if they did, they missed the Acropolis. We'll never know. And the problem is, these ancient sites continue to affect sensitive people today, tourists as well as locals. Anyway, sorry to interrupt. Please go on.'

'This is where Paul comes in. We learn from his own writings and from Acts that the Nazoraeans gave him some training. Even so, I didn't understand how he fitted into the picture until I read his letters and discovered he had at least one mystical experience. His chapters on love are typical of someone who directly sensed the overwhelming sympathy and compassion that is the essence of the Supreme Being, the Great Creator.

'Paul is a controversial figure, particularly today, and I must admit I didn't much like him at first. Arrogant and bad-tempered, a man quite prepared to use or condone violence for his own ends, as evidenced by his attempts to destroy the Jesus-followers.

'We can deduce from his writings, however, that he gradually changed after his encounter on the road to Damascus, although the transition wasn't immediate. His dogmatic conceit is still obvious in his clashes with Peter and others, but over time, presumably through the influence of Jesus, he begins to show some appreciation of contrary views, a greater humility.

'Much of what we know about him is based on his written communications, even though he only wrote seven of the thirteen letters attributed to him. And some of these have later insertions from conservative followers, who voice the usual Roman need to keep women in their place—and especially after the Revolt, to abhor the rebellious Jews and all their practices.

'When Paul, who was proud of his heritage, talks about "my own people", that section is probably authentic, even if he disagrees with other Jews as he so often does. The use of the term "the Jews" requires one to question the identity of the writer.

'And rather than denigrate the spiritual capacities of women, we should remember he worked with Phoebe and Thecla on equal and respectful terms. Some of his followers changed the writings to protect conservative Roman ideas rather than allow his more liberal approach.

'He claimed Jesus was with him, influencing him and eventually, as I learned more of the real man, especially the later one, I believed him. Through him, the core knowledge of love and kindness filtered into the Roman world, quietly, carefully, like a slow rising tide that would flood the shores of the earth.

'The pure teachings, as lived by the Movement in Judaea, would never have survived in the Greco-Roman world, especially after the Revolt, and in reality I don't think they were expected to do so. They were intended to help end the rule of evil, but the failure required a different approach for the future.

'The beliefs and precepts that evolved during Paul's missionary journeys were culturally more attuned to the Gentiles, more sympathetic to their way of life. When combined with the later gospels, enough of the "pure teachings", the concepts of compassion and concern for one's fellow man, interlaced the other Hellenistic ideas. In time, the yeast permeated the dough, the message so successful we now firmly believe that Jesus brought the principle of love your neighbour into our civilisation.

'Slowly the Empire absorbed the lessons, although it didn't change overnight. At first, it persecuted the new faith that mesmerised the Roman people, especially Roman women, with notions of charity and care for others. Yet within three hundred years, Christianity became the preferred belief system.

'Constantine saw a cross over the sun before a battle and believed Jesus gave him the victory, a rather surprising gift from the peaceful, nonviolent Saviour. However, it was enough for the emperor who saw an opportunity to use the religion as a means of control over the many races populating his dominions. But he soon discovered an explosion of diverging paths within the evolving religion that created more division than unity.

'As with ancient Judaism, many streams flowed from the source of Christianity, with one important difference. Judaism, in the Second Temple era, accepted discussion and nonconformity. The concept of heresy didn't develop until later. The various sects, although they argued and sometimes detested each other, were essentially brothers.

'In the new western religion, this liberality was unacceptable. The Emperor engaged the full, military weight of the Empire to enforce conformity. The persecutions used by the pagans against the fledgling faith subsequently became, for Christian emperors, the preferred method they employed against those who disagreed with the declared orthodoxy. Unity, both secular and religious, was paramount. No room for descent. The result was lethal.

'Jews, Christians, Protestants, and Catholics all died in their turn. Four hundred years after his crucifixion, they were fighting to the death in the streets of Alexandria over whether Jesus was man or God.

'The history of our faith is one of violence, persecutions, and wars, much of it originating from our Roman Empire heritage. Our record isn't one of which we might be proud: the crusades; the years of European religious belligerence where each side fought in the name of Christ; the bloody Inquisition, which unbelievably is still in place although under a different name; the destruction of cultures with the excuse of spreading Christianity; the consistent two thousand year spread of a virulent, religious anti-Semitism that inevitably led to the gas chambers of the Holocaust.

'How far have we come in two thousand years? How successful was plan B?

'Today's ordinary man, with some obvious exceptions, doesn't exhibit the bloodlust prevalent among the Coliseum crowds, in the days of the Empire, and there is no doubt Christianity has contributed to a greater concern for our fellow man. In particular, the effects, over recent time, of Christian social teaching, gives me hope that plan B is proceeding in the desired direction.

'Released from temporal concerns by the unification of Italy and the loss of the Papal States, Leo XIII turned his mind to the conditions of working people, and his encyclical *Rerum Novarum*, *published* in 1891, created shockwaves when he condemned rich industrialists for treating their workers practically as slaves, "mere instruments for the unrestrained acquisition of profits".

'Other encyclicals followed over the last one hundred-plus years. Core principles emerged: a just wage, decent working conditions, ideas founded on the concept of the "common good", and strongly favoured by Aristotle, Augustine, and Aquinas. Over the years they evolved, at first intended for Catholics, until the charismatic John XXIII, through his *Pacem in Terra* in 1963 spoke to the world, "to all people of goodwill".

'The encyclicals challenged political opinion, influencing both left and right, certainly in Britain. The topics embraced "all those social conditions which favour the full development of human personality", according to John XXIII. They established concepts: the market can't work unchecked; the primacy of people over things, of labour over capital; the right of workers to join trade unions; the dignity of the individual; human rights; the dangers of unbridled capitalism.'

'New ways of thinking came forward for the undeveloped world: relief for third-world debt; everyone's right to affirm their own culture; economic justice is essential for peace; the differences between the northern and southern hemispheres; the indirect employer where the western consumer looks for something cheap; the misuse of the surplus wealth of rich countries directed into the arms trade while millions are hungry and destitute; and so forth.

'The ideas essentially examined modes of defence for the weak against the predations of the powerful, a goal Jesus would have approved. The Christian church is fulfilling, to a greater extent, its primary purpose to persuade people to care for our neighbours, our brothers and sisters.

'Nevertheless, even with the rise of democratic institutions, we still find the desire for empire in both the temporal and religious arenas, this feverish desire for power, the need to impose our will on others, to control their thoughts, actions, and beliefs.

'It is arrogant to think one's path is the only one. There are many roads into the realms of the Creator, multiple gates by which to enter, just as there are uncounted clans, tribes, peoples, and nations, each with their own traditions of living together on this earth.

'We can't tell whether more was expected of Christianity. The task, to root out evil and encourage genuine consideration for others, is difficult. If Mary is right, and another attempt is made to end the rule of evil in our time, we still have a long way to go.

'And then I remembered the parable of the weeds. An enemy comes in and sows weeds among the newly sown wheat. The servants ask if they should pull them out. But the landowner says, "No. Let them grow together. Otherwise, the good wheat will be pulled out with the weeds. At the time of the harvest, we will separate the good from the bad".

'Were the inauspicious beginnings of Gentile Christianity

only to be expected? The grain must swell, blossom, mature, and proliferate. The truths of love and compassion needed time to permeate the everyday thinking of human beings. But the big question still remains. Have we evolved enough to eliminate evil in our time?'

'Perhaps I can help here, Cathrina,' Jean said. 'Our Guides taught us that such transitions depend on timing, and one "spiritual year" has passed since Jesus walked the shores of the Sea of Galilee. Now is the opportune time to change, although it won't happen quickly. It will be gradual, our own age moving imperceptibly into the one to come.

'You might be surprised to know that the transformation began some years ago. As a race, we've already made important choices. In the 1980s we stepped back from the brink of all-out nuclear war, the destruction of our civilisation, if not our species, and the prospect of enormous parts of the earth being left uninhabitable.

'And recently, we initiated efforts to control the manmade component of global warming in an attempt to protect our environment. Although, as we know, there are still those in positions of political power who try to obstruct this new thinking, especially if it interferes with their plans to attain further material riches. Unfortunately, they have little interest in the welfare of the generations to come.

'There is also considerable evidence that we are more compassionate towards our fellow man. Even the violent fundamentalism that regularly flashes across our TV screens involves a small minority of our world population and will gradually die away.

'Much can be attributed to the ease of communication and the speed with which information and ideas spread. Something happens on the other side of the world, and within a few minutes, we learn of it. Through TV, travel, and the Internet, we absorb knowledge and understanding of other people, their customs, and their way of life.

'This stimulates the growth of sympathy and a stronger desire to give aid when a natural disaster occurs, like the Boxing Day tsunami or the Ebola outbreak in West Africa. Today's disastrous and ongoing Covid pandemic has abolished, forever, the notion that we are separate entities, either as individuals or nations. We are interlaced and interdependent, and what affects one affects all of us. We need to learn how to care for each other.

'As for Satan, men and women of spiritual courage will inevitably continue the work Jesus began when he saved desecrated souls in Judaea. Gradually, the lower realms will empty. Satan will be isolated, his armour of malice and hostility will evaporate, and he will elevate. But this is only part of the story. All humanity is involved. Must be involved.

'While in our pre-human animal state, we proto-humans, like all other animals, evolved within a group soul. We experienced our first major transition when we reached the point of reflection, when we thought about ourselves, our actions, and used these reflections to decide a future course. We had acquired intellectual freedom of choice, options apart from the dictates of purely instinctive behaviour.

'Through evolution we became a different entity. From our group soul or group consciousness, we individuated into separate spiritual beings, newborn and fragile, but still the most advanced living species on Earth.

'Satan is a product of that transition, a man of phenomenal powers but impelled, in the infancy of his spirit, by instinctual drives. His continued presence among us helped speed our own evolvement, because we learn more quickly and deeply through suffering. Unfortunately, he will stay with us, in his unrealised state, until we neutralise the malice and hostility that he and his followers disseminate throughout humanity. The future of our species and our world is in our own hands. It's up to us. To succeed, in fact to survive, we must deliberately choose to encourage the transition into a kinder, caring world.

'It brings us back to the physical effects of concentrated minds. Human thought can modify material reality. Concentrated minds can change the world. The only thing holding us back is the negativity arising from greed, hatred, and malice.

'The Great Creator said the Word and the universe came into being. At the core of each of us dwells a spark of the Creator. We, as a species, through concentrated thought, can recreate the earth. We are not simply passive observers. We participate in our own evolution and that of the world around us.

'Within us lies phenomenal potential. As Jesus told us, we could move mountains if we truly wished to, and our scientists tell us we only use a small proportion of our brain. Yet so much of our energy and strength is wasted, either in our attempts to destroy others or in their attempts to defend themselves against our attack, against our anger and malice.

'Imagine our lives if that power was released for a life without limits or fear. Think of our children, our grandchildren and the generations coming after them. What would happen to them if we deepened the pool of loving kindness in our world?

'This time, however, our power won't be directed through one magnificent, though vulnerable, white and golden Holy Sanctuary on a hill in Jerusalem. It will rise from millions upon millions of humble and loving homes, from chapels, churches, synagogues, mosques, cathedrals, and temples.

Our love will ascend to the Great Creator from all over the

earth, a store of pure light to be redirected to save humanity, as Jesus and his followers tried to do two thousand years ago, a treasury of purest gold to bring in the kingdom of heaven, to pave the road to the brotherhood of man.

33

Jerusalem: A Parting

On the feast of Pentecost, the Nazoraeans of Jerusalem assembled, and Mary said final farewells to many old and dear friends.

Arrangements for the voyage to Ephesus were complete, and they spent the last few weeks quietly as the family gathered around her. James and Simeon sat with her at the big table, talking, laughing, remembering. Jude, with his wife and children, came most days, and in the final week, Hannah arrived with Isaac and their three oldest.

When Mary saw the steady, serious Natan, his resemblance to Yeshu at the same age filled her eyes with tears, and the boy regarded her with careful interest, this grandmother who had spoken to a real angel, a messenger of the Most High. He questioned her assiduously during the days that followed, drinking in the knowledge, his intelligence and maturity filling her with delight and pride.

The lovable Joses was so different, full of laughter and fun. He climbed all over her, up onto her knees and into her arms, chattering endlessly. His mother tried to take him away, thinking him too boisterous, but Mary stopped her.

'Leave him. Let him stay.'

She found her granddaughter utterly adorable, as well as

beautiful, and asked Hannah not to be too hard on her. Her daughter laughed, admitting she spoiled the child dreadfully. Salome was fascinated by this tiny little lady who had accomplished so much and travelled so far. She wanted to be exactly like her when she grew up and was heartbroken when they had to return to Perea, tears streaming from her lovely dark eyes.

Mary was careful. She kept herself strictly under control and didn't allow the inevitable grief to affect her health. Having made a promise to go back to the mountain, she wouldn't let anything stop her.

On the final morning, the family walked down the steep street to where the mule cart waited in the valley below, the baggage already packed. Mary went to James and held him for a long time. She kissed him and searched his tear-filled eyes.

'God bless you, my beloved James. May the Father always care for you and guide you.'

Turning to the inconsolable Jude, she wrapped her arms tightly around him, whispering words of love and comfort until he mastered his distress. Then she blessed him and kissed him farewell. Simeon lifted her up into her seat and joined her on the other side. John followed.

Once again, she waved goodbye to those she loved until the cart went through the Gate of the Essenes, and they were finally lost to her. Yet her eyes were dry. In her mind she'd said her farewells some days before, determined not to destroy her last sights of Jerusalem with unnecessary tears.

She examined everything around her, the defensive walls, the sturdy lookout towers, the spring green of the gardens and meadows, the people walking, the children playing. And when they reached the hills to the north, she looked back as the sun sparkled on the white and golden Sanctuary.

'Goodbye, my Jerusalem, my Holy City. May the Father always guard and keep you.'

They spent a few hours with Hannah in Beth Horon, then pressed on for the pass. This time, it held no fears for her, although she admitted she found it a distressing, even malevolent place. She smiled when she climbed into a soft, comfortable bed that night in the lower village. Simeon observed her carefully the next morning, and after a late breakfast, they travelled on, stayed in Lydda that night, and knocked on Simon's door at noon the following day.

The ship hadn't arrived in port as yet. While Mary went to her room to rest, John helped his cousin with the animals and brought the baggage into the house, ready to be transferred to the *Galilee*. Looking forward to standing on her deck as they sailed north, he smiled. It was all so different to those days of fear when they fled Jerusalem, to face an unknown future in a strange land.

He was glad they'd come home. It confirmed his mission in Anatolia: examining the temples and elevating desecrated souls, work he loved. It would make such a difference to all who lived there. And for him the departure wasn't final. He would return, one day, to Judaea.

Mary's leaving was different. It meant farewell to both her family and the land. To his surprise, she appeared serene and content. During recent months she had grown strong mentally, and although her body weakened, she learned to cope better, to take care of herself physically and emotionally. He thought with a smile of the Jacobs; with the stock of drinks from the herbalist in Jerusalem and the attention of the physician in Ephesus, she might still live a long and peaceful life.

Simon arrived at dawn, and after an afternoon rest, Mary and her son spent the remainder of the day together, walking the cliffs behind the port, gazing over the waves. They found a rock and sat down to watch the blazing yellow sun dip into the coral, western sea. They talked of their hopes for the years ahead, not only for the work to eliminate evil, but their dreams for the family, her grandchildren, Simeon's nephews and nieces. What would the future hold for them in that tormented land?

Later that night, he came with them to the harbour and they said their last goodbyes on the dock. For Mary, however, the most enduring conversations occurred during those hours together on the heights as they watched the seas to the west. She went on board, found her old cabin prepared, and lay down on her bunk, feeling blessed in the love of her family.

Peaceful days followed, filled with contentment. The southern breezes blew strong, speeding them up the coast, and at night, as usual, they anchored in little coves, giving Amos the opportunity to show off his cooking. They bypassed Cyprus and wondered would they ever see Marcus again. After a quiet night in Rhodes, the *Galilee* surged on through green Aegean waters, almost home.

Mary relaxed in her usual berth at the stern and thought back over her life, amazed at all the twists and turns of fortune, the successes and failures, the joys and despair, everything leading to this final sea journey north.

Seven days after leaving Joppa, they entered the straits between Samos and Mycale. She searched the mountain until she found her ridge and then sat back, content, as the ship sailed on through the bay and into Ephesus harbour.

34

Home to Koressos

The Galileans waited on the dock, and soon afterwards, familiar mules trotted towards them. James had sighted the ship, with John at the helm, earlier in the bay and warned the synagogue president. A message was sent to Jacob.

Impatient, Martha jumped to the ground and ran to Mary, wrapping the tiny figure in her arms, lifting her off her feet. Joseph and Hannah came more sedately, smiling with quiet pleasure to find them all together again. They stowed the baskets and baggage in the mule cart, and the physician's wife invited everyone back, asking Simon to join them later, promising to send someone to collect him. He grinned and accepted, pleased to see how nicely his friends had settled into life in the city.

At Martha's, Mary went to rest, tired with excitement, and in the cool courtyard the others gathered at a table for snacks and cold drinks. When the servants left, John told the tale of their journey and Mary's physical collapse. Afterwards, the discussions centred on the angel's message and the man, Saul, who departed the Holy City with a mission to teach the concepts of loving kindness to the Gentiles.

The physician read and reread the scroll before passing it around. 'How do we fit into this?'

'Let me explain our thinking. It appears we didn't fail as badly as we thought. The Evil One is weakened and possibly injured. As you know, our most difficult elevation was the guard at the northern gate, one of his four protectors. That soul might still be elevated. We don't know. It was far too dangerous to examine him.

'Our friends in Jerusalem will continue with the other three guards, and groups are preparing to disperse throughout the Empire, to Rome, Alexandria, Greece, and even into Parthia. Other cities will be assigned when new workers become more experienced. We will concentrate on Anatolia.

'The entities in the temples receive worship from the peoples, and that power supports Satan, the source of his strength. The neutralisation of the temple gods will weaken the desecrated souls on the levels below them. That will have a debilitating effect downwards to his main guards. We hope to reach the stage that the three are sufficiently impaired for James to hold them for elevation.'

Jacob asked the question on all their minds. 'And if we don't succeed?'

'That's the real problem. Mary believes it will be two thousand years before the next attempt will be made. She first received this information when she had the entity. It came to her again with the message at Gibeon. We couldn't see how evil could penetrate the holy place; the upper vibrations are far too strong. So we believe she's correct. It was one of the reasons we supported Saul's venture with the Gentiles. If the temples are no longer centres of lower power, it will be much easier for loving kindness to spread.'

While Mary slept, they planned their campaign. As the apostle was the only one capable of obtaining the name from an evil spirit, he would go to the cities. The identified souls would be raised by the whole group back in Ephesus. He needed companions, however. They mustn't repeat the near disaster of the Artemision.

Smyrna was first on the list with the temples of Nemesis, Athena, and that of the Imperial cult, where they worshipped the goddess Roma and the 'genus' of the Emperor Augustus. Afterwards, a visit to Sardis to see Lucius and Esther. As Martha would stay on the mountain, Jacob offered to go with him.

James and Mathias would accompany him later to Pergamon, and Joseph and Hannah elected to make the third journey into the interior, to Laodicea and Philadelphia. They had contacts there in the synagogues.

By the time they finished and Mary joined them, Simon arrived. They settled down to a relaxed and enjoyable dinner that evening, and as she told John later, although she would miss her own family all the days of her life, she thanked the Father she still had these special friends.

The next morning they left for Koressos and arrived at Rachel's in the middle of the afternoon. As she had gone to market, Jacob brought them over to the valley. Susannah came to the door when she heard the commotion and ran to Mary with tears of delight. The two went inside, asking questions, telling the news, pleased to be back together.

Later, when his aunt grew tired and went to rest, John explained her condition to Susannah. It would be her responsibility, in the future, to watch for signs of strain when he was away. He would come up more often, and she should go to Rachel if she was worried. Enough of the herbal drink remained to last a few more weeks and then she would be in Jacob's care. Poor Susannah. For a moment, fear overwhelmed her, but her common sense prevailed as she remembered how her father suffered in a similar manner. She asked him to let her speak to the physician, and he promised to arrange it.

When Rachel returned from market and found her home invaded, she called over to invite them to dinner. Mary was sleeping, so John walked back with her to the farm where Jacob and Martha were already installed on the terrace with a jug of Rhodian wine and a table covered with appetising food.

The story of Mary's illness and the rest of the news from Jerusalem was told once more: the angel's message, the groups dispersing throughout the Empire, the mission to the Gentiles.

Rachel sat quietly, absorbing all the details, envisaging the panoramic organisation of the various branches of activity. 'I presume Saul's work will be of major importance if James doesn't succeed with the guards.'

'They are very powerful, Rachel. You remember the entity with Mary, the one you confronted at the pool. These evil spirits are on the same level and I don't envy him trying to hold one of them. And he has to deal with three.

'Then there's Saul: even before he contacted us, Simeon thought we should do something about the nations. He was concerned with the suffering they will endure if we are forced to wait another two thousand years. He believed the knowledge of loving kindness would help them, as well as making it more likely that the next attempt succeeds. Obviously, Yeshu agreed with him.

'We might still be successful, but if we are not, any work we accomplish now will make a difference in the future. The temples are always in major cities, contaminating everyone who lives there, and at least we can neutralise that desecration in Anatolia. Our work will be difficult and dangerous. It's important we remain strong and disciplined. I'm glad we have each other. We're a very solid group.

'I have to admit I feel great sympathy for Saul. He's on his own, at the moment, with an enormous task ahead of him. Although he's a Jew, he's familiar with the Gentiles and knows how they think. Peter and James told us of an impenetrable toughness around his spirit, possibly the result of his more violent past. It may help him survive initially, but I hope, for his own sake, it dissolves. It won't be an easy path for him.

'Our own task is very different. We are the sons and daughters of Light and we will directly confront the darkness in the realms of the damned. Perhaps in years to come, battalions of holy Gentiles will join us in projecting the power of love and compassion to eliminate evil forever. As the angel told us, the kingdom will not be forced on us. We must choose it freely and with all our hearts.'

Within days Mary recovered most of her strength and experienced the deeper benefits of her time at sea. She pottered around the house or ventured out into her gardens where flowers dressed trees and bushes, drenching the valley in perfume. The bees buzzed back and forth from bush to hive and honey was plentiful that summer. Her baby goats played at her feet in the cool of the evening, and when John carried her up to her pavilion overlooking the Aegean, she was in heaven itself.

Filled with peace and happiness, time slowed and almost stopped. On occasions, he glimpsed the sparkle in the air around her, and she emanated an effervescence he associated with the higher reaches of the blessed realms. Sometimes he wondered if her spirit was leaving, but her physical form remained solid, and when Jacob examined her, he told the apostle there was no need for concern. As long as she persevered with the herbs and didn't overstrain her heart, she would live for some years.

After a few weeks, the men returned to Ephesus, and over the summer, Mary strengthened into something like her former self. There were permanent changes, however: she was unable to walk too far, needed help to climb to the clifftop, could no longer do much housework, tired easily, and rested more often.

Yet her spiritual being was strong, happy to accept whatever the future might bring. Sometimes the holy ones surrounded her, although she didn't sense either Joseph or Yeshu, and she waited patiently to learn what she still had to do. By autumn she decided to begin the meetings again, ready to become involved once more.

While her friends were away, Rachel spent time in the city working with the others on elevations assigned to them by John and she progressed to a considerable level of competence. Her fears left her, dissipated by her success at the pool when she fought the entity for her friend's soul. With Mary's training, she advanced still further and they elevated some demanding souls.

Time passed slowly. John came up every Shabbat and stayed two days, often bringing James and Mathias with him, and on several occasions Joseph and Hannah came and stayed at the farm. They worked solidly throughout the winter months, and when spring came, he told them they were capable of dealing with whatever he identified in Smyrna.

And so began work which involved them for years to come. If the entity wasn't too strong, one or other of the groups conducted the elevation; for a powerful evil spirit, they gathered on the mountain and worked in Rachel's home.

John would bring his aunt over on the donkey, and her

companions watched and learned: her deft handling of the often violent and vicious entities who screamed filth and obscenities; her ability to persuade the soul to accept some little offering, the first step on the long road to recovery; her compassion and understanding for the one who had fallen.

They assimilated the techniques of soul elevation, but mostly they recognised how consistent, quiet kindness and powerful love can disarm even the greatest evil. The lessons deepened their experience and confidence. She became the calm centre of their activity especially on the mountain where a strong nucleus of Jewish families protected and sheltered her, sensing the blessing of her presence among them.

35

The Other James

Out in the orchard, Susannah searched for something tasty for the evening meal. Perhaps, after the sweltering day, they would eat in the pavilion and catch the cool breezes blowing in from the sea. With her basket filled with grapes, apricots, figs, and radishes, she returned to the house and heard voices and laughter in the distance. John she recognised but not his companion, and forgetting everything else, she ran to alert her mistress to visitors.

With only moments to splash water on her face and adjust her veil, Mary came to listen. Her face creased in delight. He was home and safe. She rushed down the path to wrap her other nephew tightly in her arms.

'James. Thanks be to the Most High.'

He had arrived on the *Galilee* at dawn and planned to stay a few months, at least until Simon returned. And that evening, when Mary watched the two together, she was so happy for them. Although John rarely mentioned him, she knew how much he missed his brother.

Slight and elegant in a short, Greek-style tunic, he was clean-shaven with curls cropped to form a dark halo around his head. His eyes, large and nearly black, were usually crumpled in amusement, and the aquiline nose contributed to the distinction of his handsome face. Grief and the years, however, levied a tax. Grey hairs grew among the black curls and deep lines, around the mouth and eyes, spoke of suffering.

He told them some of the history of his voyage to the western Mediterranean but soon broke off, more interested in their own exploits. He'd heard most of the news coming up the hill and was aware of Mary's ongoing weakness, yet her spiritual condition amazed him, so elevated compared to the desperate, grieving woman in Jerusalem.

They stayed on Koressos for more than a month and gathered fruit and vegetables from the well-stocked garden. Drawn to his aunt like a child to his mother, he began to lose, in her warmth and sympathy, the crackling barrier of pain which surrounded him. She had always been a strong anchor in his life, one that was broken so tragically in the grief-stricken years after Yeshu's death and now, by some miracle, was here again in the need and dread of his adult years.

Both John and Mary realised something was terribly wrong, although neither spoke of it. On occasion, one caught the concern on the other's face and exchanged a glance of understanding; they recognised they mustn't push James too early. It would all come tumbling out in time.

He kept himself almost frenetically busy, either in the orchard cutting grass and pruning trees or, on his knees in the garden, hoeing and weeding. And when he finished, he dragged his brother off to fish in the local streams or walked over to Reuben's to help on the farm, milking goats, collecting and stacking wood for the winter.

He grew fond of Rachel, spending afternoons on her terrace,

talking of his travels and listening to the story of Mary's arrival in the valley, the haven where she stopped her grieving, regained her equilibrium, and launched her spiritual group. He told the tales of his childhood, the exciting years of the work with Yeshu, and the heartbreaking horrors of the crucifixion. During this final revelation, tears rolled down his cheeks, sobs erupted, the racking pain, bottled up for so long, punctured his defences, and the festering wound burst at last.

Rachel ran to sit beside him and pulled him into her arms, as a mother would a beloved child. But his breakdown embarrassed him, and within moments he controlled his emotions and struggled out of her hold. Rising to his feet, he apologised and excused himself, striding quickly from the terrace.

She chewed her lips. *Oh dear. I handled that badly.*

Later in the afternoon, John called and she told him what happened.

'You did well to break through to him. We've known something was wrong, but he won't talk about it. Perhaps he will now. I'm sorry if he offended you.'

'Oh no. He didn't. I wanted to help and I tried too hard. I hope he won't be upset with me.'

'Don't even think about it, Rachel. Hopefully it's the very thing he needed. Thank you for your kindness to him. I'll find him.'

James wasn't at Mary's or Reuben's. Suddenly aware of where he might be, the apostle walked up to the pool. There he was, crouched by the water, his arms tightly wrapped around his legs, holding in all the horrors of his world.

John decided to force the issue if necessary. He went over, sat beside him, and waited.

'Is Rachel upset? I didn't mean to hurt her feelings.'

'Of course not. She was only concerned for you. What's wrong? Can you tell me? Let me help.' A long silence ensued.

'I had a dream about Mary when I was in Hispania. She said you were going home to Judaea.'

'Yes. You told me on our way up the mountain.'

'She said something else. She warned me not to go to Jerusalem. If I did I would face death. That was all. Just that I would face death.' A shudder went through him and a rasping wail erupted from the shaking, crouched body. All the fears and loneliness of the years away from home poured out in broken sobs.

John's mouth tightened. *All that suffering and he was on his own. Was that why he came back?*

He pulled his brother into his arms, holding him tight, rocking him back and forth until he quietened. He smoothed his curls, kissed his brow, and hoped the sharing of the burden would help him. What did it mean? Why had she given such a warning?

When James recovered, John asked him the questions on his mind.

'I don't know why I came home. I was so cut off with no contact. At least you had Simon, and having Mary was like bringing home with you. I reached the point where I couldn't stay away any longer. It's so difficult when you're on your own, with no one to talk to or remember like we do. I went among the Jews and the God-fearers, exorcising evil spirits, doing everything I could, yet I felt I had failed, even though the initial desire to go was so strong.

'Eventually, I had neither the strength or motivation to go on. I decided to come home. I was at the harbour, ready to board the ship the next morning, when I had the dream. I didn't want to go back, so I came to find you. When I arrived in Joppa, I waited for the captain, and he told me where you were and now I'm here.'

They sat silently for a while, John's arm around James's shoulder, hugging him close.

'Look, I'm glad I told you. The fear has gone. Whatever comes will come. I must put my trust in the Father and not worry about it. I can't live with the dread. It was destroying me.'

John examined his face, aware of the new sense of peace and an acceptance of what was to come. He would face the future with courage.

James stood and straightened, once more the big brother, full of determination and decision. 'Now tell me about your work on elevations and your new group. And I want to talk to you about the angel's message. Mary showed it to me. Have you decided how you will implement the instructions?'

The younger apostle grinned, glad to follow his brother's lead. He had already recounted briefly the near, disastrous confrontation with Artemis, but now told the story in much greater detail. The journey over the Tmolus followed, the possible formation of a group there, the elevations in the city and on the mountain. James listened with knowledgeable attention, asking pertinent questions as John explained.

'I've no interest in dealing directly with the Gentiles. We've met quite a few God-fearers, some with prominent positions locally. I'm sure the wisdom will spread through such as these.

'My work is among our own people. We've planned what to do in the immediate future. We'll go to the main cities in Anatolia, identify the strongest evil spirits at the temples, and raise them here in Ephesus. We've been to Smyrna twice now, once to get the names of the souls, and the second time to make sure the sites are cleared. The difference here is already noticeable.

'We next go to Hieropolis. Mathias is coming with me and we'll meet Lucius of Sardis there. He's friendly with the president of the synagogue and that should make it easier. There is so much to do, and that will be my future, the way I can be most effective.'

James smiled, impressed. 'Perhaps I should remain and help. I might like Ephesus.'

'Would you? Nothing would make me happier. You can stay with Mary or come down with me to the city. I usually come up for a few days around Shabbat. It would be like old times.'

His brother grinned. 'We'll see. Come on. Let's get back and find out what Susannah's cooking. I'm starving.'

The cloud of despair had dissipated. His old amusing self, he spent the evening discussing the plans for the Anatolian cities, and the next morning, he visited Rachel to explain, asking for nothing to be said, as yet, about the dream. They would tell Mary when the time was right.

Several days later they were relaxing after breakfast when Rachel called over with Jacob, Martha, and their daughters. Delighted greetings and kisses of welcome followed. James was introduced, stools found and the adults settled around the table chatting, while the girls went off with Susannah to see the latest donkey foal and the new kids, the sensible married Eliana as eager as her younger sister.

The visitors plied James with questions about Hispania and his years there. He was forthright about his perceived failure and listened carefully to the methods of healing, both spiritual and physical, they used in Ephesus, Sardis, and more recently in Smyrna.

Although a strong exorcist, he wasn't a healer, and he

wondered if that inability had hampered his activities in the west. The combination of exorcism, healing to the physical body with the medical attentions of a trained physician, struck him as a phenomenal integration, especially when followed by the elevation of the exorcised soul. He understood the value of the arrangement. If he found companions with the necessary gifts, he would return and try again. Where to find them was the question.

He decided that afternoon to remain and discover more about this method of working. If the Most High willed it, he would find a way to help the people of the west. He became a welcome and experienced addition to the group, and it gave Mary joy to have both her nephews with her, members of her own family as dear to her as her own children.

There were times, however, when a shadow passed over his face and she realised he hadn't found his place, as had his brother in Anatolia or her own sons in Judaea. He was unfulfilled. She watched and waited, in dread of something she couldn't explain, and when John asked her why she was so worried, she told him of her fears. He confessed the story of her warning in the dream but promised her that James was not going back to Jerusalem.

Understanding the reason for her misgivings, she was relieved, although she wished she could do more for him. She filled him with love and over the following months something settled within his soul, the restless unhappiness diminished, the empty void, carved during the long years of isolation, was replenished. The brother and aunt cared for him in their own special way, and eventually, the strong, determined man of his more youthful years returned to them.

The seasons passed. James made his decision to return to Hispania and begin again.

'You were going to find companions to go with you. Have you changed your mind?'

'I think so, John. Those I left behind will be enough for the moment. Your work here has been an inspiration. The way everything works together. I'll find others to help me. I'm a competent exorcist and I can train new people.

'What's more, I'm much stronger. Seeing Mary so happy has helped me deal with Yeshu's death. I couldn't do that until now. I'm at peace, and I feel I must go back and carry out the task he gave me. There'll be a connection for Hispania in Rhodes. If not there, Caesarea or Joppa. It's time for me to leave.'

Nothing was said to their aunt until Simon arrived a month later, and the brothers climbed Koressos to let James say his farewells. He went to see Rachel while John brought Mary up to the pavilion to tell her what was happening.

'He won't go to Jerusalem, will he?' she asked, tears in her eyes.

'No. He promised he wouldn't. He'll find a ship for the west. They are in and out of ports every day.'

When his brother arrived, John left them together and went to warn Susannah, hoping the parting wouldn't affect his aunt's health. When they walked down the valley the next day, a dry-eyed Mary stood at the gate watching until they were gone. She knew she would never see James again.

She tried to contain her emotions, but she feared for him, an invasive, irrational terror, unconnected with possible shipwrecks or drownings. As she couldn't identify or rationalise the source, neither was she able to brush it aside or soothe the sting by thinking it through. It burrowed deep within her and festered.

Dear Father, look after him. Take care of him.

Rachel came over later to find her in bed, white-faced and ill. She took her cold hands and held them tightly. 'You can't protect him forever, Mary. Whatever will happen, will happen. You can't prevent it. We don't know why you warned him. Perhaps the danger has already passed. But no matter what happens, you need to regain your connection with the Most High. Your fear will harm your nephew; it certainly won't help him. You must be strong now. Let your love and spiritual vitality pour into him and cast a cloak of protection around him. Forget your worries. Don't anticipate disaster or you'll bring it directly to him. Be careful, Mary.'

As she spoke, Mary's grip tightened. Her head fell back on the pillows, colour flooded her cheeks, and her breathing eased. Gradually she settled, the handhold slackened, and she slept. Her friend stayed a little longer to make sure and then rose and slipped from the room.

Later that evening, Mary awoke and lay thinking. Her fears had subsided. As Rachel, dear Rachel suggested, she pushed them firmly from her mind. There was nothing more she could do, and she gave her beloved nephew into the hands of the Holy One.

36

The Dream

Some weeks later, John and James left on a second journey to Hieropolis and afterwards crossed the mountain passes to follow the Hermus River to Sardis. They stayed two months with Lucius and Esther, and over three months passed before they returned to Ephesus, worn out yet happy with how much they'd accomplished.

John went to see Jacob and Martha; he immediately realised something was wrong. 'Is it Mary? Tell me.'

She took him by the arm and brought him to the stool at the table in the kitchen.

The physician sat beside him. 'It isn't your aunt. It's your brother, I'm afraid. Simon came. James went north to Bethsaida and was arrested. He's dead, my dear friend. I'm so sorry.'

John looked at him, his eyes wide, his mouth open, not believing what they told him, dazed. James dead? He couldn't be. What happened? Why did he go home?

His mind reeled, refusing to believe, knowing his only brother had gone, the shock leaving him sick and nauseated. 'Does Mary know?'

'No. That's your decision, what to tell her and how. We're heartbroken to bring you this news. Apparently there were no ships going west from Rhodes, even though they waited several days. So they went on to Joppa. Simon managed to arrange a passage with a captain he knew. As he had to leave first, your brother remained with Susannah. There was a week's delay, and he decided to hire a mule and ride up to Galilee. Agrippa's soldiers arrested him and took him to Jerusalem.

'He's not the only one they executed; others died too. Simeon, your cousin, came to the port with the news, hoping to find the captain. It was another month before Simon returned and discovered what happened. Mathias has letters explaining everything. I'm so sorry. We liked James very much. He was a good man.'

John tried to take it in. 'Did you know about the dream?'

'Rachel told us. I suppose he thought it would be safe to go north to the Lake.'

John's head dropped into his hands, his elbows on the kitchen table. Exhaustion left him bemused.

Remembering his collapse after the work on Artemis, the physician had a room prepared and gave his friend a mild sleeping draft, mixed into a cup of tirosh. Weak from the journey and shock, he lay on the bed and, within minutes, fell asleep. Later Jacob removed his tunic, pulled a light coverlet over him, and gave his clothes to a servant to wash, checking every few hours to make sure his sleep remained deep and natural.

When he woke the following evening, he tried to place the unfamiliar bedroom. Then the memories flooded back, and with them the heartache.

Acceptance had replaced the initial despair, bereavement a familiar companion: his mother's the greatest and most painful loss, followed soon after by that of his beloved wife and then

Zebedee. Years later he suffered through the capture and crucifixion of Yeshu and the destruction of other dear friends in the early years of persecution. Grief no longer touched him to the same extent.

He rose, washed his face and hands in a bowl of cold water, and found his garments draped over the couch. Taking them, he went out to the bathhouse and bathed until refreshed. He returned to his room and sat on the bed, wondering what he should do. No point in going to Jerusalem. Mary's sons would have claimed and buried his body, and furthermore, he couldn't judge what the situation would be like in the city. Better to wait and talk to Simon, take his advice.

Mary was the greater and more immediate problem; she would be heartbroken, as if she had lost another son. He would need Jacob to help with her physical condition.

Yet what disturbed him most of all was that he hadn't felt the loss. His brother was killed and he didn't hear the cry of his soul or sense his departure from this world. He felt nothing, knew nothing. James left without a sound, without any spiritual disturbance. Not even a whisper.

His head in his hands, he sat on the bed for a long time, simply sending his brother all his love, hoping he was safe. After a while, he glimpsed a sparkle of light, a glimmer of a smiling, well-loved face, and then the full-bodied effervescence of James's soul come to comfort the one he had left behind. Within moments, Yeshu followed to take him home again and reassure his cousin that all was well.

Although only for a moment, their presence give him deep and lasting peace. James had gone to the blessed realms of the Father, where John hoped one day to join him.

Later, as twilight approached, he went to find his friends in the garden. Martha jumped from her seat and ran to meet him, searching his face to see how he was. He smiled, and the peace emanating from him reassured her. She called a servant, arranged for a meal to be prepared, and asked for bread and olive oil to be brought immediately.

The physician examined him quietly, taking in his calm demeanour. Neither said much, the comfortable silence of close friends. Some hours later, the Galileans came and John read the letters, from Simeon and Simon, that explained the circumstances but gave no further information. They spent the evening remembering their time with James. It gave the apostle the opportunity to retell all their adventures and relive the memories of life in Galilee and the years working with Yeshu.

To the others, it was a chance to listen to the precious stories that would pass from generation to generation, tales of two brothers who followed and revered Yeshua, the Messenger of the Most High. Although initiated by grief, it was a magical night, full of knowledge and experience, a night that helped John say farewell to the brother he loved.

He didn't climb the mountain for several weeks, waiting until his self-control was stronger. Jacob and Martha came with him, arriving at Rachel's late one morning. They walked over to the valley, the four of them, and the physician brought his medicine bag with special herbs for the heart, just in case.

Mary was up in the pavilion, and they climbed the steps to find her sleeping peacefully in the shade. With their approach, she awoke and her eyes immediately searched John's.

'It's James, isn't it?' When he nodded, she reached up, and he fell to his knees by her side, sobbing into her lap. She smoothed his curls and tried to soothe him.

'I've known for a while. He came to me in a dream and told me to look after you. He was with Yeshu, so I realised he was gone. Don't tell me what happened. I don't want to know. It doesn't matter now. He's safe, and whatever was done to him physically, it hasn't harmed his soul. He was bright, cheerful, and strong.

'He said to tell you he would now do the work in Hispania that he planned with you. So don't be too unhappy. He has the chance to finish the task he began, not here on earth but in the blessed realms. From there, no doubt, he will influence and guide his friends in the west.'

Her demeanour helped compose him, and as he listened to her voice, remembering how much she loved his brother, he found a way to incorporate his loss. It penetrated his resistance, and he finally accepted it was over. He would never meet James again in this world, but like his beloved wife, he would find him in his dreams, and one day they would be together again.

Mary's calm and loving acceptance of the death amazed the others. She told them everything she recollected from the dream, but her perception that passing over was no more than walking from one room into another impressed them deeply. The evening in the clifftop pavilion became a peaceful gathering, and they spoke of James as if he was still with him, discussing the possibilities for his mission in Hispania.

And Rachel wasn't the only one who sensed the powerful effervescence or absorbed the love and care of the Holy Ones that surrounded them.

37

The Temple Priest

In the spring of her 64th year, Mary's last visitor arrived, Marcus of Cyprus, the benefactor of their initial journey north. It was Shabbat: her nephew was already in the valley, and James and Mathias were installed in their orchard tent. They intended staying for several days.

The Cypriot's visit was unexpected. He arrived at Rachel's with Jacob and Martha, having joined the *Galilee* in Paphos with the specific goal of seeing Mary and John. On docking, Simon hurried to the physician with a bitter story. His patron's son, Josephus, was knifed to death in Jerusalem, only a few months after his marriage to a beautiful young girl from the family of Ananus, the high priest. Marcus was ill and in despair.

He left immediately to collect his old friend, shocked at his deterioration. The self-satisfied hedonist, the apostle so accurately described, was no more. The man he met was a thin, strained, suffering stranger. His wife remained behind on the island to care for their other two sons, as well as the pregnant bride who had insisted on returning with them to her husband's birthplace.

Marcus was unable to settle back into the carefree life he enjoyed before the disaster, and the sight of his daughter-in-law every day made the situation worse. Even though he recognised the injustice of his thinking, he couldn't forgive her.

They didn't catch the killer. Because they were Roman citizens of the equestrian elite and personally connected to the imperial family, no theory was left untested, no stone unturned in the attempt to discover what happened; suspects were flogged and tortured without obtaining a definite identity.

Who was really to blame? He had seen with his own eyes the potential cauldron within the Holy City, aware of the antagonism between the people and the detested high priests. Not only did they collaborate with the Romans and Herodians to control and terrorise the people but turned on the minor priesthood, including his own relatives, stealing their tithes, starving their families while they lived off the fat of the land and their share of the Judaean taxes collected for Rome.

His own ambition led to his son's death. The alliance with the family of Ananus had seduced him totally. His son grew to care for the lovely young girl he married, yet Marcus was honest enough to admit, at least to himself, that if he had acted in time, he might have pushed him in another direction, despite the desires of Evia's father who initiated the connection.

The old story: ambitious family alliances built on money and greed; children used as pawns to satisfy a demand for power; sons and daughters sacrificed for honours and prestige. Guilt paralysed him, and the sight of his pregnant daughter-in-law walking around the villa in Paphos became unbearable. He needed to escape, and the *Galilee* was a life-saving rope to a drowning man.

Immediately he realised Simon was sailing for Ephesus, he remembered John and particularly Mary, who lost her own son in Jerusalem, another sacrifice to the rule of Rome. Perhaps if he talked to them, he might find a way to accept his loss. Yet he wondered if he would ever forgive himself for his son's destruction.

That first night, Jacob listened to Marcus after the evening meal and realised guilt was unravelling his old friend's hold on reason. He quickly transferred responsibility for his patients to his son and son-in-law and soon after dawn the following morning, the mule cart made the familiar journey to Koressos.

The unruffled Rachel immediately organised rooms and took her guests to the terrace where Deborah arranged drinks and snacks. She welcomed her Cypriot guest with sympathy, recognising the signs of strain and nervous exhaustion. Jacob persuaded him to lie down for a few hours and brought him to his room. He gave him a sleeping draught, made sure he had everything he needed, and left him to rest.

Downstairs, he joined Martha as she explained the whole sad story to Rachel.

'Poor Marcus. How terrible to lose a child in such a cruel and useless way. What about his wife, Jacob? How is she dealing with this?'

'At home in Paphos, apparently, looking after her other sons and the pregnant widow. As for Marcus, he's in a bad state, drowning in guilt. Blames himself for giving in to his father-in-law's ambitions and his own, he admits, to marry into the high priest's family. He wants to talk to Mary and thinks she might be able to help him. How is she, Rachel?'

'Physically deteriorating as we know, but her spirit is strong. I think she'll deal with this. What do you want to do? Go over to them?'

'I think we should all go. Why don't you tell Devorah to look after Marcus. I've given him something to make him sleep well into the evening. Ask her to check on him every few hours.'

Rachel collected her cloak, spoke to Deborah, and they left for the valley.

Laughter and familiar voices echoed down the path and James smiled.

That's a relief. It might be useful to have us all here.

Mary was delighted to see her friends, and soon they were sitting around the table, listening to the story of the marriage and subsequent murder in Jerusalem.

She clasped her hands tightly in her lap, the horror bringing tears to her eyes. 'Evia? How is she?'

'She's grieving, of course, and looking after Antonius, Tiberius, and the widowed bride who is expecting a child.'

'So she's on her own with no one to help her. Poor Evia.'

'What about Marcus?' the apostle asked, realising there was more to the situation.

'He's not so good. Frankly, he isn't the man you met all those years ago. He is seriously deteriorated both physically and spiritually. I'm not sure if it's an evil spirit or profound grief, but something is wrong. He blames himself for allowing the marriage. Ananus is incredibly wealthy, and in Marcus's mind, he sacrificed his son to greed and ambition. He'll go mad with guilt if he isn't helped. He wants to talk to you both; he believes you can help him.'

'I see,' John said, looking over for Mary's reaction.

'I'll do whatever I can,' she replied immediately. 'They were very kind to us when we were there. I can do no less, especially for Evia. We need to send him back in a condition to support her. What do you suggest, Jacob?'

'I don't know, Mary. You have a better grasp of this than me. It's guilt, more than ordinary grief.'

'Can we meet him today?'

'I've given him something to make him sleep, but he'll be awake in the evening. More importantly, are you sure you are strong enough for this? I must warn you; he's in a bad condition.'

'No, that's no problem. I'll deal with it. Why doesn't John go over to you after our meal and bring him back? I'd like him to see the house, this wonderful home we've made. We'll find out then how we can help him. Poor Marcus.'

Talk eventually drifted to other subjects, but Jacob kept an eye on Mary, concerned for her welfare. Even though her hands trembled at times, he didn't think it too important. Her colour was good, she participated in the conversation and derived considerable enjoyment from the company.

John noted the surveillance and caught his friend's eye. They went outside. 'What do you think?'

'She's still strong. I am not too worried at this stage, but if she tires you must cut the visit short.'

That evening, when John met Marcus at the farm, the deterioration shocked him. Cheek jowls hung from the blue-tinged face and dark-shadowed red eyes contributed to the hollow, emaciated look. He rose with difficulty to greet the apostle, his thin body bent and stiff, a caricature of the happy, confident man in Cyprus all those years before. Around him lay a thick, heavy cloud of despair, black, gritty, and opaque, although without the attachment of an evil spirit. Even so, if they didn't deal with his self-recrimination, he would weaken and fall.

They needed to proceed slowly. Treat him kindly and let him relax without sending the sympathy too strongly. He was sensitive; in his present depletion, he might feel the kindness as painful stabs. With time, he would absorb the strength more easily. Too much at the moment might force a complete withdrawal.

Mary too was startled when her nephew brought their guest into the living room. She took his hand and showed him around her much-loved home and gardens. They saw the goats, met the donkey with her foal, and walked a little way up the valley as she chatted happily, giving him time to relax until, at last, she caught the glimmer of a smile.

She brought him to some rocks, not far from the pool, and they sat. The comfortable silence increased. Although she sensed a despair, not unlike her own after Yeshu's death, it wasn't totally destructive. He would recover. More quickly than she did.

Eventually, he raised his gaze to her face; this time the smile was genuine and reached his eyes.

'Tell me what happened, Marcus. Tell me everything.'

He fixed his attention on the cool mountain pool and talked, relating the events as he lived them at the time: receiving the news from Evia's father of the proposed marriage into the family of Ananus the high priest, the alliance considered favourably by old man himself. Such euphoria, a blessing for his son and a marvellous opportunity for the Cypriot mines. He made no apology for his delight in the business opportunities and told the story without the horror and regret that followed.

Simon's *Galilee* was chartered to bring them to Judaea. They would stay in Jerusalem for four months. His daughter, Joanna, was expecting her first child in late summer. Afterwards, the autumn festivals and the wedding.

Evia wanted to be noticed, to make an impression on the social elite of the city, but with taste, he explained with an affectionate smile. She spent a fortune: new clothes for themselves and the children; presents for the bride and her relatives; more gifts for her own and his families, those still residing in the city. She packed the *Galilee's* hold with boxes and crates, determined all would go according to plan.

Simon cared for the boys, honing their sailing skills, keeping them under control. They even called into Caesarea Maritima, where he donned his toga and went to Herod's Promontory Palace to call on the procurator. He made sure Fadus recognised him as a Roman citizen and an Equestrian with strong connections to the imperial house.

'In my youth, Mary, my father sent me to Rome. Through our contacts, I befriended Gaius, the grandson of the first emperor. Even after his heir's tragic death, Augustus maintained the connection, and my family have benefited enormously. We retained ownership of our mines when other Cypriot holdings were confiscated, and he assigned us important contracts.'

Suitably impressed, Fadus sent a message to the tribune in the city, alerting him to the presence of this influential friend of the Emperor. He invited Marcus and the family to dinner one evening when he was at the palace in Jerusalem. The Cypriot returned to the ship, delighted with the visit and pleased with his Roman connections. It contributed to his self-satisfaction and further confirmed his pleasure in his son's marriage.

In Joppa, they paid for mule carts to bring everything to a well-appointed house in the old city. Hired for four months, it was their base for the birth of their first grandchild, the autumn festivals and the wedding celebrations beyond.

His pride in his family and his important connections with the Roman world were immense and shone through subtly, and sometimes not so subtly, during his four-month progress. For once, he ignored the hunger and vermin of the poor, those who were banished so aggressively from the clean streets and comfortable houses of the wealthy and socially prominent. The whispers of anger, the hatred for the Romans and the Jewish high priests passed over him unheard, his mind closed to all that didn't contribute to his dream of success for his eldest son and to his own triumphant return to the land of his ancestors.

They left Josephus and his wife installed in a lovely old house in the best part of the city, their wedding present to the couple, everything set for a bright future within the priesthood and the Temple. He was delighted, pleased with his own shrewdness and the efforts of Solomon, Evia's perspicacious father. What a victory!

A year later, all their plans and hopes crashed down around them. His son, his gentle, studious Josephus, knifed while walking to the Holy Sanctuary from his own home, in streets thought safe and tranquil. The authorities presumed it was one of the Sicarii, an extremist group of zealots who carried *sicae,* small daggers, concealed under their cloaks. At public gatherings, they attacked anyone who supported the Empire and disappeared afterwards into the crowds.

'Why did they stab my son? I couldn't understand. I was told there were probably two reasons. Although Jewish, we were Roman citizens, members of the Equestrian nobility, and personal friends of the imperial family. After all, I told everyone, boasted about it, so of course they knew.

'Secondly, he had married the granddaughter of Ananus, one of the hated high priests, servants of Rome, living on the taxes wrung from the poor and the tithes stolen from the minor priests, like many in my own family.

'I handed him over to his death, Mary, blinded by greed and a desire for position. I can't forgive myself. My beloved boy. I gave him up as a sacrifice. An innocent, good man, dedicated to the Most High. It's all my fault.'

His head fell into his hands, and he sobbed uncontrollably, the dam burst at last.

She sat with him, tears of sympathy and understanding streaming down her cheeks. She thought of another innocent, dedicated to the Most High, another good man sacrificed to Rome's insane desire to rule the world. Not so long ago, she wept like Marcus, full of regrets, blaming herself for Yeshu's death, carrying the burdens of the evil-infested future on her own shoulders.

Wiping the tears from her eyes, she examined him and found him calmer, although exhausted by the overwhelming power of his confession. Much of the heavy miasma around him had already dissipated, leaving a severe exhaustion and a deep, spiritual fragility. Suddenly, she realised the cause of the problem.

She reached over, placed a gentle hand on his shoulder and called him with all her strength, reached out to the lost and grieving spirit who wandered in some unmapped wilderness in the outer spheres of the universe.

'Marcus, come back. You must come home. Come back to me. Come back.'

He was alone and abandoned, cold and shivering, hungry and thirsty in a dark uninhabited desert, where sharp stones ripped and sliced his unshod feet. No matter: he mustn't stop. The search must continue. His son was lost and it was his, Marcus's, fault. If only he had taken better care of him. He needed to find him.

Again he called, 'Josephus, Josephus. Where are you?' For aeons and aeons of time, he searched and searched in vain.

Then, in the distance, he heard a call, a warm, loving voice telling him to come back. Someone had found him. He'd come home.

Marcus returned to his senses and found a vaguely familiar woman sitting by his side at the edge of a mountain pool. Confused, he stared at her. Where was he? What happened? She took him by the arm and led him down a path away from the pool. His steps faltered, unsure. He stopped and gazed around him. She pleaded with him and he continued a little further until finally they reached a house, where a young man stood at the door.

Realising she was at the end of her strength, he caught her up in his arms and called Marcus to follow. He carried her down to the house and into her room, laid her on the bed, reached for a cup and poured a measure of the herbal drink. He raised her head, held it to her mouth and persuaded her to swallow a little at a time, until a slight wash of colour returned to her cheeks. Then he ran for Jacob.

Pale and exhausted, her heartbeat was irregular and weak. The physician kindled the kitchen fire to boil water and infuse stronger herbs. John came to help, his eyes questioning.

'I can't tell you anything, at the moment. We were well aware of her condition. Perhaps we shouldn't have allowed her to do this, whatever it was. Has she told you?'

'No, not yet. She was already collapsing when I caught sight of her on the path. And you must realise it was impossible to stop her. No one could have. She did what she had to do, no matter the cost.'

Jacob smiled. Her determination amazed him sometimes. 'Well, let's hope she doesn't pay too much this time.'

In the meantime, the others brought Marcus back to the farm and out to the terrace, still bewildered but recovering. Rachel gently questioned him; he remembered his son's marriage and death in Jerusalem but told them of his shock to awaken, as if from a deep sleep and find himself sitting by a pool with a woman he only met once in his life, many years ago. Then to discover he was in Anatolia, not at the villa in Cyprus.

She explained why he came to Ephesus, how he wanted to see John and Mary in the hope they would help him deal with the death of his son.

'What was I doing at the pool?'

'I don't know, Marcus. Try not to worry. We'll find out soon.'

His mental state worried her, and she persuaded him to go to bed and rest. In the morning, hopefully, they would have more information. She gave him the sleeping draught left by her nephew, making sure he drank it in her presence. The Galileans helped him to his room and remained with him until he slept. Then, with Rachel, they returned to Mary's, leaving Devorah once again in charge of the sleeping man.

John, Jacob, and Martha were in the living room talking quietly, while Susannah stayed with Mary. It was a troubled sleep. Rearranging the pillows and raising her head a little higher eased her breathing; she slept more soundly. Jacob went in regularly, taking her pulse, and checking her heart-rate until the immediate crisis ended.

After a while James and Matthias left for their tent in the orchard. Martha and Rachel went home soon afterwards, and

Jacob followed. The heart had responded to the stronger herbs, and the outlook appeared brighter. Susannah stayed a little longer but John told her to go to bed while he kept watch by his aunt's bedside. He knew she hadn't too much time. She would go soon and he would miss her.

The situation with Marcus intrigued him. The heavy cloud of blackness had left. She must've pushed it away and that probably weakened her.

He looked up and found her watching him with a smile. 'I'm feeling better, John. Go to bed. You must be tired. How is he?'

'Dazed. He doesn't know where he is. Can you tell me what happened?'

'His spirit had almost completely gone. It was the shock of his son's death. I only recognised the problem after he told me the whole story. As he went through everything and faced his pain, he pushed away the guilt and self-recrimination. He was so weak, I realised the major part of his soul had gone somewhere else. I called it back, and the calling took the rest of my strength. I didn't think I would make it home. I was so glad to see you standing at the door.'

He pulled over his stool and took her hand. What a determined little lady she was. 'You've done enough for one day,' he said, smiling down at her. 'Go to sleep now.'

'You go to bed too, John. Don't worry about me. I'll still be here in the morning.'

He laughed and checked her pulse as Jacob taught him. It was strong and steady. He decided to take her advice. 'I'll leave my door open. Call me if you need me. I'll hear you.' He kissed her brow. 'Sleep well.'

38

The Holy Child

By the next morning, she had improved. Soon after dawn, Jacob's voice alerted John and he rose to let him in. Mary was still asleep, but her colour was good, her pulse strong.

'Make sure she stays in bed until tomorrow.' John closed her bedroom door and went to the kitchen to bring drinks to the table. He told Jacob about the loss of Marcus's spirit and how, years before in Galilee, they dealt with similar situations with Yeshu.

It fascinated the physician, and he wondered if this explained some types of mental deterioration with patients after an accident or severe shock.

'How did she know it was gone?'

'When he faced the reasons for agreeing to the marriage, he pushed the desecration away and cleared. Afterwards, she couldn't feel much of the strong personality she met in Cyprus. Some of him must've gone elsewhere. She called him and sensed the soul returning. It drained her strength.'

'Ah. I wonder if I've done the wrong thing. We gave Marcus more of the sleeping herbs last night. Do you think that will harm him? I know a considerable amount of the spirit leaves when we sleep but would a draught force more of him out and if so what happens?'

John gazed off into the distance and thought. 'I'm not sure. I think it might. We'd better be careful with him. Don't use one again.

'By the way, how long are you staying?'

'As long as Marcus is here. I can't leave him to Rachel. So tell me what I should do.'

'Surround him with kindness. The returned essence is weak. We need to strengthen it, encourage its reabsorption. Remind him of his youth. Stimulate his memory of the man you knew when you were young. That will help the reintegration. We'll need to talk to him about his son, but later, not yet. Let's decide when we see how he is.'

'Does all the spirit leave?'

'Only in death. In Marcus's case, only some of it left but persuading the new part to return and stay can be difficult. I'm sure when he understands the situation, he'll want to help himself.'

They sat talking until Susannah came through from her room to commence her day. Jacob checked again on Mary and left for the farm. John finally went to bed.

The sun was high in the sky when he awoke. He took clean clothes up to the pool and remained for some time, pushing away all the exhaustion and worry of the previous day, determined to be clear and strong when he went to see his aunt. He no longer worried about her condition, leaving her health and her life in the hands of the Father. Helping Marcus, at the moment, seemed more important, and he wanted to discuss his thoughts with her.

On his return, he went to her and immediately sensed the change. She had regained most of her spiritual energy, but the episode had drained her physical power. She examined his face, noting the shadow that followed his initial delight.

He sat by her bed and she took his hand. 'John, don't darken my last days with unneeded regrets. We both know I haven't much time left. Yeshu told me I had one more thing to do, and I believe it's with Marcus. He is my final task, and you must help me complete it.

'His son came to me in a dream last night, the blessed Josephus, and he carried in his arms a holy child who will be born into the world. This is the boy his bride carries. Because of his wisdom and discernment, he will be named Solomon and will achieve wonderful things for the Most High. His mother, however, must not return to Jerusalem. She will stay with her husband's parents in Cyprus. There, under his grandfather's tutelage, the babe will grow in power and understanding.

'Teach Marcus what Yeshu taught you. Enlighten him about loving kindness, and tell him his son begs him to care for his wife. He loved her very dearly and knew from the moment he laid eyes on her that their union was destined. He wants his father to safeguard his only child and lead him towards the light of the Holy One.

'This is my last task, John. The child will help in the years to come, and we have to prepare Marcus so he can educate and strengthen his grandson for his future destiny.'

She lifted her hand and touched his beloved face. 'I will be here for a while, my dear one. Don't despair. We still have time. The summer awaits us. Try to be happy for me.'

He struggled to control the tears. He wouldn't let them fall and give in to his grief. He would do exactly as she asked. 'Do you want to see him?'

'Not yet. Give me a few more days, and then I'll talk to him. You must teach him, though. Remember he is sensitive and will understand much of what you tell him. However, don't allow him to stay too long. He has to return to Cyprus soon, certainly before the birth. The babe must enter a home of gladness, not a place of despair.'

The effort to communicate tired her. Glad the message was passed, she relaxed into the pillows, her eyes closed and the grip on his hand released. Her breathing developed a steady rhythm; he placed her hand on her mother's coverlet, leaned over to kiss her brow, and left, aware of the continued presence of the Holy Ones.

He joined Susannah for breakfast and told her of the improvement in his aunt's condition, clearing the worried expression from her face. She smiled hopefully and by the time they finished eating, she was planning everything that needed to be done, especially with so much activity between the two houses. She wouldn't disappoint her mistress.

He walked over to the farm to find all his friends on the terrace. Marcus had slept the night through and came down earlier for something to eat. He'd gone back to bed a short time before, still tired, but much improved. John told them of Mary's dream with Josephus and the new baby.

'How wonderful,' Martha said, in awe. 'A holy child to be born. That will bring purpose back into his life.'

'I hope so. I'm glad we're all here. I need your help with Marcus. There is a lot of knowledge to impart and I think, when he's stronger, we will need to show him how to elevate an evil spirit. He's highly sensitive, and that's to our advantage. We don't have much time because Mary insists he returns to Cyprus before the baby is born.'

Later, Marcus joined them on the terrace, and after initial greetings, the others withdrew, leaving John and Jacob to talk to him. The dark cloud had dissipated, his spirit present but weak, no longer exhibiting the bright, sparkling power of the man in

Cyprus. No contamination, just weakness caused by stress and grief.

He realised they were examining him, the way he so often assessed others. He smiled and looked up. 'Well, what do you think? Have I gone completely mad?'

John laughed. 'No, Marcus. There's no need to worry. You have been through a stressful time. Thankfully you found your way to us for help.'

He told him everything that happened at the pool: what he said about his son's death, how he blamed himself, the dislocation of his spirit, and how Mary realised what happened and called it back.

'It's important you rebuild your strength now and recover from the shock.'

The Cypriot sat quietly, his head bowed. 'How can I ever forgive myself for what I did? An intelligent, gentle boy, full of promise, and I sent him into the hands of a murderer. In what way can I come to terms with that?'

John quickly moved to the chair next to him. 'Marcus, you must try to put this all behind you, especially your grief for Josephus. A new grandson is coming. You have to care for him and teach him all you know.'

'I can't even look at my daughter-in-law. She reminds me, and I wish she hadn't come home with us.'

He suddenly raised his head and stared at the man sitting beside him, hard aggression in his eyes. 'How could you possibly know it's a boy?'

Then he learned about Mary dream, the child in the arms of Josephus, one who would accomplish marvellous things for the Most High, a holy babe to be named Solomon. As John spoke, Marcus's eyes widened in wonder, and joy once more pierced his frozen heart. His son had forgiven him; he was in the blessed realms, not languishing in an underworld. A grandson for whom he was responsible.

'Your son trusts you with this special child destined to be born. Into your care he has been given. Preparation is important. Grow strong spiritually and learn how to help him. Mary told us he has a task to accomplish for the Creator. We'll help you regain your powers before you return to Cyprus; then you can begin your new work.'

The joy of forgiveness, the realisation that the wedding of his son was meant to be, flowed through him like a cleansing stream. Tears came to his eyes, this time overwhelming tears of bliss. Feeling embarrassed, he rose from his seat and walked down to the bottom of the garden. He leaned on the wall, like so many before him, and looked across the valley to the blue Aegean and beyond. And a long time passed before he composed himself.

John watched and waited. When Marcus straightened up to return, he went to meet him, walked with him down through the gardens, and talked of what he should do in the days to come.

Later, Mary would speak to him of everything she experienced in the dream.

'Did I harm her? I wasn't well when I arrived, and I don't even remember going to the pool.'

'There is nothing to regret, Marcus. She wanted to help you, and when she decides to do something, nothing stops her. She just needs to rest. So don't worry. You must concentrate on getting well. Talk to the others. They will show you the way.'

He went back with him to the terrace and then turned for home to Mary.

Over the next days, Marcus worked on his recovery and became a kindly and amusing guest. When Matthias and James went back to the city, Jacob and Martha brought him for walks into the mountains every morning, rebuilding his physical strength and endurance. He returned exhausted but pleased with himself.

After breakfast, John came over and they gathered on the terrace to hear the stories of Yeshu and his teachings. The concept of the rule of evil fascinated Marcus, especially as the tradition had passed down in his own family. He questioned the apostle on the neutralisation of wickedness, and had to see the whole process in action.

Persuaded, John held, for elevation, an evil spirit identified earlier in Hieropolis. Initially, aggression and belligerence battered them as the entity rejected the loving thoughts. Yet within a short time, the antagonism diminished and he spoke more quietly. The sensitive Cypriot was aware of all the changes, amazed at how the black, gritty heaviness gradually transformed into tingling effervescence and how light replaced the darkness. As the soul elevated, he sensed the departure and was convinced.

He asked how they knew if the elevation was successful and learned of the examination after seven days. Sometimes the holy soul was pulled down, and work had to begin again.

It was a period of learning, an opening of his mind to new knowledge and new ways of looking at traditional beliefs, especially that of the underworld and the last judgement. Yeshu himself, for instance, created quite a stir when he appeared to so many after his crucifixion, seeming to indicate that the rule of evil was over and the great judgement of the Most High was about to commence.

Marcus was confused and asked John for an explanation. 'The rule of evil hasn't ended, and one's spiritual assessment is individual and comes soon after death. There is no interim underworld. Your son, for example, must've been a righteous man because Mary said he was in the blessed realms. Yet the entity we raised came from the realms of the damned. Through loving kindness, he pushed aside the evil surrounding him and ascended to his original home in the gardens of the Holy One.'

The days passed. Marcus absorbed the teachings and grew strong. His visit to Mary gave him profound peace. While he sat with her, he sensed the presence of a holy soul, whom she identified as Josephus. He felt blessed with the heavenly privilege and the weeks on Koressos gave solace to his tortured but recovering mind and spirit. She worried, however, that time was passing. She told him he needed to return to Evia and his daughter-in-law to give them comfort and prepare for the coming of the holy child.

When he was ready to go, he left friends who had learned to love him dearly. Jacob and Martha brought him down the mountain, and although the *Galilee* was not in port, they found another ship leaving for Cyprus within a few days. He stayed with them for that final interval, talking and reminiscing.

They went to the synagogue where they met Joseph and Hannah and learned of their association with John and Mary. The exorcisms among the Jews and the Gentiles made an amazing difference to the city. No longer did the possessed live in hunger and desperation outside the walls of Ephesus but returned restored, to their grateful relatives.

The physician spoke plainly and told his old friend how the letter of introduction that John brought all those years ago, had changed his life immeasurably. Every day from deep within his heart, he thanked his friend for thinking of him. Marcus was impressed, not only with the physician and his wife but also with the thoughtful, synagogue president and his kindly spouse. It banished any residual doubts; when he boarded the ship for home, he planned the future in his mind.

39

The Final Days

John remained on the mountain with Mary; Martha and Jacob came to visit, bringing with them James and Mathias or, on occasions, Joseph and Hannah. Unlike the sweltering heat of the city, breezes cooled Koressos, and they came as often as they could. They said little, but time was short, and they had an underlying desire to enjoy whatever remained.

Rachel and Susannah would join them in the valley when they packed the donkey's baskets full of food and took their breakfast up to the pool in the mountains. Mary rode the donkey; the foal, the nanny goat, and all the latest baby goats came too. They spent a few relaxing hours by the cool waters until they banished the laughing John, and the women bathed and washed their clothes.

Evenings passed in the clifftop pavilion or on the terrace at the farm. As Mary couldn't walk very far, the donkey took her over or her nephew carried her up the steps to sit for hours, gazing down at the Aegean Sea which Joachim had known so well.

It was her last summer, and she was content. Her life had been difficult but fulfilling, and although they hadn't ended the rule of evil, they brought important wisdom to mankind, knowledge that would lead, one day, to a peaceful world.

The times of regret were bygone memories, replaced by days

of quiet appreciation for dear and steadfast friends, with the snuffling of the ageing donkey as she reached over the fence to touch Mary's hands, with the bleats of little black and white kids and the anxious eyes of the watchful nanny, with the pavilion on the heights and the mountain pool, but mainly with the loving care of Susannah and the cheerful John.

Towards the end of the summer, she awoke during the night to find him leaning over her. He held up her head and shoulders and persuaded her to sip a few drops of a special mixture of herbs and drugs the physician created for such a time as this. Her mouth twisted in pain.

Susannah came running in her nightclothes. John told her to dress, find Rachel, and ask Reuben to go immediately for Jacob.

Calm and quiet, he raised her, slipped in behind and rested her body against his chest. He persisted with the herbal drink and managed to get her to swallow some drops. He let her rest for a while before he tried and tried again, until he gave her the specific dose prescribed. She slept, a disturbed, rasping sleep. Her body sometimes trembled, and she moaned quietly.

She was leaving at last, her long fight with life nearly at an end. While she dozed in his arms, enclosing her with love, Joseph came to stand by the bed, waiting patiently.

Rachel arrived first and, soon after, Susannah with Adora. It was the beginning of a long few days. Mary eventually fell into a deeper, less troubled sleep, and Rachel helped raise her so John could stack more pillows behind her. It made it easier for her to breathe. Jacob and Martha came at noon, and alerted by Jacob's servants, Joseph, Hannah and the Galileans joined them a few hours later.

During that day and into the night, the news spread that she was dying. Small groups gathered in the gardens, in the paddock with the goats and donkeys and under the trees in the orchard. Darkness fell and little oil lamps were lit. The valley filled with flickering lights as more and more came: families aided by an exorcism or a healing; acquaintances known at the market; neighbours who had grown to love her; all wishing to give the respect they believed was due to the mother of Yeshua the Healer, a Man of God, a Messenger of the Most High, a good man crucified by the Romans.

All that day and the next, well into the second night, they kept vigil. Near sunrise the next morning, John, waiting by her bedside, saw light brighten the room and thought dawn had arrived. It was Yeshu standing beside him; he smiled and placed a warm, comforting hand on his cousin's shoulder. The illumination intensified for a moment and then vanished. Her breathing stopped.

He kept her hand in his, even though it was over.

Jacob felt for the pulse on her neck but there was nothing. He realised John understood by the look on his face. Glancing over at the others waiting beside the bed, he shook his head.

Susannah began to cry, and Rachel wrapped her in her arms, holding her tight. Martha leaned over and kissed Mary on the cheek, whispering how much she had always cherished her; she would miss her every day.

Reuben stood at the back of the room, his cap crushed in his hand, and slow tears ran down his cheeks. He had loved and greatly respected the little Galilean lady since she came to live on Koressos. No more would he call to see her, talk about the garden and what needed planting, walk among the trees planning the pruning, or discuss the extension of the grape trellis for the following season. He would have to do something about her bees now, unless John stayed on the mountain. But nothing would ever be the same, now that Mary was gone.

Rachel brought the sobbing Susannah out to Adora and talked for a moment with those waiting outside. Yes, she was dead, and yes, the funeral would be later in the day, towards sunset probably, everything already arranged. She would lie in a cave up in the mountains, not far from the mountain pool. Reuben and Avram prepared her resting place some time ago. All was ready, but John would make the final decisions.

Finally, she managed to escape and returned to the room where Mary lay, knowing how much she would miss this wonderful little lady who taught her so much, laughed with her so often, and became her dearest friend. She leaned over, kissed her brow, gently patted her cheek, and said her final farewells.

She glanced over at John sitting beside the bed. Aware of her glance, he looked up into grieving eyes and his own filled with tears. She came round to him and tried to persuade him to come out, at least for a rest, but he said no, not quite yet.

He wanted to wait for a little while, even though she no longer remained with him. Now, there was no one to run to when, as a child, he grazed his knee, no one to come to when his mother and then his only love died, no one to share the pain after Yeshu had gone, or to talk to into the night when plans were made and decisions taken. His most beloved aunt and friend had left him, and life would be different now: empty.

Unknowing, he echoed Reuben's thoughts: *Nothing will ever be the same, now that Mary is gone.*

EPILOGUE

In 62 CE, James, Mary's second child and the leader of the Nazoraeans, was thrown from the steps of the Temple and stoned to death at the instigation of Ananus, the high priest, son of Ananus the elder and brother-in law to Caiphus. Simeon, nearby, tried to intervene, but by the time he reached his brother, he was already dead, his head bashed in by a fuller's club.

A detailed description from Josephus outlines the reaction of the people of Jerusalem, especially the leading citizens, to what they saw as an unlawful killing, and we begin to understand the mood in the city, only four years before the outbreak of the Great Revolt

During the reign of the Agrippa II, Festus the Roman procurator died and Nero appointed Albinus as successor. The king had removed the high priest Joseph from office and replaced him with the younger Ananus, a man, according to Josephus, of rash and insolent character. It was illegal for the Judaean rulers to pronounce the extreme penalty without Roman sanction, yet the new chief priest took advantage of the interregnum. While Albinus travelled, he called a Sanhedrin. James and some others came before them, charged with breaking the law. They were condemned to die by stoning, the sentence carried out immediately.

An uproar ensued in the Holy City. Some of the prominent

citizens complained to Agrippa and travelled to meet Albinus who wrote to Ananus in a rage, threatening to punish him. This forced the king to remove his puppet, even though he had only ruled for three months.

The expelled high priest, however, received no further Roman punishment. Despite his initial fury, the new procurator soon succumbed to the bribes of Ananus's immensely wealthy father, the head of the clan.

Why did they kill James? This is more difficult, although there are some indications. One theory ascribes his death to Agrippa's anger over the Temple Wall Affair. The Nazoraean led the unofficial opposition to the establishment, and the king appointed the obstreperous Ananus in the hope he would eliminate this opponent. He didn't expect it to be easy; the "Ziddick" had a strong following both among the priests in the Sanctuary and the ordinary people of the Holy City.

The Temple Wall Affair gives some evidence of the antagonism that existed between the administration, on one side, and the anti-Roman, nationalistic, and messianic groupings ranged against them, a situation that grew over the next few years into full revolution.

It might explain James's death, but it doesn't mean he supported the frenzy of destruction into which the revolution descended. Like his elder brother, he believed violence strengthened Satan and would have encouraged his followers to walk the difficult, narrow line between a desire for justice and physical force.

Some scholars attribute the particularly, vicious murder of Ananus and the burning of his palace during the rebellion, to revenge for the death of James, the man the people of Jerusalem revered as a Just Man.

How Did the Jewish Revolt Affect the Jesus-Followers?

Eusebius, an early Church writer, tells us that, before it broke out in 66 CE, an oracle warned the Nazoraeans to escape to Pella in Perea, to their traditional homeland east of the Jordan. There they stayed, under the leadership of Simeon, Mary's third son, until they returned to Mount Sion in 73 CE.

Not many of the followers managed to escape to the north. The majority remained and met their deaths during the siege or the ensuing massacre and destruction. Few survived. Those who did leave in time, and later returned, found Mount Sion in ruins, like the rest of the city. Led by Simeon and other members of the *Desposyni*, the family of Jesus, they began to reconstruct their lives out of the devastation. They rebuilt their synagogue on the site of the old Essene guesthouse where they celebrated the Last Supper.

The new building faced the place of the Resurrection, not the ruined Sanctuary, and they used some of the beautiful "ashlars", carefully sculpted Herodian stones, from the Temple itself, stones which can still be seen today under the present Cenacle.

Over the years and centuries, they extended the synagogue, and although destroyed and restored on several occasions, it became revered as the Church of the Apostles, the "mother of churches". Later, the Benedictines built a monastery, the Dormiton Abbey, over the house where Mary and her family lived in the difficult years after the crucifixion.

What Happened to Simeon, Jude, and Mary's Other Descendants?

Even after the death of James, the trials of Mary's family didn't cease. Eusebius tells us this:

'Vespasian, after the capture of Jerusalem, issued an order to ensure that no one who was of royal stock should be left among the Jews, that all the descendants of David should be ferreted out and destroyed and for this reason a further widespread persecution was again inflicted upon the Jews' (EH 3.12, 3.20 1–4).

The decree confirms that Vespasian recognised the uprising against Rome as messianic, but no other information is given about this imperial instruction or its results. His second son, the Emperor Domitian, issued another order for the execution of all those of David's line. This resulted in the identification of Simeon, Mary's philosopher, as a descendant of David. Tortured and crucified in Judaea, the witnesses marvelled that he could bear such pain.

The Syriac Apostolic Constitutions reveal that Jude Thaddaeus, the last brother of Jesus, went to preach to the Edessians in Armenia and founded the Armenian Christian Church. There are various stories about his death, but both the Constitutions and Hippolytus tell us that he died a martyr in Berytus, present-day Beirut, and was buried there.

Jude's progeny were equally sought. Eusebius says they worked tirelessly with the early organisation of the Nazoraean Assembly, known as the Jewish Christian Church, but Rome pursued them relentlessly.

'The descendants of Jude, as the brother of the Lord according to the flesh, because they were of the family of David and as such related to Christ were brought to Domitian.' Apparently they were farmers. 'The hardness of their bodies and the calluses on their hands was evidence of their labour.'

Questioned about their uncle's teachings, especially about his kingdom, they explained it was 'not of this world, not earthly but heavenly and angelic.' Domitian, despising them as simpletons, commanded them to be released and by imperial order terminated the persecution.

Later, the Emperor Trajan ordered the arrest and execution of Jude's male descendants. Their names were Zoker and James (EH 3.20.5, EH 3.32.3-6).

Nothing is reported about Mary's line of descent through her own daughter or the female children of Jude. Only the fate of the males is recorded. We do know that, while the Roman army came south on its march of death and destruction from the Galilee to Jerusalem, the Greeks in Pella of Perea turned on their Jewish neighbours and killed many.

The writings also tell us, however, that Simeon and others returned from Pella, surviving the attacks there, possibly saved by the strength of the Nazoraean presence in their own homelands.

Perhaps the direct line continued through Mary's female descendants. Accordingly to Eusebius, the Nazoraeans continued into the fourth century, living in the lands east of the Jordan right up as far as Aleppo in Syria.

The *Desposyni*, or family of Jesus, provided bishops for the early Jewish Christian Church, centred on Mount Sion. Fifteen followed James and Simeon and all lived very short lives. Was it due to persecution? Eventually, they were absorbed by the emerging Gentile Christian Church.

Finally, what of the Jewish people?

The Revolt became a total disaster for the Jews and for the aims of the original Jerusalem Church.

The Romans destroyed the city and the Temple. According to Josephus, 1,100,000 Jews died and 97,000 became slaves, although modern estimates would reduce these figures. Their traditional

Caesarean protection ceased. Declared rebels like the Dacians of present day Romania, Rome had no mercy. Today we call it genocide.

The gold and treasures dedicated to the Most High, plundered from the burning Temple, were taken and melted down by Vespasian to pay for the Roman Coliseum, that notorious Amphitheatre used for bloodthirsty games and the destruction of Christian martyrs.

The Revolt directly affected the Gentile Church which expanded from the synagogue God-fearers into the empire's population. Women, in particular, were attracted to the Jewish principles of care and compassion for the needy, the widow and the orphan, concepts in contrast to Rome's indifference, if not contempt.

The early converts, keen to increase numbers among the higher echelons of society, soon realised they couldn't blame the Empire for the death of Jesus. They transferred responsibility to the Jewish people, and from then on, punished them for acts directly perpetrated by Rome or her representatives, the Herodians and high priests, the Vichy Government of their time.

Early Christian writings, with the exception of Paul's letters but including the Gospels, were written by Gentiles after the Revolt. Influenced by a desire to acquit Rome of blame, they even absolved Pilate himself. We know he was recalled in disgrace in 36 CE. A deluge of complaints from both Judaea and Samaria detailed Pilate's many murders and his disastrous rule. He was a cold, cruel man. The crucifixion of Jesus, one among many thousands he condemned to die on a cross, wouldn't have cost him a thought.

The Roman, and later Christian, attitude to the Jews became a virulent, theological anti-Semitism, sustained in Europe throughout two thousand years. It allowed Hitler to develop his Final Solution without too much opposition and led to the gas chambers of the Holocaust. The historical lie, that the Jews killed Jesus, is still perpetuated from our Christian pulpits.

Today's premier Jesus scholar, John Dominic Crossan, professor emeritus of religious studies at DePaul University of Chicago and a former ordained priest, poses some penetrating questions in his book, 'Who Killed Jesus?'

As he examines the New Testament stories where Pilate is declared innocent and the Jews guilty of killing Jesus, Crossan argues convincingly that these gospel accounts are early Christian propaganda, not Roman history. In the aftermath of the Jewish Revolt against Rome, it was probably the one way the early Christians were able to protect themselves. He continues:

'But once the Roman empire became Christian, that fiction became lethal. In the light of later Christian anti-Judaism and eventually of genocidal antisemitism, it is no longer possible in retrospect to think of that passion fiction as relatively benign propaganda. However explicable its origins, defensible its invectives, and understandable its motives among Christians fighting for survival, its repetition has now become the longest lie, and for our own integrity, we Christians must at last name it as such.'

'Think now, of those passion-resurrection stories as heard in a predominantly Christian world. Did those stories of ours send certain people out to kill? ('Who Killed Jesus? Page XII)

In more recent years, some popes have begun to undo the damage of two millennia. John XXIII, as papal nuncio in France during World War 2, witnessed the Nazi purge of French Jews and later abolished the accusation of deicide or 'Christ killing'. He began the process of communication with Judaism.

John Paul II called the Jewish people our 'elder brothers,' and the present Pope Francis said: 'Because of our common roots, a true Christian cannot be anti-Semitic.'

It's a beginning at least.

Lightning Source UK Ltd.
Milton Keynes UK
UKHW011951290322
400790UK00001B/14